The Tamsyn Webb Chronicles #1

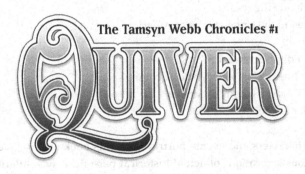

Jason Fischer

Published by Outland Entertainment LLC
3119 Gillham Road
Kansas City, MO 64109

Founder/Creative Director: Jeremy D. Mohler
Editor-in-Chief: Alana Joli Abbott

Paperback ISBN: 978-1-954255-37-1
Ebook ISBN: 978-1-954255-38-8
Worldwide Rights
Created in the United States of America

Copy Editor: Scott Colby
Cover Illustration: Ann Marie Cochran
Cover Design: Jeremy D. Mohler
Interior Layout: Mikael Brodu

Printed and bound in the United States of America.

Visit **outlandentertainment.com** to see more, or follow us on our Facebook Page **facebook.com/outlandentertainment/**

For Kate, Logan, and Lottie - my everything.

PART #1:
GRAVESEND

— I —

Breath pluming in the chill, Tamsyn scanned the streets below. Things had been quiet for the last few weeks, but Council had insisted the watch rosters be kept. Tower watch was the worst.

It was cold up in the clock tower, and not even three layers of clothing could keep out the late autumn chill. She wanted to close some of the louvers just to eliminate the biting breeze. But that was the point of it all; the Jubilee Clock Tower had a commanding view of the south-east corner. From here she could see right over the barricade of cars and rubbish blocking off Milton Road and the Grove, and several hundred yards of empty street beyond the Safe Zone.

There. She could see movement, someone shuffling forward in the middle of the laneway. A young woman, looking a little lost. She cut a pathetic figure, and Tamsyn thumbed the focus dial on the binoculars till the image became clear.

Dead. Her hair was matted and wild, and what was left of her waitress's uniform was patched with mould and filth. The woman's right forearm ended in a snapped mess of bones, jutting like an obscene pair of chopsticks held wrong. Great chunks of flesh were missing from her neck and face, and her eyes were blasted orbs, milky and vacant.

"Shuffle on, love," Tamsyn said. "No restaurants here for you."

She picked up the hammer, ready to strike the dead clock's bells. The sound would bring people running, ready to fend off an undead assault. But after a long moment she hung the hammer back on its hook. This zombie was alone, just wandering aimlessly as they often did.

It had been months since the last survivor made it to Gravesend, Kent.

Braving the chill, she eased off her gloves. It was lonely up in the tower, and she had nothing much to do for the next two hours.

She began to sketch the dead waitress in her notebook. It was tricky drawing things through the binoculars, and she'd often peer down to check on what she was doing. Over the last few months, she'd noticed that some of the zombies ambling around the area were regulars. Previous pages in her notebook held drawings of Construction Guy, Armless Schoolgirl, Necrotic Nanna, and the heart-wrenching tragedy that was Toddler Tim.

Tamsyn was working on the waitress's face when the zombie suddenly looked directly at her. For one long moment their eyes met, and the dead thing seemed to smile, or twist its mouth into a snarl. Though it was at least a hundred yards away, the sudden scare caused her to drop the binoculars. Jerking back, she fell, inches from the edge of the stairwell. Scrabbling to her feet, she wished she had a rifle, furious that some broken dead thing had put such a fright into her.

"Checking the time, were you?" Tamsyn yelled out through the slats, her heart racing. She pointed up at the motionless clock-face above her, its hands frosted with ice. The zombie had reached the head-high barrier of junk and, bumping into it, couldn't find an easy way through. The dead waitress casually turned and wandered off in the opposite direction.

"Bloody hell," she grumbled, sitting back down. She'd marked the drawing with a clumsy scratch and fumbled for an eraser with her cold fingers. "Must have seen the sun on the lens or something. They're not that smart."

She heard the clumping of feet on the steps and put her notebook and pens away. No sense being caught napping on the job, not when she'd made a point of wanting to be taken seriously. Guards got extra rations, and she meant to keep her strength up, as well as Mal's.

"Tam!" someone called out from below. "You all right?"

"Yeah," she yelled down the steps. "Just telling a zombie to nick off."

"Good," the voice said, and Ali's broad grin appeared above the ledge. "You tell enough of them, and hopefully you'll clear Britain in a week or two."

They'd been in the same year at school. Gravesend Grammar crawled with dead things now, but the concept of education still limped along behind the town barricades. What children had survived those first panicked days continued their lessons by candlelight, huddled up in St George's Church.

"They should let us have a kerosine heater up here," he said, settling himself down on a stack of quilts. "I'd stay up here for days then."

"I don't think they want the guards getting too comfortable," she said. "You wouldn't spot anything anyway. Too busy reading girlie mags and sleeping."

"You kidding? I'd get a rifle up here, and pow!" he mimed, taking up a sniper's stance at the window. "I could drop hundreds of them."

"And bring thousands more, you idiot. How many bullets do you think we have left?"

"Enough to take back the school. I left my laptop there. And think of all the rubbish food sitting in the tuck shop. Seriously, that shit's got enough preservatives to last till doomsday."

Tamsyn opened her mouth, but nothing came out. She pointed at Milton Road, hand trembling, gaping at the solid block of corpses walking up it. The wave of dead things stretched from one side of the road to the other, shuffling forward and growling in a hungry chorus.

"Oh God. There's some kids outside the wall!" she said, scrambling for the binoculars, and sure enough there were three youngsters just ahead of the zombie pack, running for their lives. One of them was perhaps six years old, pushing on a scooter. He was only just keeping up with his mates.

"Shit! Ring it," Ali said. "Ring the bell!"

She was only meant to strike the bell once for each zombie, as a signal to the other defenders. There were at least fifty approaching the wall, moving quicker now.

"Bloody hell!" she said, snatching up the hammer. She didn't bother counting, beating at the bells until the noise was deafening.

She pointed at the stairs, and, giving a nod, Ali began to climb back down. He was rushing, taking two steps at a time, and somewhere near the bottom he slipped on the steep steps. He fell to the floor, hard. Tamsyn winced as she saw him land heavily on one ankle.

"Are you okay?" she shouted. He looked up at her from the floor of the tower, pale but nodding. Carefully she reached the ground and helped him stand up.

"It really hurts," he said, gingerly putting some weight on it. He screamed in pain, sliding to the floor, sucking in great hissing gasps between his teeth.

"It's broken, it's gotta be. I'm so stupid."

"Yes, yes you are," Tamsyn said. "Stay in here and bolt the door." She picked up her compound bow and kit from where it leaned beside the doorway and made sure he was locked inside the tower.

She made it to the eastern barricade on Milton Street, just in time to see the first of the kids scrambling through a tight gap in the packed wall of wreckage. It was Jake Hammond, tearaway and recent orphan. One of his mates followed, panting and terrified.

"Quick, you gotta help him!" Jake said. Gripping the last little boy by the wrists, Tamsyn helped to pull him through. The boys moved a loose sheet of tin to cover the gap.

"Are you lot stupid? What the hell were you doing out there?" Tamsyn yelled, trying to shore up the hole with something a bit more substantial. The zombies were almost at the wall now, and with some relief she saw a few people come running at the sound of the bells, weapons in hand.

There was no more time for questions. A solid phalanx of dead things were beating against the barricade. The undead were stupid, but they knew how to break things. Given enough time, they could force through the thick wall, find a way around all the cars and junked washing machines. Or they'd step mindlessly all over each other, until their filthy human pyramid lifted a slavering murderer up and over.

"What game are you playing at, Tamsyn Webb?" said Dr. Murray, unshaven and reeking of booze. "You ring that thing enough times, it becomes a bloody dinner bell. One ring per zombie! There's a reason for that rule."

"I didn't ring it nearly enough," she said. "There must be fifty zombies out there. Where are all the other guards?"

"West wall. They've got bigger problems than us," Murray said, feeding shells into a shotgun. He'd been a vet once, but it was a long time since he'd used the gun on an ailing horse.

She could hear the faint cries of terror in the distance. The distant crack of a pistol cut through that din, and then another.

"Where's my dad?" she asked.

"Doing his job is where he's at," Murray growled. "Be ready now."

They climbed the painter's scaffolding that ran behind the junk wall, and Tamsyn thought she was going to be sick. There were dozens of dead people pushing against the stack of cars and fridges, and when she was noticed up above the wall, the mob went feral. They screeched, snapping their teeth, pounding their rotten fists against unyielding metal.

The stink rising up from the horde was horrific. The handful of others who'd rushed to defend the wall had scarves across their faces, dipped in vinegar.

"Don't just stand there, girl, have at them!" Murray yelled, his shotgun barking into the upturned faces of the walking dead. Ears ringing and hands shaking, she nocked an arrow, aimed it at the forehead of a dead little girl. Her shot went wide, and the arrow slammed into the mottled thigh of an obese naked woman.

"Head shots! Don't waste your arrows," someone else said.

Tamsyn breathed away her panic until the whole universe slowed for her, and her vision narrowed down to her hands, to the little nubs that were the adjustable sights on the bow. She sent arrow after arrow into the pale faces of the dead things, even as they climbed the wall, reaching, stretching for her warm flesh.

A rotting priest pushed in through the children's secret pathway, even as the first zombie reached the top of the wall. Tamsyn got lucky and sent an arrow through the dead man's brain, pinning him to the side of a filing cabinet.

Everything after that was the madness of close combat, one last frantic push as the zombies reached the scaffolding. The guns gave way to cricket bats, sharpened pool cues, even a fireman's sharp axe. Anything that could crush, snap, or sever the brains of these resurrected monsters.

"The barbarians are at the gate," Tamsyn said numbly, taking up a wicked little hatchet that someone thrust into her hands.

Later, even as the corpse-fires burned, those who'd died in the defence of the town were prepared for burial. Whether out of grim necessity, or superstition, a rail-road spike was applied to the frontal lobe. Sometimes, a terrified man or woman would be held down moments after a zombie bite, begging for life, for a chance. There were never any chances; the bitten always turned. If they were lucky, their former allies would spare the poor sod a bullet, give them a quick death.

For most there was the economical spike, its heavy point resting between their eyes, their last sight on God's green earth the swift descent of the hammer. Then, oblivion. Still, it was a clean death, and better than rising an hour or two later, mindless and hungering for human flesh.

Gravesend no longer had a man of the cloth. Reverend Gibb had taken a bite in the first month, and so they'd stopped with the proper burials. They cited lack of space in the churchyard, hygiene concerns, no one able to make a coffin to the right specifications. A variety of excuses were invented and tabled in Council to assuage their own consciences. No one wanted to deal with a friend or neighbour, somehow alive and scrabbling upwards through the earth. There was no sense in keeping a potential enemy behind town walls.

These days, those who died in service of the town were wrapped in a hessian sack weighted down with rocks. A boat would take them out to the deepest part of the river, and they were dumped into the water without any further ceremony. At first the burial parties gave a quick reading from the Common Book of Prayer, but no one bothered with that anymore.

Mal Webb volunteered for corpse duty. No one enjoyed consigning the bodies of their friends and neighbours into the murk of the Thames, but Mal never complained. It was necessary. He even helped hold down old Frank Roberson, who had a chunk taken out of his shin by some dead thing he was in the process of braining. He'd limped away from the fighting and hidden himself in the loading dock of Marks and Spencer.

"Please Mal, not you," he said, but Mal had simply nodded sadly.

"They'll do it on three, Frank. It will be quick," he promised. The poor old baker looked up at the fat spike resting between his eyes, sobbing and shaking. A wet patch spread on the front of his trousers.

"Ready? One," Mal said, and the hammer fell. They never made it to two.

Tamsyn had the nightmare again. The zombie attacks always brought it on, but she never dreamt about the undead. This was the only small kindness her subconscious granted her.

As always, it was with perfect clarity that she relived the worst day of her life. The bus was about to come, and her mother had just thrust a five pound note into her hand, telling her to buy the damn magazine and to stop pestering her.

"Be quick about it," she'd snapped at her. Not *I love you*, or *I'm so proud of you, Tam*. Be quick about it.

Walking back from the newsagency, Tamsyn could only watch in horror as the car rounded the corner way too fast, losing traction, overcorrecting. It was an old estate wagon, covered in faded blue paint and rust.

The car ploughed into the packed bus shelter, scattering bodies like autumn leaves. A frail old lady was thrown nearly twenty yards down the street, bouncing and rolling and finally settling into a tangle of broken limbs and ruptured paper-thin skin, right in front of Tamsyn.

She couldn't spare the shattered body of the elderly woman more than a glance because, caught up between the fender of the car and the metal frame of the shelter, body bent to an impossible angle, screaming in agony because *oh my god she's still alive,* were the broken leftovers of Jenny Webb.

"Mum!" she screamed, teen heartthrob magazine fluttering to the ground. There was nothing she could do, nothing to free her mum from the wreckage. She could do nothing but watch her lifeblood pour out, listen to her scream, and beg and wail then her final rattling gasp as death took her.

A furious mob was hauling the driver out of the car, a man so drunk that he couldn't even stand. If it wasn't for the timely arrival of the police, they might well have beaten him bloody.

And their eyes met, now as then, each and every time she had this awful nightmare. Simon Dawes, the man who'd killed her mother. She'd sat in that courtroom through months of adjournments and legal tweakings, hating the man, wishing a horrid death upon him, every muscle in her aching for justice.

"Tam, it's okay," Mal said, gently shaking her awake. He must have heard her screams, even from the other end of their borrowed terrace house. For a long moment she trembled and tears streamed down her face.

"Come on, love, I'll make you a hot drink," he said, and led her by candlelight down to the kitchen.

They lived in a dead man's house; the Webb house lay well outside of the Safe Zone, and they'd had to abandon everything they owned.

"I'm sorry you're still having the dreams," Mal said.

"Not your fault," she said, shivering in her dressing gown. "Anyway, there's not a lot we can do, because my psychiatrist is dead and walking around. Probably still billing you, too."

Mal grinned. He had a big scratch running down his forearm, and a bruise on his right cheek that was already going greeny-purple. The fight to defend the west side of town had been long and bloody and had taken everyone Gravesend could spare to put the horde down.

"I don't like this place, Dad," Tamsyn said. "I miss our stuff."

"I'm not a fan of it either," Mal said, putting more wood into the old stove in the living room. It had been purely decorative until Mal cleaned out the flue and put it back into usage.

"Can't we try and get some of our gear back? What if a forage team goes near our house? We could tell them to pick up some of our things."

"You know we can't do that, love," Mal said. "They do that for us, they'll have to do it for everyone else. Their job is dangerous enough."

He picked up the saucepan of water on the stovetop and judging it to be hot enough, he mixed up a drink for Tamsyn.

"It's the last of the chocolate drink, so make the most of it," he said, handing her a steaming mug.

"It would mean a lot to me, going back," she said. "That's the only family photo we have." Tamsyn pointed to the photo from Mal's wallet, crease folds pushed flat and sitting in a frame on the mantle.

"Sorry love," Mal said. "It's hard all round. At least we're alive."

They sat in silence, with nothing but the ticking of the metal stove, a faint rustle as the hot coals shifted and settled.

"In a way, I'm glad your mother didn't see this day," Mal said, looking at the photo from a long-forgotten family trip. "She had family in Folkestone, and I doubt they lived past the first day of the outbreak."

Tamsyn watched Mal, warming his hands in front of the little stove. In the daylight he was full of vigour, organising work-teams, making plans, corralling the children and providing them with a focus. It was only in the cold of night, in the intimacy of this false home, that she saw her father for what he truly was. A tired, scared man, hair made prematurely white by the events of the past year.

"Damn Government," Mal sighed. "Too slow to blow the Channel Tunnel, and now this."

"They weren't to know, Dad," she said, wishing for the millionth time that she hadn't gone for that magazine.

In a dark corner of her heart, she wished she'd been standing with her mum when Simon Dawes roared around the corner. She could have shared that death, a clean death, back when the world didn't crawl with monsters.

"None of us were to know."

— 2 —

Interregnum," Mal said. Except they were in school now and he was Mr. Webb for her, same as everyone else.

The school was set up in the old St George's Church, the only place Mal had deemed as suitable. The acoustics were perfect, he told the Council. But the truth was that it was easily defensible, and close enough to the river that what remained of Gravesend's children could quickly get to the boats.

"It's a Latin term meaning 'between the kings' and was sometimes applied to the Dark Ages," he continued, pacing around in front of the pulpit. "When the Roman Empire fell, much of their knowledge was believed lost. Going by Petrarch's rose-coloured nostalgia, the ancient Romans had a civilisation like nothing the western world had ever seen.

"Widespread literacy. Engineering projects that had never been imagined, made possible by science. Siege machinery that was ahead of its time. Medicine. I could go on."

Tamsyn looked around and saw that some of the other kids were distracted. Eddie Jacobs was nudging one of his mates in the side and laughing. It was easy enough to pass stupid notes behind the pews, thinking that Mal didn't know.

He knew all too well and let the kids get away with it. It was hard enough to get them to turn up at all, and these days it was wisest to let certain things slide.

"When the Roman Empire fell, it was said to have set the course of western science back for one thousand years. *One thousand years,*" he repeated. "Outside of monasteries, it was believed that few in Europe even knew how to read and write. If you bought into this Roman nostalgia, why, it stayed that way until the Renaissance."

"Of course, none of this was true," Mal continued. "Civilisation went on. Science, rational thought, trade. Art. People find ways to fill the gaps. There was never really a dark age, not in the ways that Petrarch meant."

Perhaps he realised that he'd lost some of the class because he stopped mid-lecture. Sighing, he sat down on the steps of the sanctuary and looked up at the ceiling.

"I know it's hard for some of you. The last place you want to be is in here," and some of the class mumbled their agreement. "I've heard some of the parents say that there isn't much point to even having a school."

There were just under thirty children in the classroom, of all ages. Most of the old schools were outside of the Safe Zone, and the kids who'd survived the first wave of the zombie outbreak had either been home sick, playing hooky, or home-schooled.

Tamsyn had been over at Maidstone, visiting Dr. Clarke for one of their weekly chats. Mal had come to pick her up, and she had been grateful. She'd been feeling fragile that day and had asked him to drive her home. Had she tried to catch the Gravesend bus, she would now be outside with the stinkers, pounding on the wall and slavering for human flesh.

"I won't make you stay here. If you want to work instead, I can have a chat to Council, assign you to some of the forage crews or work teams. I only want you here if you're prepared to learn."

That certainly shut a few people up. Boring as school might be, it was an easy way out from having to work on reclamation projects, most of which revolved around thankless manual labour.

"The reason that I'm so hard on you kids is this," Mal continued. "It's unlikely that anyone's coming to save us. There's been no sign of the government or the army, and apart from a few places like Gravesend, there's nothing left of Britain."

Silence. The facts were enough to depress anyone, let alone a room full of youngsters. *Good one, Dad*, Tamsyn thought. *We're scared enough without having to hear that.*

"It's gonna be up to you kids one day. You need to learn more now than you ever did before. Once you could have become beauticians or computer programmers. But you have to realise that your old comfortable world is gone."

"You'll all need to learn as much as you can. Medicine. Agriculture. Engineering. Maths and science. Even textiles and weaving. You'll be making your own clothes someday soon."

The tiny class sat still and looked at the ceiling, the floor, anywhere but at the man delivering a series of uncomfortable truths.

"Make no mistake, the human race is in serious trouble. And the biggest threat isn't what's outside of the walls trying to get in. No. What keeps me awake at night is this simple fact: we are perhaps two generations away from an actual Dark Age."

Tamsyn was out in the churchyard, sketching the Pocahontas memorial statue. It was one of her favourite subjects, and she'd drawn it in her notebook several times.

The first few were straight sketches, attempts to capture the statue in different shades of light. Lately, she'd inserted Pocahontas into bizarre fantastical settings, like a boat in the middle of the Thames, the distant riverbank aflame. This time around Tamsyn was working her into a futuristic cityscape, a great oversized Madonna looking down upon the zipping air-cars and sky-bridges.

Ali limped his way over, propping himself crutches and all on the bench next to her. He shifted his plaster-cast foot into a comfortable position. It was a sloppy casting which reflected Dr. Murray's expertise at setting animal's bones, not children's.

"Hey Tam, why are you obsessed with this statue? I mean, it's cool and all, but it's a bit strange."

"Ali, my poor ignorant friend. This is Pocahontas."

"I know, I saw the Disney movie. What's your point?"

"This woman was a princess to her people, and she gave it all up to be with a white man, to pray to his god. She sailed halfway around the world to meet with a king. And what happens to her?"

"What?" Ali said, scratching inside his cast with her ruler.

"They leave London, showered with gifts, the toast of the season. They set sail down the Thames, and she falls ill. Very sudden, and turns out it's smallpox. So they pull up here, and during the night she dies. The most interesting thing to happen in Gravesend, Kent, is that a native princess came here to die."

"Oh," Ali said. "Still doesn't explain why you've got a boner for this dead chick."

"I've also come here from a foreign land, and I'm most likely going to die here too," Tamsyn said. "And it will be even more pointless, because there won't be anyone left to make a statue."

"Bet you're wishing you'd never moved here."

"Makes no difference. This virus or whatever it is, it's worldwide."

"Look on the bright side, Tam. Camberwell Arts isn't having an intake any time soon, but there's nothing to stop you from sailing up the Thames and nicking some priceless artworks."

"Nothing except eight million or so zombies prowling the streets, you mean."

She remembered a still day last spring, sitting with Mal on the end of the pier. Even though Greater London was 25 miles away, they could hear the zombies. Millions of them moaning at once, and if she tried really hard, she could pretend that they sounded like the faint roar of traffic.

"Hey, it's Trampsyn!" someone yelled, and she groaned. It was Eddie Jacobs and a bunch of his mates, kicking a football and shoving each other. One of them booted the ball past her head, and it rebounded from Pocahontas's face to a resounding cheer. The ball rolled to a stop at Ali's feet.

"Hey curry-muncher, pass us the ball!" Eddie yelled, but Ali ignored him. The burly lad came across the lawn to pick up the ball, stepping over Ali's legs and roughly knocking his plaster cast. Ali breathed in sharply, trying not to cry out.

"Sorry 'bout that, champ," Eddie smirked.

"What the hell is wrong with you?" Tamsyn said, on her feet now. She got into Eddie's personal space and glared up at him.

He's just a stupid bully, she told herself. *He needs to be put in his place.*

"It's a free country. Sorry, did you want some private time with your foreign boyfriend?" he laughed.

"Piss off, he's not my boyfriend," Tamsyn said. "And you are a racist piece of shit."

"What did you say?"

"Racist," she said slowly, poking him in the chest with each word. "Piece. Of. Shit."

Bright red spots appeared on his broad cheeks, and Eddie ground his teeth. She was a girl, nearly half his size, and few were game to stand up to him. He was genuinely confused.

"Smash her!" one of his mates yelled out.

"Grab her tits!" another said, and they fell about laughing.

"Enough!" she heard Mal yell out as he came running from the church's rear entrance. The other kids scarpered, leaving just

Eddie and her standing toe to toe in front of Ali. A frozen tableau, under the serene smile of Pocahontas.

"What in the bloody hell is going on here?" Mal demanded.

"Nothing, Mr. Webb. Me and Tam were just having a little chat," Eddie said, bouncing the ball from hand to hand.

"Ali?" Mal asked, but he looked down at his cast, cheeks flushing. Tamsyn guessed it was humiliating, having a girl fight your battles for you.

"It's all right," Tamsyn said. "Eddie and I have an understanding." Mal ignored her. Grabbing her by the arm, he put himself between her and Eddie.

"Look here, Jacobs, I won't have you acting like a thug around my school. Your 1,000 word essay just became 2,000 words," he said, to Eddie's rather vocal dismay. He pulled a spiral notepad out of his pocket, rapidly scribbling out a note. He waved it in front of Eddie's nose.

"I expect you to take this note home and get it signed by your father. Hopefully he can give you some of the discipline you so badly need."

"This school is a joke," Eddie said, crumpling the paper in his fist. Staring at Mal, he jammed the note into his pocket and left.

"Are you okay?" Mal asked, but she shrugged her way out of his concerned hands.

"Dad, I was fine! He's just a stupid kid."

"That 'stupid kid' was about to belt five shades of shit out of you. Or worse."

"Relax, Dad. It's not *Lord of the Flies* just yet."

All that Mal Webb had ever asked from his daughter was that she be politically aware, and even in these chaotic times she was dragged along to every sitting of the Gravesend Council. Most of the Borough of Gravesham was a stomping ground for corpses, so it was deemed pointless to refer to anything outside of the town itself.

This enclave of survivors had quickly ratified a new town constitution, elected some public officials, and continued to bicker in the grand tradition of British local government.

"All I'm saying is that we need to gather information," Terry Jacobs said, absently tugging at the dead mayor's sash with his greasy hands. He'd been a lorry driver before the outbreak and was elected on the grounds of his barricade plan. The Safe Zone.

"It's a stupid idea," Dr. Murray said. "You ask me, we shouldn't be attracting attention to ourselves."

"Well no one's asking you, are they?" Jacobs said. He was up, pacing the room and scowling at tonight's pack of naysayers. "What if the London zombies are migrating? What came at us last night, what very nearly *wiped us out*, that was nothing."

Tamsyn could have heard a pin drop in the new Council Chambers, formerly known as The Three Daws Pub. An old smuggler's haunt. She always thought this Council looked second-rate, sitting around a trestle table on plastic chairs.

There was a big block-mounted map on the wall, lifted from the Tourist Centre. It showed most of Kent, and the Council had attacked it with felt tip pens. The initial movements of the zombie hordes were marked in, spreading out from Folkestone like a gang of fat black worms. The towns confirmed as no-go zones had crosses through them.

A big angry circle surrounded Greater London, up in the top left of the map. 8 MILLION DEAD AND WALKING, Jacobs had scrawled next to it.

"We need to send a party towards London, to spot any large zombie movements," Jacobs continued. He jabbed at the map with the mayoral sceptre, captured from Cygnet House along with the other trappings of an honest government. This special raid had killed two people.

"That's daft," someone called from the back. "No one's gonna volunteer for that. Poor sods will end up eaten."

"I didn't say it had to be on foot," Jacobs said. "They can take a boat and be safe as babes in the middle of the Thames."

There was a general rumble of agreement. There were only a handful of working boats left to the town; hundreds of amateur sailors had taken to the waters in that first mad panic. Several boats had crashed and sunk within sight of the Pier.

Those who stayed hadn't been game to leave their food supply, didn't know any safe places to go. Wasn't the whole world like this anyway?

"I want to send a boat all the way into London itself," Jacobs said. "They can spot for signs of the government, of the army. Hell, they can even look for some supplies while they're out on their pleasure cruise."

The motion for a naval expedition was seconded and carried. A team of scouts would be kitted out and sent upriver at dawn.

"Bet you a chocolate bar they won't make it back in one piece," Mal whispered.

"Do I look mad?" Tamsyn whispered furiously. "I'm not taking that bet. They're toast."

Next was a report from Communications. This was a glorified way of describing Mr. Wakefield's ham radio rig. The work crews had built him a shelter in the unfinished apartment complex by the river, his mess of aerials bristling from the exposed girders a good 100 metres above the ground.

"I've lost contact with the survivors in Luton," Wakefield wheezed. Tam had never seen him without a cigarette. "They lost nine last week, so it doesn't look good for them."

"What about the mob to the north?"

"Manchester says not to approach them. They're holding tight for now, but the dead things are swarming up there, thicker than fleas on a dog's arse. Hundreds of thousands, they reckon."

"How are Tilbury going?"

"They lost three on a trip to the shops. Say they're running low on food, and have fuel to trade."

There was a small group of thirty or so across the river, hiding on a damaged cargo ship up in drydock. The *Paraclete*. All the other working ships at Tilbury's deep-water port had taken to the seas at the first sign of trouble.

"I'll give bugger all to them stevedores. Offer half what we offered last time."

Tam was sure that Jacobs's bravado masked a very real fear. The town inventory was never tabled in Council, and folks were starting to get nervous. How much food did Gravesend actually have left?

"Any more word from the Isle of Sheppy?"

"Nothing new," Wakefield said. "They just repeat that same phrase whenever I hail them, and then they sign off."

Warning. Do not approach the Island. Intruders will be shot on sight. Unfortunately, this was true. The only bridge onto the island had been completely destroyed. The first group sent downriver with trade goods had been fired upon. The shooters had been wearing HM Prison Service uniforms.

"Damn those swampies. We should be helping each other," Dr. Murray growled. "I hope all them murderers and rapists break loose and give 'em what they got coming."

"Next item. Food rations will be increased this month," Jacobs announced to a delighted murmur. "We've got to eat all the frozen meat before it spoils. Plus the generators are using too much fuel for us to keep the freezers working."

The meeting broke into excited chatter, but the mayor hollered above the din, thumping the table until everyone was silent.

"Oy! The meeting's not over yet. One more thing I want to discuss."

Tamsyn had a horrible feeling in her gut. Jacobs had been eyeing off Mal the whole meeting. Now he'd buttered up the town and was ready to strike.

You shouldn't have punished his kid, she thought.

"Mal Webb's school. I've been against it since the word go, and I haven't changed my mind. It's time we closed it down."

"This is madness," Mal said, on his feet now, and he was shouted down by some of the others. The mayor bashed his sceptre against the table until it had a dent in one side and the mob had gone quiet.

"We're about survival now," Jacobs said. "Education is a luxury, and I say we can't afford it."

"We can't afford *not* to teach the kids," Mal said. "Do you want your grandkids to be throwing spears and telling fairy tales about aeroplanes?"

"Rubbish. The kids will be fine. We need them, Webb. There's work needs to be done, and not enough hands to do it."

"Oh, like the garden allotments that are doing so well? How much food did we grow this year, Terry?"

A cold snap earlier that month had killed nearly everything. The first harvest had been dismal, and with winter arriving there'd be no plantings till the spring thaw.

"Mind your bloody tongue, Webb. It's all trial and error. You want to stay in this town, you need to respect the Council's decisions."

The vote went slightly in Jacobs's favour, and so with a final bang of the battered sceptre the meeting was brought to an end. The Gravesend School was now officially closed, and Mal Webb found himself without a job.

— 3 —

Will Dwyer came for her just before dawn. He was a familiar face, a neighbour from their old street. Tamsyn remembered his sweet young wife and their new baby girl, who'd never made it to the barricades that first awful night.

Will's face was badly scarred, and his eyes spoke of deeper horrors. He'd had an easy smile once, but Tamsyn couldn't remember what it looked like.

"I'm sorry, Mal, but the rules are the rules. They drew her name out of the hat, fair and square."

"She's just a kid, Will!" Mal argued.

"But Tam's on the guard roster, and she's agreed to fight wherever Council needs her to. She's coming on the boat."

"I'll go in her place, then."

"No dice, it's her assignment."

"It's okay, Dad," Tam said at his elbow, still blinking away sleep. "It will be all right."

"Mal, Jacobs put me in charge of this fool's errand. I promise you, I'll look after your little girl as if she were my own."

There was a long awkward moment, and Mal nodded.

Will gave her enough time to quickly wash up and get dressed. Council had rigged up some water stills, but the line-ups were always too long, so whenever it rained the Webbs caught the runoff from their roof, boiled it just to be sure. That was yesterday, and the water in the saucepan was already icy cold. Awareness came back to her, shortly followed by a panic that gripped her insides and squeezed.

Keep it together, she thought. *It's just a boat ride, nothing serious.*

She put on a thick denim jacket and her ski gloves, strapped an archery bracer onto each arm for added protection. She pushed the handle of a claw hammer through her belt and strapped a quiver of arrows to the other side. Will was shaking his head as she came down the stairs.

"Leave the bow at home, love. We'll kit you out with a gun."

"No guns," she said. "Anyway, I'm a better shot with this."

"All right, Robin Hood, have it your way," Will said.

Tam grabbed a small satchel and stuffed it with food, and an old soda bottle they'd filled with rainwater. She jammed her spare notepad in there too, and some pens. *I'd hate to drop months of work into the river,* she thought. *I can glue these pages in later.*

"Quick now, they're waiting," Will said. The three of them walked briskly through the empty streets, Will's flashlight showing the way. The streetlights were now nothing more than dark monuments to a kinder time.

They were at the Gravesend Pier, the motorboat already full of people with guns. Tamsyn thought the boat looked awfully low in the water, probably overloaded or leaking.

"Watch your step," Will said, holding Tamsyn's hand as she gingerly stepped across the gap between the boat and the pier. Someone handed her the compound bow, and she found herself nestled on the floor of the boat, grateful for the warmth of those around her.

She recognised a few of the people onboard and got a nod and a nervous smile from Naomi Higgins. The old butch had once been a netball friend of her mum's, and after the accident she'd visited the Webbs with a care basket once a week or so.

"Men are next to useless. They can't even look after themselves, let alone a little one," the enormous black woman had said at the time, hamming up the man-hating act as she often did. Naomi's cooking was barely edible, but fine cuisine had been far from their minds at the time.

Drifting back to the present, she noticed a handful of people stood on the end of the Pier to see them off. The group of well-wishers stood by the edge of the historic wrought-iron structure, shuffling their feet and rubbing their hands. Mal stood to one side, tight-lipped and white. Mayor Jacobs was nowhere to be seen.

What? No brass band?

"Let's go," Will said. Naomi fiddled with something up the front, the outboard motor roaring into life. The sound was eerie and echoed across the silent pitch-black of the Thames. Tamsyn hoped that zombies wouldn't be drawn by the noise.

Then they were away and powering upriver, the belly of the boat slapping against the murky water. Naomi switched on a bank of spotlights, steering the boat carefully around the wreckage that littered the Thames.

Prows and masts poked from the murk, more evidence of the panic. At one stage they had to slow the boat right down, and one bloke climbed onto the prow to clear a path, pushing wreckage away with an oar.

An ocean liner had crashed into the far bank just out of the Tilbury port. It lay tilted in the water, the pre-dawn light showing a great hole torn in the hull by the collision.

Tamsyn could see someone moving around on the deck—several someones. A figure dropped over the rail and into the water, then another. She thought she could hear a faint keening from the beached liner, but the sound was soon lost to the chill whip of wind, the deep chugging of the motor behind them.

When the sun lifted above the horizon, Tamsyn unpacked her notepad and pens. She sketched the scenery as it rolled by, deft little drawings of the dead towns and the uncaring river that flowed past them.

"Hey Seb, she's gonna put you out of a job," one of the others said. A young man who wasn't much older than her had a digital camera out, snapping photos of every town they passed.

The zombies were already more numerous and active than they were at Gravesend. Dozens of them stared dumbly at the boat as it droned by, and the man next to Tam aimed a rifle at the shore. A dead man in a crumbling tuxedo reached for them with the stub of an arm, dropping face first into the water.

"Everyone, save your bullets," Will called out. "They can't hurt us from there."

As far back as Tam could see, the streets and roads were full of rotting corpses slowly shuffling away from the city. When the occasional town became the uninterrupted outskirts of London itself, their numbers climbed dramatically.

The undead exodus was plain to see. Thousands and thousands of murderous flesh-eaters, on a slow march towards Gravesend.

After an hour or so they reached the Tower Bridge. It was choked with traffic, cars long since abandoned. Many of them still had doors and trunks hanging open, this still scene speaking volumes of the long-ago panic.

Tam imagined the terrified mob, screaming and pushing. Perhaps some of them trusted their safety to the waters far below or pushed their children out to die before the blank-faced man-eaters could get to them.

Without realising it she'd drawn out the imagined scene in amazing detail, and Seb looked over her handiwork.

"Damn, girl, you really have replaced me." He took his photos anyway, the actual scene eerie and still but for the slow movement of a handful of zombies. Naomi put the throttle to full, weaving the boat left and right as they passed under the bridge. The undead became visibly excited by the sound of their motor, pressed right up to the edge and staring down at them.

The gangling leftovers of a school girl pinwheeled down from the sky, glancing from the edge of the prow with a sickening snap. The zombie thrashed and sank behind them, the rotten gingham dress vanishing into the gloomy water.

Tamsyn had her bow up and an arrow ready, her heart pounding. If that *thing* had fallen into the boat, they'd all be dead now.

Millions of rotting monsters packed the inner city, thicker than ants, slowly crossing the bridges. The walking corpses jostled with each other in the crowded streets, aping the commuters they'd perhaps once been. It was a sick parody, and the moment a forage team stepped into the streets, they would be torn apart.

London was no longer a city. It was a living tomb.

"Well, that's torn it," Will said.

The boat sat silently in the middle of the Thames, pointed at the ruins of the Westminster Bridge. The whole thing had been collapsed, and sharp points of rubble breached the surface, even at high tide. Only some fragments of the supports remained above the waterline, and there was no safe way of getting the boat through.

"Must've been the army what blew it up," someone else offered. "You know, to keep the zombies out."

"Fat lot of good that did," Seb said. He was madly clicking away, taking photos of the Westminster Palace, the London Eye, the hands of the clock tower forever frozen at seven minutes past ten.

Mr. Wakefield had set them up with a portable radio transmitter, and they tried for long minutes to raise anyone at all on any frequency. Here in the heart of the city, surely any survivors with even a cheap walkie-talkie would hail them.

They sent up flares, even set off one of those things that spewed out coloured smoke. Apart from luring dozens of undead towards their boat and into the water, they got zero interest.

"Typical pollies, never around when you need 'em," Will said, pointing to the Houses of Parliament. The flags were rotting, the grounds crawling with undead.

"What about Buckingham Palace?"

"You wanna go through that crowd for a look, you can be my guest."

Everywhere, the mobile corpses of Londoners trampled the rubbish. Big Ben might stand forever silent, but here the dead were a murmuring multitude, and the noise rose and fell like a football crowd. This far into the city, the stink was unbelievable, an eye-watering miasma of rot.

Tamsyn finished drawing the statue of Boudica, her defiant figure overlooking the ruined bridge, her proud nation finally overrun by death itself.

"Filthy things," she whispered, sketching in her entourage of corpses. They were so thick now, pressing up against the base of her statue, that from Tam's perspective Boudica's chariot seemed to be aloft on a sea of the undead.

"Will, let's get the hell out of here," Naomi said, and he nodded. The engine roared back into life, and she wheeled the boat around, throwing up a large wake of rotting body parts and other muck stirred up from the depths.

The little recon party sat morose as they headed for home, and Tam wondered what the reactions would be to their bad news. *Probably build a bigger wall, plant more veggies,* she silently scoffed. *We need to move somewhere safer!*

"Hey!" Will said. "Gunshots!"

Tam could hear it too, a faint stutter just audible above the endless chorus of dead throats, the tinny chug of the motor.

"Other survivors!" Tam cried out. "We've gotta help them."

Naomi slammed the throttle to full, and the deep chug became a whine, the boat slapping and lurching as it leapt across the murk. No subtlety now, nothing but speed and hope.

Someone is alive in all this!

The return trip seemed to take forever, and Will swept the binoculars frantically, left and right. They soared past the shattered boroughs, still crowded with undead. Seb let off the last of their flares, hoping to draw the attention of whoever had been shooting.

"Come on!" Will shouted to Naomi. "If we're too late to save them, I'll never forgive myself."

Nothing. The gunfire had stopped. There was no way of knowing where it had come from, just somewhere downriver. *If someone is still alive and hiding in London, perhaps they've crawled back into their bolthole,* Tamsyn thought. *You'd be mad to linger long in these streets.*

"Fuck it," Will cried, slamming his hand against the rail. Tamsyn was surprised to see tears welling up in the big man's eyes. She put her hand on his shoulder, but he grunted, shrugged off her touch.

"Straight for home," he yelled to Naomi. "Don't stop for no one or nothing. We've seen enough."

Rounding the Isle of Dogs, they once more approached the Tower Bridge, Naomi running the launch as hard as she could. If there were any coffin-dodgers looking to hitch a ride on this boat, they'd find it hard to land on it at that speed. But there were no zombies anywhere to be seen on the bridge. The dockside fronting onto the Tower was also free of undead traffic.

"Where did they all go?" Seb said, photographing the empty promenade. Tam was looking for signs of anything, dead or otherwise, when everyone started shouting. Naomi swung the boat around in a tight arc, cutting the throttle. Tam fought hard to keep her balance and could almost see herself slipping into the foul water. There were bodies floating in the river, she saw. Some of the half-submerged ghouls were still twitching, surrounded by their own guts and gore.

As the boat righted itself, she saw the cause for the alarm. Dangling from the bridge like a pair of green spiders were two men. Soldiers, abseiling down lengths of rope. They halted their descent, assault rifles trained casually down on their little group.

"Put down your weapons," a crackling instruction came from above. Tam could see a handful of figures on the bridge above them, including the man with the megaphone. More soldiers.

"What's going on?" Will called out through his cupped hands. No one answered him.

"We're going to send out a boat," said the same faceless man above them. "You are to place your weapons and supplies into our custody."

"What are we gonna do?" Seb said, raising his camera. Will snatched it out of his hands.

"Don't you dare take another photo," he hissed. "We are in deep enough shit without you antagonising these goons."

Heart pounding, Tam took a good look at the men on the abseils. They looked gaunt, skeletal. The nearest soldier had grown a scraggly beard, and with some alarm she noted that they'd removed all insignia from their uniforms.

They're starving, she realised.

"Will, they're not soldiers," Tam said. "They're robbers!"

"I know, I know," he said. "Not much we can do about it."

"We can't just give them our stuff," she protested. "What if they just kill us anyway? What if they torture one of us, and we tell them where we came from?"

The old Traitor's Gate eased itself open, and a little punt came putting out onto the river, a pair of men in army greens on board. In perhaps a minute they would pull up alongside them.

Seems this mob had looked on the Tower as a good holdout. Perfectly defensible, tall walls, good visibility. Pity the London forage scene was such a bitch. Hence, their clever little trap. Knowing the river was blocked, knowing that anyone on a boat would have to come back past here, carrying food and what have you.

Stand and deliver. They weren't even pretending to be the real army anymore. What had happened to them? Were they here when the city fell? Had this broken little squad huddled in the Tower, listening as the ghouls murdered thousands, millions of people within earshot?

"They don't deserve a crumb," Tam shouted. "We cannot sit here and let these bastards rob us!"

She could feel a panic attack coming on. God, what if they were going to keep her, make her their slave? Or worse?

"Go, Naomi, go!" she shrieked, pushing past the huddle in the middle of the boat, lurching into the woman's broad back. Whether by accident or design, Naomi pushed the throttle right forward. *We're committed to it now!*

"No!" Will yelled. The men on the ropes opened fire as they passed between them. Bullets bit into the sides of the boat, and Tam heard someone screaming. The quicker ones returned fire with their old bird guns and pistols, insignificant *pops!* against the murderous chatter of the assault rifles.

One of the soldiers seemed to be having trouble aiming his weapon, swaying around on the rope, bullets spraying into the water. Before he could right himself, Tamsyn was at the stern of the boat, drawing back an arrow, aiming blind. No time to adjust the sights, nothing but pull and release.

The arrow sunk deep into the man's belly, and he howled in pain, clutching at the shaft. Her next arrow went wide, but the man nearest her finished the soldier off with a rifle shot. The soldier was limp now, an obscene marionette twirling on the rope, big gun slipping into the waters below.

I just shot that man, Tam thought, hands trembling.

The men at the punt were shooting at them now, and as they passed under the bridge gunfire came from above. Keeping low behind the wheel, Naomi wriggled the boat left and right. Tam cried out as a near miss punched a hole in the bottom of the boat. It missed her leg by inches. The gunshots slowed and stopped, and it seemed the boat had made it to a safe distance.

"Oh God, that was close," she said to Seb, clutching his arm. "Look, the punt can't keep up."

She looked over at him and screamed, backpedalling away from the boy. A great hole had been torn out of Seb's throat, and he leaned over the gunwale, flopping and pale, his life-blood spilling in their wake. Even as she choked, working her mouth in shock, Will Dwyer seized her by the shoulders, shook her hard.

"You stupid girl! You just killed these men."

"They were gonna hurt us," she sobbed. "We had to run."

Through a film of tears, Tam looked at the butcher's nightmare that was their boat. The packed mess of men had been riddled with bullets, and at least three other people were dead. It was a miracle she'd escaped unharmed.

"We just had to give them our food," Will said, shaking with rage, eyes flashing with fury. "Then we could have gone on our merry little way."

Tam thought he was going to hit her. She opened her mouth to say something, anything, knowing that her platitudes would do nothing to bring back Seb and the others.

He had the front of her jacket bunched up in one hand, and slowly, expectantly, Tamsyn saw his other hand curl up into a fist.

"Will, don't," Tam started, and then Will Dwyer's head seemed to burst outwards, spraying her with bits of brain and bone. Screaming, she pushed him away, panic lending her strength. He went over the back of the boat. There was a horrible grinding sound, and then the motor choked, died.

"Oh my god, oh my god, I've just put Will through the propeller!" Tam shrieked. Someone pulled her down into the bloody floor of the boat, water seeping in by the second. She heard another whipcrack, felt the impact of a bullet striking the boat.

"Stay down! There's a sniper in the Tower," Naomi shouted.

"Move this boat, the others are catching up to us," someone said. Peering through a bullet hole in the side, Tamsyn saw the slow passage of that ridiculous barge, patiently working its way towards them. A man stood on the deck, raising a mean looking gun. Was it an Uzi? Tam didn't know enough to tell.

"The motor's all jammed up!" Naomi said. "Something's blocking it."

Another snap, and a man was screaming, clutching at his thigh. The water was rising slowly, and there were several inches in the bottom of the boat now. They'd have to start bailing it out soon, or they'd never make it back to Gravesend.

One man braved the sniper to fire a shotgun at the punt. The shot was wasted, out of range. The soldier replied with a quick burst from his submachine gun. He wasn't close enough to do much damage, but at least one metallic thud told of a bullet striking the motor.

"We are fucked, so fucked," Tam said. "All my fault."

She put down her bow, waited for the distant rifleman to fire his gun, waste seconds reloading. The moment she heard the report, she was over the side and into the icy-cold water, with only time to snatch a quick breath.

I've gotta clear the propeller! she thought. *If they can start the motor again, we have a chance.* She felt her way along the bottom of the boat, trying to see through the disgusting murk.

Lungs starting to ache, she found the propeller, found the jumble of mincemeat that was once Will Dwyer, the pleasant family man from two houses down. The blades had snagged themselves in his stomach, great ribbons of intestine spiralling out from the wound.

Tam felt the rather odd sensation of her lungs struggling to draw in breath, while at the same time her stomach wanted to purge everything she'd ever eaten.

I'm so sorry Will, she thought, trying to jerk the big man free of the blades. She could see a black shape gliding overhead; the soldier's barge, getting closer. Bullets punched through the water, and bubbles burst from her lips when hot fire licked her side.

I've been shot.

Choking on the foul water, she finally dislodged the body of her Dad's old lawn bowls partner, and he drifted away from the boat, already bobbing towards the surface. She kicked to the far side of the boat, trying to put it between her and the sniper.

The engine fired as she reached the surface, her lungs burning and vision blurred. It was all she could do to grip the side, hanging on for dear life, unseen hands pulling her up when it was safe to do so.

The Tower and the Bridge faded from view, and Tamsyn knew that she would never set eyes on them ever again, that London was a fool's dream.

No one was coming to rescue them. Gravesend was as good as it got.

Tamsyn felt like she was dying, and she probably was. She'd come down with a fever from diving into the freezing Thames, or from swallowing down a gutful of diseased water. The river had been bad enough twelve months ago, and now it was little more than a conduit for corpses.

Mal dragged her mattress downstairs, setting her up in front of the potbelly stove. He fed it with palings torn from the back fence, kept the room heated to the point of being uncomfortable, yet Tamsyn still shivered.

A line of stitches ran across her right hip, and Dr. Murray called her "luckier than a boxful of horseshoes." The bullet had only creased her young skin, parting it like a puckered kiss.

The wound was puffy now, infected. There were no antibiotics left in the Safe Zone, and all she had to combat the sickness was a half-packet of paracetamol, doled out carefully by her father.

Soon she had no idea what was going on. When her body wasn't burning up, she felt like a girl carved from ice. She whimpered, grew delirious, was convinced that zombies had gotten into the house. Argued with her mum.

Mal came and went, and every now and then cold water slid down her aching throat. Once she thought she saw Naomi by her bedside, but she drifted off. When she woke, the warm, broad hands that had been mopping her brow were gone.

The nightmare of her mother's death came again, but everything had changed. The bus shelter was full of people that she knew, who'd gone for a boat ride and never come home. Will Dwyer chatted with Seb, who was showing him some photos on his camera. The other young men wore football scarves, singing together drunkenly.

Her mother stood in the middle of all this, somehow separate from this camaraderie. She was looking straight at her daughter, shaking her head, a disappointed look on her face. Jenny Webb paid no attention to the dead men around her.

Simon Dawes shot the corner, overcorrecting. His car slammed into the shelter and sent them all flying, bags of meat that broke apart on impact. Will's head crumpled, his guts running out of him like fat blue worms. Seb's throat was torn out on a piece of glass, his blood painting the pavement slick with red.

Simon Dawes staggered out of the car, laughing, crying, calling for help. The others were already rising as the undead, even her mother. Only Will lay headless and eviscerated, a feast for the football fans.

Looking down at her hands, Tamsyn saw that she held a bow. Not the rubbish bow she'd looted from the camping store, but her good competition shooter from home. The one she'd won all the trophies with.

She had one arrow in her quiver, no more. A cruel, barb-tipped shaft, a thing of war. The means to end one life.

Simon Dawes slid against the side of his car, too drunk to even stand up. Seb and her mother were closing in on him, and in moments they would fall upon him, tearing and biting.

It was an awful way to die.

She drew the arrow back, sent it soaring towards Dawes. She did not go for a headshot, though she knew in the logic of this dream that she would not miss. It buried itself deep into his gut, a belly shot like the soldier on the bridge, punching through Dawes's back and into the car door behind him. Pinned, he could do nothing but scream hysterically as the undead reached for him...

Someone was shaking her awake. Looking up, she saw the concerned faces of Dr. Murray and Mal. She was in the sitting room of the borrowed house, her bedclothes and nightgown drenched with sweat.

"You're okay, sweetheart," Mal said, running a damp washcloth over her forehead. "It's all right, you're safe."

"Thought you were going to bust a vein," Murray said. "All tensed up, hands bunched into fists. Shouting at some poor bugger."

"Here, swallow this," Mal said, putting a large pill in her mouth. She took the glass of water and tried to swallow, the huge tablet scraping her swollen throat on the way down.

"What was that?" she gasped. Dr. Murray held up a plastic vial, shook the contents.

"Antibiotics," he said with a huge grin. "You're not to tell a soul we have these, you hear?"

"We asked Jacobs to send a forage team to the hospital," Mal said. "We lost a few people on that trip, so no one can know about anything I kept for myself."

Even their hoard of food under the floorboards was illegal, punishable by banishment from the town. Mal had taken a hell of a risk, stealing valuable medicine from under the eyes of Jacobs's goons.

"You went on the forage?" she asked, and he nodded. "I thought the hospital was crawling with coffin-dodgers."

"You were really sick, Tam," he said. "You needed this medicine, and I'm glad to see it's started working."

"What do you mean? How many of these have I had? How long have I been in bed?"

"It's been eight days, Tam," her father said, voice breaking. "We almost lost you."

— 4 —

Tamsyn was still too sick to go to Council, so Ali sat with her. He usually lived in the haberdashery on New Street, under the care of Naomi and Monica, a timid woman with a shocking frizz of red hair.

Ali never talked about his parents, and Tam didn't pry into his grief. He'd skipped school to see Terminator 5, and while this had saved his life, he didn't have anyone now. Council had assigned him to the care of the women.

Monica had worked the till at the haberdasher's, and come doomsday (and the permanent disappearance of her manager) she'd wasted no time in converting the store into a rather liveable house. Fabric was hung from floor to ceiling, making a maze of temporary walls and rooms. There were stacks of blankets and quilts for bedding, and staying there felt like camping.

"I'm just glad to spend one evening away from those horrible old lesbians," Ali said, dodging the pillow that she threw at him.

"Don't be awful," Tam said. "I think it's nice they've found each other. Monica lost her partner in the outbreak, you horrible shit."

She went back to gluing the pages from the disastrous London trip into her main notebook. The book had gotten a good soaking in the bottom of the boat, but most of her drawings were still legible. Loose sheets were arranged in front of the potbelly stove, drying, some of the ink smudged. Tam thought she could redraw some of the more damaged pictures.

"Don't get me wrong, I don't care that they're gay," Ali said, shovelling down the contents of a lukewarm can of Irish stew. "I just don't need to hear old people having sex."

There was knocking at the door, and they both jumped. She recognised Mal's code and relaxed. The meeting must have ended late, and he'd been expected two hours ago.

Ali picked up his crutches and limped down the hallway, struggling to unbar the door one-handed. Mal had installed strong brackets to each side of the jamb, and they kept it wedged shut with the iron bar from a weights set. Mal came in, a chill wind following him inside. He was on the guard register now and set his rifle by the front door.

"This town is run by idiots," he said, shivering and teeth chattering. "It's a miracle we haven't starved to death or been overrun."

"What did they say?" Tam asked.

"Bigger walls. More forage parties. Send raiding parties to take the Tilbury oil by force. Idiots."

"Dig more frozen gardens!" Ali laughed. "Pack the entire town up and risk the guns of Sheppy."

"You get the general idea." Mal grinned. "Also, Council said they need your drawings, Tam. Seb's camera ended up in the drink, and your soggy notes are the only record of that damned mess of a boat ride."

"Okay," she said, "just as long as I get them back. They're mine and they belong to me. I can do copies if they want to keep those."

"I think they just want to look at them," Mal said, settling down on the uncomfortable settee. He rubbed his arms furiously, covered his legs with a spare blanket.

"What else did they say?"

Mal said nothing for a long moment, either because he was still defrosting or because he was gathering his thoughts. *Goddamnit Dad, I need to know,* Tamsyn thought. *Does the town blame me for what happened?*

"Naomi spoke up for you at the meeting, says it's not your fault," Mal said. "That the robbers would have shot everyone anyway."

Silence. Ali cleared his throat, and they both looked at him. He reached for his crutches and made to stand up.

"I should get going," he said.

"Rubbish," Mal said. "You'll freeze before you get out the front gate. You're staying and that's the end of it."

Mal disappeared upstairs for a minute, and with much thumping and cursing he brought his mattress down the staircase. He set it up next to Tamsyn's, threw some blankets and a pillow at Ali.

"No hanky-panky, you two."

"Shut up, Dad!" she groaned, wishing she could sink right through the mattress and the floor. "That's not even funny."

Ali wriggled into his nest of blankets, blushing. *And now he's thinking about it. Thanks Dad. Last thing I need is a mate mooning over me, writing bad poems and whatever.*

Dousing the candles, Mal stretched out on the settee, the springs squeaking as he settled his weight. Tam could hear nothing but the howl of the wind outside, the shaking windows, the ticking of the old stove as it fought off the impending winter chill.

"Listen, there's something else you kids need to know about," Mal said in the darkness. "Something that Wakefield picked up on his radio."

"Other survivors?" Ali said.

"No. It was a recording, an automatic message that loops over and over. Very faint."

"What did it say?" Tam asked.

"It's not so much what it says, but where it's from. The transmission claims to be from America."

He told them what the message said, word for word. There wasn't much sleep in the Webb house that night, and it was fair to say that most of Gravesend spent a sleepless night too.

"What if the message is true?" Tamsyn said. "We've got to get to America!"

"How?" Ali said, limping along beside her. "You gonna book a flight at Heathrow? Tell the zombie pilot to take you to the moon while he's at it."

"What about a boat?"

Mal had told them about the heated discussions at Council. When the wording of the "American" transmission had sunk in, there'd been a handful of people keen to load up in what motor-boats and barges they had and just hare off across the Atlantic there and then.

Mayor Jacobs had called them suicidal idiots, "dreaming that our little toy boats could ever make it across the ocean. With winter coming on."

Much as it pained Mal to do so, he agreed with Jacobs. They were a town of photocopier technicians, of accountants and bus drivers. There wasn't anyone experienced enough to pilot them across the ocean safely, or a boat that could hope to survive the battering.

"You're mad," Ali scoffed. "There's icebergs and shit out there. Didn't you see *Titanic*?"

They were making their way to the Pier, with news that the ferry was coming over from Tilbury. They joined a crowd of bored onlookers, mostly kids with nothing better to do.

Tamsyn had been going stir-crazy and was glad to be outdoors. She felt like a train wreck on legs, but at least her fever had passed. Her hip still hurt like hell, though, and Dr. Murray's fresh supply of ibuprofen from the hospital wasn't doing much for her.

Eddie Jacobs was there, cradling a shotgun and watching the crowd with a bored eye. When he saw Tamsyn he held the gun at crotch level, hand working the barrel suggestively. He licked his lips and laughed.

"Idiot," Tam said, giving him the bird. "Whoever gave him a gun should be shot."

"Well, you'd better shoot the mayor, then," Ali said. "Daddy signed him up as a Council thug."

"Would the ferry make it across to America?" she said out loud, looking over the MV Duchess. The rusty old tub chugged across the water, blue smoke billowing from its exhaust. The engine sounded rough.

"I'll be surprised if it makes it across the river," Ali said. "Besides, you'd only be able to fit fifty or sixty people on that. And what about all our food and stuff?"

"All right, genius. I didn't say it was a good idea."

The ferry swung in towards the port, and she could see the deck and cabin packed with people. She did a rough count and realised that the Tilbury mob had brought their whole group across the Thames. There were a pair of men on the roof with guns, and a mob of sullen-faced people hefting iron pipes and other impro-vised weapons.

"What the hell?" Ali said. "Normally they only send a couple of old blokes over for a trade."

By the time the ferry pulled alongside the pier, Mayor Jacobs was there, and a strong force of what passed for the constabulary. Council goons. No one was pointing a gun at anyone else, but the atmosphere was far from friendly.

"What are you lot up to?" Jacobs yelled. As always, he had his grotty sash and battered sceptre, the mayoral effect lost when one took in his ratty anorak and his greasy, half-bald head.

"We want sanctuary," said Marcus Riley, the Tilbury mob's elected representative. He was an old union rep, and the bulk of his crew were stevedores, the handful quick enough to hole up on the drydocked *Paraclete* the day the world ended.

"Have you lost your bleeding minds? We can barely feed ourselves."

"Look, Jacobs, we've had to give up the docks. There's no food we can get to safely, and we can't stay there. For the love of God, let us off this boat."

"The deal was you come over for a trade. We're not a refugee camp, Riley, and the moment I let you stevedores in you'll be trying to run the show. I say you can all piss off."

A thick, silent moment. The weight of guns and other, cruder weapons, in the hands of scared people who could barely remember law and order. The parts of Riley's face that weren't hidden by his bushy white beard were a thundercloud.

"I hope those dead things push your walls over, and that you all die in your sleep," Riley said, spitting over the side of the boat. "We're human beings, just like you lot."

If we send them away, they're gonna die, Tamsyn realised. She looked around, saw the shame on many people's faces. But no one said anything. No one lifted a finger to stop this travesty.

And then Mal Webb climbed onto the bonnet of a junked car, put his fingers in his teeth and let out an ear-piercing whistle.

"Enough. Stop this, Jacobs. This isn't right and you know it."

"Watch your tongue, Webb," the mayor snarled. "I've got the mandate to run this town however I want, and I've made my decision."

"Well, we've still got the right to criticise our government when we think they're making bad decisions. And this is the stupidest thing you've done since we were stupid enough to vote you in."

There were scattered catcalls, a ragged cheer, some booing. Mal had successfully taken the wind out of Jacobs's sails.

"That's it, you're finished," Jacobs said, signalling to his goons to seize Mal. The press of the crowd prevented them from closing in, and Mal continued to heckle the mayor.

"One year ago, you were watching TV and scratching your balls, and now you're about to kill these people," Mal shouted above the crowd. "How can you have fallen so far, so quickly? You're not fit to run this town."

The crowd erupted into a passionate fury, everyone shouting at once. Those on the boat simply looked on in disbelief, unsure whether they were welcome or not.

Someone called out one simple word, "election!" and the word was repeated by others. In moments things got very ugly.

Mal was frogmarched to the Three Daws Pub and spent the night under Council arrest. A large mob rallied around the old pub, beating on the doors and calling for his release.

Sometime close to lunch, the Council gave in. The ex-teacher emerged, battered and bruised, but smiling. Tamsyn hugged him fiercely, tears rolling down her face.

"I thought they were gonna kill you, or throw us over the walls," she sobbed.

"No fear of that," he said, kissing her and hugging her till she thought her ribs would crack. "Your old man knew civil disobedience back when it was cool."

"Terry Jacobs has agreed to a new Council election," Mal announced to his rescuers. "One fortnight from today. And I will be standing for office as mayor."

There was a great cheer, and Tamsyn thought her heart would burst in her chest. When they'd dragged her dad away, she thought her world had ended. Now, there was hope.

He could really win this! Tam thought, looking around at those who'd rallied in support of Malcolm Webb. Well over half the town was there. *Gravesend just might become a place worth living in.*

The Tilbury ferry was permitted to stay in dock while the question of their sanctuary was chewed over. Tamsyn went visiting with Mal, who was keen to assure the refugees that things were looking up for them.

"We thought of going to the Canvey Islands, or even Foulness," Riley said over a shared cigarette. "But the water's not deep enough to keep the zombies out. Not worth going to Sheppy unless you want a bullet, so Gravesend seemed the safest place."

"Gravesend isn't going to be safe for much longer," Mal said. "More zombies are heading downriver every day, and before the year is out we'll need to consider relocating the town. I've got an idea, one that Jacobs doesn't agree with."

He pointed across the river to where the old Tilbury Fort lay huddled underneath the dormant power station. Marcus Riley had a moment best described as relieved stupidity.

"I can't believe we didn't think of it," he said. "We thought it was just a stupid old ruin."

"That stupid old ruin has got strong walls and a moat," Mal said. "And one little bridge to get in and out. There'd need to be some houses built, and we'd need to port over all of our supplies, but we could all fit in there."

They talked about the American radio message. Riley's radio guy had picked up the transmission from the deck of the *Paraclete*, their whole mob frustrated that the cargo ship was out of commission.

"Every other ship hightailed it out of the docks when those things appeared. Only place left to hide was a broken ship. Safe enough place when we raised the gangway, but thirty people worked through the ship's supplies pretty quickly."

"What's wrong with it?"

"Beats me. Manifest says engine trouble, but we're not talking a Mini here. There's whole engine rooms down below decks, as complicated as you like."

"You know, we've got a mechanic," Mal said. "Bloke called Gilly who used to fix trucks, crop harvesters, whatever. He might be able to help."

"Mate, he would have to be an engineering Houdini to get me near those docks again. They're overrun. We'd have a fight on our hands to reclaim that old tub."

"Speaking of which, do you know how to drive one of those things?" Mal asked.

"You ever been in the bridge of a big ship?" Riley said. "I couldn't tell you what half of those controls are. There's a manual up there and I read it twice, still don't make any sense."

"I guess there's no point fixing it," Mal conceded. "We might have the boat, but we don't have the captain."

Dr. Murray cleared Tamsyn for guard patrol. The drunken old sot wasn't happy about giving her a clean bill of health, but food needed to be earnt. The Webbs weren't on the mayoral gravy train just yet.

She spent the day on perimeter watch, pacing the southern border of the Safe Zone, trying to walk off her sore hip. The full loop took her behind Bath Street's cinderblock barricade, around a crooked dog leg of blocked-off streets, and then up past the clock tower till she got to the Thames again.

The southern boundary of the Safe Zone was the train line that bisected Gravesend, the embankment steep enough to keep the undead out. Anything stupid enough to wander across the tracks was easy to spot, easy to hear as they kicked the ballast around.

All the overpasses were blocked off, but the train station itself was a weak point. The platform was a mess of barricades and sandbags manned 24 hours a day.

Naomi was there, sharing some moonshine with the guards, and when she spotted Tamsyn she waved her over.

"Have a look at that," the stocky woman said, pointing down the line. Tamsyn couldn't believe her eyes; it was the dead waitress she'd sketched from the clock tower, stumbling along the track. When it saw the shooters behind their barricade it moaned with excitement, moved along a little quicker. It tripped over the track but righted itself, arms raised, mouth spread in hunger.

"Target practice, Tam," Naomi said. "What do you say, boys? Is some dead sheila even worth a bullet?"

The guards laughed. Tamsyn nocked an arrow to the bow and waited for the zombie to get a little closer. She was a little nervous and wished there wasn't anyone else watching her.

She tried for a headshot but it went wide, and the arrow clattered against the stones. Her next arrow buried itself just under the zombie's collarbone, while the next one sprouted from its thigh. Two more in its belly, and she put one through its arm before giving up.

"I'm not used to this stupid bow! The tension is set too high," she said, throwing down her bow.

"Don't blame your tools. I thought your dad said you'd won archery trophies or some such."

Tamsyn picked up a sharpened broom handle and used the blunt end to pry the zombie waitress from the edge of the platform. It was trying to climb up to them, gnashing its teeth and moaning like a constipated cow. There was no anger in its face, just dumb hunger.

It looked pathetic. Less than an animal.

The undead thing was gnawing at the other end of the broom handle, and a handful of rotten teeth fell out of its mouth.

"Go on, piss off!" she yelled, giving the zombie a great big shove. It tripped over the track and fell onto its backside, looking up at them with confusion.

"We don't want you here! Get lost!" she said.

"You tell 'em, girly!" one of the guards chuckled, and they joined in, waving their hands and yelling at the creature. "Go on, scat. Ya great stinky bitch."

The zombie climbed to its feet, and to everyone's astonishment it held its head high and turned away, for all the world as if trying to hold together some dignity. Bristling with arrows, it shuffled away from the town, heading west.

"Well, I'll be," Naomi said. "Biggest hedgehog I ever saw."

Tamsyn later visited the abandoned camping store. All the ammo had been rounded up by Council, but the archery gear was left on the shelves. She stocked up on arrows and looked again for a bow with a lighter pull, but had no success.

If I could just go home and get my OWN bow, this would be a lot easier.

Leaning a competition target against the base of the Pocahontas statue, Tamsyn hit the centre ring nearly every time. She was good, just as good as she'd ever been.

Archery had been Mal's idea, something to occupy her time after the car accident. She'd turned a hobby into a competitive interest and had a shelf full of trophies in the bedroom of their abandoned house.

Shortly before it all went toes-up, she'd earnt a spot on the Commonwealth Games archery squad, her proudest hour. Youngest female archer Britain had ever fielded, but she never got to go up to Glasgow in 2014 to earn a medal.

"I should be like bloody Legolas," Tamsyn said. "So what's wrong with me?"

Can't shoot something that looks back at you, she realised. She thought about the soldier she'd shot, and how he spun on the rope, screaming and clutching at the arrow in his gut. *A lucky shot. And your life DID depend on it.* Gritting her teeth, she retrieved the arrows and started again.

"Can we watch?" she heard someone say behind her. She turned to see little Jake Hammond and his mates, playing with their scooters in the church yard. One of them had found a BMX somewhere and was trying to do a wheelie.

"Okay, but be careful. Stay behind me," she said. She put another six arrows into the centre ring, and the boys cheered. She gave a flourish and bowed.

"You're really good, Tamsyn," Jake said. "Me, I go *pow pow!* with a gun. I hit the monsters in the head, and I never ever miss."

"Really?" she said, trying to hide her smile. "You have a gun?"

"Yep. We're a gang. We ain't scared of nothing."

The trio of kids gave a gangster pose, contorting their hands into an elaborate club sign. Tamsyn nearly burst out laughing but managed to maintain her composure.

"Well then. I think you boys would give the Crips and the Bloods a run for their money."

"You could join our gang if you want," one of the other kids said shyly. The others nodded in agreement.

"I don't know," Tam said. "You're a pretty hard mob, and I don't know if I'm tough enough. What would I need to do to join? There aren't any working cars left to steal."

"You need to sneak past the walls and get something for us."

"What?"

"Sweets. You need to bring back a whole bunch of sweets, and then you're allowed to join our gang."

"Where am I gonna find sweets?"

"That shop round the corner from the hospital. You know, the one that the Indian family owns?"

"Except you can't go there," one of the other tykes piped up. "We took all them sweets."

"We found some cigarettes too, but they're gross."

"Billy threw up!"

"Did not!"

"Are you serious?" Tam asked. "You sneak out of town to go looking for *lollies*?"

"We do it all the time," Jake said proudly.

At her urging, they showed her several ways to sneak out of the barricaded Safe Zone. One of the terrace houses right at the edge had loose palings in the back fence. There was a little pipe that ran above the train line, which Jake assured her she could shimmy across. If you climbed under the Gravesend Pier, there was a low railing that ran all the way along the bank, through to the abandoned West Pier on the other side of the wall.

She told the work crews about the broken fence, but kept her mouth shut about the other sneaky ways out of Gravesend.

I won't be looking for sweets, she thought.

She dreamt about Simon Dawes again. She was a little puzzled as the dream unfolded; she was walking with her mum, and the statue of Pocahontas was there and *walking* on her other side.

They linked arms with her, their grips cold and hard. Pocahontas's face was nightmarish, the bronze pockmarked and aged, her features faded. Her eyelids were mere ideas, her mouth a thin lipless line that worked but made no sound.

They were walking through the old Tilbury Fort, as she remembered it from a half-forgotten family trip. Her father had been absorbed with the history of the place, dragging his long-suffering wife and bored teenage daughter all over the abandoned fortress.

The cannons were still there, but no longer welded lumps of iron for the tourists. They were in full operation, crewed by a ragtag mixture of red-coat soldiers and various survivors from Gravesend. The guns spewed fire and wrath onto the Thames, but no shattering echo accompanied the barrage. The place was eerily silent, just three women taking a gentle stroll across a parade ground.

"Be quick about it," her mum said, pointing. There was a post standing upright in the ground, a flogging post if she remembered rightly. Someone was tied to it, but even from this distance she knew the man. She'd never forget his clean-shaven face, his buzz-cut hair, and the neatly pressed suit to make a good impression on the jury.

"Be quick about it," her mother said again, and the dream lurched, space folded. They were but ten paces from Dawes, who looked up, fear in his eyes, lip trembling. He'd slid down the pole, head on his chest, tears streaming down his face.

Pocahontas handed her the bow. Tamsyn looked down, saw the jagged tip of the killing arrow in her free hand. She understood that the native princess had blessed her hand, and there was no way she could miss her shot.

"Be quick about it!" Tamsyn's mother urged her, cold, dead fingers biting into her forearm. She turned, saw the cannons continue to blossom in silent fury. The gunnery crews were frantic now, pulling out pistols, the redcoats ramming powder into their muskets. A wave of the undead were over the tall walls, an impossible feat. The cannons were lost, the ragged line of defenders retreating backwards.

There was no time left. She had to deal with Simon Dawes, punish him while this moment remained for her. The shade of her mother sobbed, pointed, begged for vengeance even as her killer looked up, terrified.

"Be quick about it!" her mother screamed. She made to say more but could not seem to frame her desires into new words.

"Please, Tamsyn," Dawes croaked. A foul mess of snot and muck coated his face, eyes red, cheeks slick with tears. "I'm so sorry."

"Not good enough, Dawes," she said, bow raised, arrow nocked. Just a quick pull and release, and she would bury the arrow squarely between his eyes. It would be a clean death, natural justice at last. His pathetic little life was hers.

"Go home, Tam."

Tamsyn blinked at his words, confused, standing there like Diana with an arrow drawn back to full extension. She met Dawes's gaze, and his lip quivered.

"I can help you. I can help all of you. You need to go home."

Confused, she eased back the tension in her bow. Before he could say anything else, there was the rattle of distant gunfire, the silent tableau shattered. She was suddenly awake, muzzy-headed in the sitting room. Mal's radio crackled at the same time that some poor frozen sod was hammering on the clock bells.

"Hundreds of them!" the radio squelched. "Get your arses *out here*, God they're everywhere. Coming all directions."

It was like a strong coffee had instantly wormed its way through her veins, and a little electric fire danced through her gut, right down to her toes. Mal and Tam were dressed in seconds and ran out into the foggy pre-dawn streets, padded and protected and ready to fight.

"Where do we go, Dad?" Tamsyn asked. Her dad shooshed her with one finger, holding up the radio to his ear. The batteries were going flat, and he frowned as he tried to make out the instructions.

"Pick a spot. They're about to overrun the train station, and west and east are in the proverbial. Look-out reckons there's hundreds."

There was a spirited defence of the clocktower corner and not so many places left on the scaffold where they could get a good shot. There was little they could do to help here. Running along the southern boundary of the Safe Zone, they reached the train station.

Reinforcements had arrived, and someone opened up with one of the rare semi-automatics. Mal grimaced as the gun chattered through countless precious bullets, few of them telling.

There must have been close to four or even five hundred shambling bodies above them, a slow parade of blank-faced killers. They emerged from a bank of fog on the far side of the train embankment, frustrated by the blocked off overpasses. Bodies started falling over the edge, a waterfall of rotting flesh.

"Stop shooting, they're not close enough!" Mal yelled to the young man riding the big bucking gun. What was left of a young woman wearing gym gear made it out of the mad tangle of twitching bodies. The putrid clothes were falling apart, one breast hanging free from the ruins of a sports bra. It was purple and swollen, threaded with the black lines of her veins.

The dead woman looked up at Tamsyn for one long, horrid moment, long enough for her to take in the lank greasy hair, the blank expression, the bite-sized holes in the right bicep. Then the semi-automatic gave another coughing stutter, and the zombie's head disappeared in a spray of rotten meat and gunk.

That was someone's girlfriend, someone's daughter, Tam thought, sighting in her bow, trying to breathe away the panic. *If someone says "What a waste" I swear I'll shoot them and call it an accident.*

Pulse racing, she tried to fight off a growing surge of panic. Hundreds of foul, snapping mouths, and nothing but a stack of sandbags and cinderblocks to keep them out. Guns roared to her left and right, and her ears rang. The reek of dead flesh competed with the stink of cordite, and people were shouting.

Tamsyn went somewhere else in her head, somewhere beyond their instructions, their terror. She somehow found her centre, or became too numb to care. Her arrows flew true. The zombies she butchered sank to the stones, mostly twitching, sometimes folding in on themselves like babes at rest.

Then her scrabbling fingers could find no arrow to fit to her bow. She gently put down the useless weapon, closed her hands around a tire iron that some faceless ally passed to her.

A wall of rotten meat, rising over their own manmade wall, Death itself come for a very personal visit. Then there was nothing else for Tam, nothing but the rise and fall of her arm, diseased hands grabbing for her, the sickening crunch as she drove the unholy life out of each and every skull.

Thirty-seven people dead.

Some fool had tried to set fire to a walking zombie, and it clambered above the sandbags, a burning weapon. No one could get close enough to dispatch it, the vomitous stench and the heat driving them back.

The burning creature fell upon a portly old chap who was too slow. Hunched over the burning, screaming man, the flaming monster tore great chunks out of his face and neck, ignorant of the fact that it was a moving bonfire. The others were forced to keep their distance, the brutal spectacle ending only when the monster's brain finally melted into jelly.

The west wall had actually crumbled in two places, the shoddy masonry unable to withstand the press of hundreds of bodies. It was all the defenders could do to mass at the gaps, to push an uncaring enemy back. Each extra moment was paid for in blood, as people were dragged kicking and screaming into the ranks of the hungry dead.

Terry Jacobs himself saved the day, blasting along the wall in a forklift that he'd liberated from Tesco's loading dock, dumping a junked car into the first gap. Wheels spinning on the icy ground, he made it to the second breach and used the machine as a weapon, spearing heads on the tines, sweeping them back and forth till the petrol ran out.

The east wall held.

Thirty-seven dead.

Before the exhausted defenders of the train station could pour petrol over the walls and set the purging fires, Tamsyn asked them to wait. She fished a set of pliers out of her pocket and shimmied over the wall on a rope ladder.

Under the watchful eyes of several shooters, Tamsyn stepped through the piles of broken, twitching corpses. She had a claw hammer ready, tense and waiting. With every step she imagined a cold hand closing around her ankles, dragging her down, screaming, helpless...

Nothing happened. The fight had been brutal, every blow telling. Blasted eyes stared up at her from twice-dead faces, skulls caved in or blown to bits.

"Coffin-dodging freaks," she muttered, nudging rotten limbs with her sneakers.

There. Under the bulk of a dead window cleaner she saw one of her arrows, jutting from the eye socket of a little girl. She gagged a little, holding her hands up to the vinegar-soaked bandanna covering her mouth. This close, the smell of rot was horrendous.

Lord knows what diseases are crawling all over this lot, Tamsyn thought. *Bloody good reason to have a bon-fire.*

She put her boot on the side of the little zombie's head and wrapped her pliers around the base of the arrow shaft. It was stuck in the bone, and it took a bit of effort to work it free. The arrow came out coated in grey sludge.

"Gross," Tam said. "Looks like it's a boiling pot of water for you, my little pointy friend."

"Hurry up," someone shouted. "We want to get the fire going."

"Burn this," she mumbled, flipping them the bird. She continued with her grim task, eventually extracting fourteen whole arrows.

The rest were either broken, lodged too deep for her to pull loose, or invisible beneath the mounds of dead flesh.

"Betcha Legolas never had to do this," she grumbled, securing the tainted arrows and climbing back up to safety.

The entire guard force was kept on high alert. Even though the bulk of the mindless horde had been put down, there were still stragglers, the occasional wanderer who'd followed the moaning crowd down the traffic-jammed tarmac of the A2.

Small parties were sent over the walls to hunt for more leftovers, kill them before they found the town and brought others in their wake.

Tam stood nervously at the bottom of the ladder with her bow while the others put their guns away in favour of silent weapons. She knew some of the others on her crew, most of whom were friendly with her dad.

Over the next two hours they dropped twelve more, lone zombies and some small packs. Silent, quick kills, and several close calls. They only lost Marty Willard, who'd been careless, walking right into a cluster of dead things. The undead tore his throat out before the cavalry arrived, but Marty copped a spike to the brain, just to make sure.

That seemed to be the worst of it. There were some other zombies still out there. Locals. Gravesend's indigenous zombies kept to themselves, roaming their old neighbourhoods.

At one point, her little group of scouts passed within a few blocks of their old house, over in what was left of Singlewell. She briefly considered slipping away from the group, making a run for it, but she was mentally and physically exhausted.

I'm just too knackered, she thought. *Doubt this lot will wait for me while I lug out photo albums and Mum's Royal Doulton. I'll have to come back.*

By the time Tamsyn's patrol made it around the blocked over-passes and back to the west wall, a steady drizzle had turned into a heavy downpour. She stood with the others, soaked right through and wet hair hanging in her eyes. They shouted for the ladders, cursing the sluggish speed of those set to watch for their return.

Mal was up on the scaffolds in a plastic poncho, scanning the streets with binoculars. He spotted them, threw the rope ladders over.

The rest of the guard huddled underneath the walkways, backs against the wall as if they were in the trenches, catnapping before Jerry launched another offensive. They were sullen-eyed, exhausted. Two men whispered, throwing fearful glances their way.

What was that all about?

"Any more out there?" Mal asked, bringing her under a tarpaulin they'd rigged to keep the rain out. The changing winds brought sheets of icy spray in every direction anyways, and it provided little shelter.

"No," she said, shivering. Her hip was aching again, and she could feel her throat starting to ache. *Great, now I'm sick again.*

"We're on double shifts for the next week," Mal said. "Stinkers mob together, so we'll probably get another visit like this real soon."

"Well, they won't follow this lot," she said, launching into a coughing fit. The wind and the rain did little to block out the corpse-fires, and Tamsyn briefly entertained the thought of huddling over the smoking husks, warming herself over the charred torsos crackling away on the other side of the wall.

"Get home, love. You've done enough," Mal said. "I mean it."

Someone had brought out a box of brand new yellow macs, and Tamsyn shrugged into one. It was several sizes too large, and she felt slightly ridiculous.

"Paddington Bear will see you at home, Dad. Stay safe."

He nodded, climbing back up to his post even as she darted out from cover, running through the streets with all her gear. The gutters were overflowing now, and her sneakers were saturated by the time she got to her street. The wind picked up, and she felt like it would blow her away. Even though her front door was in sight, she ducked into the nearest doorway.

And ran straight into Eddie Jacobs.

"What the hell?" she said, disgusted that she'd brushed up against him. "What are you doing, you sick freak? Are you watching my house?"

Eddie pushed her away with a meaty paw, and she pushed back. The torrent of rain was coming down hard now, cats and dogs and everything else too. The shelter provided by the tiny alcove was the only thing keeping her this close to him.

"In your dreams, Trampsyn. I've got better things to do than follow you around."

"Likely story. Porch-lurker."

They stood together in silence for long moments, browbeaten by the ferocity of the elements. It must have been nearly midday, but it was dark and bitterly cold.

"You got a smart mouth on you," he said, eyes narrowed. He was a thunderhead posing as a football hooligan. "There's gonna be a day, real soon, when you discover there's only one use for your mouth in *my* town. I'll see to it that you learn some respect. Personally."

The rain eased up some, and Tamsyn took the opportunity to knee Eddie in the balls. Before he could recover, she ran under his flailing arms and down the street, throwing her front door open. She stood in her front yard, an arrow nocked and drawn.

If he takes one more step, I swear to God I will shoot this fucker dead.

Eddie Jacobs stood there in the street, clutching his crotch and watching her for a long moment, before slinking off through the rain like a wounded animal.

Three hours after she'd let Mal back into the house, dog-tired and stumbling around like a dead thing himself, there was a great commotion that stirred Tamsyn from her solid slumber. She was instantly alert, up and shouting for her dad. Someone was trying to kick the door in.

Mal was already standing in the hallway in his nightshirt, rifle levelled at the doorway. The iron bar was bent slightly, and thick chunks of wood were splintered off from the swinging edge of the solid door.

The battering stopped, and someone stuck their hand into the gap, reaching for the bar. Mal lunged against the door, slamming it shut and pinning the man's hand. The intruder screamed on the other side of the door, fingers shaking as he tried to wriggle loose. Mal grabbed the man's hand and twisted the fingers back towards his hairy wrist. Blows rained on the door, more than one person trying to bust it open now.

"Fuck off, the lot of you!" Mal yelled. "I'll break his wrist, I swear it."

There was the sound of breaking glass from the kitchen. Tam hefted her gore-stained hammer and stood in the hallway uncertainly. The place was cramped, and there wasn't enough room inside to use her bow without knocking it against a ceiling or wall, fouling the shot.

"Go!" Mal said. "Before they break through. Up to your room, put all the furniture up against the door."

Tam heard wood splintering and ran to the darkened kitchen. The window above the rusting sink was broken, glass on the sill and all over the draining board. When they'd moved in, her dad had boarded up all the ground floor windows, inside and out.

One of these boards was hanging loose now, and she could see the sharp curve of a pry bar, jammed in between two more planks as the faceless attacker strained to loosen them.

She rummaged in the hallway closet, finding a pack of nails by feel, spilling half of them in her mad dash back to the kitchen. As fast as she could, she hammered them into the boards, reinforcing the ones that had been knocked loose.

There was a sharp crack as Mal fired his rifle, deafening inside the cramped hallway. Someone shrieked in agony, and in a heartbeat Mal was next to her, gun jammed through the broken window and barking out into the night.

Someone swore, and then she heard the scuffle of running feet, the creak of old wood as several people vaulted the side fence.

The house was once more still, and the Webbs stood in their kitchen, breathing from their exertions. They faced each other in what slits of moonlight made it through the boarding.

"So nice to see our elected officials hard at work," Mal said, hugging her with his free arm. He did not let go of the gun, and Tamsyn saw that he was holding it knuckle tight.

When the sun came up, they surveyed the damage. The front door was nearly off its hinges, and the bathroom window had also been smashed, pry marks speaking of a thwarted break-in attempt.

"Well, that's just dandy," Mal said, pulling open the door to test the hinges. Blazoned across it in red spray paint were two words: DEAD MAN.

"If Jacobs thinks he can scare me away from the election..." Mal muttered. He wriggled into his anorak, putting a handful of bullets into his inside pocket. The last of his allotment. He sat cross-legged on the front step with his cleaning kit, pulling apart the gun, scrubbing away at the built-up powder and filth.

A tired old teacher pushed too far, making ready for war, Tamsyn thought. Even as he was reassembling the weapon, she came stomping down the staircase with her bow and a quiverful of arrows still crusted with rot.

"If I don't take 'em out with the first shot, at least they'll die a horrible, lingering death," Tamsyn said, puffed up with false bravado. She was scared shitless. Jacobs had showed his thuggish hand, and there was no telling what he might try next.

"No," Mal said quietly. He slid back the bolt-action, feeding a bullet into the open breech. "You're to stay here."

Tam opened her mouth but saw that he meant business. He pointed inside, scowling.

"How are you going to get back in, then?"

"Leave my bedroom window open," he said with an eye to the street, *sotto voce.* No telling who was keeping an eye on them.

She bit back her protests, eyes brimming with tears. Mal put his hand on her shoulder and squeezed. Then he was walking down the garden path, shoulders tense, gun to the ready.

I'm never going to see him again, she thought, forcing the battered door closed. She barred the door, looking distrustfully at the bent piece of metal, eventually pushing the bureau up flush against the whole mess.

That should buy me a minute, she thought. *When they kill my father and come for me, that should be just long enough to kill myself.*

"No," she said with vehemence, shaking away the dark thoughts. Hands clenched into fists. "I'm gonna go *Home Alone* on their arses."

Tamsyn put on a full patrol rig, packed a bag full of weapons and supplies. She pulled down the hatch to the attic, sliding the ladder down. She heaved the compound bow up into the darkness and lugged up a bottle of water and a thick quilt.

Hours of waiting in the cold dark, settled uncomfortably across the ribs of her house. Every settling sound of the old terrace the creak of a rapist's footstep, a creeping killer come just for her.

She held her bow sideways and ready, listening for the creak of feet on stairs. The moment that someone decided to search the attic, to pull down the hatch, she would put an arrow through their sneaky eyes.

There. That was definitely someone treading on a floorboard. They'd found a way into the house. She heard a door open, then another. They were in her bedroom.

I'm Boudica and Pocahontas rolled into one, motherfuckers, she thought, heart hammering in her chest and stomach clenching.

Hands scrabbled at the access hatch, and a beam of torchlight blinded her. Tamsyn pulled back the deadly arc of her bow, tense and wide-eyed, taking sharp, shallow breaths. It had come to this. The person below began to climb up the steps, their shadow jumping, looming tall on the ceiling.

She very nearly put an arrow through her father's head, and a last-minute twitch of her arm sent it past his ear, whizzing down the stairwell.

"You stupid idiot!" she yelled, throwing the bow down at him. It bounced against the steps and clattered to the floor. "I almost killed you. Why didn't you say something?"

"I didn't know you were going to shoot at me."

"What else was I going to do?"

A tense pause, and then they both broke into nervous laughter. She was just glad to see him alive and in one piece.

"Come down from there, kiddo," he said. "You need to pack up all your stuff. We're leaving."

Mal was serious. He levered up the floorboards, pulling out their secret stash of food. Checking that the coast was clear, he quickly dug up the secondary cache at the bottom of the backyard.

There wasn't much else to take. She had a couple of changes of clothes and her art stuff. Mal had even less. He pulled apart the frame holding their family photo, folding it up along its old creases. He handed it to Tamsyn.

"Best you hold onto this," he said. She carefully slid it into her notebook.

"Dad, tell me what the hell is going on!"

"No time now. Quick, we don't want to be here when night falls."

Hefting all their worldly belongings, Tam and Mal left the grimy little terrace house. Mal left the door wide open, and Tamsyn understood then that they were not coming back.

The streets were completely empty of people. Mal was hustling her along, casting a worried eye in all directions.

They were near the centre of the Safe Zone, on High Street. Uncomfortably close to the Three Daws Pub. She recognised Dr. Murray's house, a Trust-listed terrace standing alone in a sea of half-finished, trendy kit homes. The old drunk was openly happy that the apocalypse had stalled the controversial revamp of the town centre.

Mal pounded frantically on the door, and a moment later Murray appeared with a propane lamp, ushering them inside. He closed the door on their heels.

"Were you seen?" he asked, and Mal shook his head.

"You'll get me killed," Murray grumbled, leading them into his house. Tamsyn had never been inside before and goggled at the row of mounted animal heads along the hallway and the elephant foot umbrella stand. The whole place was an exercise in taxidermy and stank of dust and old man smell.

"Have you thought about what I said?" Mal asked. Dr. Murray steered them into his living room and pointed them towards his settee, a lumpy nightmare of velour crush. Tamsyn couldn't look away from the tiger-skin rug, complete with head.

"I'm too old, Webb. As long as Jacobs finds me useful, I'm safe enough here." He fussed about with a decanter and poured himself and Mal a drink. He made to pour a third glass for Tamsyn but thought better of it.

"They don't deserve you, Clem," her dad said. Tamsyn didn't even know Dr. Murray *had* a first name.

"This place is finished anyway. Everywhere is. I might as well live out my last few days in comfortable surroundings," he said, pouring liquor down his gravelly old throat.

"Will someone please tell me what the hell is going on?" Tamsyn said. "I mean it. I'm getting pissed off."

"Well then," Dr. Murray said. "Young lady, it seems your father isn't keen to admit failure. He's lost the town."

"Tamsyn," Mal said slowly. "There's not going to be an election. Last night was only the start of the ugliness."

"You're as much the villain," the old vet said. "I bandaged up Jacobs's man, the one you put a bullet in. They only meant to put a scare into you, but they're after blood now."

"Man's got a right to defend his family," Mal said, a little huffily. He sipped at his drink, staring into the red glow of Murray's kerosene heater.

"What do you mean, no election?" Tamsyn said. "Half this town's behind you, Dad. You always taught me to stand up to bullies."

"People have been killed," Mal snapped. He took a deep breath, leaned over, and patted Tamsyn's hand before continuing. "Most of the hunting parties sent over the wall were people who openly supported me for mayor. They weren't allowed back in."

"They were left out there to die?" Tamsyn said, a sob catching in her throat. She'd gone out in a hunting party, and thankfully Mal had spotted their return. Jacobs had marked her for death.

"He's playing dirty, Tam, and I won't be the cause of any more killings. We have to leave Gravesend. For good."

Dr. Murray let Tamsyn kip out in his spare room, and she left Mal to snatch what sleep he could, huddled up on the lumpy old settee under the unblinking gaze of a dozen dead animals.

They were leaving just before dawn. A sack full of baked beans and ramen noodles would hopefully buy them sanctuary on the Tilbury ferry and a safe ticket out of the town.

Once we get past the Council thugs guarding it. Great plan, Dad.

The room was freezing cold, and she wriggled around under the nest of quilts and blankets. Her mind ticked over, and she tossed and turned. Tamsyn was exhausted, numb to the core, but sleep was impossible.

Jacobs would be a no one if we somehow got to America, she realised. *Just a fat, obnoxious Manc, but he's king here.*

No wonder he wants Mal out of the way.

Most of all, she thought about their house. About all the memories, everything that was the Webb family. *We're leaving everything behind! Leaving it for these thugs to pick over.*

That decided her. Tamsyn threw the bedding aside, fully clothed against the cold. She tugged on her shoes. It was hours still before dawn arrived, plenty of time to sneak over the wall, make a mad dash for home. Mal would be furious, but the sight of their precious memories should calm him down.

She emptied her backpack onto the bed, making a neat stack of cans and clothes. Feeling for her weapons in the dim light, she tucked her hammer behind her belt. Dad had found a tomahawk for her last week, sharp and weighty. It just fit into the front pocket of her denim jacket.

Tamsyn tested the window. The wood was old, jammed into the frame, and she put all her strength into it.

"Come on," she whispered. The frame gave with a terrific squeal, and instantly cold air blasted into the room. She could feel the icy tickle of snow.

Tamsyn waited a long, tense moment, and cracked open the door. She heard the sounds of Mal snoring, and a deeper rumble from the far end of the house that was Dr. Murray.

"Well, I feel safe. I might as well walk out the front door," she grumbled. Easing the window shut, she crept up the hallway.

Peering through the front windows, she couldn't see anyone. In fact, it was so dark she could hardly see past her nose. Tamsyn gently opened the door, making sure it was unlocked before closing it behind her.

Tugging her beanie down around her ears, she shivered. The wall guards would be huddled around their fires, and Jacobs's farce of a constabulary wouldn't stir from the pub in this weather.

I can do this, she thought, teeth chattering as she walked, hugging the walls along High Street. It was next to pitch black, but she didn't want to take any chances. Thinking of little Jake Hammond and his adventures, Tamsyn made her way to the southern boundary of the Safe Zone.

Checking that the way was clear of guards, she found the water pipe that crossed the train line. Tucking her bow up behind her backpack, she climbed the waist-high mesh fence, stepped over to the edge of the embankment.

A girl could bust her head open, she thought, spotting the twin streaks of the train-tracks below. *Bugger it. If an eight-year-old can get across this, I sure can.*

Leaning forward, Tam could feel the chill of the metal through her gloves, and when she gripped the pipe with her thighs she thought she was going to pass out. *Man alive, that's COLD.*

She inched her way forward, determined to get across before she froze solid. Her jeans were slick with moisture from the ice, and as she realised just how dangerous it all was, she slipped.

Gasping, Tamsyn locked her arms around, held on as she rolled around to the underside of the pipe. Her numb legs slipped and scrabbled for purchase, until finally it was just her locked arms frantically hugging the pipe, legs dangling beneath her.

"Fuck!" she sobbed, kicking upwards until she got her legs back around the pipe. She gripped onto it like a bad boyfriend, knew that her knees were probably bruised to hell. She shuffled along as quick as she could, gasping and terrified and expecting to fall twenty or thirty feet at any second...

Then she felt the press of earth under her back. She'd made it across. Tamsyn let go of the pipe, trembling all over.

"I'm so fucking stupid," she said, crying softly as bitter little snowflakes fell on her face. There was no way in hell she was coming back this way.

Stifling a cough, she sat up, instantly aware that she was in no-man's land. The coffin-dodgers moved a little slower in winter, and she hoped to outrun any that she spotted.

If I don't die of exposure first, she thought, shivering right through. *I need to get out of this cold.*

She was probably a mile and a half from home. St. Francis Avenue might as well be in another country, and in fact it now was. Zombie country.

Tamsyn checked her kit. Her bow was still tucked up behind her pack, in perfect nick even though she'd been lying on it. A quick check of her quiver brought a curse—half her arrows had fallen out. There was no way she could get down to the train track without breaking her neck or drawing the attention of the guards.

The hammer and tomahawk were still there. She was good to go. Vaulting the low crash-barrier, Tamsyn moved down the rubbish-strewn streets, darting from cover to cover. A thin layer of slush was already coating the pavements.

Tamsyn heard the moan of a coffin-dodger somewhere close, guttural and low. Frustrated, maybe angry. She dropped to her knees and scrambled behind a rusted-out rubbish bin, heart pounding. With numb fingers she struggled to fit an arrow to her bow. Ever so slowly, she peered around the side of the bin, gagging slightly from the stink of the year-old garbage.

There. A lone zombie, pushing a silent lawnmower across a front yard choked with weeds. What remained of this stocky man still wore a rotten dressing gown, falling apart on his shoulders.

This undead gardener wrestled with the uncooperative mower, the blade snagging on the tangle of undergrowth. Even though the snow blew into the creature's blasted eyes, even though it could barely see, it tried its best to finish the yardwork.

Tamsyn just didn't have the heart to kill it. She waited until its pointless circuit took it toward the house, windows smashed and door ajar. She slipped from cover, watching where she stepped. She barely made a sound.

This worked for two houses, and then she nearly ran straight into the zombie that stepped out from a tree. The gaunt remains of an old woman bedecked in a mouldering floral-pattern smock, rake in hand, trying to move the black sludge of rotting leaves from a driveway. It came for her in ignorant hunger, garden tool raised like a polearm, mouth wide and leathery tongue-scrap flapping.

In one fluid motion, Tamsyn sent an arrow through its temple. The mindless creature crumbled in the driveway, twitching hand lifted, reaching for the offending object lodged in its head. A final, pitiful yowl.

This was enough to bring others. The lawnmowing zombie, and another trailing garden shears from a half-severed hand. A kid clutching a mouldering teddy bear. Dozens of them, crying out in wordless excitement. More of them appearing by the second.

She ran for her life. Dodged the outstretched hands, clawing at her. Her bow was caught, wrenched out of her grip, and with a curse she abandoned it. One coffin-dodger snagged her by the jacket, and she lashed out, cracking its forehead with her hammer. Tamsyn leapt over the body, shuddering. Those dead hands, grabbing and snatching at her...

Legs pumping, eyes burning, she found herself on St. Francis Avenue. A little sedan was crumpled around a bollard, doors thrown open. Without pause she dove underneath the car, drew her legs right in so that she couldn't be seen.

Tamsyn saw them rounding the corner. A crowd of undead were hunting her now, dozens of lurching corpses that would tear her apart like a chicken. With one hand firmly clasped over her mouth she fought her heaving lungs, terrified that the sound would betray her.

With her free hand she worked the tomahawk out of her pocket and gripped its handle tight. There wasn't much room to get a good swing under the car, but she'd bury the sharp blade into the first thing to reach for her. And then the next, until they dragged her out, pinned her down, leering and snapping their rotten peg-teeth...

This is it, she thought. She could see dozens of legs surrounding the car, rotting and bent wrong. The car rocked slightly as the dead things brushed against it.

And then they were gone. They'd passed her by.

When the large pack had disappeared around the corner, Tamsyn slowly rolled out from underneath the car wreck. Hatchet to the ready, she ran across the street to the nearest house, vaulting over a low brick wall.

It was the Dwyers' front yard.

She looked over her shoulder at the house, door split from its hinges, a year's worth of leaves and filth collected in the hallway.

If Mrs Dwyer or little Emmie are still here–and Tamsyn quashed the thought. If they came for her, she knew she would falter. Scrambling to her feet, she got the hell out of there. With one mad final dash, Tamsyn Webb was home.

Their house was intact. Doors and windows were still fastened, the blinds drawn. Happiness washed over her, for a brief moment eclipsing her fear.

I never thought I'd see this place again, she thought. Carefully creeping down the side of the two-story semi-detached, she found the garden bed that contained her Mum's gnome collection. She tipped over the one with the fishing rod, plucked out the plastic key-hider.

The keys were still there. With a shaking hand she unlocked the kitchen door, easing the door open. It stuck a little, but opened without too much of a struggle.

The house was pitch black, and Tamsyn was a little scared. Logic told her that the house would be free of zombies, but it took a long moment before she could step over the threshold, carefully locking the door behind her.

The house stank from a year's worth of stale air, and the rotten dishes from their last meal that were still in the sink. Fumbling through the kitchen drawers she found a candle, and eventually the matches to light it with.

Home. Even as the feeble light danced over familiar surroundings, Tamsyn wanted to cry. She saw furniture that her mum had picked out, worn out board games, favourite books, photos on every wall.

This was home, and Tamsyn knew she could never come back. This was her one chance to carry away memories, tokens of the lives they'd led before the end of the world.

Thinking frantically, trying to estimate how much time she had left before dawn, Tamsyn began to stuff things into her pack. The camcorder that Mal never managed to erase, still full of family holidays and happier days. The power cords for it, in case they managed to find a generator.

"Need a photo album," she said, looking wistfully at some of the framed photos. Too bulky, not enough room in her pack.

She went up to her bedroom, floor still scattered with dirty socks and teenage magazines. Her favourite teddy bear went into the backpack. She pulled some storage tubs out of her wardrobe, packing some fresh art markers and another notebook.

Another container was full of photos and papers, and Tamsyn quickly extricated a stack of albums. She jammed as many of them into her pack as she could fit.

"If Dad's gonna kill me, better make it worth my while," she said, and then stopped. There, in the rat's nest of papers and curios, a stack of court documents.

His trial. The day that Simon Dawes fronted the court, accused of Jenny Webb's death. Mal didn't want to keep anything that reminded him of the accident, but Tamsyn had squirreled away everything to do with the court case. It was the last connection with her Mum, and much as it all pained her, she could never bear to throw it out.

"I wish I could stop thinking about you. You complete and utter bastard," she said. The candle was starting to burn low, and she'd have to go soon. There was no time left to pore over old hurts.

But she found herself flicking through the pages, drawn to her victim's statement, the words of the other witnesses. The court transcript. She had a duplicate of the whole brief in her hands, a hush-hush copy from a sympathetic prosecutor.

"Hardly seems important, what with the zombies and all," she said, trying to be wry. But it still mattered, more than she could ever admit to Mal, to Ali, even to zombie Dr. Clarke if she dropped by for a consult.

She was reading the page detailing Dawe's sentence: five years imprisonment to be served at HMP Swaleside, non-parole period of three years. Swaleside...

"No, no. NO! Dawes, you rotten bastard!" Tamsyn cried.

HMP Swaleside was on the Isle of Sheppey. The prison guards were turning outsiders away, and all the bridges were destroyed. As far as anyone knew, they'd all survived the zombie outbreak intact. Dawes was probably still alive!

Furious, Tamsyn tore through the paperwork, cursing the sputtering candlelight. She found his prisoner intake form and scanned it anxiously.

There. He'd been eligible for parole six months ago. Useless details, like his address, date of birth, previous criminal convictions, his–

Occupation. It leapt out at her. She'd known this all along, her dreams trying to tell her what she'd forgotten.

Simon Dawes had been a merchant seaman. Master Mariner, dishonourably discharged from the Merchant Navy. First, he'd crashed a big boat while drunk, then he'd murdered a bus stop full of people, and now–

"Now you're living in comfort, safe on that bloody island," Tamsyn seethed, twisting the paper in her hands.

It gave Tamysn great pleasure to pick up her competition bow. The tension was set much lower than the bow she'd looted in Gravesend, but it was still powerful enough to put an arrow through a human skull. She tested everything out, made some adjustments to account for a year of neglect.

Pack bulging with mementoes, Tamsyn left their house for the last time. Pointless as it was, she locked the back door, put the keys back under the gnome. It felt right to leave everything intact, a monument to the Webbs-that-were.

The snow was falling much heavier now. Tamsyn had changed into her own clothes, briefly considering her ski coat but discarding it in favour of a tough leather jacket from her brief period as a goth. It fit her snug, would protect her forearms from a festering bite or two. The bracers went on over this, and a Man U scarf completed the look.

She poked her head into the garage by the rear laneway. In the dim light Tamsyn could just make out her mum's old Astra, but she was pretty sure the battery would be dead by now. With an eye to the door she fetched her old bicycle, fumbled around in the gloom for a pump. It was the work of a moment to get the tires good and firm, and after strapping the bow to her backpack she was ready to go.

"Let's see you catch me now, stinkers," Tam said. With nary a wobble she was off and rolling, wheels slipping a little in the slush but the houses flying past.

Tamsyn nearly lost control when a pair of decomposing arms snatched at her. She caught a glimpse of a naked dead man, lurching at her from behind a phone box. Fighting the wobbles until she had the bike running level again, she carefully pulled her hammer out, steering one-handed.

Turning a corner, she almost ran straight into the original pack of zombies. The lawnmowing zombie, the one with the shears, all of the old neighbourhood turned out to eat her. Hours later they were still hunting for her, and as one they reached out, stretching across the road like a fleshy hedge. Pedalling like a mad thing, she feinted left then right, and most of the zombies took the bait. She buried the tines of the claw hammer in the outmost zombie's eye socket, felt it wrenched out of her grasp as she passed by.

And then she was free. She kept to the middle of the streets, dodging the occasional morgue-lurker, making good time.

Rounding a corner, she slammed on the brakes, heart pounding. An enormous horde of zombies, thousands upon thousands of them, filling every street and laneway, as far as she could see. They were already converging on the west wall, rifle fire spitting futilely into their ranks.

The London zombies had arrived in force. There was no way anyone was walking away from this. Gravesend was finished.

Tamsyn wouldn't be able to get to the seawall pipe. She needed to find another way to slip inside the Safe Zone, and fast. She followed the train line back east, away from the horde. Risking a peek over her shoulder, she saw a flood of rot, rank after rank of the undead, pushing, jostling, flowing around the Safe Zone. The town was slowly being surrounded.

Despite the snow, Tamsyn felt hot, punishing her legs as her bicycle flew along the abandoned streets. The local zombies were being drawn out by the commotion, abandoning their pointless loitering to join up with the greater pack.

She briefly considered the water pipe spanning the train line, but a thick dusting of snow already coated it from end to end. There was no way she could cross that without slipping and falling.

There had to be another way. She thought of the clock tower corner, of the tiny gaps in between the wall of cars and junk. She wasn't much bigger than Jake Hammond. Maybe she would fit through.

Then she remembered the guards who'd left her outside to die, and quickly wrote off the idea. Someone in the mayor's pocket would be keeping an eye out for the Webbs. Most likely she would be shot "accidentally."

For these reasons Tamsyn found herself on the wrong side of someone's back fence, cursing herself for telling the work crews about the loose palings. Cursing the hammer that lay miles away, embedded in a dead man's face.

She hacked away with the tomahawk, making one hell of a racket, blunting it against the thick boards. As far as she could tell, she wasn't making much of a difference.

When she saw a trio of dead things shuffling up the laneway, arms spread and foul mouths yawning, she redoubled her efforts. Finally, she snapped the bottom half of a board loose, and hurling her stuff over the fence she wriggled through, ribs hurting as she squeezed through the tiny gap.

They'll never get through that, she thought, pushing a rubbish bin and some other junk up against the tiny hole. She paused only to snatch up her belongings before dashing off.

The ghouls tore at the fence in wordless hunger, vice-like hands yanking at the boards. More joined them, dozens of corpses that had been in slow pursuit of Tamsyn, and then the fence could do nothing but snap under their combined weight. Even as distant guns popped and the survivors yelled ragged defiance, a steady stream of dead cannibals poured into the heart of Gravesend.

"Where in the bloody hell have you been?" Mal yelled. "I've been worried sick!"

"I went home, Dad," Tamsyn said. "I went home."

They stood toe to toe in Dr. Murray's kitchen, he staring at her, taking in her old clothes, the fancy bow. She popped open her bag, and a glimpse of the stack of photo albums had him wordless, tears welling in his eyes.

"You wilful mule of a girl," he eventually said, wrapping her in a bear-hug. "You really did it. You went back for our stuff."

"Someone had to," she managed, snuffling. There was the priming sound of a shotgun behind them, and she turned in alarm.

"This is a nice moment," Dr. Murray said, "but you need to shit or get off the pot. I've got things to do and you can't stay here."

"Dad, Dr. Murray, you need to know something," Tamsyn said, rifling through her bag. She produced the sheaf of paper that was the court brief.

"There's a sea captain on the Isle of Sheppey. Someone that can take us to America." She explained what she had found.

"Simon Dawes," Mal said, the words coming out like something sour.

"If that's not Dickensian, I don't know what is," Dr. Murray said. "Well, he certainly owes you two."

"We don't even know if he's still at Sheppey, or if the prisoners survived the outbreak." Mal said.

"Not to mention those screws will bloody shoot at us," Dr. Murray said. "Right-o then. Just give me five minutes to pack a bag."

"You're coming with us?" Tamsyn said.

"Lass, a thread of hope is better than dying here."

The trio stepped cautiously out of Dr. Murray's house and into the foul weather, weapons at the ready. The clock tower was still ringing, a steady dirge calling for all hands to defend the walls. The two-way in Dr. Murray's pocket squawked frantically until he turned it off.

"We all knew this was coming," the vet rumbled. "That Mancunian wanker has killed us all. The monsters will break in within hours."

A man ran past them at a flat sprint, nearly losing his balance on the ice-slick road. There was a shot somewhere behind them, and a long, ragged scream.

Tamsyn risked a glance back, and that was when she saw the first zombie, a forlorn looking figure in a ragged two-piece suit. It stood at the street corner, chewing on a bloody hunk of flesh.

It looked up and saw them, gave a rattling, husky moan. The street rapidly filled with undead, some of whom were gnawing on severed limbs, another dragging a torso behind it by a fistful of intestines. They walked on legs that were stiff and slow, but relentless. Dead jelly eyes fixed onto the living.

Like everyone else, the Webbs and Dr. Murray ran for the boats. Everything was lost.

"How did they get inside the Safe Zone?" Dr. Murray panted. Tamsyn's heart sank when she realised the truth. She'd led some zombies to a weak point, even helped weaken the barricade for them. And they were like ants when the promise of food was involved. One would bring thousands.

I'm so stupid. So much blood on my hands, Tamsyn thought. *I've killed everyone, all over some photos!* She knew she could never tell a soul about this, and shame burned away in her chest. She bit back on the hysterical sob that threatened to burst out of her at any moment.

I should just lie down in the street and let them eat me. It's all I deserve now.

Tamsyn never got the chance. Her dad held her upper arm in a vice grip, hauling her along. In moments they were at the Pier, a scene of chaos. The embargoed Tilbury ferry was trying to put to, fighting off a throng of Gravesenders that threatened to overload the vessel. Every boat was filled to capacity, and several of them already sat out in the middle of the Thames, ignoring the cries and curses of those onshore, these amateur sailors uncertain of where they should actually go now.

The zombies could be seen emerging from every street, every little alley and pokey corner, their slow march converging on the seething mass of humanity at the Pier.

People panicked, fell into the freezing cold water. Blows were exchanged, there was a gun shot, and the ferry finally succeeded in casting off.

"Riley!" Mal yelled out till he was hoarse. He waved frantically, and the old stevedore saw him, shrugged his shoulders helplessly. He couldn't come back to shore without being mobbed by dozens of people. The rusty old boat was dangerously overloaded as it was.

"Go back to the *Paraclete!* We've found a captain." Whether the man heard him or not he couldn't say, but the ferry slowly pulled away from the bank, heading cross-river.

"Ali!" Tamsyn cried. The boy was limping just ahead of the slavering pack, Naomi and Monica trying to help him. He'd cast his crutches down in frustration, and the women had him in an awkward kind of fireman's lift.

Monica stumbled, and they all went down. They were instantly enveloped in a tide of grey flesh and diseased hands until all that Tam could see was the broad back of Naomi trying to free her lover, fighting off the mindless ghouls with nothing but her own blocky fists.

Pragmatism kicked in, and Naomi had to leave them behind, could do nothing but run as the monsters tore her loved ones apart, still alive and screaming for mercy.

I killed Ali, Tamsyn thought, despondent, firing arrows into that slow advance. Each shot told, and still it meant nothing. *My friend is worse than dead now, and I brought this to him.*

"Let us onto a boat, you bastards!" Dr. Murray yelled. Somehow, they got old Dr. Murray onto one of the last boats; having saved everyone's life at least once probably secured him the berth. There was no room left for the Webbs.

People were firing the last of their bullets into the packed mass of zombies, trying to halt the inevitable. Others were launching themselves into the Thames, braving the icy flow. Even if they made it across the river, they'd die of exposure. Or something in that filthy water would kill them slowly. Or the zombies, reaching for them even as they clambered from the opposite bank.

Terry Jacobs was pulled out of his motor-launch before it could clear the dock, people pouring onto the boat until it nearly capsized. He was handed overhead, a crazy crowd surf above which he choked, red with rage, lashing out with his ridiculous sceptre like Punch given life. He fell into the mob, who became a flurry of fists; pipes and axe-handles rose and fell.

"Quick, this way," Mal said, and Tamsyn allowed herself to be drawn away from the chaos, uncaring of her fate.

The last Tamsyn saw of the mayor of Gravesend was a red smear on the docks, and she could not tell if he was alive or dead before the zombies reached him.

— 6 —

There was one boat left in Gravesend, and Mal knew about it. He threw back the snow-covered tarp, and Tamsyn groaned.

It was the death boat from the London expedition. Council had ordered it drawn up onto the unused Royal Terrace Pier, hoping to repair it for later use. The blood-stained hull was still riddled with bullet holes, and a round hole as big as a 50p coin was punched through the housing of the outboard motor.

"Quickly now, we don't have much time," Mal said, even as the first zombie stepped onto the pier. Tamsyn sent an arrow through its skull, fixing it to an information sign. It lay there shivering, like a live moth pinned to the board.

They pushed the boat into the water, both of them leaping in. Water began trickling in from a dozen places, even as Mal wrestled with the motor.

"Bail as fast as you can," he said. "Don't stop."

The motor roared into life, sounding like it had half a dozen ball bearings rattling around inside it. Tamsyn bailed water with a bucket and could not hope to keep up. The water was rising gradually, already up to her ankles. Mal held a course close to the south bank, running the boat as fast as he dared.

The weak sunlight was trying to fight through the winter sky, the snowfall easing off and then stopping. The wind whipping past her ears was freezing cold, and Tamsyn wrapped the scarf around her face. The other end of it was dangled in the water, which was up around her hips now. The boat was riding awfully low in the water, and it would sink within minutes.

"I need to find a place to junk this thing," Mal called out over his shoulder. A worrying plume of blue smoke was pouring out of the motor, and it was beginning to misfire. Mal wound the throttle right down, let the boat limp along the shoreline.

The motor gave a final death rattle and conked out. Mal let the last of their momentum guide the boat to the shore. They'd made it to Allhallows-On-Sea, and a small group of undead could be seen wending its way through the holiday cabins, drawn by the noise.

"Well, look at this then," she heard Mal say, and turned to see him extracting a bundle of orange plastic from under the driver's chair. A life raft.

"Grab those oars, love. Looks like we're going to pick up Simon Dawes the hard way."

The boat inflated in seconds, and Mal pushed them away from the bank, even as the first inquisitive dead thing shuffled through the snow and grit, still wearing bathers.

It seemed to take them hours, even with the current washing them down towards the sea. Then they were near the mouth of the river, and the ocean fought them every step of the way. Spray washed over them with every breaking wave, and they were soaked through. Tamsyn felt cold and miserable, and no longer cared if they made it to safety. A dark part of her hoped that the raft would sink, hoped that drowning wouldn't hurt too much. She cried even as she carved at the waters with her paddle, wept for Ali, for her guilt in betraying Gravesend, for the hopeless mess they were in now.

And then, just as her spirits were at their lowest, the grey bulk of the Isle came into view, looming out of the spray and fog. They'd made it. Father and daughter renewed their efforts, slowly pulling towards the shore. Sheerness was soon in sight, and the faint glow of streetlights could be seen.

"Geez, would you look at that. It's just like Normandy," Mal said, white-faced and straining at the oar. The shore was a mad tangle of barbed wire, cement barricades, and great rolls of mesh fencing fixed into place.

"Not at all friendly," Tam said. "Hope we can talk our way past all that."

The shore was in sight, but as they struggled to beach the cumbersome inflatable, a shot rang out. She looked up to see a line of hard faces peering over the fortifications, guns to the ready.

"Turn your boat around now or we will fire upon you," someone said through a megaphone. At least ten guns were trained on them, and Tamsyn noted wearily that more gunmen were arriving by the second.

Most of them were wearing the uniforms of prison guards. Some were in civilian clothes, and here and there could be seen the orange jumpsuit of a prisoner.

Trusties?

"Please," Mal called out. "I need to speak to whoever's in charge."

"Turn around now!" the same man bellowed out. He was some sort of ranking officer, judging by his uniform.

"What the hell is wrong with you people?" Mal shouted, fighting the drift of the boat. They were being buffeted around by the waves, and a strong wind caught the inflatable, started to blow them offshore. "We're not infected. We don't even want to stay."

"You've got five seconds, mate," the officer said.

Ignoring him, Mal was over the side of the boat, thigh-deep in the waters, struggling to lug the raft onto the shore. He held up an arm, the one still holding the paddle, and Tamsyn saw him smile, knew that he was about to say something eloquent, something that would convince these idiots to do the right thing.

And then with a whip-crack his chest burst open, and Mal Webb slid down into the water with a surprised grunt, the words never leaving his lips. In moments the thrashing foam was pink with his blood, and from an immense distance Tamsyn heard a gut-wrenching scream, which she realised was coming from her.

"Cease fire! Cease fire!" someone shouted. Tamsyn sat in shock, watching her father drifting to the shore in a face-down bob, washing up onto the sand. A distant part of her noted the men peeling back a section of razor wire, a pair of prison guards rolling her father onto his back, attempting CPR.

Others were pulling the inflatable all the way onto the sand. Several hands tried to lift her out of the boat, and she was instantly filled with a savage rage, kicking and scratching and swearing into their surprised faces.

"I thought he had a gun," she heard a man protest.

"It was an oar, you stupid thug," someone else said.

She struggled loose from her captors, and ran across the sand, falling to her knees next to the prone figure of her father. They'd torn open his shirt while trying to resuscitate him, and she could see the brutal wound where a bullet had punched through his chest. He stared up at that egg-white winter's sky, his eyes nothing but dead jelly now, frozen into their last regard of this world.

All the fight went out of her then, and she didn't resist as faceless hands ushered her away from the body, wrapping her up in a blanket. She craned her neck, looked back at her dad until someone draped a tarpaulin over him.

The prison guards led her through the clean streets of Sheerness, the streetlamps glowing, sputtering intermittently. The welcoming glow of electrical light spilled from every window, and soon she found herself sitting in front of a radiator, a mug of cocoa in her hands. She stared at nothing for what seemed like hours, eyes unfocused.

"It was a regrettable accident," she heard someone saying. It was the prison guard from the beach, the one who'd been shouting at them through the megaphone. The clean-shaven man sat in a chair opposite her, peaked hat in his hands. There was a police officer next to him taking notes, and she realised that she was in some sort of waiting room, presumably in the police station.

"We're not monsters here, miss. We've only ever intended to scare people away."

"You've got electricity," Tamsyn stated.

"Why, yes," the man said, somewhat surprised. He smiled. "We've captured the Grain station across the way. The fuel will run out one day, but we've enough to tide us over till we can get the wind farm working properly."

"There are people out there," Tamsyn said calmly, "who are starving to death."

There was an uncomfortable silence, and the two men looked at each other. Finally, the police officer spoke.

"You have to understand that we have limited resources here. We let one person in, we let thousands in."

"You lot should be ashamed of yourselves," Tamsyn said, standing up. "And your kind words and fucking cocoa will not bring my father back."

"Miss, I understand that you're upset now," the policeman said, gripping her by the shoulders and trying to steer her back into the seat. "You need to sit down and rest. We'll take care of you."

"Take your hands off me," Tamsyn said, her voice barely under control. She gave the cop her best death glare, and he actually took a step back.

"I didn't come here looking for a home!" she said, glaring up at the man, punctuating her final word with a vicious finger-jab to his ribs. "And I certainly don't want to live here now."

Tamsyn felt like the throbbing pulse of anger was the only thing keeping her upright. She was a grieving warrior-queen, Ripley from Aliens, Boudica pushed too far by the Romans.

"I want to speak to whoever's in charge. Then I'll be leaving."

It was a prison van that took her to HMP Swaleside, the first vehicle she'd seen in almost a year that wasn't jammed into a barricade or abandoned. Tamsyn almost felt surreal as she swept across the bleak Isle in minutes, passing a work crew of prisoners who were clearing snow from the roads.

The three prisons rose above the marshlands, and soon they were passing through the main gates of Swaleside itself. Gate after gate opened before them, and then she and her escort were out of the van and walking through the prison.

Swaleside was very much in full operation. Prisoners wolf-whistled as she passed their cells, and she heard profanities that made her skin crawl. She was very glad that these people were still under lock and key, even here at the world's end.

"Governor's through here," the guard accompanying her said, and she was let into an austere office, all panelled walls and straight edges. A hard-faced woman stood up from behind a desk and bid her to enter. Tam took the seat that was offered to her. GVNR. JOAN BRIDGELY declared the brass nameplate attached to her desk.

"Miss Webb. I've already heard the report. I'm appalled at this senseless accident, and you have my full apologies. The man responsible will be punished."

"That won't change anything," Tamsyn said, and the woman nodded, steepling her fingers. They sat in silence for a long moment.

"No doubt you think we are monsters," the Governor said. "We have food on Sheppey, electricity, communications. Ample labour. Surely we are holding out on those who've survived, out of spite alone?"

"You're the government, or whatever's left of it. It's your responsibility to fix this mess."

"Too true," Bridgely said. "And we are."

A guard arrived with a tea tray, and the Governor poured them both a cup. Tamsyn fell onto the plate of biscuits like a starving waif, stuffing her face.

"We're building more greenhouses," the Governor continued, "working on reclaiming the marshlands for settlements, trying to generate our own electricity. The moment that we are truly self-sufficient, then—"

"Bullshit," Tamsyn said through a spray of biscuit crumbs. "Yeah, then you'll open your gates and welcome all with hugs and kisses. Well, I've got news for you, everyone's dead."

"Do you think the blockade was an easy decision? I'm responsible for hundreds of rapists and murderers. And thousands of townsfolk, villagers, farmers. They all rely on me."

"But what about the—"

"The Queen's laws are upheld. These scum are still serving their sentences. Everyone has enough to eat. I sleep at night, young lady, and if you ask me, I think I'm doing a bloody marvellous job."

Tamsyn nursed her tea and gazed deep into its tannic depths. She felt like a naughty kid in the principal's office, and despite her mixed feelings she knew the woman was right. Had done the right thing, by her people at least.

Rifling through her papers, the Governor extracted a fat file and dropped it onto the desk in front of Tamsyn. The label running down the side of it read DAWES, SIMON #356876.

"Dawes finished his sentence four months ago. He's a free citizen, and as such he may do as he pleases. Even go on your fool's errand, if you can convince him."

"You've heard the American transmission?"

"Yes. Pointless. What guarantees are there that things haven't changed? I wouldn't gamble everything on that recording."

"There's at least a hundred people out there, and a boat that might make it. If you won't feed them, the Yanks will."

"We're on half-rations as is," the Governor said. "The answer is still no. We've a place here for you, but no one else."

Tamsyn thought about the overloaded boats fleeing Gravesend. Their safe haven was overrun with walking horrors, and it was all her fault. It just wouldn't be right for her to stay, but she was so tired...

"Society continues here, and with it, England," the Governor said. "Take my advice, girl: forget about America."

There was a long, awkward moment, filled with nothing but the ticking of a wall clock.

"At least we've been given a chance," Tamsyn finally told the Governor. "This whole island is a damn prison, and you're welcome to it."

After a nondescript church service, they buried Mal Webb in the back corner of the Sheerness cemetery. The local reverend was an anaemic looking man who droned his way through a graveside Bible reading. No one mentioned the violent manner of Mal's passing, and everyone gave Tamsyn a wide berth.

She stayed to watch two prisoners wrestle the pile of frozen clay back into the grave as the small crowd filed out through the neat rows of headstones, presumably into the warmth of the pub. Finally, she was alone with the tamped mound of slush, facing the wooden marker that read MALCOLM WEBB, 1962-2013.

"Just like Pocahontas," she whispered. Her father had never set foot on the Isle of Sheppey his whole life, and now he would stay here forever.

"They should give him a headstone, something more respectful," a man said from beside her. "A proper monument, like."

She turned, and her heart skipped a beat. There, in a denim outfit plastered with clay, was Simon Dawes. He held a cap in between his hands, shifting from foot to foot in the cold.

"It's the least these rotten bastards can do," he said, giving Tamsyn a weak smile.

"You don't get to speak," Tamsyn managed, shaking all over. She thought she might vomit. "My entire family is dead because of you."

He nodded and left her to collect herself. It might have been hours later, but she eventually left the grave, numb inside and out. Dawes was waiting for her just outside the tiny gate, a rose arch made bare by winter.

Without a word, they walked together through the light snowfall. She had a room near the esplanade, and she let them in. Her things had been retrieved from the boat and left there for her. Half the photos were ruined, and the camcorder was destroyed after its salt-water soaking. Tam had everything spread out in front of the radiator, hoping to save what she could.

Her art books were completely destroyed, a sodden wad of paper and ink. Years' worth of work, and nothing to show for it.

Tamsyn cried then, great heaving waves of sorrow that rose from her belly. Curled up on the floor of the bedsit, she wept until there were no tears left to her.

There was a polite coughing behind her, and Tamsyn looked up. Dawes had been standing just inside the door, waiting for Tamsyn to finish.

Climbing to her aching legs, Tamsyn pointed at a kitchen chair. They sat down at the poky little table. She squinted a little, unused to the electric light.

"We have a boat, a big cargo boat. They might be able to fix it, but no one knows how to pilot a ship that big. You're a sea captain. We need you to get us to America."

"America?"

He genuinely didn't know. The Governor hadn't told these people anything. With an annoyed sigh, Tamsyn brought him up to speed.

"Oh." Dawes scratched his salt-and-pepper beard, lost in thought. She looked him in the eye.

"You'd better say you'll do it, you rotten shit," Tamsyn shouted, slamming her fist against the table. "Those people are depending on you. I'm depending on you. If my father wasted his life, so help me I'll—"

"Tamsyn, I'll do it. I'll do anything," he said quietly, holding up one broad hand to calm her down. "I can't ever make up for what I've done to you, but I can help your friends."

"The ship's got broken engines," she said, still spoiling for a fight. He laced his fingers and leaned forward onto the table, meeting her contempt with a steady gaze. Dawes had a sad twinkle in his blue eyes, and Tamsyn made herself look at him.

She took in a leathery old face marked with hard living, thick worry lines around his eyes, the receding hairline. There was the faint white of jagged scars framing either end of his mouth. Seems his cellmates had given him a Glasgow smile.

Dawes wasn't a monster. He was just a sad old drunk, already punished for his addiction, shoulders slumped from years of guilt.

"I've worked all over ships, everything from scrubbing the loos to steering the damn things," he said. "I'm not an expert, but I know a bit of everything. We'll get your boat going."

It was snowing again, the day they slipped the *Paraclete* out of dry dock. They had to use the Tilbury ferry as a tugboat and nearly strained the old crate to bits by the time the big cargo ship was out and clear.

For as long as she could stand the cold, Tamsyn stood in the prow. The river was starting to ice over near the banks, and every building and street she could see was dusted with thick snow.

"I can't believe this is really happening," said Naomi, ruffling her hair. Tamsyn smiled up at the enormous woman, noted her eyes still washed red from crying, a smile that didn't sit true. They'd all lost someone, and Naomi was putting a brave face on things.

Carefully easing past the wreckage of the cruise liner, Dawes guided the ship out into the centre of the river. The walls of old Tilbury Fort were lined with those who'd chosen to stay, waving and shouting out to them. From the bridge, Dawes hauled on the ship's whistle, the sound cutting across the frozen landscape.

"Those people have the good sense to starve here, rather than dying stranded on the ocean," Dr. Murray said, going belowdecks in a huff. He'd been especially cranky since the booze had run out.

The damn coffin-dodgers were everywhere now, tracking through the deep snow drifts like ants, sluggish with the cold. They didn't seem so menacing from here. Just sad, a little lost. Forever walking, never arriving.

Finally, the freezing winds got too much for Tamsyn, so she headed up to the bridge. She passed Eddie Jacobs napping in an alcove and resisted the urge to kick him in the ribs. He did nothing but lurk around, pouting and getting in people's way, but his old man was dead and people still far too forgiving. The Gravesend dream was finished, and Eddie was just another scared orphan.

Climbing up to the bridge, Tamsyn knocked on the hatch. Marcus Riley wound open the door, beaming when he saw who it was.

"Never thought I'd see the day we got it working," chortled the old stevedore. "She's not the QE2, but she'll do the job."

Behind the ship's wheel, Dawes nodded at Tamsyn. She went and stood by the helm, watching as he slowly guided the ship around the larger islands of frozen rubbish.

"I could probably plough right through all this muck, but I don't want to risk it," Dawes said. "We've still got a long way to go."

The *Paraclete* thrummed with power, all the controls glowing with life, the engines chugging away far beneath them.

"The number one engine is still firing a bit rough, but it should get us there," Dawes said. "Be it limping or crawling, we'll arrive."

They cleared the Thames estuary, rounding the Isle of Sheppey. From up here the lit-up towns and villages looked miserly, one shabby little island against the world. Finding the whistle cord, Tamsyn gave Sheppey a long, defiant tooting.

Then onto the Channel, and rougher seas. Dawes and Riley looked calm, while Tamsyn wanted to vomit every scrap of food she'd ever eaten. She began to play with the radio, hoping to distract herself.

"Show me how to play this across the whole ship," she asked Dawes, who showed her the correct switches to push. She dialled the radio into the emergency broadcast channel, and the crackling American voice filled the ship.

The *Paraclete* sailed past the white cliffs of Dover, even as the mysterious message ended and looped to the beginning. Swallowing her bile, Tamsyn smiled up at Dawes, patted him on the arm.

"I might just get my sea legs yet," she said.

Eighty-three survivors left England that day, an island mausoleum crawling from end to end. There was nothing for anyone there. The real answer was in America, and if one word of the broadcast was true, an exciting possibility was waiting for them.

"We're going home," Tamsyn said, deftly sketching the pale cliffs on her new notepad. "Never been to America, but we're going home."

PART 2:
CORPUS CHRISTI

— 7 —

I f a ship was becalmed in the old days," Dr. Murray shouted, "they'd dump all the cargo, all the ballast. They'd drown all their horses, too."

Tamsyn Webb nodded, fighting off a full-body shiver. She was wrapped in several layers of clothing, with most of her face covered by a fisherman's scarf, greasy and older than her. She wore a slicker over this, but it only kept out some of the spray.

There were perhaps twenty fishing lines strung out across the rail of the poop deck, every rod and hand reel that they could scrounge from the crew quarters and the hold. Her eyes watering in the wind, Tamsyn tried to spot any movement that might indicate a hooked fish. The rain was coming in almost sideways, and each gust whipped the lines around mercilessly.

"Waste of a fine animal, but ye olde sailors would dump 'em just the same, and pray for wind," Dr. Murray continued, his leathery old face poking out of a nest of scarves and hoods. "Maybe it's the old vet in me, but I can't stand the thought of killing a horse for no good reason."

Great walls of icy water broke against the sides of the drifting cargo ship; hammer-blows against its thick steel skin. Squinting against the wind, Tamsyn spotted an enormous iceberg some miles off, drifting along on its own slow voyage.

Even the Titanic had the means to dodge one of those things, Tamsyn thought. *God, I hope it hits us.*

Once they had limped away from England, the engines on the old ship had given up the ghost. For three weeks now, the *Paraclete* had been dead in the middle of the Atlantic Ocean. The world was a stomping ground for hungry corpses, and no one was coming to rescue them.

"Today, I would eat a horse, hoofs and all," Dr. Murray said. It wasn't his turn to watch the lines, but he kept Tamsyn company, rigging up a tarpaulin to keep some of the rain out. They took it in turns to brave the weather, playing out the lines, checking them for snags and tangles.

"Look!" Tamsyn said, scrambling for a rod that shifted. The line jerked, moving several inches. The rod flexed under the weight of something heavy, and she laughed as she rapidly worked the reel.

Then, a release as the weight was suddenly gone from the line. Slipping on the wet deck, Tamsyn landed heavily on her side. The ocean chose that moment to launch an icy barrage against the ship, and she slipped further; her head striking the iron rail as she slid underneath it. Pain shot through her skull as she dangled over the edge, the rod spilling out of her numb fingers.

A rough hand wrapped around her wrist, and Dr. Murray dragged her backwards, even as the fishing rod struck the waters far below.

"Big fish," Dr. Murray said. Tamsyn trembled, her heart racing. By the time a lifeboat could have got to her, the chill waters would have done what the zombies had failed to do.

At least it would have been a clean death, she thought, looking at the edge of the deck and fighting back the tears. *I won't come back as one of those mindless things. I'd rather kill myself.*

"Be easy, lass, you're all right," he said. "Look on the bright side. Our dinner might still be down there, testing our hooks."

Dad would have loved this, Tamsyn thought, massaging the egg-lump on her forehead. *Even floating out here, starving to death on a dead boat, he could have fished to his heart's content.*

Grief crushed her heart, and she tried to concentrate on her job, tried to push the image of Mal Webb's limp body from her thoughts.

"Could be a big salmon, maybe a mackerel or something," Dr. Murray said.

Her stomach rumbled at the thought. The fishing lines occasionally supplemented their dwindling food supplies, and on a good day the smell from the galley was positively mouth-watering.

Another line jumped. Dr. Murray roared with delight, fighting the fish as it bent his rod almost double.

"Get the net ready," he shouted, and Tamsyn raced for the rails, looking down as an enormous head split the foam, thrashing and bucking. The line snapped before the animal could be cleared of the water. Dr. Murray laughed fit to burst, his florid drunk's face squeezed tight. Finally, wheezing and hacking, he found his breath.

"It was a bloody shark," he finally managed.

June and Clarry Debenham eventually relieved them from the tedious job. The couple had once run a florist's shop in Gravesend, and now they timidly followed their neighbours from one disaster to the next. Tamsyn still didn't know how the pair of myopic fusspots had survived the end of the world.

"How exciting, I've never even been on a boat-ride," June Debenham had said, back when the *Paraclete* was working and food wasn't yet a dirty word.

Tamsyn and Dr. Murray retreated inside the *Paraclete*, the outer hatch sealing away the foul weather. The retired vet bid her goodnight and limped towards the mess, dripping water all over the deck. His wet cough echoed against the metal walls as he hacked phlegm into his hanky.

That doesn't sound good at all, she thought. *But it's not like he was in the best of health when we escaped. Or young.*

Lucky old bugger. He might not live long enough to starve.

She climbed down to her small room in the crew quarters, dripping water everywhere. The safety lights wired along the passageway flickered and once again died. Cursing in the dark, she fished out a flashlight from a jacket pocket, thumped it into life against a bulkhead when it wouldn't cooperate.

The lamp was half-filled with water and cast a weak light, ripples of shadow licking the walls and floor. Her journey became surreal, as if she was walking through a sunken wreck on the ocean floor. She was surrounded by the echoing clatter of her footsteps, the creaking of the boat as its iron skeleton fought the stresses of the elements.

Passing through the old crew quarters, she thought she heard someone crying, and a muffled argument. Tamsyn hurried to her door, hoping not to bump into anyone else. Conversations were becoming awkward with the other passengers, and she didn't miss any of the dark looks cast in her direction. People with sunken eyes whispered in dark corners.

Tamsyn had found them a captain who could fix this leaky old ship, talked these people into chasing the mysterious radio broadcast coming from America. Even before they raised anchor, everyone coming aboard had made their own choice.

At the end of the day, though, they were stranded here because of her. And everybody knew that the food was running out.

The *Paraclete* carried eighty-four frightened souls, which meant that the sleeping quarters were all full and sometimes doubled-up.

Some families had set up sleeping areas in the hold or claimed equipment rooms for themselves. Tamsyn shared a cabin with Naomi Higgins, an old netball friend of her mother's. She'd lived three streets away from them, in Gravesend, Kent.

That feels like about five lifetimes ago, Tamsyn thought, lighting a candle-stub on the tiny table she and Naomi shared. She doused the torch, leaning it upside down to let the water drain out.

The enormous black woman was curled up in her bunk, snoring fitfully. Tamsyn winced; there was no way she'd be getting any sleep in here tonight.

She shed the wet layers of clothing, wringing them out over a sluice grate and hanging them on wall pegs and chair backs. She wrapped the scarf around the radiator like a dull brown snake–if they got the power up again, maybe it would help dry it quicker.

Every stitch was soaked, and Tamsyn quickly stripped down, attacking her damp skin with a scratchy towel. As she rifled through her footlocker for dry clothes, she noted that her ribs stuck out a little bit more, that her pelvis was more pronounced today.

"We're starving, Naomi," she said. "Well, *I* am. You're just losing a dress size or two."

Her roommate answered her with a canvas-ripping snore, her broad nostrils drawing in a fat rattle of air. Tamsyn threw a balled-up pair of socks at her, but the snoring continued.

"Honestly," she said as she dressed. For a while she worked on her sketchbook by candlelight, pouring her attention into a series of still lifes. The drawing helped keep her mind off things.

She'd drawn Dr. Murray playing solitaire. Simon Dawes wearing the old captain's hat they'd found, posing with a grin, one hand resting on the ship's wheel. Eddie Jacobs, skulking around in the little galley when she'd busted him looking for hidden food.

She was still working on a large sketch–the final moments of Gravesend, Kent, the docks overrun by the walking dead. The horrid things filled the streets, pushing a panicked crowd towards the icy Thames. Bodies were falling into the filthy water, and a knot of zombies had just descended upon Ali, her best friend. Poor Monica was fighting to free him, and Naomi was trying to wrest her girlfriend from the ranks of murderous corpses.

Before the world had gone belly-up, before dead people hunted the living, Tamsyn had been about to begin a scholarship, accepted into Camberwell Arts at seventeen. She'd captured the scene in almost perfect detail, and it broke her heart.

Naomi whimpered in her sleep then, and Tamsyn looked up. The woman was balling her fists up, releasing them, sobbing quietly. Tamsyn had bad dreams too, almost every night.

I caused all this, Tamsyn thought, remembering how she'd panicked while outside the Safe Zone; led the horde of zombies to a weak spot in the barricade. *I made a stupid mistake and now people are dead.*

And I can never tell a soul.

Frowning, she packed up her sketchbook and left Naomi to her troubled sleep, heading down into the bowels of the ship. They'd still be awake in the engine room, Dawes and Marcus Riley, and maybe she could do something useful down there.

Tamsyn was carefully descending a ladder when the lights came back on, and she smiled. A moment later, there was a loud bang, and the ship was once more in darkness. By wavering torchlight she found them, the engine room full of smoke. Marcus Riley threw a spanner and cursed, coughing and waving away the fumes. His bushy white beard was streaked with grease and filth.

"So, all right then?" she asked, and the old stevedore looked at her with barely veiled fury. Simon Dawes shared her grin, a twinkle in his blue eyes, face twisted by the scars of his Glasgow smile.

Their eyes met, and her smile froze, retreating into thin lips that she worried at with her teeth. *He's a good man now,* she thought. *I've got to let it go.*

The first time Tamsyn ever laid eyes on Simon Dawes, it was as he'd crawled out of the wreckage of a car, too drunk to even walk. He'd ploughed into a bus shelter, crumpling it like a Coke can, her mother pinned underneath the car, screaming, bleeding -

"It's gone to custard, is what," Riley said, snapping her out of her morbid train of thought. "There's no fixing this bloody mess."

"The number one engine is completely burnt out," Dawes explained. "We've stripped it for parts, but number two engine keeps misfiring and conking out. We had to cannibalise one of the generators too, but it's not enough."

"You've gotta keep trying," Tamsyn said. "Give me a spanner or something. How can I help?"

"It's broken, love. We can't fix it," Dawes sighed. "This boat's over fifty years old. I'd never have set out in this, had we a better choice."

"Well, we didn't."

The three of them regarded the massive engine, lit by emergency lamps and partially disassembled. The room stank of burnt oil and melted plastic.

"It gets worse, Tam," Dawes said. "I was checking the radio today, to see if there were other ships within hailing distance, that sort of thing."

"What's wrong?" Tamsyn said, her stomach suddenly very queasy. Simon Dawes was a man of few words, and normally didn't beat around the bush.

"The emergency transmission that we're following, the automatic one coming from America. I can't raise it on any channel. It's stopped."

Up on the bridge, the radio gave a static hiss on every channel. The world was running on radio silence.

Tamsyn knew the message by heart, had listened to it countless times. A simple message that ran on a loop, the words faint and hard to hear, but enough to get them all on a broken boat, enough for them to brave the Atlantic Ocean mid-winter.

We're hurting, but America stands strong, a nameless woman said, the hint of a southern lilt coming through the static crackle. *If y'all can hear this, know that there's hope. We have a cure for the infection.*

Come to Texas. Come to Corpus Christi.

"Perhaps this Corpus Christi got overrun by the coffin-dodgers," she mused. "The transmission kept running automatically, and then the batteries or whatever ran out."

"We have to tell everyone," Dawes said.

"Are you mad?" Riley said. "That mob will go berserk."

"I agree," Tamsyn said. "Some of those folks were already unhinged when they got on the boat. They're likely to turn cannibal or something."

"They deserve to know that we're finished. We can't catch enough fish to feed eighty-four people. God, we've only got a fort-night's worth of fresh water left."

"There's going to be a panic," Tamsyn said. "There's going to be killings, they'll bust into the food store, you name it."

"The food ran out this morning," Dawes said calmly. "There's not a crumb left on this boat."

They stood there in silence, the fact sinking in.

"We have to try the lifeboats," Riley said. "Surely we can reach the shore, any shore. It's gotta be worth a shot."

"We're here," Dawes said, pointing out their position on the nav chart. They were roughly in the centre of the Atlantic Ocean, hundreds of miles from any land mass.

"You won't make one hundred miles in those leaky punts they call life-boats. You may as well just strip off and jump straight into the water."

Tamsyn felt the beginnings of a panic attack, felt the terror start to gently squeeze her throat. Here they were, as far from the undead as possible, but there wasn't even the hope of America, of living past the week. All options were gone.

"People need to prepare themselves," Dawes said gently, a determined look in his eyes. "I'm going to be blunt, Tamsyn. We all need to choose how we want to die."

It was several hours till ration time, when the trouble was likely to start. Calling up Naomi and Dr. Murray to the captain's cabin, they talked at great length, argued and measured distances and finally realised that it was over.

Huddled around the tiny table, the five of them formed a suicide committee, and tried to blunt this stomach-churning task with logistics.

"We don't have enough bullets to do everyone," Naomi said, tired eyes scanning her notes, her head sunk in defeat. She was what passed for a quartermaster on the *Paraclete*. Naomi toted a clipboard filled with ruffled sheets, detailing every item on board the ship.

"There's going to be people who fight this," Dr. Murray wheezed, face a blend of mottled gray skin and rough stubble. "We'll need to get all the guns up here. We shoot the troublemakers, and those who want to nibble on the rest of us."

"Agreed. All we've got left is our dignity," Dawes said. "Everyone dies today."

"We've got rat poison and the like, but it's a nasty end," Dr. Murray said. "I can give syringes of bleach to people, but it's not much better."

Reefing a hip flask out of his pocket, he took a long pull, shuddering as he swallowed.

"Where did you get that?" Naomi demanded. "I thought there was no alcohol left onboard. Is someone running a still?"

"Metho," the old drunk gasped. "Figure I won't live long enough to go blind or insane."

Dawes nodded at the old man and eyed the flask himself for a long moment. He took a deep breath and raised his eyes.

You pretend you're not, but you're still a drunk, Tamsyn thought. *Don't worry, Dawes. My mum will be having words with you by sunset— right before you slip into hell.*

"We can get together all the meds and some people can overdose," Tamsyn heard herself saying, lips moving but somehow not connected to her. In the dark months following the death of her mother, she'd often considered taking her own life. But she'd always hung on, always fought the dark thoughts, even as the world rotted around her.

Now, she had to do it, had to pick a way. All her instincts screamed that it was the wrong way; that after all they'd been through it was unjust to surrender at life.

I saw Dr. Clarke every week to stop cutting myself, Tamsyn thought. *She'd have a screaming fit if she were here.*

Nooses. A railway spike, hammered between the eyes. Drowning. A live wire, to bring a quick electrocution from the one working generator. All these things were talked about calmly, added to the list as they sipped at the last of the tea.

"Tamsyn can get her bow and arrows and shoot some folks in the head," she heard Riley say.

"I won't do it," Tamsyn said woodenly. "I can't."

"She doesn't have to," Dawes said. "At point blank, anyone can fire the damn thing. And we can reuse the arrows."

Arrow to the head was added to the death list.

"Everyone's got their jobs, so go and do them," Dawes said. "Get all the guns and ammo up here, soon as you can. And quietly."

The five of them stood; the de facto crew of a floating tomb. They faced each other in the white glow of the fluoro lamp, and Tamsyn thought they already looked like corpses, faces sunken and washed of colour.

"Until I say so, no one hears about this. When we're holed up, I'll make an announcement over the intercom."

They left the captain's cabin to do their final errands. Tamsyn felt numb as she walked down the stairs, the lights cutting in and out as the backup generator began to fail. She banged her shin once in the darkness and hardly felt it.

Reaching her cabin, she poked around in the piles of junk and dirty clothes, finally coming up with her compound bow, a competition shooter that won her several trophies before entering service as a silent zombie killer. She had a quiver half-full of arrows, several bent out of true, still marked with pliers from where they'd been yanked out of skulls.

These days, she couldn't be too picky about what she went shooting with. She took a long moment to run her hands over the carbon-fibre frame, the pulleys and sights. It was a beautiful piece, custom made for her, and it had cost her dad a mint. With one smooth motion she attached the string, tested the tension.

What's the point in all this palaver? she thought. *It's just gotta hit some poor sod at point blank, kneeling on the floor, waiting for the sound of the string, the air whistling around the feathers.*

Will they hear it before they die?

Fighting off the morbid thoughts, trying to focus, she left the cabin, putting one foot in front of the other. She didn't see the man step out of the shadows, blocking her pathway.

"Oi, wait up there," he said, and by the flickering safety lights Tamsyn saw that it was Darryl Gunderson. He'd been one of the last to escape from Gravesend, with his heavily pregnant wife

Tara. Little Milly had been born one week out from England, a joyous occasion.

"Let's hope this little one never sees a zombie," Dr. Murray said, peeling off his bloody latex gloves and beaming like everyone else.

She never will, Tamsyn thought.

"Hi, Mr. Gunderson," she said, holding the bow alongside her body. She hoped he wouldn't see it in the darkness, ask any awkward questions.

"Listen Tamsyn, you gotta help us. You're in good with the captain, and that horrible black bitch running the food stores. Please."

"I'm sorry," she said. "We're all running short. We'll hopefully get the boat going soon."

He hovered in front of her, his hopeful smile turning into a desperate rictus, wringing his calloused hands, moving to block her path. He'd been a road worker back home, and she was conscious of the way he loomed over her, broad shoulders blocking out the weak light from the nearby fitting.

"Please. There's got to be some milk, even some powder stuff that the captain is keeping for his tea. Just something."

"There's no milk left. I asked Naomi to check. There was only some sour stuff, too curdled for anything. There's nothing else I can do."

"Please! I'm not asking for me," he sobbed, pacing back and forth in the corridor. "My missus is so hungry that she can't even give milk. You ever heard a hungry baby crying for hours on end, knowing that there's nothing you can bloody do?"

"I'm sorry," Tamsyn said, and meant it. She'd given all she could to the Gundersons, even though she felt like fainting most of the time. Tara's eyes were puffy and almost black, and she wolfed down every crumb pushed into her hands, whispering her thanks to a parade of starving people that were killing themselves to help her.

"It cuts through my fucking skull like a drill, that crying. I don't know what I'm meant to do," the man said. He pushed her back, pinning her shoulder to the bulkhead. Tamsyn fought against him, dropping the bow with a clamour.

"Stop it, stop it!" she cried, her panic rising. "Don't you touch me!"

"We know you lot are looking after yourselves," he shouted, the desperate smile replaced with fury. "We were stupid enough to follow your daft plan, and now you're fucking killing us!"

Pushing up at his chin with the flat of her palm, she struck him once, the way her dad had shown her. Reeling from the pain, he slapped her, hard. She tried to knee him in the groin, but he blocked her strike with his free hand. Reeling, she snaked a hand down into the quiver at her hip. A sharp arrow was in her hand, and she lifted it, ready to drive up into his gut...

There was a flurry of movement, and suddenly Gunderson was gone. In the darkness were scuffling sounds, the grunting of two men, the meaty sound of a fist striking a body, a pained groan.

The light flickered, revealing Eddie Jacobs. Gravesend's favourite young thug was aiming a kick at the retreating Gunderson, who limped and sobbed and weaved his way up the corridor.

"Go on now! Fuck off!" Eddie said, and it was probably the first time in her life that Tamsyn was actually glad to see him.

Eddie flipping Jacobs, she thought. *I cannot believe he just saved me from a beating.*

"Follow me," Eddie said, jerking a thumb towards the stairwell. "I've got things to say to you, I have."

Nodding, Tamsyn slid the arrow back into the quiver, picked up the bow with shaking hands.

She followed Eddie upstairs towards the deck, looking around nervously as they passed doorways and corridors. They didn't pass anyone on the way, but she was glad of his presence. Eddie was a stocky lad, a skinhead with quick fists and a short fuse.

"Don't worry, Tam, them folks will be laying low if they know what's good for 'em." He opened the outer hatchway, pulling the hood of his greasy anorak up around his ears.

The lifeboats formed a windbreak, and it was here that Eddie led her, leaning up against the flimsy rowboats that were less than useless.

"I needed to talk to you, all private like," Eddie said. "Don't fancy the chance of a quiet word anywhere down there. We're all living in each other's farts and such."

"Thanks. For saving me," Tamsyn said. He snorted and pulled a face.

"Those Gundersons are idiots," Eddie said. "If you can't feed 'em, don't breed 'em, is what I say."

"Eddie, that's just... oh my god, you're actually right. They were mad to have a kid."

They sat inside the curve of the boat, shielded from the wind and rain. For long moments they sat there, until Eddie blinked, cracked his knuckles.

"I wanted to say I'm sorry. About your dad and that," he finally managed. "Weren't right, what happened back in Gravesend."

"You mean how your father shut down my dad's school, or when he tried to have us killed?" Tamsyn said. "Coz I'm not sure which thing you're apologising for."

Eddie's face clouded over, and he turned away. She saw a tear leak out of his eye, and sighed. *Oh Tam, you bloody idiot. He lost his dad too.*

Eddie might put out those soccer hooligan vibes, but really? He's just a scared kid who misses his dad.

"I'm sorry, Eddie," she said, patting him on the arm. "Past is past, okay?"

"Okay," he mumbled, wiping his nose on his sleeve. "Look, I know it's all gone to shit. Right? Be honest with me, Tam. We're finished, aren't we?"

Considering Dawes's warning, Tamsyn looked at Eddie, at his piggish eyes and crooked nose, skin chapped from the constant cold. He seemed...accepting of things. She nodded.

"I'm not gonna wait to starve out," he said. "Got me old man's switch-back razor. It'll be quick."

"Can I borrow it after you?" Tamsyn said after a moment. "I'll probably still sterilize it first."

Looking at each other, they fell about laughing. Sides heaving, Tamsyn slipped forward, arrows spilling out everywhere. Eddie caught her wrist and helped her up.

"Should we shag then?" he said. "If we're dead anyway."

"Oh, grow up." Tamsyn punched him in the arm and started gathering up her gear.

"You know, Eddie, I reckon your dad would have been proud of you," she said. "I thought you were always going to end up as a hitman or something, but you turned out okay."

"All right then," Eddie said, hiding his smile. *A hard man to the last.* They shook hands. "Well, I'll see you at the Kool-Aid queue."

They made their way back to the outer hatch, Tamsyn eyeing the thrashing sea about them. Great sheets of ice washing about in the waves, and the enormous berg still dominated the horizon.

So this will be our floating tomb, she thought. *Our bodies will freeze here, forever safe from the walking dead.*

That was when she saw another shape, sliding out from behind the wall of ice. At first she thought it was more ice, a sliver that had broken free of the larger berg. And then she saw the row of windows in its side, the brown panelling of a ship's deck.

"Wouldn't read about it," Eddie said, whistling softly. "That's a bloody boat right there."

The lifeboat was quickly filling up with water, and those who weren't struggling with the oars were working the bailing buckets furiously. The freezing waves buffeted the boat, lifting it metres high, then dropping it like a toddler frustrated with his toy.

We are idiots, Tamsyn thought numbly. *Starving idiots.*

"We're almost there," Dawes shouted from the prow. "Get ready."

The wave dropped to reveal the enormous superyacht, several figures moving around on the upper decks. *Petty Cash,* read the nameplate on the side of the prow.

Look how many decks are on that thing, Tamsyn thought. *It's more like a wedding cake than a boat.* Someone threw a grapple-hook, and it fell short.

"Again!" Dawes yelled. The world seemed to give a sickening heave, and in one terrifying moment a surging wave threw them up against the side of the ship. They were thrown around in the life raft, and Tamsyn fell into a tangle of limbs, her elbow slamming painfully into the gunwale. There was a loud snap, and two of the oars were broken.

"Quick, grab that rope!" Tamsyn did not know who was shouting. A horrific scream cut through the waves and driving wind, and Tamsyn saw that Clarry Debenham had his arm trapped between the two vessels. He was slowly being crushed as the lifeboat ground up against the ship, and the trapped florist wailed and screamed in agony.

Another wave slapped the flimsy lifeboat, and they were washed towards the rear of the ship. A swim deck led down to the water level, tantalisingly close. A small runabout was moored there, tipped over, half submerged as the freezing swell mercilessly battered everything.

Naomi swung the grappling hook and caught it on a railing. Hands shaking, fingers numb, Tamsyn joined in the frantic group hauling on the line, drawing them closer to the bottom steps.

Even as they reached out to tie up the boat, it shook around them. A final barrage from the ocean, a bad one, and the back of the lifeboat went completely under. Tamsyn wrapped both hands around the bench seat beneath her, gasping as the water washed over her. Others held on, but a woman screamed as she was pushed overboard, dragged away by tonnes of water.

"We have to save her!" a man shouted.

"She's already dead," Dawes yelled. "Do you want to kill the rest of us?"

Arms flailing, the poor woman yelled and thrashed, fighting to keep afloat. In moments she'd crested the first wave, a terrified figure wrapped in a life vest. The next second, she was gone from sight.

"They're here!" someone else cried. Several zombies were already descending the steps, teeth bared, hands bunched into tortured claws. Tamsyn could already hear the damned moaning, the sharp cries of frustration. Of unending hunger.

Repel all boarders, Tamsyn thought, scrabbling for her bow. She breathed a sigh of relief when she found it wedged up against the empty life vest locker. Half her arrows were rolling around in the bottom of the boat, and she had no time to collect them all.

Dawes finally had the boat lashed up against the swim deck. The boarding party clambered out as quick as they could manage, fighting to keep their balance against the knee-deep waves that scoured the platform.

"Get ready!" Dr. Murray shouted, closing the breech of his vet's shotgun. *Two rounds, maybe ten more in his pockets*, Tamsyn thought, nocking an arrow to her string. She ignored the sighting pegs; this was going to be up close and far too personal. She wouldn't miss; couldn't miss. Death itself came staggering down the stairs, a thick crowd that wobbled on stiff joints, snarling at the intruders.

Dawes readied a long dead policeman's revolver, and Riley struggled with the bolt action of an old bird gun. That was as much firepower as they were packing. Everyone else nervously gripped at hatchets, iron pipes, cricket bats.

Darryl Gunderson had the last of the emergency flares and sent it spiralling up the packed staircase. A loud bang and a white flash of phosphor brought a pair of twitching corpses rolling down the steps, landing awkwardly on the swim deck. Dawes looked down grimly at the unholy things, pistol held level as they dragged their smoking bodies forward, snapping their teeth at him.

Frowning, he stomped forwards in his work boots, breaking in teeth, stomping their skulls into paste. In moments the rotten corpses lay still, their spreading gore drifting with the sweep of the water, blackened fingers twitching weakly.

Fear was a luxury for the living, and the zombies kept coming. Tamsyn could see the first of these coffin-dodgers clearly now, the desiccated remains of a man wearing filthy rags, once board-shorts. The skin was taut over its ribs, punctured in places.

Tamsyn drew back on the bowstring, felt the tension even as the pulleys countered the immense force. She breathed out, released, and a feathery shaft punched its way through the zombie's eye. It slid down the stairs with a surprised look on its face, hands scrabbling at the quivering shaft in one final moment of confusion.

The others looked at her, amazed. The zombie had been perhaps thirty feet away, up a staircase. It was a perfect shot.

"They're all still in their bathers," she said, teeth chattering. "Don't they know it's bloody freezing?"

"Murray, get here," Dawes said. "The rest of you, up that ladder there. We've gotta get off this deck, now."

A series of steel rungs led up to the lower decks. Riley was the first up the ladder, rifle at the ready. The others climbed up behind him, some struggling with their improvised weapons. One or two of them dropped what they carried, the better to deal with the climb.

"Don't drop your stuff, you idiots!" Tamsyn yelled, shaking her head as she readied her bow. Standing behind Dawes, she tapped him on the shoulder with the tip of her arrow. He got the message, knelt in the water to give her a clear field of fire.

The three of them held the stairs, sent a volley of death up into the packed ranks of the undead. The growing blanket of moans was drowned out by the ear-rattling roar of the shotgun, the popping of the revolver. Tamsyn felt the thrum of her bow, the satisfying flex of its power as her shafts flew forward.

Somewhere above them, a rifle shot, screams, the breaking of glass.

Don't think of skulls. Just think of popping eggshells, Tamsyn told herself, fighting back her bile. Bodies toppled down the steps, a parade of rotting flesh wrapped in bikinis, crew uniforms, even the threadbare remains of a safari suit. Still the undead kept advancing, until they were climbing over the stack of shattered corpses, shuffling unsteadily across the swim deck itself.

"I'm out of arrows!" Tamsyn said, throwing her bow at the ravaged remains of a topless sunbather. The corpse actually caught the weapon, testing the carbon fibre with a mouthful of foul teeth. "We gotta go!"

They climbed the rung ladder, Dawes emptying his gun to buy them time. Tamsyn pulled herself up onto the first deck, to a scene of complete chaos.

Bodies littered the outer concourse, tangled up in deck chairs, leaning through the outer rails. Not all of them were zombies; Tamsyn recognised a chemist named Yvonne, throat torn out, tangled up with what was left of her undead assailant. Tamsyn took in this final, almost intimate embrace, and drew the claw hammer from her belt. She stepped over the blood-slick boards.

"They didn't finish the job," Tamsyn said to Dr. Murray, and even as Yvonne's dead eyes opened, her hammer fell. It took three solid hits to the temple to stop that awful sound, a wordless cry that spoke of betrayal, of hunger.

What was left of the boarding party was scattered across the enormous ship, a running fight that nearly turned against them. They regrouped in the fifty-seat theatre, lost two more people in the bar, and worked through all five levels of the sprawling luxury cruiser, clearing every cabin and wardroom and storage closet.

The captain's cabin was locked, and Eddie Jacobs shouldered his way in. The captain hadn't bothered leaving a note; his putrefied body lay slumped in a chair, a plume of gore painting the wall behind him.

"You're such a ghoul," Tamsyn said as Eddie prised the pistol out of the dead man's grip.

"What?" he said. "I'm commandeering it. Yeah, I know a big word. Whatever."

It was done. They'd lost eight people in the taking of the *Petty Cash*, but it was theirs. Satisfied that all the zombies onboard were disposed of, Dawes ordered that the corpses be tipped overboard.

During the clean-up, Tamsyn found the topless zombie wandering the rear of the vessel, still gnawing on her bow. Eyeing Tamsyn through a veil of lank hair and peeling skin, it dropped the bow and advanced on her, snarling.

"Honestly love, you need to put a top on," she told the walking corpse. "The boys will respect you more."

Even as the zombie reached out for her face, mouth wide open and dripping black slime, Tamsyn ducked under its flailing arms and drove the claw-end of the hammer into an eye socket.

With a final sigh, the creature fell onto what was once a shapely backside, holding its head in its hands.

"I'm sorry," Tamsyn said, pinning the zombie's head to the deck with her boot, wrenching the gore-soaked hammer loose from its skull. "Sometimes, the truth hurts."

The engines of the *Petty Cash* were in good order, but the fuel tanks were completely dry. Near as Naomi could figure from the logbooks, they'd fled from land at the first sign of the outbreak, not realising an infected person had boarded.

"It would have happened quick," Naomi said, "all munch-munch, and pass us the brains, thanks. So the captain gives up the bridge, right," and here Naomi mimed a pistol to the roof of the mouth, "but the boat must have still been going, and it just drifted around until it ran out of fuel."

The boarding party scanned the ship deck by deck, taking inventory. Tamsyn couldn't believe their good fortune. The dead passengers had all been wealthy people, and they'd left behind cabins filled with jewellery, expensive watches, amazing dresses, thousand-dollar suits, wallets stuffed with American currency, and dozens of credit cards worth just as little.

Tamsyn's clothes were saturated from the boat ride, and with teeth chattering she quickly changed into the outfit of someone too dead to need it: khakis, a nice silk shirt, and a thick cashmere sweater. She found some dry socks, and a pair of canvas tennis shoes.

"For all the good it will do you," Naomi said, shaking her head as Tamsyn showed off a fat diamond encrusted bracelet. "You planning on eating that?"

Wading through the scattered chaos of the spacious galley, Tamsyn opened the door to the cold-room. The smell that wafted out of the huge refrigerator was stomach churning, and she staggered away, coughing and gagging.

Enormous cuts of meat hung from hooks, blackened and crawling with worms. The shelves were filled with food, all of it ruined, furry with mould and slime. Large trays were arrayed on a central bench, dozens of unrecognisable desserts ready for service.

"What's for supper, eh?" Eddie said at her elbow, startling her. She was so furious that she actually took a swing at him. He stepped back from her wild haymaker, chuckling, hands raised in mock defence.

"It's not funny!" Tamsyn shouted, kicking a dented saucepan. "There's nothing to bloody eat. We're completely stuffed."

"Don't be so sure," Naomi called out, clearing a stainless-steel bench, sweeping crockery and foul pots to the floor. Reaching into a low cupboard, she began to stack boxes, packets, tin after tin onto the bench.

"Enough pancake mix here to feed an army. Flour, gravy, more beans than I ever want to see. Nothing fancy here, but it sure beats eating my fingernails."

Rifling through the other cupboards, Tamsyn smiled, broke into laughter. She triumphantly held aloft a carton of long-life milk.

"There's dozens of these!" she crowed. "Someone tell Mr. Gunderson!"

Emptied of furniture, the mate's cabin was earmarked for secure storage, and with stomachs growling the boarding party ported all of the food into it. Only Dawes was to have the key, for which Tamsyn was grateful. She didn't want to be connected to any more unpopular decisions.

Even as the last corpse was dragged out of the bridge, Riley managed to patch a radio call through to the *Paraclete*. The cargo ship was to be abandoned, and everyone transferred over to the *Petty Cash*. Every lifeboat into the sea, with as many drums of fuel and water as could safely fit.

"And leave all your shit behind," Dawes said, taking the radio from Riley's hands. "You better come off those boats with only the clothes on your back."

The ship had been adrift for almost two years but was in surprisingly good condition; the main corridors stank of old death, but many of the cabins were still clean. Wearing a vinegar-soaked bandana over her mouth and nose, Tamsyn mopped the rot-blackened deck with disinfectant.

Some of the passengers had been killed in their sleep, and several gore-stained mattresses were soon pushed overboard, a flotilla of white lozenges washing around in the furious waves.

"What are you doing?" Dawes shouted, as Naomi and Tamsyn wrestled another mattress over the rail. "What the hell are you doing, pushing all that junk out into the water?"

"You said to clean up," Tamsyn said through gritted teeth. "You said 'get all the diseased muck and tip it overboard.'"

"I didn't mean mattresses!" Dawes said, the Joker-style scars around his mouth all the more hideous on his angry face. "The boats are on their way and now they've got to get through that! You've got a brain, Tam, why don't you use it?"

You'd know all about killing people, Tamsyn wanted to say, but bit her tongue. *Killed my mum, and as good as killed my poor dad.*

Despite her best intentions, Tamsyn was finding forgiveness hard to stick to. She realised that she still hated Simon Dawes, even after everything he'd done to redeem himself.

You can't unkill my parents, you bastard.

The first of the remaining lifeboats was soon spotted, barely visible against the violent sea. Another one followed, and two more behind that. Four boats, dangerously overloaded, and Tamsyn thought she could make out some drums in the middle, lashed down with ropes.

The boarding party raced to the stern, clearing the swim deck of debris, pulling the little tin runabout up onto the boards and out of the way.

"Those boats are awful low!" Riley shouted over the crashing water. "Send them back, Dawes! We can make more trips if we need to."

"No time," Dawes said, pointing to the sky. A black bank of cloud was rolling in from the north, rapidly filling the sky. "We get everything over now or we lose the chance. Once that storm hits, this ship will be miles away from the *Paraclete*. We'll never find it again."

The first boat was closer. Tamsyn could see the worried faces of those onboard, some of them two to an oar. The boat was taking on water quicker than they could bail it out.

"Be ready with the ropes," Dawes said, handing out lengths of ship line, fastening loose ends to the deck with expert knot-work. "We need to lash everything down as fast as possible."

A strong wave caused the lifeboat to overshoot them, and it took a great deal of oar-work to get them back. Ropes were played out, yellow snakes dancing across the cold foam. Everything condensed down to a minute of frantic hauling, where the universe became a rope and the slippery deck, and the palms of Tamsyn's hands seemed to be stripped of skin. After a tense eternity the boat was safely tied up, and people were climbing on the *Petty Cash*, laughing, weeping with joy.

"Quick, get that fuel in!" Dawes shouted. Canisters and drums of the stuff were ferried into the guts of the boat. Some plastic tubs of drinking water were ported towards the storage room.

Someone cried out, and Tamsyn looked up to see the cause of the commotion. Barely three hundred yards from the *Petty Cash* a boat had broken in the rough waters, split in two, the wreckage surrounded by bobbing containers, and little forms in yellow life vests waving frantically.

"We've got to save them!" Tamsyn shouted at Dawes. "Quickly!"

"No," Dawes yelled back. "I can't risk losing any more people. It's too late for them."

"You're scum," she shouted, shoving him in the chest. "They're right there, and you're happy to watch them die? Fuck you, Dawes."

She signalled to Riley and started to pull the runabout towards the water. The stevedore pushed it out into the sea, hauling on the ripcord as Tamsyn got behind the wheel. There was a lick of fuel in the tank of the outboard motor, enough for it to cough into life.

Eddie climbed into the tin dinghy after her, pushing her out of the way. He waved a hand at her protests.

"You even driven a boat?" he said. "Figures. Move over, you daft cow."

She gripped the bench-seat, teeth gritted, blinking against the spray as Eddie threw the throttle to full. Motor whining, they climbed from wave to wave, slamming into the swell with spine-jarring force.

Then they were amongst the wreckage. The lifeboat was already sunk. Bobbing drums of water crashed into the sides of the runabout with hollow booms. Above the pounding ocean came the wails, the frenzied cries for help.

"There!" she said, and soon Eddie was slowly guiding the dinghy toward a cluster of yellow life jackets, already pushed some distance from the sunken lifeboat.

Tamsyn leaned over the side and clutched the shivering hands of someone already too weak to climb over the gunwale. Eddie helped drag the man in, and then they were leaning out with gaff poles, dragging aboard anyone with the strength to reach out and hold on.

Some of those they poked simply bobbed in the water, faces serenely still, arms spread out just below the chill surface. If they weren't already dead, they soon would be.

"We have to leave them," Eddie said, throwing a wet tarp over the gasping survivors. They clutched at it, desperate for any warmth.

"God, no," Tamsyn said. "Eddie, you've got to bring the boat around."

Gently bumping aside dead people, Eddie pulled them up alongside a small figure, a huddle of limbs wrapped around a life vest, unfastened for use as a flotation device. Her soaked hair sweeping around her like a blanket, Tara Gunderson did not respond to a frantic prodding in the ribs with the gaff, did not reach up for salvation.

"Tara! Wake up," Tamsyn screamed. "Where's Milly?"

Eddie stretched out his gaff pole, hooked the vest through an arm hole. At first it did not move. Tara's frozen fingers clung to the edges, but finally she gave up her grip and sank into the depths of the Atlantic.

Tara's hair slid back as the ocean swallowed her, revealing Milly Gunderson, wrapped in a thick swaddle of blankets, bobbing away on the life vest. Tears blinding her, Tamsyn leaned over the side of the boat, plucking the infant from the vest as Eddie carefully guided it in with the pole.

Stripping away the sodden wrappings, Tamsyn held the baby against her, rubbing her little arms and legs vigorously, even putting Milly up inside her shirt for warmth. She felt the feeble movement of limbs, a first cough that preceded an earth-shattering wail.

Eddie fought back to the *Petty Cash* through the mad ocean, butting hard up against the packed swim deck in his rush. Blankets were there, waiting for the handful of survivors that they'd managed to pluck from the waters.

Darryl Gunderson held his daughter as if she were some screaming alien thing, his face slack and mouth working, scanning the runabout for any sign of his wife. Even as people dashed around him, carrying the rescued to safety, he stood there in shock, finally letting someone pluck the wailing infant from his hands.

One more lifeboat arrived with a handful of terrified people onboard. Five people had been washed overboard, and only two of them had been wearing life jackets. They'd gone back for them, wasted precious minutes chasing the pair from wave to wave.

When they plucked the men out of the water, they were already dead.

No one saw what happened to the last lifeboat, and when the storm hit, the grey bulk of the distant *Paraclete* was soon lost from sight. They never saw the cargo ship again.

"We've tested the engines, and they work perfectly," Dawes told them over supper. He'd found the captain's dress suit, and the gold-braided white jacket seemed disturbing when combined with his scarred face, the dark wells of his haunted eyes.

"He looks like a Bond villain," Tamsyn whispered to Naomi, who coughed on her packaged mash potato, fanned her face as she jiggled with barely contained laughter.

The grand dining room had been aired, the tables put to rights, and most of the chairs matched. The room could easily seat one hundred, but only thirty-eight people had survived the boarding of the *Petty Cash*. They wolfed down a subdued meal in looted finery, blinking under the bright lights of the chandeliers.

"At a conservative estimate, we've enough fuel left to reach landfall anywhere that touches the Atlantic Ocean," Dawes continued. "We don't have to go to America."

"Makes no difference—everywhere's shit," Dr. Murray slurred, waving a tumbler of whiskey into the air. Someone had found him a dinner suit in his size, complete with tails and top hat. Since donning it, he'd spent several hours single-handedly trying to drink the impressive bar selection dry.

"I've heard that some people aren't happy with the way I'm doing things," Dawes continued, ignoring the cackling old drunk. He met Tamsyn's glare calmly, and with a scowl she resumed her attack on the stack of pancakes in front of her. "I'm doing what I promised. I got you out of England, and I'll get you wherever you want to go. So let's talk about that."

Suggestions were thrown around the room and mostly discarded. Africa, Europe, the Americas. It was all the same. They'd land the boat and die draped in jewels—the entire world had been overrun by the dead, after all.

"What about some island somewhere?" Marcus Riley said. "We just pick an island and that's where we stay."

It seemed to be the most popular decision, and calling out through mouthfuls of reconstituted glug, most of the passengers voiced their approval.

"No," Tamsyn said, slamming her fork on the table and standing. "No way."

"What do you mean?" Dawes said. "It's the only safe thing we can do."

"If we wanted to slowly die out on some tin-pot island, we could have done that back home," Tamsyn said. "What are we going to do-- pick coconuts, pop out a few kids? Even the smallest inhabitable island will still have a bunch of people on it. They'll be zombies now, and we'll have to kill every single one. How many bullets we got left, cowboys?"

No one answered. People fiddled with their food, looked anywhere but in her direction.

"I say we go on to America, to Corpus Christi. I say we find out what happened there, why they stopped the broadcast. They had a bloody cure for the zombie virus, for crying out loud!"

An argument erupted, and the victory supper devolved into a shout-fest. Shaking her head, Tamsyn left the dining room, feather boa trailing behind her, a small fortune in bangles dancing around on arms made bare by her looted evening gown.

She was alone in the ship's cinema, halfway through "Sex and the City 4" and working her way through a box of dubious chocolate clinkers when Eddie Jacobs sat down in the plush recliner next to hers. Tamsyn offered him the box.

"Well past their due date, but they smell all right," she said. Eddie poured them into his mouth, munching on them with relish.

"I hate chick flicks. You got your period or something?" Eddie mumbled through a mouthful of candy. She snorted, rolled her eyes.

"Put a war movie on or something, I don't care," Tamsyn said. "It's been so long, I'll watch anything."

"Me too," he said, and they sat there in a comfortable silence, the light of the projector flickering overhead as the story followed to its formulaic conclusion.

There was a faint rumble around them, barely detectable against the acoustically deadened cinema walls, the upbeat soundtrack, the interplay of characters dealing with the problems of a world now gone.

"I wonder if Sarah Jessica Parker is dead," Tamsyn mused as the credits rolled. "Or if she's out there, ripping people's faces off."

"When we get to America, we can find out," Eddie said. "I sure hope there's some sort of bounty on that stupid bitch."

"What?"

"Come on. That movie was utter shite."

"No, what do you mean, 'when we get to America?'"

"Oh, yeah. They've all decided that you were right. Dawes has fired up this bad boy, and we're sailing there right now."

"When were you thinking of telling me this, Eddie Jacobs?" She regarded him with amusement, the skinhead in a sports jacket and black skivvy. *You look like a strip club bouncer,* she thought.

"You looked like you were having a good old sulk. Seemed criminal to interrupt it."

They watched "Hot Fuzz" until both of them began to nod off in the recliners, and Tamsyn switched off the projector, filed the movie back into the impressive video library. Eddie said goodnight, hands in his jacket pockets, strutting along the outer concourse as if he were a rich playboy. She drifted back to her cabin with a smile on her face.

Clem Murray was a small boy during the Blitz, and his first memories were of war-time London: blackout curtains, the distant sound of bombs and the anti-aircraft batteries. They'd fled to the country like many others, but the feather of fear had never left his soul, from that day until now.

Even as their train pulled out of the station, a young Clem looked out as they passed through one of the largest cities on earth, everything around them dark and cold. Father had taken a bullet in the night some months ago, trapped with thousands of poor Tommies at Dunkirk.

For years, Clem had been terrified of the dark, of the absence of life that it stood for. He'd been sneaking drinks since the age of twelve, and it helped a little. Alcoholism crept up on him during his adult years, and now in the twilight of his life it had almost consumed him.

He was the first of the Murray boys who did not enlist, and instead turned to birthing lambs and shooting lame horses for a crust. For thirty years he'd been a respected figure in the estuary districts, even if he wasn't fit to drive to house calls most of the time. On the day that the court took his driver's licence away from him, Clem Murray decided to quit the veterinary business in order to bring his full focus onto drinking.

"Rat-arsed bastards," he slurred, rapping on the bulkheads with the tip of his cane. "There's enough to go around."

He staggered through the lower levels of the *Petty Cash*, his suit rumpled, top hat sliding around on his head. They'd closed the bar to him when he'd gotten too rowdy, and when he took a swing at Marcus Riley they booted him out of the dining room altogether.

Murray was a canny old drunk. He knew, deep in his pickled hindbrain, that Simon Dawes would now deny him access to that impressive array of liquor in the main bar. It would all be locked up, doled out to him in quantities that wouldn't keep the terror at bay.

"If there's anything I know about sailors, it's that they always have a secret stash of hooch," he slurred. Murray continued to bellow out show tunes, poking his head into various crannies, searching for hiding places. He found a flask of bourbon hidden inside a fuse box, an inch of brown heaven still left in the bottom.

"I was right!" he laughed, making short work of this find. He sneezed, eyes bugging as the heady liquor burned his demons away. "That's a good start."

There were thick slicks of ice on the bottom level where several water pipes had frozen over and burst, but Dr. Murray was so drunk that he did not feel the cold. He slipped once, hitting the floor grates hard. A dark patch of blood spread out on the knee of his crisp dress pants.

Groaning, he found his feet, felt his way onwards. The ice was worst by the bilge-pumps, up behind the main engine room. Murray was wise enough to keep his mouth shut as he passed by, and sure enough he heard the voices of Dawes and Riley, arguing over some engineering point.

It looked like a good hiding place, lots of compartments and removable panels. He began his search, his too-large dress shoes slipping in the large runnels of water as the engines warmed the ice.

If he hadn't been near blind drunk, he might have seen the corpse: what was left of a young woman with a ravaged neck, the lower half of its slender body trapped in the ice. If he'd been sober, he wouldn't have dismissed the low moan as a ship noise, and he certainly wouldn't have let a trapped monster snatch at him, sharp teeth savaging his forearm.

Struggling free of that clammy embrace, Dr. Murray drove the tip of his cane through the zombie's eye socket, and the unnatural thing fell back into ice and silence.

"Fucker bit me," Murray whispered, and knew what was coming. If he'd been sober, he might have gone back to Dawes, told him, shown him the wound. Or he could have found a different kind of courage, and kissed his old shotgun, or taken a long swim in a big ocean.

But he was drunk, it was dark near the bilge pumps, and the vet had seen enough pre-emptive executions, the frenzy with which former allies would drive the life out of the bitten.

He'd delivered the clean death to other poor sods. A bullet if you were lucky. If you weren't, a railway spike, hammered into the temple, or right between the eyes.

"It might be all right," he said, eyeing off the teeth marks on his forearm. The skin was broken, but not too deeply. Reeling and sweating, he made it back up to the sick bay, recently claimed as his room. He cleaned the bite thoroughly, stitched a loose flap of skin closed. *It's just three stitches. Nothing really.* For good measure he bound his entire forearm in a plaster cast.

"I fell over and broke it," he snapped at Riley, who'd come by later with a bottle of 10-year-old Glenfiddich - a peace offering. "And I really wish you'd brought this round earlier."

For the first time in months, Tamsyn had a nightmare. Zombies always brought them on, but they rarely made an appearance themselves. Things much worse than the walking dead waited in the depths of her subconscious–the coffin-dodgers just helped it all bubble up to the surface.

Back in Gravesend now, and she was in the world of school and boys, a sunny place where televisions worked and you could still get McDonalds. She was in front of the bus shelter. Realising what was to come, she tried to look away as Simon Dawes's estate wagon ploughed through the flimsy metal shell. But she couldn't.

This time, in her dream, everybody got back up. Tamsyn's mother; the old lady on her way back from visiting her sister; everyone who'd died that day. They all shuffled with the broken gait of the dead, given an awful second life. Coffin-dodgers, one and all. But their eyes...their eyes were all too aware.

They pulled the drunken Dawes out of the wreck and smothered him in an obscene embrace, nuzzling him like a rock star. And then he rose, a blood-drenched messiah.

"Tamsyn," he said, pointing down the street, towards the Thames and the old pier. "The cure–it's here."

The *Petty Cash* had just docked, the superyacht overshadowing the small town of Gravesend. Dozens of dead things were descending the gangplank, hundreds more on the deck of the ship. As she woke up gasping, she realised that the monstrous arrivals had all been crying out with joy, their arms raised in benediction as they swarmed towards her.

— 8 —

In a matter of days Dawes had piloted them out of the brutal winter seas, bringing them into calmer waters. They were in the subtropics now, but despite the warmer weather Tamsyn still wore a light windbreaker on deck—particularly when she'd just braved the salt water swimming pool.

"Dawes reckons we'll see land today," Naomi said from her deckchair, baby Milly nestled against the large swell of her bust. They'd found her a nursing bottle with clean teats, and she was thriving on the long-life milk, chugging it down with gusto.

"Where's her dad?" Tamsyn said, and Naomi frowned.

"I see more of her than he does," she said. "Darryl's more of a ghost than a man right now. Lord knows, he doesn't often have the patience to deal with tears and nappies. Poor man just lost his wife."

"My dad did all right, though, didn't he? After–after mum?"

"Mal Webb barely knew where the kitchen was, but he managed. Your dad was a good man, Tam."

Dr. Murray wandered past then, mumbled a brief pleasantry. He looked ashen today, skin swimming with sweat, thinning hair lank and greasy. The skin on his face seemed to have drawn in tightly, and his cheekbones were pronounced.

"He looks bloody awful," Tamsyn said when he rounded the next corner. "Even for a tired old drunk living on dehydrated crap."

"I'm surprised he's still here," Naomi said. "Silly old bugger. And now he's falling down all over the place too. I mean, when old people start busting their hips on the back doorstep, it's all over, right?"

"Dr. Murray is the least of our problems. What's at the other end of this boat ride, Naomi?" Tamsyn said, running her fingers through Milly's fine hair. The baby blinked up at the two women, confused by these smiling strangers, and decided to ignore them in favour of draining her bottle dry.

"Undead cowboys. Big trucks, and lotsa guns," Naomi said, a mangled attempt at a drawling American accent. "Hopefully not the KKK."

"Yeehaw, little lady," Tamsyn said, mimicking the shooting of two six-guns into the sky.

"Uh-oh. Someone's got a ripe backside, and it ain't me," Naomi said. She waved Milly's posterior at Tamsyn, who recoiled in horror.

"You wipe your own arse, what's the difference?" the stocky woman chortled, burping the baby over her shoulder as she went.

Tamsyn stayed at the rail for a long time, watching the waves lick at the prow, scanning the horizon for sight of land. *How far away is it now?* She could go up to the bridge and ask Dawes, check the GPS, look at the map.

No way. I'm not even staying in the same room as that maniac, she thought.

She sat there for hours, half realising that she was sun-burnt. She loved it, drank in every warm ray. It felt like the cold of England was being sloughed off, the deep bone chill of this horrifying journey some sort of false memory.

The afternoon sun sank before them, as if the *Petty Cash* was pointed straight into its honey-gold eye. Bearing pure west then– they'd reached the right latitude. Tamsyn tried to remember her geography, knew that they'd be passing Puerto Rico and Cuba, straight into the Gulf of Mexico.

"Wonder if there's still all that oil and shit in the water?" Eddie said, appearing at her side. He was wearing a t-shirt and jeans, his too-white arms almost the colour of the rail. Their elbows touched briefly, and Tamsyn felt her heart flutter a little, her mouth go dry.

You CANNOT like Eddie Jacobs, she thought with alarm. *Get a grip, Tam! You've definitely been at sea too long.*

"Did they finish cleaning that oil spill before it all went to custard? Still, doesn't matter much now." Eddie cracked his knuckles and then lit up a cigarette. He offered one to Tamsyn, who shook her head, frowning. The wind blew the smoke straight into Tamsyn's face, making her eyes water.

"Look! I can see something," he said, leaning in close as he pointed. Waving away cigarette smoke and squinting against the setting sun, she could see a little whisker on the horizon, a smudge of something that could have been anything.

I never thought we'd see land again, Tamsyn thought.

"I can see—yep. It's definitely a McDonalds."

"Idiot."

The *Petty Cash* sailed through the Bahamas, and as the sun dipped down over the horizon, they were passing south of the Florida Keys. Tamsyn noticed that Dawes did not take them close to any of the islands and grudgingly agreed with this decision.

One sign of palm trees and this mob will drop the anchor, she thought. *We need to keep going.*

The horizon was dotted with a row of large cruise ships, over-shadowing the islands they were still tethered to. One had run aground, listing at an awkward angle, ropes and the ruin of knotted bedsheets trailing down from the rails towards the beach below.

As the sun kissed the far horizon, it turned these enormous cruisers into dollhouses, boxes lined with windows. Through a borrowed pair of binoculars, Tamsyn could just make out dozens of figures pacing the decks of the nearest liner, a slow ant-march that had long ago scoured all life and purpose from the vessel.

Dawes did not sleep. He drove the *Petty Cash* through the night, and all of the next day too. In a little over 24 hours they'd crossed the entire Gulf of Mexico. Word got out of their imminent arrival in Texas, and most of the passengers lined the decks by sunset, shivering against the dusk winds, eyes shaded as they watched the horizon.

The luxury yacht passed between the hulks of abandoned oil rigs. Once, Dawes had to correct their course to avoid a drifting shrimp boat—its mast snapped, all the windows smashed. There was no sign of anyone on board, living or otherwise. They did not stop.

Tamsyn made small talk with Naomi and the others, but the conversation was forced, the mood tense. There'd been nothing but signs of ruin, every island, every little scrap of land overrun by the living dead.

What's waiting for us in Corpus Christi?

"GPS says we'll see Texas soon," Riley called out, huffing his way down from the bridge, steaming thermos in hand. "Within the hour."

The ocean swallowed the last sliver of sunlight, but there was an excited murmur amongst those on the decks. It was almost impossible to make out, but there was a faint glow on the horizon. It remained long after the burnt orange of dusk gave way to a true night sky.

Within twenty minutes the first lights could be seen—bright beacons against the darkness of the land. Soon they were close enough to make out a haze of streetlights, lit up high-rise buildings: bright ropes of light that stretched across the horizon, mirroring the star-dusted sky.

People around her gasped, and then there was laughter, chatter, even some crying. It had taken two terrifying months, and the loss of over half their number, but they'd made it.

So this is Corpus Christi, Texas, Tamsyn thought. *In the Good Ol' US of A.*

"There's people, Tam! It's a flipping city!" Eddie said enthusiastically, grabbing her around the shoulders. Naomi engulfed the skinhead in her formidable embrace, planting a kiss square on his lips to much laughter. Someone popped a champagne cork, and a party broke out on the deck of the *Petty Cash.*

Tamsyn slipped away from the celebration and made her way upstairs to the bridge. The lights were off, and Dawes was hunched over the helm, a low lamp illuminating the map-table. She said nothing for many minutes, watching as he powered the boat down, negotiating them through the thin strip of peninsula facing the ocean.

He flicked the ship's lights on briefly as he navigated the ruins of a shipping lane, but the moon was out and soon he turned the lights off.

"You're running under darkness," Tamsyn finally said, and Dawes nodded.

"Figure it best that we don't advertise that we're here. We don't know what's waiting for us."

"Thought of using the radio, numbnuts?"

Dawes looked over at her and gestured to the radio. "Have a listen for yourself. Just don't transmit anything."

She scanned the radio band and picked up on a hundred mundane conversations. She overheard nothing of note, but her heart lifted.

"I've never been so happy to hear ham radio nerds in all my life," she said. "There's really people here! And they've got the time to do boring things. A true civilisation!"

"This set can't pick up any of the official channels, they're all just coming across as gobbledy-gook. Encrypted. Couldn't tell you what the law is up to, or if there's a trigger-happy Navy lurking about."

"Don't be such a goose," Tamsyn said. "We'll have to chat to someone sooner or later. You should turn on all the lights, call out to anyone who'll listen."

"Righto," Dawes said. "I'll tell 'em to put the kettle on, yeah?"

Tamsyn smiled, and after a moment so did Dawes.

"I'm sorry for—for being such a moody bitch," Tamsyn said. "Thanks for saving us."

"It's the least I can do, Tam," Simon Dawes said with a heavy sigh, his whole body seeming to deflate. He looked completely exhausted, the skin around his eyes puffy and dark. "I owe you big time, kiddo."

Lit up like a Christmas tree, the *Petty Cash* was approaching the main docks of Corpus Christi when the first helicopter appeared. The loud chatter of its rotors broke the quiet sky, and a searchlight quickly painted the luxury boat where it was, rapidly carving through the dark water. Blinking, half-blinded, Tamsyn spotted two more helicopters en route.

"I don't like this," Tamsyn said to Dawes. "What the hell are they doing?"

He shrugged, easing the throttle back. The emergency channel was silent, but he thumbed the switch, spoke into the handset.

"This is the *Petty Cash*, requesting asylum. Repeat, this is the *Petty Cash*, we are British citizens and we are requesting asylum. Over."

There was a long moment of silence, and then the radio crackled into life, a strident American accent filling the bridge.

"*Petty Cash*, you are ordered to heave to," the voice announced. There was a long pause.

"*Petty Cash*, prepare to be boarded. These are Republican Marines. Any sign of aggression will be responded to in kind. Out."

"What the hell is this?" Dawes demanded into the handset. "We're bloody refugees. Don't you dare send your goons onto this ship."

There was the faintest crackle; a breath as if someone was about to say something. Then nothing but silence, no matter how Dawes cursed and railed at the anonymous voice.

Tamsyn was out and down the stairs, loose hair flapping about her face as the first helicopter buzzed the *Petty Cash*, the deafening chatter of its rotors drowning out the confused cries of the people milling around on the deck.

"They're gonna board us!" Tamsyn shouted. "Soldiers."

Eddie reached into his waistband, and Tamsyn saw his hand closing around the butt of his pistol. She dragged him into a doorway, blinking as the searchlight swept over them.

"Don't be an idiot!" she cried out. "Drop that right now. If you pull out a gun, they'll kill you!"

Fury passed over his fist-sculpted face, and then something that might have been shrewdness, perhaps a lick of common sense. He dropped the pistol to the ground, kicking it underneath a lifebuoy. A moment later the searchlight fixed onto the deck.

It was all over in seconds. A dozen fat ropes struck the deck, and black shapes rappelled from the helicopters, impossible to see properly against the glare from above.

They were surrounded by shouting shapes who dashed about the deck, assault rifles at the ready. "On the deck, now!" a man shouted into Tamsyn's face, and forced her onto her knees, wrenching her arms behind her back. She felt the pinch of a zip-tie around her wrists.

"Hey, it's too tight!" she cried, but then her captor pushed her forward, and her head bumped against the planks of the decking. Tamsyn risked a quick glance up and saw that everybody had been treated the same. The Marines paced around the restrained passengers, talking into their headsets.

With shock Tamsyn suddenly felt hands running along her arms, felt fingers prodding along her body. Her dress began to slide up her legs, and with her heart racing she realised that the soldier had nearly reached her inner thighs. She exploded into fury, rolling onto her back and kicking up at the man. She caught him on the chin, a neat snap kick that sent the man reeling backwards.

"Don't you touch me!" she screamed, even as she was surrounded by bellowing Marines, the business end of several firearms pointed right at her head.

"Stand down, civilian!" a thick-set man shouted at her. He looked thoroughly pissed off. "We will shoot to kill."

There was a long tense moment, and Tamsyn fought the urge to scream, the fat barrels of the rifles poised, ready to cough death at her. A second helicopter deposited another team of gunmen, who unclipped from their lines and poured into the gang-ways of the Petty Cash. A trio of men made their way towards the bridge, sliding around the corners and covering each other as they passed the various hatches and passageways en route.

One of the new arrivals talked quickly with several of the soldiers on the deck. He was an enormous black man, head shaved smooth, thick neck corded with muscle. From his insignia he appeared to be an officer of some sort. He unclipped a megaphone from his belt.

"Listen here. You will be still, or you will be dead," he said through the mouthpiece, his deep rumble audible even above the helicopter engines. "We have orders to search each of you for bites, wounds, or signs of infection. If you resist this, we will assume that you are infected and act accordingly."

Tamsyn let her head sag back down onto the deck. These Marines weren't mucking around. Several hands rolled her back onto her stomach, and they finished frisking her. She looked up into the eyes of Eddie Jacobs, and he was wincing as a man knelt in the small of his back, patting him down.

Thank God you ditched the gun, she thought.

When they were satisfied that she wasn't a threat, she was allowed to sit up. She saw Dr. Murray being helped to his knees, and he was as pale as a ghost, thin body shaking as a coughing fit seized him. It was obvious that he was in very poor shape, and a Marine stood directly behind him, assault rifle held level.

Even stranger was the Marine pacing amongst them, eyeing off the prisoners carefully. He bore no firearm and held one of those nooses on a stick that dog catchers used.

What's the point of that guy? Tamsyn thought.

Next she saw the Marines leading Riley and Dawes down from the bridge, the stevedore struggling until he was clipped across the head with a gun barrel. Dawes did not resist the soldiers, and Tamsyn supposed that it was easy for him to slip back into prisoner mode.

The officer was back now, speaking intently to Dawes. A pair of soldiers forced the tired man to his knees, but he did not fight them, holding very still as his hands were zip-tied behind his back. The big officer interrogating Dawes was a slab of ebony muscle, easily six and a half feet tall. His hands alone looked as large as Tamsyn's head, and the megaphone in his hands looked like a toy.

"We are taking command of this vessel," the man said, voice distorting as the wind buffeted the deck. "Your captain here tells me that none of you have identity papers, so you will be detained at Corpus Christi Naval Base until further notice."

"We're refugees, we have rights!" Riley yelled, struggling to get to his feet. A moment later the gruff stevedore fell, gasping, as two Marines administered a swift rhythm of boots and rifle butts to his stomach.

"Without papers you might as well be best buddies with Bin Laden," the officer said. "Any other comments?"

As if we had time to go hunting for our passports, Tamsyn thought. *We barely made it out of Gravesend with the clothes on our backs.*

After the beating that Marcus Riley had received, no one else spoke up. Tamsyn felt the rumble of the engines through the deck, and soon they were moving through the water. One helicopter kept pace with the yacht, spotlight still dancing around the group of prisoners on the deck. The other two helicopters veered off on a different trajectory, leaping forward like a pair of predatory birds as they headed inland.

The Marines steered the *Petty Cash* away from the civilian docks and made for the sprawl of the nearby Naval base. Tamsyn took in several enormous buildings ringed with lights, hundreds of uniformed people scurrying about. They passed an entire airfield, lined with rows of mean-looking helicopters. An open hangar door revealed many more in various stages of repair. They looked like a colony of wasps.

The Navy docks were lined with patrol boats and civilian vessels, and even a large war ship, deck bristling with gun turrets and rocket launchers.

Their captors guided the superyacht into dock, herding the prisoners down a gangplank and through a confusing maze of warehouses and squat pre-fab barracks buildings. Ahead, a high-walled compound, and even as the gaggle of exhausted prisoners were herded towards it a light was flashing, a sturdy gate slowly rolling to one side.

The building was clearly a military prison of some sort. With swift efficiency the prisoners were separated by gender, all their belongings confiscated. The handful of children who'd survived the voyage on the *Paraclete* were taken elsewhere, and a medic peeled the wailing Milly out of Darryl Gunderson's hands. He did not so much as resist or even look up as his baby was taken away from him.

I would have fought tooth and nail for that kid, Tamsyn thought. *Something's not right in his head.*

A woman in uniform shouted at Tamsyn to strip, and next thing she knew she was wearing a pair of orange overalls, crammed into a crowded cell with all of the female passengers.

There were no walls, no privacy whatsoever, nothing but rows of bars, the cold concrete floor, and a stainless-steel toilet in the corner. Pacing the corridors were hard-eyed men with guns. The two cells adjoining theirs contained the men of Gravesend, milling about in prison garb, whispering to each other when they thought the guards weren't looking.

Not the welcome I expected, Tamsyn thought.

"So, they love their flag here, yeah?" Naomi whispered to Tamsyn. They'd even found an orange jumpsuit in her size. "You know, they were always yakking about the stars and stripes on the telly, and they got all tetchy when the Arabs were running around burning the things."

Hours had passed. There'd been a change of guards, and a box of stale sandwiches delivered to each cell. Tamsyn watched as a bored-looking young man paced alongside their cell, assault rifle cradled in his arms. Every now and then he would tap the barrel against the bars, warning someone not to talk.

"Their flag isn't high on my list of things to give a shit about," Tamsyn whispered.

"Well, we just got frog-marched into a military prison, and I have not seen one single American flag. It's flipping weird, is what it is, Tam."

With some shock, she realised that Naomi was right. They'd passed several flagpoles on their terrifying march through the base, but the stars and stripes was not in evidence. She couldn't remember what they'd flown in its place, so she waited for the guard to make his rounds, leaning against the bars as she quickly looked over his uniform.

There. On the breast of his shirt and on the upper arms, the flag was different. It was a single white star on a blue field, not the red, white, and blue. One of the badges had been sewn on slightly crooked, and she could see the faded square where another badge had recently been unpicked.

"Eyes down," the guard barked.

"What happened to your flag?" she asked without thinking, and the look on the man's face showed that she'd just invited trouble. Suspicion, and a gun to back it up.

She backed away, looking at the floor. *Stupid, Tam. These people aren't into chatting.* There was a jingle as the man reached for the keys on his belt, and it seemed she was about to be taken somewhere worse.

"Guard, quick! We need help!" someone was shouting, and the Marine wheeled, gun raised. It was one of the men in the cell block adjoining theirs. The guards went running, half a dozen Marines milling around the entrance to the cell. One of their number paused by the lock, radioing in for instructions.

"He's not breathing," someone else said. Tamsyn couldn't see much from where she was, but several people were crowded around somebody lying on the floor. There was an excited buzz, and someone began shouting out the wrong way to do CPR.

"Give him some air, you daft buggers!" Naomi called out. "Back off!"

Oh no, Tamsyn thought. It couldn't be anyone else but poor old Dr. Murray. She ran to the bars, for all the good she could do him. He'd saved her life once, back in Gravesend, had been a friend to her and her dad when everyone else had abandoned them.

The gruff old drunk had been a constant fixture in her life since the world ended and had been especially kind to Tamsyn after her father was shot. Some days his dry sense of humour was all that had kept her going. It seemed somehow unjust that he'd survived everything, only to die on the floor of a crowded prison cell.

It can't be Dr. Murray. Please, just let it be someone else, she prayed.

"Help him!" she screamed at the guards, who still hadn't received whatever confirmation they were waiting on. Everyone was screaming at them now, and the guard with the keys bit his lip nervously, fumbling with the lock. He threw the door open, and a trio of Marines forced their way through the human press, shouting and elbowing their way in. The cell was packed to capacity, and the going was slow.

There was some sort of commotion, and the people that had been pressed around the stricken man pushed away, the crowd fighting to escape through the press of their cellmates.

"Argh! Let go! Let go of me!" a man screamed.

"He bit me!"

"Fucker's turned! Zombie!"

The pushing and jostling turned into a mad panic, and soon people were being pushed into the bars, struggling to breathe as those behind them tried to get to the outside of the cell. Good people wrestled with each other, tried to put friends between them and the monster in their midst.

The Marines already in the cell reversed their direction, pushing back for the door. Their buddies used boots and rifle butts to keep the prisoners in the cell, and soon the others were out and clear.

They locked the door behind them.

"What the hell is wrong with you lot?" Tamsyn shouted. "Shoot the bloody zombie! There's people still in there, you sickos! Kill it!"

Once more the frenzied call into their radios, and finally several footsteps could be heard. For what it was worth, the reinforcements had arrived.

There were more terrified screams from those still trapped in the cell, prayers and curses, and then Tamsyn heard it. The snarls of a monster, of a dead man given a vicious new life.

The prisoners rushed as a single body to the far end of the cell, and for just one second Tamsyn saw him. It was Dr. Murray, chin running red with blood, face frozen into a mad grimace. He lurched about with short jerky movements, hands stretched into stiff claws, grabbing at anybody within reach. In all the madness, somebody knocked an older man to the ground, and in moments what was left of Dr. Murray straddled him, tearing at his face with a gore-streaked mouth.

Once more the cell door was opened, and the newest group of Marines entered. They were mobbed, but someone let off a gunshot, and with brutal efficiency they forced their way through the crowd. Tamsyn could see these new guards were carrying the same dog-catchers as the man on the boat, and with one fluid motion two of them snared the zombie Dr. Murray, hauling him way from his sobbing victim.

This man was also snared, and three others. As these people were taken from the cell, Tamsyn saw that they'd all been bitten, and knew that they were all as good as dead.

Someone had strapped a wire-mesh muzzle around Dr. Murray's head, and it took two soldiers to control him. As he passed Tamsyn, he suddenly snatched at her, brushing at her with his cold hands. He snarled at her through his metal mask, dashing his face against the bars, furious as the soldiers dragged him away, denying him his meal.

Sobbing, Tamsyn almost didn't notice the last man to be forced out of the cell in a noose. Through a film of tears, she saw Simon Dawes, his face a mess of blood and torn skin. Their eyes met briefly, and then his captors led him away.

Tamsyn tried to hear the gunshots above the sounds of weeping and the frightened whispers of the prisoners, but she never heard a thing.

After a restless night on the cold floor with a thin blanket, the guard called for Tamsyn in the morning. Her arms ziptied behind her once more, she was marched through the military prison with Naomi, Marcus Riley, and Eddie Jacobs.

Their escort would not answer questions, depositing them into a bland office. Four steel chairs were arranged in a horseshoe in front of a plain desk, and the woman behind the length of Formica and paperwork indicated that they should sit.

She was the first person Tamsyn had seen in the Naval Base that wasn't in a uniform of some sort. The woman was dressed in a crisp power suit and radiated a quiet confidence. Her hair was immaculately styled, and she wore a few deft touches of makeup, enough to negate some worry lines and crow's feet.

"I'm sure the warden won't mind me borrowing his office, now," she said in a Texan drawl. "Please, sit down."

Tamsyn and the others sat. It was an awkward descent with their wrists still bound behind their backs. Naomi collapsed into her seat with a grunt, and for a moment it looked like she would tip the whole thing over. Their two escorts still flanked the door, faces blank and guns at hand. Clearly, they were taking no chances.

"Your captain, ah, Simon Dawes. He says that you four can speak for the rest of your ship. Is this correct?"

"Where is Dawes?" Tamsyn said. "What have you lot done with him?"

"He's infected now, sugar," the woman said, giving off a folksy air that didn't quite ring true. "Please, just listen. There's a lot of ground to cover and we don't really have a lot of time. I'll let y'all pick my brain when we're done here, 'kay?"

Tamsyn mumbled something that passed for an apology and slouched in her chair. The woman smiled and continued.

"I've read all the reports, and I'm sorry for what happened in the cells. Navy SOP is quite clear though: our fighting men and women cannot engage the undead without a catcher."

"Your lot locked them in there and left them all to die!" Naomi cried. "They were right there with guns, for heaven's sake. You should be ashamed of yourselves. You're monsters."

"Well, we didn't know that you were attempting to smuggle infected people into our country, so I guess we're even," the well-dressed woman said, now with an edge of iron to her voice. "Which brings me to the crux of our pleasant little chat. We've been a little wary of visitors just lately, and we still don't even know who the hell you people are."

"Look, we were just following your radio transmission," Tamsyn said. "You were the person who recorded that, weren't you? I recognise your voice."

"Yes, I was, honey. We stopped transmitting the message over a month ago. Things have changed here... uh... it's Tamsyn, isn't it?" she said, briefly referring to the notes in front of her.

"Listen here, lady!" Tamsyn growled. "We got together a boat-load full of people because of you. We limped across the Atlantic Ocean in a broken ship, and half of us died because of your promise. Don't you dare tell me that America will turn us away now."

"I'd keep a civil tongue in that pretty little head," the woman said. "For starters, you're not in the United States. They might welcome you, but I doubt it."

"What?"

"Oh, where are my manners? Allow me to introduce myself. I'm Clarice Feickert, President of the Republic of Texas. And you might say that our immigration policy has changed."

"It's salt," President Feickert said. "The new oil. Lordy, it's worth more than gold now. Can't believe you Brits didn't work it out for yourselves."

Tamsyn was numb all over. The big cure, the secret weapon against the unnatural hordes, and it was sitting on supermarket shelves, in shakers in restaurants, even in the sea. It was stupidly simple.

They knew it, and they kept it secret, Tamsyn thought. *This information could have saved lives.*

I trust this bitch as far as I can throw her.

"Here's our ride," she said, indicating the Humvee waiting in the courtyard. "Can someone cut their damn zip-ties already? We're on home soil, it's not Afghanistan here."

With their hands untied they were loaded up into the vehicle, wedged in with numerous personnel—each of whom carried enough weaponry to start a one-man war. Feickert settled into the centre of the rearward-facing seat, flicking through a folder. An airman came running with a steaming thermos, and she smiled gratefully at the man.

"These service folks brew a mean coffee," Feickert said. "Now settle in, boys and girls. What I'm about to show you changes everything."

The Humvee passed through several checkpoints without pause. They were waved through a boom-gate to the base hospital. A pair of airmen opened the car doors and saluted smartly as the President emerged. She was out and walking briskly through the sliding doors and along the hallways of the hospital, the prisoners and guards trailing in her wake.

"He's in here," Feickert said, gesturing at a ward door. Two armed Marines flanked the door, a pair of saluting statues. "Well, go in, y'all. You came a long way to see this."

Tamsyn pushed at the door tentatively and saw that an entire ward had been emptied of all but one bed, flanked by two more Marines.

Strapped to the bed was the filmy grey corpse of Dr. Clem Murray, straining against his bonds, thrashing around violently. He was connected to an IV bag of clear fluid, half emptied.

One moment the zombie was thrashing around, and then what was left of Dr. Murray arched his back as far as the thick leather straps would allow. Tamsyn flinched at the inhuman wailing that came bubbling out past the blue-gray lips. The sound was pure agony.

"Now, I bet you never heard that before," Feickert said, trying to make herself heard above the racket. "These critters are known for all their moaning and groaning, but they don't ever squeal."

Murray's corpse looked as if it was in the grip of a powerful seizure. Only the whites of his dead eyes showed, and a slimy foam was dribbling out of the corners of his mouth.

"I mean you can blow them apart, an inch at a time, and they'll never make a goddamn sound. But this, this they feel."

"STOP IT!" Tamsyn found herself shouting, caught up in the unyielding arms of a Marine as she threw herself forward. "Get that thing out of him! You're hurting him."

"Turn it off," Feickert called out calmly, and a medic appeared from somewhere, fiddling with the valves on the IV. Eventually the zombie stopped shaking, and the head rolled to one side. Dr. Murray's infected corpse lay perfectly still, and Naomi started crying, great heaving sobs.

"You're bloody monsters!" Eddie yelled. "You should put a bullet into the poor sod's head. Whatever this is, it's just cruel."

"There's two sides to every coin," Feickert said, facing down the snarling skinhead with complete self-assurance. "Here's a fact, mister: you shoot a zombie in Texas without due cause, you'll end up in court. We'd call you the monster."

Tamsyn gasped. Dr. Murray had opened his dead-fish eyes and looked at her with something approaching calmness. Clarity. He moaned softly, a low sigh.

"You see it, don't you?" Feickert said, looking at Tamsyn carefully. "Your friend is still in there."

The President signalled to the medic, who opened up the valves again. The screeching resumed, as did the violent seizure.

"We never said that it was a gentle cure, but we've beaten this thing," Feickert said, her hand on Tamsyn's shoulder. "It takes about five pounds of salt, and a few days of this rather painful procedure, but we can bring back every single person."

"Bring back?" Tamsyn said.

"Oh yes. Soon you'll be able to talk with him, and most of all he won't try to bite you. The Re-Humans have to keep taking doses of salt, but they're perfectly safe."

Re-Humans?

"So far they're readjusting well to their new circumstances. We've got a population of five thousand Re-Humans, and they've got churches, schools, there's even some light industry in their own neighbourhood."

"So you've put 'em in a ghetto, yeah?" Naomi said.

"I'm not proud of everything I've ever done," President Feickert said. "Politics is a damn dirty game, and I don't have a clean nose. But we are the only place in the world doing this. The only place trying to save them. The ghettos are not my choice, but they are a political necessity."

She signalled, and again the medic cut off the saline supply, the screechings cut off into instant silence. Tamsyn noticed that Feickert was checking her watch, realised that they were dosing

Murray on a schedule, and giving him regular breaks from the all-encompassing pain.

"It's not torture," Tamsyn said. "It's a treatment. It's like chemo or something."

Feickert nodded, smiling.

"I could never destroy one of these creatures, not knowing that there's still a person trapped inside," the President said. "What's left of our neighbour to the north does not agree with this sentiment. It's not the only bone of contention, but it's the chief reason for our secession from the Union.

"The vast majority of Texans voted that we raise our own flag, do things our way. Too many folks remembered shooting their own loved ones, back before we knew about the salt. Now, we try to cure this horrible affliction."

President Feickert looked down upon Dr. Murray, the gritted face muscles, the clenched fists. His screeches were coming out now as a series of low sobs, and the seizure was now a gentle trembling of the limbs.

"Five pounds of salt to save a life," Feickert said. "Turns out that nothing worth a damn comes cheap."

"We were trading with Cleveland for salt, but they started making excuses, and now they won't even return our calls, so to speak," Feickert said. They were in the hospital mess, eating greasy hamburgers and drinking sodas. Tamsyn had never tasted anything so good.

"It's damn Palin's fault. If the woman had an ounce of sense, she'd never have tried to boost morale. She should have been in a bunker, wrapped in bubble-wrap. Damn fool of a woman."

She must have noticed their blank stares, because she immediately backtracked.

"Um, President Palin was bit during a morale-boosting tour of the infected zones and put a bullet through her own brain. The VP got spooked, and up and evacuated to Hawaii, took most of the Air Force and Navy with him. They tried to quietly airlift the Congress off-shore, but word got out. Mind if I smoke?" Feickert said.

Without waiting for confirmation, the President opened up a slim cigarette case, gold worked through with a prominent eagle design, some sort of military emblem. She deftly tapped out a single cigarette, offered them to the others. Only Tamsyn turned her down. A Zippo quickly did the rounds, and Feickert pressed a saucer into service as an ashtray.

I'm pretty sure no one's meant to be smoking in a hospital, she thought. *Just 'cause you're President of whatever the hell this place is now.*

"So there's Vice President Wycliffe, sunning it up in paradise with what's left of our military assets, while good Americans were stuck in hell. The infected just ripped through everything we had on the ground: the Army, the National Guard, the cops, even the Uncle Bob militias.

"By the time the dust settles, we got nothing left but a bunch of armed enclaves, full of the fortified and terrified. Too scared to do anything but waste bullets and form committees. The government is still hooked up to the broken-up platoons by sat phone, telling 'em to sit tight, hold the bases, protect the civilians. Cavalry's on its way, and all that."

The President drew back on her cigarette, burning it down to the filter. Coughing slightly, she immediately lit up another one.

"I'll tell you where the cavalry is. It's still scratching its balls over in Waikiki, eating Spam, making godawful plans to recapture the west coast, issuing pointless standing orders to anyone still listening. The duly elected government of the United States of America has abandoned its people to die, and I cannot forgive that.

"So we got everyone left behaving like it's the Black Death. Guess it is. Nothing left to the USA but a bunch of walled-off towns and strong-points, cut off from the outside world. The major cities are still no-go zones, and everything between them is a walking graveyard. The Deadlands."

Feickert's hands shook for just a second, and Tamsyn realised that the woman's steely resolve was not so unflappable. Under the fluorescent lights, the makeup did little to hide the bags under her eyes, the growing spread of wrinkles, and it was obvious that the strain was getting to her.

"I was the Governor of Texas when it all went to shit. I personally pulled everything back here when we lost Houston and found myself sitting on top of the world's largest helicopter repair facility. I didn't hear squat from that sack of shit in Hawaii, so I sent out everyone who could fly a whirlybird. It burnt up a lot of fuel, but we evacuated nearly three hundred thousand people here.

"That's when it all went pear-shaped. The outer walls of Christi weren't even finished yet when we got the orders. All of our military assets were to be relocated to Hawaii, along with our stockpiles of salt. Turns out that our practice of resurrecting the 'enemy' was to stop too.

"We were ordered to destroy all of our Re-Humans immediately. Our husbands, wives, sons, and daughters. I told Vice President Wycliffe to go fuck himself," Feickert laughed. "Sour old bastard. One week later, and the Texans vote their way out of the Union. Yankees are still busy unstitching one star, but we just up and burnt the whole damn flag."

"How did you find out about the salt?" Tamsyn asked.

"Our own R&D boys came up with that one," Feickert said. "We shared the find with our superiors, who decided it was a better use of salt to incapacitate, rather than rehabilitate.

"We've got a different salt philosophy, but sugar, we have gone through tonnes of the stuff. Those undead that we snare, we give the treatment. It's our law. The ones in the Re-Human zone, well... we gotta dose 'em daily.

"We got something like two or three million of the hungry dead roaming the Deadlands around Corpus Christi. So many living here, the smell and the noise draws the dead. They try to bust through our wall, wave after wave of them.

"We pump salt water up from the bay to a bunch of riot cannons, squirt the shit out of them. Ain't nothing gonna grow on that ground now worth a damn, let me tell you. But the water guns can't be everywhere, and it uses too much fuel to drop water from the choppers."

"You need more watches," Eddie said, blowing out a wreath of smoke. "You've got thousands of geezers just sitting around. Don't you Texans all have five guns each?" Feickert snorted, her lips tight as she flicked the ash of her cigarette with some emphasis.

"I'm sure that back home when the deadheads came a-knocking, y'all went Rambo on their asses. It's different here. We look on it like someone shooting their handicapped cousin. They all can't help what they are."

A moment of silence. President Feickert ground her cigarette out into the saucer. She weighed the case in her hand, but slid it back into her pocket, followed by the lighter.

"Let's get down to brass tacks, folks. You're illegal immigrants, and last I checked we weren't exactly signed up to the United Nations Refugee Charter. We can keep you locked up until you rot, if we see fit."

Tamsyn quickly glanced at the other three and saw that they all looked as worried as her. Even Eddie kept mum. *This woman's got a cast iron pair of nuts,* she thought. *What's she getting at?*

Why is the President herself personally involved in this? What's her angle?

"So that's your situation, but I'll raise you a situation," Feickert continued. "I got a bunch of scared folks out there, hiding behind a wall that's getting pounded day and night. And even if the barricades hold, no one knows what we'll all be eating in six months.

"We're digging canals that will surround Corpus Christi within a ring of sea-water moats, but the work is slow. Evaporation saltpans are being constructed right now, but it will be weeks, maybe months before we can harvest the salt. And we may not collect enough to keep the Re-Humans dosed, or to convert the ones we capture.

"On top of that, there are elements calling to impeach me, a large percentage calling our secession illegal, and quite a few folks that want to put all our Re-Humans back in the ground. Right now, I can't so much as scratch myself without three reports being tabled in our Congress and the press crawling up my ass."

"What do you want from us?" Tamsyn asked quietly.

"I need a lot of salt, I need it quickly, and most of all... I need it done quietly," Feickert said.

The President held up her hand and waved, and the doors swung open at the rear of the mess. Tamsyn looked up to see an enormous black man striding towards their table. He was in civilian clothing, and his white t-shirt did nothing to hide the fact that every inch of his frame was thickly corded with muscle.

He stood to attention at the end of their table, towering over everybody there. He had to be approaching seven feet in height. Tamsyn recognised him, and took in the man's imposing face, broken nose, acne-scarred skin, clean-shaven scalp and face.

It's the officer who boarded the Petty Cash.

"At ease, Colonel. You're technically on leave, so why don't you get that stick out of your ass and grab a seat? Folks, this is Colonel Reuben Dekker of the Republican Marines."

Dekker dragged over a chair and perched on the edge of it. He looked like a man visiting the children's table at Christmas, and everything was out of proportion for him. He crossed his tree-trunk arms across his chest.

"What we've got in mind would get me crucified if I sent our own," Feickert said. "A squad of Marines is put to better use on the walls, or manning security at the Re-Human zone.

"So that's where you come in. I send you out to run this errand, with Dekker here to babysit you. Y'all go out to the Deadlands, bring back enough salt to see us through, and we'll consider that your citizenship exam. For all of you. Interested?"

Tamsyn looked at Naomi, who was absolutely terrified. Eddie Jacobs mumbled something, and Marcus Riley stared at the floor.

"All right, keep your knickers on. We'll do it," Tamsyn said. "We'll fetch your bleeding salt."

"A modified Sikorsky helicopter will drop us off *here*," Dekker said, painting part of the projected map with a laser pointer. "Place called Salt Flat."

Tamsyn and the others sat in the front row of the large briefing room, wedged behind small folding desks. They'd changed into new clothes that they'd been issued with for this covert trip. Thick motorbike leathers with high collared jackets; reinforced, knee-high boots; and fine leather gloves that fit snug. Everything was interwoven with a tough mesh, and it was hopefully enough to stop a zombie bite from penetrating.

Dekker wore the same outfit as them, with no insignia or any other identifying markings. This trip was as unofficial as it got.

Think I preferred the orange onesies, Tamsyn said, eyeing off the lazy wobble of the ceiling fans. *It's damn hot in here.* She peeled off her sweat-slick gloves, thought wistfully of the summer dresses she'd worn onboard the *Petty Cash.*

"You. Put your damn gloves back on," Dekker boomed at her. "From here on out, you will eat, shit and sleep in your protective gear. Am I understood?" Tamsyn frowned, sliding the gloves back onto her sweaty hands.

"I said, am I understood?" the officer roared, barking loud enough to be heard over gunfire, helicopters, the whole box and dice. They all jumped in their seats.

"Yes," she mumbled. Dekker glared at her for a moment longer, and then returned to his projector, clicking the remote to key up the next slide.

"We've taken aerial footage of other salt production facilities, hoping to find something closer. This is Houston, with at least two locations of interest."

Two photos flashed up, the first a series of warehouses, the second a factory flanked by tarpaulin covered mounds. One of the tarps had become unsecured, pulled aside to reveal a white pyramid of salt.

The photo was dotted with people, roaming along the roads, coming in and out of the buildings. There must have been at least two hundred figures in the photo.

They're not people, Tam. You dumb-arse.

"Houston is only two hundred miles away, but it's got a static zombie population of four million. We've done salt retrievals via helicopter but it's using more fuel than it's worth. We lost five Navy Seals that last trip, and Command has ruled out Houston as a salt source."

Another slide, and this one showed what appeared to be a satellite photo. The topography was brown and bare, dusted with vast fields of white. Lonely roads bisected the area, and the only town anywhere near the place was a tiny collection of farms, some twenty miles to the north.

The next photo was zoomed right in and showed the intersection of two roads with a handful of buildings clustered together. A blacktop cut through the dusty plain, a straight arrow to places less forsaken.

"Looks like Vegas without the casinos," Dekker said. "We sure as hell ain't going to Salt Flat for kicks. But we should be left alone long enough to harvest this salt. That's where you folks come in. I have agreed to babysit your civilian asses, and you will work like dogs till I decide we are done."

Dekker clicked the remote, and the next slide showed a small facility, linked to the highway by a long and winding driveway. It faced onto the salt flats itself, and several pieces of equipment could be seen sitting outside of the rusty sheds.

"Near as we can tell, this salt-scrape outfit has been out of commission for decades," Dekker said. "We will probably have to repair several of these machines, which is my first job for you, Mister Riley. We will also need to locate a truck, a big one."

Colonel Dekker took the four Brits from the briefing room to a waiting jeep, which whisked them to the base's firing range. The place had been emptied of all personnel, and as they entered the guards left, locking the doors behind them.

"First rule," Dekker said. "Anyone points a firearm at me, I will kill them and kill them hard. I am much faster than any of you, I suggest that you do not test this."

Each booth was set up with an arsenal of firearms, and several boxes of bullets stacked neatly to one side.

"We are going in as a black op," Dekker said. "That means no support at all, and no laws. If a zombie comes at you, you drop it; the mission comes first. No one here needs to know what we do out there."

He picked up a pistol, a sleek looking thing. He slid a clip into the base of the gun, pulled back a sliding mechanism.

"This is the Beretta M9. By itself it's a good beginner pistol, easy to learn. Not much in the way of stopping power, but if you are required to kill one of our zombie friends, this could do the job."

Putting on her earmuffs, Tamsyn took her turn at practicing with the pistol. Her skills with the bow had never transferred to firearms, and her paper target showed a scattered grouping of glancing hits.

She hadn't made a single head shot. A quick glance at the other targets showed that Marcus Riley had tapped his target once in the temple, but the others hadn't had much luck.

"Congratulations. Between you, you've emptied four clips and stopped one zombie," Dekker said. "Good thing for you we got ourselves a secret weapon."

He opened a separate box of bullets with a huge combat knife, slicing through the purple tape binding it shut. The Colonel reefed out a single bullet and held it aloft, a solid slug of white bound by the brass shell.

"Salt bullets. Even a glancing flesh wound will incapacitate any zombie it touches. It will rust the hell out of your firearm, but this is Texas—we got plenty of guns to spare."

They tried a number of different weapons, including a combat shotgun loaded with salt crystal scattershot. Dekker even tried them out with assault rifles but found none of his new recruits could handle the large weapons with any accuracy. Tamsyn fought the bucking rifle, her bullets spraying high and low.

"Never have I seen sorrier shooting!" Dekker shouted over the final chatter of the automatic weapons. "Put down your damn guns, I've seen enough. Beats me how none of you been bit by now."

"We survived because we didn't run around shooting six-guns in the air," Tamsyn said, wincing at the pain in her shoulder, letting the heavy M16 rest back in its cradle. She felt her temper rising and stood before the enormous black man, looking up at him with her neck craned and arms crossed. Her face was only slightly higher than the man's navel.

"I can put an arrow through a zombie's head at fifty steps, and the other zombies don't hear a thing. No wonder you lot lost your bloody country—guns don't fix everything."

"Watch your mouth girl," Dekker said. "One word from me and you're back rotting in the cells."

Shut up, Tam! she thought to herself. *What are you doing?*

"I'll prove it," Tamsyn said. "I had a compound bow on the boat, my own custom rig. Get me some competition arrows and I will outshoot anything you've got, shot for shot. Put the targets back as far as you like."

It danced across his ruined face, the faintest flicker of something that might have been a smile. Then it was gone. Within twenty minutes a runner had delivered her bow, and a sheaf of blunt-headed competition flight arrows.

"So far, you're just another smart mouth," Dekker said, chambering a clip into a monstrously large pistol. "Show me what you got, Robin Hood."

Flicking the controls in the booth, Tamsyn sent the target back as far as she could, and the Marine followed suit. Testing the tension of the string, she adjusted the sights, drew her first arrow. With a soft sigh she released the string.

The arrow tore through the paper and kept going, square in the centre of the paper target's head. With an eyebrow raised, Dekker levelled the pistol with both hands and sent a large slug through his target's head.

Ten shots later, they were evenly matched. Neither had missed, both with a close scattering of hits to the head region.

"All right. You can bring that thing if you want," Dekker said, and Tamsyn realised that this was the closest she would get to praise from the man. "The rest of you, here's something else, more to your skill levels."

He pulled out several water pistols from another box and handed them around.

"Are you having a laugh?" Naomi said. "These are kid's toys."

"They're filled with saline solution," Dekker said. "Keep this on you as a last resort, but it could save your life. Aim it at their eyes. Otherwise, you might just piss them off."

It was a copy of the official report, one piece of paper bound into a manila folder. "FORM XR-27B - DEATH IN CUSTODY" it read. The text swam in front of Tamsyn's eyes, and her hands shook.

"CAUSE OF DEATH – STRANGULATION/HANGING"

"This is just to prove to you that we're not running some sort of Abu Ghraib," President Feickert said to Tamsyn. "Your boy got into an altercation with the guards, and they put him in the hole. Solitary."

"He's got a baby," Tamsyn said woodenly. "A little girl."

The report was brief, but thorough. She could almost picture the scene: Darryl Gunderson naked, orange coveralls looped tight around his neck, leaning at an awkward angle from the bars, face blotched, his tongue dry and lolling from blue lips. As per standing orders, his body had already been cremated.

"They were meant to check on him every hour. Trust me when I say that asses are being kicked over this. I'm sorry, Tamsyn. It's a clean death, at least, and that's the only comfort I can give you."

Tamsyn put the folder down on the hospital chair, took the scalding cup of coffee from the President. Whoever made it had loaded it up with cream and sugar, but Tamsyn didn't taste it, barely noticed as she burnt her tongue.

"What happens to Millie? His girl."

"She's in care like the other kids, fostered out to a service family. You do this job for me, we'll figure something out for her, I promise. You ready?"

Tamsyn nodded, standing up, clutching the hot drink like a lifeline. Feickert pushed open the door for her, ushered her in.

"I've got to get to a press conference now, but there are guards just outside this door. You holler if anything goes wrong. Good luck."

Tamsyn walked into the room, set up with a single bed, a patient strapped securely to the frame. An IV stand stood ready, a bag of saline solution hooked up and ready to go.

"Hello Tam," Simon Dawes said, giving a weak smile. He was drenched with sweat, the bite marks on his face swollen and pustulent. His skin was already a disturbing shade of grey.

"So, all right then?" Tamsyn said. "How's the food here?"

"Better than anything I've eaten lately—not that I can keep any of it down," Dawes said.

They sat still for long moments, the silence punctuated by the occasional sound from the banks of medical equipment. Tamsyn offered him the glass of water by his bedside, and he sipped at it through the straw, his cracked lips working at it clumsily.

"I'm glad you came," Dawes finally said. "I don't really deserve a bedside visit."

"Maybe you don't," Tamsyn said. "But I'm here anyway."

She looked down at the man responsible for breaking her heart, the parent-killing monster. Simon Dawes had ended her world, long before the world had actually ended. In a further display of cosmic bastardry, the hunt for this man had cost her father his life.

Years of therapy, two dead parents, and a river of fucking tears. I should put a pillow on your face, you bastard, Tamsyn thought. But she took up a damp cloth and wiped the sweat from his face. She moved a chair by his side and sat with him.

"Ha!" She snorted. "This just proves you should be careful what you wish for."

"How's that?"

"All I wanted once was the chance to see you dead."

"Hang around," he wheezed, nodding towards the IV-stand. "Show's about to start."

Each breath was becoming a struggle for him, and the sweat poured out of him quicker than Tamsyn could wipe away. One of the medics had told her a theory in the coffee room, that the zombie virus itself attempted to push out as much salt from the victim as it could.

"I've done bad things," Dawes moaned.

"Shh," Tamsyn said. She reached out her hand and held him by his sweat-slicked fingers. He gripped her hand tightly.

"I'm sorry Tam. So sorry for what I did."

"Simon, listen. Look at me," Tamsyn said, as one of the machines set off a strident beeping. The lines on his heart monitor were leaping around like surf waves, and his pulse was through the roof. "I forgive you."

Here, as his life slipped away, she found that finally, she meant these words. She felt a weight lift from her soul, the effort of hating this man finally drifting away from her like smoke.

"Don't let them bring me back," Dawes whispered.

"Do you want a bullet?" Tamsyn asked, an eye to the door. The medics would be here soon, to begin the excruciating rounds of post-death treatment. "If we get back, we'll find a way into the Re-Human ghettos, find a way to get you a gun. Bugger their stupid laws."

"No. I...I deserve to walk this earth. Out there, with all the other monsters."

"You *want* to be a zombie?"

From what they'd told her, Tamsyn knew that the procedure needed to be repeated. Small doses of salt on a regular basis. Without this treatment, he would revert back to a normal zombie within days.

"Okay. I'll do my best to get you out," Tamsyn said. "And once you're out in the Deadlands, we're all square, okay?"

Dawes tried to say more, but could not manage the words, his face twisted in pain. Tamsyn knew enough to know that he was in the grip of a massive heart attack, and she squeezed his hand tight, sat with him as he finally died. Every machine was erupting in a clamour, and in moments the medics were pushing her aside, checking that the IV-drip was ready to go, fastening a muzzle across his face.

She watched as Simon Dawes emerged into unholy life, thrashing and snapping and hungering for flesh. And she watched as the salt poured into his corpse, bringing its own cleansing fire, a world of pain that brought out an unholy scream.

9

All I'm saying is, Dekker's all man," Naomi said, wrestling with the seat harness. She needed to extend the straps as far as they could go, and even then it was a struggle to buckle her into her helicopter seat.

"As if he's gonna even look at a heifer like you," Eddie said.

"I can do more for that man than any of those skinny little white girls you dream about," Naomi said, smacking her lips loudly.

Tamsyn snorted out with laughter; it was unlikely that her mother's old netball friend was going to go against the habits of a lifetime.

Dekker climbed into the side of the large helicopter, closing the doors and signalling to the pilot with a twirling finger. *Take-off.* The hulking Marine buckled into a chair up front, talking into a headset. The rotors whipped into a frenzy, the chopper throbbing around them.

The next moment they were up, rising through the air, the Navy Base rapidly falling away beneath them. They got an excellent view of Corpus Christi, a thriving city full of life and industry. Several cars could be seen on the roads, and a baseball game was in progress on a field that they flew over.

"Look down there," Marcus Riley said, pointing down at one section. "The ghettos."

Tamsyn could see a whole section of the city fenced off, surrounded by pillboxes, guard towers, and razor wire. It looked filthy, run-down. There seemed to be more guards surrounding the ghetto than there were on the nearby city wall.

"Horrible place," the old stevedore managed over the racket of the helicopter. "We went to check in on our Dr. Murray. They treat those poor Re-Humans worse than dogs."

Naomi said that Dr. Murray was almost talking again, and certainly had recognised his visitors. The allotted visit was over in moments, several guards leading him away from the fence-line, despite all protests. The treatment had been going well, but Dr. Murray was still muzzled, still being hauled around with a dog-catch pole.

They weren't allowed to talk to any of the other Re-Humans, who kept their heads down, running the shops and factories in the fenced-in community, living the fragment of life that had been allowed them.

"Down there's our town wall," Dekker said over the speakers. "And some hopeful future citizens."

A double wall surrounded the central city and the Navy Base, bounded on two sides by the estuary. On the other side, thousands upon thousands of the dead swelled forward, swarming like bees as they pushed against the wall. A thick zombie pyramid had formed at one point, and several fire trucks formed up between the walls, spraying seawater onto the pile of twitching corpses.

"Hope it stings, suckers." Dekker disconnected the intercom with a deft jab of his forefinger, and leaned back in his chair, already dozing off.

Tamsyn saw the beginnings of a broad canal beyond the walls, a moat to block off the city from zombie attention. Far below, the yellow blobs that were construction equipment rapidly hacked away at the earth, while the two fire trucks on standby blasted back the crowds of zombies with seawater, trying to give the engineers a safe space to work.

They'll be safe enough once that's dug, Tamsyn thought. But the work crews had miles of ground left to dig, and out in the Deadlands it resembled a rock concert, a mass march. Hundreds of thousands of coffin-dodgers, an unstoppable army of rot, all driven to the sounds and lights of Corpus Christi.

"These guys don't need salt, they need atomic bombs," Tamsyn said, wondering how many Re-Humans this new Republic could maintain. They would have to truck the stuff in constantly just to keep everyone dosed up, let alone the five pounds of salt needed to bring a zombie back from foggy oblivion.

The flight to Salt Flat took a few hours, the enormous Sikorsky helicopter tearing unchallenged through the sky. Tamsyn spent her time watching the scenery unfold out the window and was not surprised to see town after town devastated, the cities crammed full of walking death.

Not much better than back home, she thought. *I don't care what these jokers say, there isn't much of a Texas worth claiming. How they can call one fortified city a Republic is beyond me.*

She took a long look at the highways beneath them, choked with traffic and cracked from disuse, and as she drifted off into a light doze, she wondered just how they were going to get a big truck through all of that mess.

"Oy! Rise and shine, sleeping beauty."

Eddie was shaking her by the shoulder, and she woke up to see that the big helicopter had landed. The others had gathered up their equipment and were wrestling their way out of the doors with packs and guns.

Tamsyn joined them on the ground, her compound bow slung neatly against the side of her pack. Strands of Tamsyn's hair blew around and got in her face until Dekker loomed in front of her, jamming a plain baseball cap down onto her head.

"It's not a fashion show. Wear your damn gear." Tamsyn poked her tongue out at the man as he stalked away but was grateful for the peaked hat. Even in winter, the sun was brutal.

The moment they were out and clear, Colonel Dekker closed the doors, thumping them twice with the flat of his hand. The Sikorsky chopper lifted off, wheeling about and heading back east at maximum speed. Several extra fuel tanks had been attached to the bottom of the chopper for this flight, but Tamsyn wondered if they'd make it back to Corpus Christi.

They'd been dropped off in the middle of the highway, five figures standing alone in a sparse landscape, a dusty tundra inter-rupted by the occasional stubborn tuft of bush. North of road lay a dirty white plain, stretching out to the horizon, gleaming and hard to look at under the noon sun.

Keep it together, Tamsyn thought. She felt a faint tickle of agora-phobia and pushed it away, focussed on her breathing like Dr. Clarke had taught her, back when an anxiety disorder was her biggest problem. There was nothing around for miles but this flat wasteland and the cracked leftovers of a highway.

How in the hell are we gonna get back?

"All right, listen up, boys and girls," Colonel Dekker said, cradling an enormous assault rifle as if it were a toy gun. "We're officially on our own now. That chopper ain't coming back. From here on in I am your fairy godmother, and you will eat up every word I utter as if it's sparkling dust descending from Tinkerbell's ass. Am I understood?"

The four Brits looked at him with a mixture of sullenness and disbelief. Marcus Riley shook his head slowly, and Eddie had his arms crossed, nose curling back into a sneer.

"Drop the attitude, son, or I will drop you," Dekker growled at Eddie, who suddenly found that his boots were a lot more interesting than the large, angry officer stepping into his personal space.

"This is the dumbest plan ever," Naomi said, already sweating under her heavy load of kit. "I don't see how we can do this. Your boss lady should have sent like fifty guys with guns, twenty helicopters, whatever. You're all bleeding mad."

"I don't like this secret squirrel bullshit any more than you do. But orders are orders. I'm gonna get me a truckload of that salt," and here he pointed with his rifle at the vast white drift, "even if I gotta haul it back home over your expedient dead asses. You got me?"

They trudged behind Dekker like a troop of foot-weary Boy Scouts, the Colonel leading them along the highway with his gun at the ready, watching every bush and rock as if it contained an enemy. He paused only to peer down at the flip-map that was fastened to his forearm, and led them off the blacktop, over to an old wire gate which sagged above a cattle-trap. A ragged driveway stretched beyond it, a miserable track overgrown with weeds that led away for a mile or two before cresting a small rise.

"This is the place," Dekker said. "Sit your asses here till I've gone and sniffed around. Tamsyn, you come with me."

While the other three pulled off their packs for makeshift seats, Tamsyn strung her compound bow. Dekker's quartermaster had found her some truly nasty hunting arrows, and she made sure the quiver was clipped securely to her hip.

Look at the barbs on that. Probably used to take down bears, or sasquatch, she thought. Nocking an arrow to the string, she made sure the pulley wheels were turning nicely.

Tamsyn and Dekker made their way along the old driveway, and she noticed that it followed alongside the salt flats. Dropping to his belly near the top of the rise, the Marine reefed out a pair of binoculars and, after a moment, handed them to Tamsyn.

Perhaps a mile or two up the driveway sat a cluster of sheds with what looked like construction equipment out in the weather and rusting. She could see what looked like a grader, and a small excavator that was half-covered by a mouldering tarpaulin.

"Anything moves, you put a damn arrow into it," Dekker whispered. "It may look quiet, but assumptions get folks killed."

Keeping low, Dekker moved forward, and Tamsyn followed, struggling with the awkward gait. They crossed the equipment yard to the nearest shed, and Dekker peered through the window, gun raised and ready to cough destruction.

Nothing. They covered the entire site with military efficiency, Tamsyn following Dekker's lead. They peered under dozers, lifted sheets of tin, even looked down an old trash-pit. While they were poking around in the main processing shed, a dark, musty place filled with conveyors and crushing equipment, Tamsyn heard a noise. A faint clatter, something scrabbling around on old tin.

Even as Tamsyn wheeled around frantically, looking for the nearest monster to put an arrow through, Dekker pounced on something, yelling triumphantly. With his free hand he emerged from the shadows, holding a yowling, spitting ball of fury that she soon realised was a starving cat.

"Looks like we got ourselves a mascot," he said, looking down on the cat with a grim smile. The mangy tabby had sunk all four claws into his leather-clad forearm with no effect and was worrying at his gloved hand with sharp fangs.

"This really is the arse-end of nowhere," Tamsyn said, taking in the broken-down facility, abandoned years before the zombie outbreak. "Probably the safest place on earth. I'm beginning to think this is a good plan."

"Well, that makes one of us," Dekker said. "Fetch the others. And get something to feed this miserable excuse for a cat."

It took the first two days to get everything cleaned up and working again. Marcus Riley's bush mechanic skills brought the excavator coughing into life, even though it sounded like it had a cupful of ball bearings in the motor. There was an old front-end loader onsite that just wouldn't work, and Riley had the engine in pieces before he admitted defeat.

"This sure would have made life easier," the old stevedore said, wiping the sweat from his brow. He was covered in dust and grease, his white beard already streaked with oil. "It's nothing now but a home for critters."

The conveyor belts in the processing shed seemed to be in good order, but the motors were wired to main power. They found a generator and jury-rigged this up to the power lines. With a bit of oil, the conveyors worked just fine, and, through trial and error, they got the big salt-crusher up and running.

"Here's the most reliable equipment in the place," Dekker said, dropping an armload of shovels and mattocks on the floor. "Found me a whole stack of wheelbarrows outside. Time for y'all to start earning your keep."

That first day of digging was torture, the least of it being the endless trudge from the salt sheds out onto the salt flats, almost a mile before the nearest usable salt. Tamsyn felt numb from the endless swinging of the mattock, and even in gloves her hands were raw, throbbing as she broke apart the thick crust on the ground.

When her wheelbarrow was full, she began the long trudge back to the shed. When an air horn sounded behind her she nearly jumped out of her skin. Eddie raced past in the rattling excavator, throwing her a salute as he roared across the flats with a bucket full of salt.

"Eddie Jacobs, I will kill you in your sleep!" Tamsyn yelled, smiling despite herself. She finally arrived back in the coolness of the shed and tipped her barrow of salt into the hopper. It was slow work, but they'd already crushed one load of salt that day. By Riley's best estimate, they'd processed almost a tonne.

A tip-truck that was nine parts rust sat next to the crusher, the engine completely disassembled. Riley and Dekker were kneeling amidst a spreading tangle of parts, scrubbing and oiling the rusty mess of cogs and rods, doing everything but scratching their heads.

"It's in poor shape, but we should be able to get it going," Riley said, examining a slight crack in the flywheel. "We might bring this bad boy home, but we'll be limping the whole way."

Dekker eventually called it a day, and they downed tools, retiring to their makeshift camp in the middle of the shed floor. Collapsing against her pack, Tamsyn poked into a satchel of the insta-cook rations that were still stamped "USMC," sharing spoonfuls of mush with the cat.

"Here you go, Scratch," she said, letting the tabby lap away at her spoon. After the mess he'd made of Dekker's leathers, the name had stuck. "That's gotta be better than mice, or whatever the hell you've been eating out here."

"We'll never get rid of that cat, the way you're encouraging it," Eddie said through a mouthful of food. "Horrible, mangy thing."

"You leave poor Scratch alone," Tamsyn said, scratching the tabby under the chin. "He's better company than you."

"You say that now, but I know you'll crawl into my sleeping bag one cold night," he scoffed, throwing an empty food tin over his shoulder. It clattered loudly in the vastness of the shed, and Dekker glared at the skinhead. "Cats can't do everything, if you know what I mean."

"Cat can clean itself with its tongue," Naomi said. "Doubt you can do much good with *yours*, boy."

Eddie blushed beneath the onslaught of laughter, opening another ration packet. Tamsyn smiled at his discomfort, and they passed the rest of the evening in good humour. Dekker even broke out a set of cards.

Right before Tamsyn slipped into exhausted slumber, she realised that almost everyone who mattered a damn to her was under this roof. She saw that Scratch was curled up into a ball on Eddie's chest and drifted off with a smile on her face.

The days of back-breaking labour dragged on into the second week, but when Tamsyn thought that her blisters were growing blisters, Dekker called everyone in for a meeting.

"Good news, folks," Dekker said. "Your soft civilian hands have dug up something like fifteen tonnes of salt. Truck's full. Get your stuff, we're heading home."

There was a subdued cheer at this news, and happy murmuring. They were too bone-tired to do much else.

"I got the truck to turn over, but we're low on diesel fuel," Riley said. "We'll probably have to stop in on that general store before we leave, and we may have to scavenge some more on the way home. Quite a drive ahead of us."

It got very squeezy up in front of the tip-truck. It had a wide bench seat, but there were five people to fill three seats, not to mention the uncomfortable explorations of Scratch the cat. The broad posterior of Naomi Higgins did not help the situation much.

"Okay, change of plans," Colonel Dekker said, after Eddie's elbow dug into his ribs for the third time. "All our gear, wrap it up in a tarp and put it back there with the salt. You and you," he pointed at Eddie and Tamsyn, "you're riding back there too."

"Sit on salt for seven hundred miles?" Eddie said. "I'll probably get dermatitis, you bloody Nazi."

"Take something to sit on, you goddamned nancy boy," Dekker said, mocking their English accents. "Call yourself a lookout if it makes you feel better. Just get the hell outta my truck."

They covered as much of the salt as they could, using tarpaulins and dust sheets. Tamsyn clambered up the ladder and started stowing the packs that were hoisted up to her.

"Drag the packs up behind the cab," Eddie called out as he climbed up. "If we have to sit back here, we might as well be comfortable."

"All ready doing it, genius," Tamsyn said, and noticed that Eddie was cradling Scratch in his arm. "Look at you, all Doctor Evil."

"I hate this stupid cat. It's just that Captain America down there didn't want Scratch 'all up in my face.'" Eddie mimicked.

"I don't believe a word of it," Tamsyn laughed, and Eddie grinned, stroking the cat's chin. With a whining chug the engine started, and Riley drove the tip-truck out of the processing shed, crunching gears the whole way.

"We do have a pretty good view from up here," Eddie admitted, leaning on the roof of the cab as he primed a shotgun with salt-crystal scatter shells. Tamsyn strung her bow, resting an arrow across the sighting pegs.

The truck bounced along the driveway and swerved onto the cracked blacktop, jarring their bones with every bump. The worn engine struggled with the full load, and blue smoke poured out of the exhausts above them. Soon they pulled into the township itself.

"One shop, which is also the garage," Eddie said. "This place makes Gravesend look like Hong Kong."

Tamsyn saw the general store, a run-down building sitting flush on the crossroads of two highways. There was an attempt to fence off a yard, and a trailer home brooding in the far corner with a pair of sheds. Apart from the abandoned salt-scrape some miles behind them, this was the entirety of Salt Flat, Texas.

"Be ready up there!" Dekker yelled out of the window. "Gonna bring out the welcome party."

Pulling the truck up in front of the fuel bowsers, Riley leaned on the air horns for a full ten seconds, splitting the silent landscape with a piercing squeal. He revved the engine loudly, as if to emphasise the point.

"There! Coffin-dodgers!" Eddie yelled, firing down onto the handful of zombies that streamed out of the buildings, moaning and confused, drawn by the cacophony. The coughing bark of his shotgun was echoed by the fusillade erupting from the windows of the truck cab beneath them.

Colonel Dekker was out of the truck and walking fearlessly amongst the dead, casually plugging them with nothing but his sidearm. Easy, economical movements, each round a clean headshot.

"Redneck zombies—now I've seen it all," Tamsyn said, putting an arrow through what was left of a fat trucker in flannelette and denim.

Is it right to kill them, knowing that they're still inside, still alive in there? she thought. *It's them or me. Besides, it's much crueller to bring them back.*

Scratch yowled in her ear so loud that it made her jump and almost lose the next arrow she'd nocked. There was a noise behind them, a tapping sound, followed by a faint scraping. She poked her head over the side of the tray to see the mummified remains of a skinny looking kid in grease-streaked overalls, halfway up the rear ladder.

The desiccated zombie roared up with murderous rage when it saw her, hand fumbling and reaching up for the next rung, the act of climbing a half-remembered thing. Tamsyn watched in horrid fascination as it climbed and howled at her, guessing that the leathery boy was probably about her age when he'd died.

"Just shoot the rotter already," Eddie said at her elbow.

"Bet you my last chocolate that it makes it all the way to the top," she said.

"You're on."

They watched its ponderous progress, even as the others began carting out goods from the store and hand-cranking the diesel pumps. She let out a triumphant whoop when their zombie finally reached the top, snapping its teeth together and staring at them with blasted eyes, only to meet the butt-end of Eddie's shotgun. He caved in its undead face with one sharp blow, and by the time it hit the ground it was just a corpse again.

Eddie reached underneath the tarp, found a pinch of salt, and let it drift down onto the body.

"That's what you get for messing with us," he said. "A salt and battery."

With a pained groan, Tamsyn punched Eddie in the bicep, hard.

"Seriously, tell another pun like that and I'll be forced to kill you."

They almost filled the fuel tank with what diesel was left at the tiny general store, and there was enough in the way of bottled water and soda drinks to replenish their dwindling supplies. Eddie threw an entire box of looted chocolate bars up to Tamsyn, who grinned like a Cheshire cat.

Loaded up, Riley put the truck into a sweeping u-turn, crushing a couple of corpses underneath the fat tires. Leaving Salt Flat forever, they powered on due east, and for hours Tamsyn saw nothing but highway and sky.

Despite the afternoon sun, the wind whipped around them mercilessly, and Tamsyn crawled into her sleeping bag. Eddie zipped up his leather jacket and burrowed into the packs, hands firmly planted in his armpits.

"Saying we do get back to Corpus Christi in one piece, what then?" Tamsyn said. "We're sitting on Feickert's lifeline, but she's only going to use it to keep those poor Re-Humans behind bars."

"Deal's a deal," Eddie said with a shiver, trying to keep his head out of the whistling wind. "We don't owe 'em nothing after this."

"Even with this lot, they still don't have enough salt. Even blind Freddy can see that the Re-Humans will be massacred within a year. They'll call it a relocation, load them up in trains, and pow," Tamsyn mimed a pistol to Eddie's head.

"It sucks, Tam, but they're already dead. What you gonna do, hold all this salt hostage, try to bargain those dead folks into nicer houses? You try telling that to GI Joe down there."

"I know it's all going to go to shit," Tamsyn said with a frown. "But I don't have to be happy about it."

The highway wound through lonely farm districts and was mostly free of traffic. Drawn by the blare of the misfiring truck engine in a silent world, zombies dotted the fields, shuffling towards the neglected blacktop.

They did not stop. When dusk fell, they hit their first town, Van Horn—a ruin crawling with the undead. Riley hit the gas, and the truck shuddered, knocking over ranks of zombies, grinding them into paste beneath its large wheels. One of the headlights broke, and the other was coated in gore, bathing the road ahead of them in a pale red light.

"Save your bullets," Tamsyn said after Eddie let off a round over the side. "Let the truck do the hard work."

The going got tough for Riley, who was forced to steer the large truck around several vehicles abandoned on the road. He had to reverse when confronted with an abandoned barricade: junked whitegoods and burnt-out cars packed into an impassable barrier.

Looks like they tried to do a Gravesend here, make a Safe Zone to live in, Tamsyn thought. *I'm guessing it didn't go so well.*

Corpses by the dozen were crowded around the truck at this point, hammering mutely at the metal sides with ruined hands, crowing at the growling machine that broke their silent world, a monster from a forgotten age.

Scraping against parked cars, nudging bins aside, Riley attempted to turn the truck around in the narrow street. For one long moment the shrill beeping of the reversing siren blared across the dead town, and then the truck coughed once, wheezed into silence.

"That did not just happen," Eddie said. "We did not just conk out here."

Perhaps fifty zombies milled around the truck now, wedged as they were in the blocked-off street. The low moans of the coffin-dodgers grew into an excited chorus, the sudden stimulus bringing plenty of others to investigate. Soon hundreds of murderous cannibals pressed up against the truck. Tamsyn knew that they would soon start climbing on top of each other; a foul human pyramid with the ones at the bottom crushed into slime.

Unimpeded, given enough time, a mob of zombies could get over any wall. People-stink always drove them into a frenzy, the urge to take the most direct path to meat.

Riley crunched the gears of the truck. Tamsyn heard the futile clicking sounds, knew that the starter motor wasn't even turning. Zombies began banging on the doors, reaching up for the handles. Gunshots went off from up front. She could hear the popping of a pistol, the ear-ringing stutter of an automatic rifle.

"We got climbers," Eddie shouted, unloading several rounds from the back of the tray. Tamsyn looked down to see three fallen zombies at the base of the rear ladder, and a time-ravaged fire-fighter still making a clumsy ascent. Tamsyn raced to the back of the cab and wrestled loose the spare shovel from its welded rack.

"Sorry, Madam President, you'll have to put this on my tab," she said, sweeping the tarp aside. With some deft shovel work, she flicked loads of salt over the sides, greeted by a cacophony of wails as the crystals dusted the ranks of zombies pushing against the truck.

"Hey Tamsyn!" Naomi shouted from up front. "You got a hair-clip I can borrow?"

"Not a good time for fixing your hair," Tamsyn yelled, madly sending drifts of salt down onto screeching dead faces. It wasn't much, but it was keeping the undead at bay. For now.

"It's a blown fuse," Naomi said. "They just need something to bridge the circuit, something metal."

Ripping the baseball cap off her head, Tamsyn felt through the tangle of her hair. *There.* She pulled the clip free, climbed on top of the cab, and leaned over the side, arms stretched out as she tried to reach Naomi's flailing fingers.

If I slip off this roof, I'm a dead woman. Look at all those hungry monsters...

She handed the metal clip to Naomi, and, pushing back from the edge with trembling arms, she slid back into the tip-tray. Minutes later the engine roared into life, and Tamsyn shivered, grinning with relief. The truck bounced and jolted as it backed over thick ranks of bodies, bones crunching and skulls popping. At one stage the wheels were spinning and slipping, unable to find a purchase in the thick layers of gore.

They escaped the town, and the next several hours devolved into a waking nightmare: a slow migration through the night of the Deadlands, nudging through dead towns and slowly heading east. They paused once on a lonely road to let the engine cool, only to fire it back into whining life when a battalion of rotters caught up with them.

Tamsyn found herself in a numb half-sleep, the freezing kiss of the wind barely felt. She noticed that her hand was wrapped around the bow in a death-grip and forced herself to put it down.

"San Antonio," Eddie mumbled groggily, reading a street sign. "Looks big."

In the dim light of the false dawn, the city looked enormous, a packed mass of skyscrapers surrounded by the sprawl of suburbia.

The closer they got to the city, the harder it got to navigate the truck; the roads were thick with abandoned vehicles, and the confusing curlicue of the on-ramps for other highways were choked—a long-silent traffic jam where all doors were opened and the cars given up to the dead.

Riley left the highway when he could, finding it quicker to manoeuvre through the side streets of San Antonio. The city was nothing now but a monument to the brash ambition of the Texas that had simply stopped.

Tamsyn flinched at the sight of the dead folks filling the streets, only so much gristle when the tip-truck struck them at speed, rank after rank of rotten meat walking.

"You missed the turn-off, numb-nuts!" Eddie shouted, pounding on the roof with the flat of his hand. They passed over the main highway heading east, and apart from the occasional wreckage it was a fairly clear run to Corpus Christi.

"I really don't like this," Tamsyn said. "Where the hell is Dekker sending us? Where—Christ, get down!"

Grabbing Eddie by the sleeve, she pulled him down behind the cab. Hanging above the city, a helicopter hovered above the rising sun for a moment, and then it fell below the skyline. She'd glimpsed the sleek lines of a gunship, a black wasp bristling with guns and missile racks under its stubby wings.

"Stop the truck!" she hollered, thumping on the back of cab. "There's a helicopter, it spotted us!"

The ancient truck kept rolling and did not slow. Tamsyn screeched over the side of the tray, hoping they would hear her through the open windows, but to no avail. Naomi and Riley would not reply to their cries.

"He must have them at gunpoint in there," Tamsyn realised. "Dekker is taking us towards that chopper!"

"Back-stabbing bastard. I should just take him out," Eddie said, holding the shotgun up against the roof of the cab. "This will get through, no problems."

"Don't you dare! I can't remember where everyone's sitting. What if you kill one of the others by accident?"

Eddie relented, and they could only watch as the truck was slowly diverted away from their intended route. When they could clearly hear the rotors of the helicopter, Tamsyn crept to the edge of the tray, peering over as the truck pulled up and stopped.

"You've gotta be kidding me," she said. "We're at the Alamo."

The murderous looking chopper hovered above the weathered stone building, the site of the infamous siege, the birthplace of this renewed nation. In the plaza in front of the building, dozens of zombies still lay twitching, and as she watched the gunship turned on some new undead arrivals with a mini-gun, churning them into mincemeat. She slid back below the lip of the tip-tray, trembling.

"How the hell do you know where we are?"

"My dad was a history teacher. Be quiet, and for god's sake keep down. I don't think they saw us back here."

Eddie got out his shaving mirror, and they used it to peer around the edge of the truck. They could see Dekker out and walking, an assault rifle held low but pointed in the direction of the cab.

"Y'all keep still," he boomed. "We've got a change of destination here. Keep your guns down and there won't be any trouble."

"Dekker, get 'em out of the goddamn truck!" came an amplified voice from the gunship. "Uncle Sam wants his salt."

Dekker's deserting? Tamsyn thought. *Maybe he's got less faith in Feickert's plan than I thought.*

And I guess we ARE sitting on a fortune back here.

"These folks are coming with us," the Marine hollered, shaking his head. Tamsyn didn't know if they could hear him up in the helicopter, but his intent was clear.

"That wasn't the plan, Colonel," the anonymous voice in the helicopter. "Waste those fuckers already."

"Oh my god, he's meant to kill us," Tamsyn whispered. "Oh shit!"

For one horrid moment, Tamsyn saw Colonel Dekker lift up his rifle, aiming it at the cabin. He seemed cold, resolved to this action. Even as she scrambled for her bow, the Marine frowned, his whole face showing the battle he fought inside.

He won't do it. He can't.

Dekker saw the gleam of Eddie's mirror, and with the ghost of a smile he winked at them. A moment later, the massive black man was rolling for cover, firing a burst on full automatic, gun aimed up at the underbelly of the helicopter.

The large Marine emptied his clip, to no apparent effect. After a surprised second the helicopter swivelled, tracking Dekker with the mini-gun. With a ferocious chatter, the air was filled with a hail of lead, and they saw Dekker torn apart, as if his body were chewed up by an invisible beast.

Hand shaking, Eddie dropped his shaving mirror over the side, and it broke apart on the ground. At Tamsyn's urging they huddled in underneath the tarpaulins, covering themselves with packs and bags. The thick salt granules got underneath their clothes, scouring their skin.

"Don't shoot!" she heard Naomi shout, but the helicopter turned again, the broadside facing the tip-truck. The mini-gun opened up, and it felt as if a giant was kicking the front of the truck, the windscreen smashing, bullets knocking dents into the thick steel of the tip-tray at their backs.

For one horrible moment they heard screams, and then there was no sound but the low whine of the helicopter rotors, the death-bird slowly coming down to rest on the ground. Then the engine died, and there was only the *whoosh* of the blades slowly beating to a halt.

Tamsyn fought back her hysterical sobs, clutching Scratch to her side, willing the cat to be silent. Eddie clutched his shotgun in a pale panic, staring up through a gap in the tarps at the dawn sky, his lips moving as if in prayer.

They're dead. Just like that, they're all dead.

And we're next.

Footsteps on the gravel. A couple of people, cautiously approaching the truck. Somewhere, the tinkle of glass shards as they fell from the shattered windshield.

"You're a goddamn moron, you know that, Jenkins?" one of the men said. "You coulda put a hole in the radiator, way you were hosing down this crew. Then where would we be?"

"Shut your damn fool mouth," Jenkins said, easing open the passenger side door to the cab. Tamsyn struggled not to breathe, ignored the urge to itch away the salt that was slowly scouring her skin. The men were mere feet away, and she heard one of them cough and spit.

"Well now, that's a lot of guns. Dekker was working to pull something on us."

"That's why his black ass is dead. And now it's half a share, not thirds."

One of the men was pacing around the outside of the truck, tapping the tip-tray with the end of something metallic. His foot ground into the remains of Eddie's mirror, and Tamsyn thought she was going to be sick. She needed the toilet real bad.

They'll have to know that we're in here! she thought. *Our only hope was to take them by surprise. If they get back into that chopper, we are dead.*

The man didn't miss a beat though and whistled as he walked towards the rear ladder. The sounds of booted feet climbing the rungs.

"Hey Simmons, sounds like it's full up to the top. Biggest payday you or I ever gonna see. I'm a have me a looksee."

Ever so slowly, Tamsyn swept back the mouldy tarpaulin that covered her. Holding the bow low across her hips, she carefully nocked one of the wickedly sharp hunting arrows. Drawing the string, Tamsyn felt the immense force at her fingertips, prayed that she would hit anything at that awkward angle.

Scratch chose that moment to leap up from their hiding place, bounding playfully across the canvas landscape to investigate the noise. The upper half of a swarthy blonde man with a crew-cut came into sight, and he flashed a flawless smile as the cat flew into his arms.

"Hey! I found me a pussy-cat!" Jenkins said, one moment before Tamsyn sent a barbed shaft into his throat. He looked at Tamsyn with shock, working his lips soundlessly, thick jets of blood gushing from the wound. A moment later he went limp and fell from sight, Scratch yowling as he fought his way loose from the dead man's hands.

Bastard. I'm just glad I missed the cat, Tamsyn thought. *Two against one, now.*

"Stop horsing around back there, Jenkins. We gotta get this truck cleaned up and moving."

Eddie rose up carefully, shotgun at the ready. He pointed towards the driver's side of the truck, mimed the action of firing downwards. Tamsyn nodded and, fitting another arrow to her string, crept forwards.

"Jenkins, I am coming back there to kick your ass," the man named Simmons shouted. "I can see five hundred zombies coming, and I will feed each of them a small piece of you."

The cab door slammed, and she could hear the footsteps of a man circling the truck, a quick, purposeful stride. She looked across at Eddie, noticed the worried look on his face, the way he was working himself up to that one desperate moment of resistance. Eddie saw Tamsyn watching him and flashed her a nervous smile.

I am in love with this man, she realised. *If we get through this in one piece, I will have Eddie Jacobs's babies, and put up with all of his bad habits.*

Eddie tensed and rose. Tamsyn followed, drawing back on the arrow as she stood. A man in a one-piece aviator's suit walked underneath them, a pistol drawn. Something must have given away their position, perhaps their shadows in the dawn light, or the white drift of salt falling from the barrel of Eddie's gun. Quicker than thought, the man fell to one knee, gun up and tracking.

She heard the whip-crack of Simmon's pistol at almost the same moment as the ear-ringing boom of Eddie's shotgun, and then something punched her in the shoulder, a fiery finger that crushed bone and sent her shot wide, the arrow passing over the helicopter and clattering into the crumbling stones of the Alamo itself.

Tamsyn saw the helicopter pilot fold over, clutching the ravages of his stomach, and then looked down to see the gunshot wound, just below her collarbone, pulsing out a thick flow of blood. Her vision swam for a long moment, and then she was on her back, lying on a bed of salt.

The crystals ate into her open wound and stung—stung like a bitch—but then everything went cold. As Eddie pressed his jacket into her wound, she tried to tell him something, anything, but a black curtain fell and everything stopped.

The night-feeds were the worst, Tamsyn soon realised. It didn't help that she only had the use of one hand. Her other arm was strapped to a slowly healing collarbone.

Eddie got up to feed baby Milly when he heard her air-raid wailing, but more often than not he would sleep through her cries. Even now, Tamsyn could hear him snoring from his room as she wrestled one-handed with the tin of formula, heating up a bottle in the microwave.

If Eddie plays his cards right, he'll be snoring in my room soon, she thought happily. The deaths of so many friends weighed heavily on her soul, but their budding romance was lifting her spirits. Tamsyn was taking it very slow with Eddie, but there were plenty of tender moments, and it soon became obvious to Tamsyn that despite his bluster, Eddie felt much the same way that she did.

What would Naomi say if she could see this, me shacked up with Eddie Jacobs? She'd just about have a conniption.

"Drink up, beautiful," Tamsyn cooed, holding the baby awkwardly in the crook of an elbow, smiling as the infant chugged her way through another feed.

The salt delivery had saved Feickert. The impeachment proceedings had commenced while they were out in the desert, and with enough salt to see out the construction of the moat, she'd held onto her fragile presidency by all of three votes.

Tamsyn had held onto her life by just as slim a margin. She awoke in the military hospital, Eddie asleep in the chair next to her bed. In groggy panic she looked up at the IV stand, only to realise that it was blood pumping into her, not saline.

For the two survivors of Dekker's salt expedition, it meant citizenship, a fancy new house, cars, and the promise of good jobs with the government. The other Brits were seeded out into the community, and it was branded a human rights triumph, even if their forced incarceration was glossed over by the local media.

"All right?" Eddie said, standing in the doorway with tousled hair. Scratch weaved between his legs, mewling for attention. At some stage Tamsyn must have dozed off; dawn was creeping in through the bay windows.

"All right," Tamsyn smiled, burping Milly one-handed. She put her back into her bassinette and gladly accepted the cup of tea.

"You sure you want to do this?" Eddie asked. "We don't have to go."

"I made a promise," Tamsyn said, and waggled her bound arm. "You'll need to drive though."

With the baby firmly strapped into a booster seat, Eddie and Tamsyn drove out to the outer walls, where a strong gate had been fitted, a temporary bridge constructed to cross the moat.

The Re-Humans were leaving Corpus Christi today, every single one, their ghetto emptied and returned to the living. The streets leading to the outer gates were lined with people, from the curious to the openly hostile, and several protestors screamed at the treated zombies as they shuffled past.

"REPEAL RE-HUMAN EMANCIPATION ACT" one hand painted sign declared. "PUT THE DEAD BACK IN THE GROUND!" read another, this one a fancy printed sign distributed to many in the crowd.

A pass got them through some military checkpoints, and they were soon at the outer gates. The saltwater cannons were clearing a path from the temporary bridge, pushing the untreated zombies away from the opened gate. All experiments had shown that the dead would not molest the Re-Humans, and they would be safe enough out there, in the Deadlands.

"Tamsyn," Dr. Murray croaked, and with her good hand she clutched at the leathery hands of her dead friend.

"I will miss you," she said, fighting back a tear. "It's not fair, they can't just send you away."

"For the best, my dear," he said. "We aren't welcome here, and it will only bring trouble. Out there, we can start our own city, clear the roads, produce salt for the Republic. It's the best thing that could have happened for us."

"Are you going to be okay?" she asked.

"Best I've felt in years, though I miss the booze. I am sure that our paths will cross again, young missy. You take care of her,

Jacobs, y'hear?" he snarled, blue lips peeling back to reveal a rotted mess of teeth and gums.

"Sod off, you old git," Eddie said, shaking the dead man's hand. He was cradling Milly in a papoose. "Don't let the door hit you where the good Lord split you."

With a cheery wave the Re-Human joined his companions, shuffling out through the gate and into the Deadlands. If the salt spray bothered them, they were stoic enough to walk away from Corpus Christi with their dead heads held high.

"There's Dawes," Eddie said, waving him over. "I'm right here Tam, if you need me."

"It's all good," she said. "I feel safe enough with hundreds of armed marines around me, but thanks for the macho sentiment."

"Whatever, you moody cow."

Simon Dawes pushed his way through the slow exodus, eventually standing on the other side of the crowd barrier. He nodded at her and stood there awkwardly, a grey-skinned shadow with a ruined face, forever locked in time.

"We're even," Tamsyn said. "We got the Act passed, and you're free. If you can keep up with the others, I hear they're starting a new settlement at Salt Flat."

"I meant what I said, Tam," Dawes said. "I'm not taking my dose anymore. Some of us are going to walk away from the Re-Humans, keep walking until the salt wears off. It's my penance, for all the lousy stuff I've done."

"I call it the coward's way out," Tamsyn said, "but there's plenty of stuff I'd like to forget too. All the best, mate," she said, offering her hand. Simon Dawes took it, and they shook hands, his cold grip surprisingly firm. Still shaking his hand, she drew Dawes in close.

"If we meet again, I'll probably have to shoot you," she told him, and he nodded mournfully, rejoining the slow parade of dead things.

When Eddie and Tamsyn returned to the sprawl of their new house, they found two letters in the post box. The first was expected, their new citizenship papers and passports. The second, a less welcome letter.

"I cannot believe this!" Eddie said. "We've just been bloody drafted."

Tamsyn took the letter, scanning it carefully. They were both eighteen now, which meant they were adults, expected to defend the Republic.

"Must be what Feickert meant by 'a good job in the government.' Last time I trust a politician."

They sat on the couch in a mild shock, playing with their blissfully oblivious foster child. Flicking on the TV, the news did little to cheer them up. Talks between the United States and the Republic of Texas had completely broken down, and sabres were not so much being rattled as being drawn and sharpened. The US military had now left the safety of Hawaii, and jet fighters had recently been spotted buzzing the Texan border.

"A civil war, flipping marvellous," Eddie said. "We get in just as the bombs start dropping, that's great."

"Someone else just dropped a bomb," Tamsyn said, screwing up her nose. "Be a dear and change this nappy."

PART 3:
ARMY CORPSE

10

Lying flat on her belly, Tamsyn attacked the chain link fence with pliers, snipping out a hole to wriggle through. The moon was full, and it hung low above the refinery like a bloated yellow eye, painting the tanks and sheds with a dull glow.

Tonight was not a good night for hiding.

"We stand out like dog's balls," Eddie whispered behind her, sliding her compound bow and quiver through the gap in the fence. Tamsyn glared back at him, pressing a finger to her lips.

She winced at the noise that he made as he pulled himself through the severed mesh, dragging a rifle behind him with a loud clatter. Keeping one worried eye to the cluster of buildings, Tamsyn quickly tested the tension on her bow, resting an arrow on the string.

Eddie Jacobs, I could kill you! she thought wearily. She scowled at the skinhead as he threw her a cheeky grin, casually checking the action of his weapon as he settled down on the ground next to her.

He infuriated her constantly and had no social graces worth mentioning. But she loved him, now that she'd discovered the human being hiding underneath the thuggish exterior.

Everyone else she'd ever given a damn about was dead now.

Eddie stank just as much as she did, his mismatched uniform stained and torn in places. The trip north had been tough on their piecemeal unit, but the trip back south was turning into an absolute disaster.

We'll be lucky to make it home alive, Tamsyn thought, ruefully considering the crude insignia stitched into both of their shirts. White star, blue field. The Republic of Texas, a new country that had recently given them refuge, citizenship, and then draft papers when a stupid civil war came calling.

So it was North vs South again, over the new moral issue: zombie rights. More specifically, the zombies that could be "cured," brought back to reason and memory. Re-Humans.

Even when the bloody Yanks weren't shooting at them, there were always the enormous hordes of the undead, mindless mobs of walking corpses that sometimes numbered in the thousands. Ignorant of the poor man's war raging in their midst, these super-packs were still scouring the country to the bone, just as hungry for human flesh as they'd ever been.

The bloody coffin-dodgers swarm like bees over here, Tamsyn thought, remembering the pointless pottering of the zombies back in England, groaning corpses pushing rusty lawnmowers, waiting for buses that hadn't run in months. *This lot can't bear to be alone, even in death.*

The refinery yard lay in silence. Going by the weeds pushing up through cracks in the asphalt, it had been silent for some time. The main gates were secured with a fat padlock, and a handful of cars and trucks were still neatly lined up in the small carpark. All the tires were flat now, with three years' worth of dust coating the windshields.

PIEDMONT BIO-DIESEL INC., a large sign read above the main works shed. The roller doors were open a crack, but the bright moonlight did not penetrate the gloom within.

There could be anything in there, Tamsyn realised, a faint tickle of fear flushing through her, pushing back at the exhaustion. She'd had something like three hours sleep over the last two days, and everything else was a haze of driving, the glow of distant bombing runs on the horizon, the furious chatter of firefights. Each time the shooting sounded closer and closer, and every delay was excruciating.

Retreating sucks, Tamsyn decided for the hundredth time, eyeing off the rows of fuel tanks. Taking the back roads to avoid the enemy advance, their unit had stumbled across this almost hidden refinery in a moment of dumb luck. Most of the garages and abandoned cars had been picked clean by other survivors in this area, and foraging for fuel was getting close to impossible.

Another man joined them in the yard, signalling that the rear was safe for now. Griffin was her fourth, out beyond the fence somewhere, hugging a tree with only a Dragunov sniper rifle for company.

So there's numb-nuts here; then Baxter, the scary one who's actually done some Army training; and Griffin, our guardian angel, the one keeping an eye on things. In the chaos of the retreat they'd changed her squad twice now, and Tamsyn had never bothered remembering anyone's names until they'd given her stripes.

Signalling that the others should follow her and keep low, Tamsyn crept forward. She'd left her army-issue boots behind, changing back into her old sneakers for this mission. Recon and secure the site if possible. The LT wouldn't let her leave her pistol, and so the heavy lump of metal flapped around on her belt, slapping against her hip and generally annoying her.

Tamsyn had ordered that they stash their heavy packs and gear in the woods, near Griffin's sniper nest. It seemed stupid to haul so much gear, knowing that they only had a ten-minute walk back to base. They needed to get in and out quickly, and she preferred to travel light, where possible.

The yard was empty so far, but Tamsyn was wary, and kept a wide berth from the parked cars. Zombies had been known to sit in cars for months or years, silent until the moment they struck, snatching out with skeletal arms at the unwary.

She raised a hand, ready to send Eddie and Baxter on a perimeter sweep, but froze, clenched her fist to signify an immediate halt. She stepped back, heart pounding. Shuffling slowly through the tank-farm were dozens of walking corpses, getting tangled up in the hoses and pumps, or just staring up at the moon and moaning softly. Many of these undead still wore hardhats and rotting coveralls.

All of the access gates were still closed, which meant that the entire refinery had fallen to the virus. All of the workers, all of the office staff, even the driver of the local lunch van, still parked by the warehouse door with shelves full of mouldy food.

"Get back," she whispered to Eddie, who craned his head around her to get a good look. "Too many."

"Can't break into a honeycomb without stirring up some bees," Eddie mused softly, patting his assault rifle like he was in an action movie. "Call it in, boss lady."

Baxter slid out from the shadow of an abandoned tanker truck, signalling that several zombies were moving on the other side of the main refinery shed. He might have been giving her the stink-eye too, which didn't surprise Tamsyn much.

I didn't want this stupid field promotion, arsehole, she thought. *You wanna be in charge so badly, it's all yours.*

She ordered the fireteam back to the entry point, grateful that dozens of murderous monsters hadn't heard them poking around. Grabbing the walkie-talkie from her webbing, she twisted the volume knob to a low setting, wincing at the squeal that erupted from the handset.

"LT, we are going to need an Article 7, over."

There was a long pause. She could just picture Lieutenant Hennesy, somewhere in their temporary camp behind the next ridge. On the off-chance that the refinery was empty or the biodiesel was spoiled, he was already redistributing the last of the fuel, effectively halving the motley collection of vehicles that were still going. They were already squeezed in, two to a seat in most of the convoy, with more folks hanging from doors and riding on the roof. Their situation was as stupid as it was hopeless.

Tamsyn couldn't think of a better way to describe Foxtrot Company, and the imbecile who'd progressively led them up shit creek. *Lieutenant Erwin Hennesy, the biggest dipshit I've ever worked for.*

After the Texan capture of Cleveland, he'd volunteered his conscript force as the vanguard for the failed push into Washington, DC. Hoping for glory, or perhaps a promotion, he'd ordered the retreat far too late, and the rout became a slaughter.

"Negative, Corporal," the Lieutenant transmitted, his voice faint and crackling. Even their field radios were second-rate. "You encounter any infected, you are to restrain them only. Lethal force is denied."

"Goddamnit," Tamsyn muttered, and then thumbed the mic. "LT, if you want this fuel, we are going to have to kill some zombies. At least fifty on the site. I don't have that many zip-cuffs, so perhaps the coffin-dodgers can chew on a volunteer while everyone else fuels up. Over."

Eddie chuckled to himself, but Baxter was less amused, frowning at Tamsyn's insubordination. The radio squealed again.

"You are way out of line, Corporal Webb!" the lieutenant yelled. "Subdue any resistance, and if you're gonna fire something, fire your X-76. Article 7 is denied."

"Well, that tears it," Tamsyn whispered. "We're not even allowed to shoot at the bloody things now."

"You're not in England anymore, Corporal," Baxter said. "We do things differently here." He hung his rifle over his shoulder and started to unfold a dog-catcher's noose.

"You're all bloody crazy," Tamsyn said. "Until they get the dose, they're murderous fucking lunatics, and I say I misheard the LT just then."

"Yep, I coulda sworn that the head-cheese approved an Article 7," Eddie said. "Radio's been playing up, know what I mean?"

Baxter watched the pair of them, eyes narrowed, as if measuring up his chances. He snapped the handle of the noose into place and pointed it at Tamsyn's nose.

"If you kill anything beyond an Article 3, I will report you, and your boyfriend," Baxter said. "You'll both be court-martialled for murder, war crimes, you name it."

"Gah. I am so sick of the flipping Undeath Act," Tamsyn said. "Do you really think we can bring all of them back?"

"Yes. We can, and we will," Baxter said. "Dropping zombies is like shooting the handicapped. You Brits make me sick."

"Kinder to put a bullet in their brains," Eddie said, stepping up to the Texan, swatting away the dog-catcher. "I don't know about you, but while we're here fiddling around with zip-cuffs and IV drips, Uncle Sam is going to find us and shoot us."

"Stop it!" Tamsyn whispered, breaking the two men apart with the swift and strategic application of her knees and elbows. "God knows why I'm in charge of you knuckleheads, but you're going to macho us right into the shit. Now listen up."

She was five foot nothing and underweight from months of short rations, but Tamsyn Webb had her temper up now, and she'd earned something of a reputation—along with several bouts in the can—for fighting dirty.

"Article 3 of the Undeath Act gives a non-com the right to execute five infected, for the purposes of meeting a mission objective. That's going to happen, so don't argue with me, Baxter," she finished, touching the tip of her bow to his solar plexus with a bit more force than necessary.

"Article 1 gives any civilian the right to kill three zombies with a firearm in self-defence. We need to do this now, and properly. If that idiot sends our backup in with nothing but butterfly nets and fucking sunshine, people are going to get killed."

She thumbed her radio and raised Griffin in her sniper nest. She was one of the sharpest shots in the company and would have no trouble putting a bead on anything that moved in the refinery yard.

"Griffin, in two minutes you will need to snipe exactly three zombies. In self-defence. And turn off your radio now. Out."

Griffin thumbed the transmit key twice in confirmation and resumed her patient silence. Just as Lieutenant Hennesy began a string of crackling obscenities and threats, Tamsyn also switched off her handset, with a smile on her face.

"Such a shame. Terrible signal here," she said. "Now, both of you sit tight. If anyone so much as farts while I'm gone, you won't be using your man-bits anytime soon. Capisce?"

Foxtrot Company was behind the nearby tree-lined ridge, carefully hidden on the valley floor on the far side. If Hennesy was going to haul her team off the mission, it would take him at least ten minutes to send the back-up through all of that.

Ignoring Eddie's farcical salute, Tamsyn stole across the cracked asphalt like a cat. Ignoring the ominous yawn of the roller door, she skirted the main shed and made for the tank-farm, twenty or so stainless-steel silos clustered together, a slight breeze rattling a catwalk overhead.

Hiding behind an equipment board, she tried to still the tremor in her chest, expecting at any moment for a cold hand to grip her shoulder, for a slimy jag of teeth to slowly close around her neck. Hands shaking, she adjusted the sights on her bow, some distantly clinical part of her mind taking into account the wind.

Just drop five of them, she thought to herself. *Then get your little surprise ready. Easy.*

Breathe. The stilling of her nerves. Before the end of the world, Tamsyn Webb was a somewhat damaged schoolgirl who had just been accepted for a spot in the UK's archery team. She was meant to compete in the next Commonwealth Games. Then everything went to shit.

She'd qualified with this same compound bow, the one her dad had bought her after the car accident, suggested by her therapist as something to keep her busy, something to keep her mind from her grief.

Even now, a lifetime later, this simple communion with a bow and arrow kept her demons at bay. Just for this moment, Tamsyn could forget about her mum, her dad, everyone else she'd seen die in this horrible new world.

On her next in-breath, she released the string, and the pulleys and gears drove a barbed hunting arrow at great velocity into the temple of a rotting secretary. The corpse fell with a soft sigh into a drain, passing from unlife with a series of tremors, one remaining stiletto heel shivering in the moonlight.

By this time her next arrow was already nocked and drawn, and Tamsyn lined the sighting pegs up with the mobile remains of a hardhatted worker. Frowning at the white curve of the plastic helmet, she dropped her aim slightly, planting a quivering shaft in between the zombie's eyes.

Even as the dead thing fell, there was a sound just behind her, a low, rattling snarl. Heart pounding madly, Tamsyn wheeled and saw it reaching for her, the remains of an obese man in a ragged suit. What was left of its face was moulded into an eternal fury, focused only on her. It had gotten within ten feet of her and she hadn't heard a thing.

"Shit, shit shit!" Tamsyn whimpered. She fumbled the next arrow, and it fell from the string. She dropped the bow with a curse and grabbed for her pistol. Her fingers closed around the handle, but then she reconsidered, knowing she didn't have enough bullets to drop the swarm of coffin-dodgers that the gunshot would surely attract.

Her hand dove into another pocket and came out trembling, clutching an innocuous looking water pistol. The X-76, the last line of defence that every Texan referred to as The Squirt.

Ducking under the flailing limbs of the undead businessman, Tamsyn got right into the creature's stink, reaching forward and squeezing the stream of liquid directly into its eyes. Even though these creatures felt nothing, would keep coming at you even if riddled with bullets, the dead man felt the saline solution.

Salt had changed everything.

The zombie squealed with pain, the sound somewhere between a stuck piglet and a boiling kettle. Clutching at its eyes and staggering around, it finally collided into a tank, falling onto its fat backside with a disgusting squish, crying and snapping its teeth blindly.

"Oh, shut the hell up," Tamsyn said, pulling out a wicked little hatchet. With two sharp blows she sent the dead thing into its final silence.

Snatching up her bow, she fell back with a curse. The wails of the stricken zombie had brought too much attention, and at least a dozen of the coffin-dodgers were making straight for her, each rotting set of lungs adding to the growing chorus of moans.

"Good one, Tam," she berated herself, and retreated the way she'd come in, all stealth abandoned. She paused only to knock over a full barrel of the biodiesel from a loading dock, striking off the cap with her hatchet and sending the pungent mess seeping across the ground.

"We could hear you from over here," Eddie said when she arrived. "Thought you was meant to be sneaky, yeah?"

"Don't get smart with me," Tamsyn said. "Same plan as I had, it's just happening sooner. Baxter, gimme your lighter."

"You owe me a new one," the Texan grumbled, but handed over a disposable cigarette lighter, yellow plastic. A solid phalanx of animated corpses was already trudging towards them, the entire plant converging on the living trio in an eerily accurate fashion.

"You two, make a racket, keep 'em interested. You know, whistling, clapping, whatever." Tamsyn tested the action of the lighter, and it took a couple of attempts to conjure up a weak flicker of flame from it.

"If it all goes to gravy, get the hell out," she said. "I won't be far behind you. Remember, you're actually allowed to shoot three of them."

As the first of the zombies started to cross the spreading pool of diesel, Tamsyn took off at a loping run, hugging the inside of the fence as she made for the far end of the tank farm. She looked over her shoulder to see the two men clapping, whistling through their teeth, and stamping their feet. Perhaps fifty of the undead were heading for them, snarling, mouths stretched wide with an unending hunger.

Taking the rattling stairs two steps at a time, Tamsyn soon found herself at the top of the catwalk, walking above the enormous steel tanks. A gantry took her halfway between the tanks and the main shed, a cluster of fat pipes rattling beneath her as she moved.

Quietly, she thought, barely daring to breathe. For one moment she thought one of them had looked up, but the small crowd continued, howling for the warm flesh that was almost within reach.

Leaning over a railing, Tamsyn tried to gauge the distance between the spilled diesel and the storage tanks, tried not to think about how much fuel she was sitting on top of.

I'm either really stupid or some sort of genius, Tamsyn thought, praying that the lighter would work. She set the little flame to its highest setting and waited until a cluster of the undead passed underneath her.

The wink of fire danced as the cigarette lighter fell, an innocent star that touched the ground and sent up a flash of flame, followed by the explosion as the fire reached what was left in the barrel itself.

By some minor miracle, none of the tanks or other barrels went up, but the fireball sent a large group of the undead sprawling. Steaming and still smoking, the creatures slowly found their feet, or simply dragged themselves forward, their desiccated flesh still burning and crackling.

Shame. Thought that much diesel would be enough to flash fry 'em, Tamsyn thought, belatedly remembering the Molotov cocktails that were quickly ruled out of Gravesend's defence plan. All this usually achieved was a burning zombie, who still came at you until its brain melted into goo and would set you on fire even as it was eating you.

I think I can safely chalk this up as another shit decision.

The wave of burning creatures staggered towards the two men, who slowly began picking off targets. There was a whipcrack from outside the compound, as Griffin dropped one zombie, and then another.

Tamsyn sent her arrows down at the flame-grilled coffin-dodgers, eventually getting the other two headshots allowed to her under Article 3, pinning a pair of crawling bodies to the ground like crispy bugs.

Article 1 gave her three more personal kills, although bows and crossbows were a grey area according to the Undeath Act. After that, they only had Article 2 to fall back on.

As many dead things as you can bust up in hand-to-hand combat, provided everyone present could vouch that it was all done in self-defence, and these witnesses were not other rednecks out for zombie-bashing thrills.

Eddie and Baxter slowly fell back towards the hole in the fence, the flame-wreathed monsters reaching for them. Eddie quickly slung his rifle over one shoulder, unfolding the camping shovel he sharpened religiously. *Old Whacky*, he called it.

"Just run!" Tamsyn shouted, heart in her throat. "There's too many!"

Then a flame shot across the sky, followed by the scream of a jet engine, so close that the catwalk trembled around her. Tamsyn barely had a moment to register that the Americans had found them when the entire horizon burst into flame, the ridge overlooking the refinery erupting into an enormous plume of fire and fury. The force of the explosion shook the gantry dangerously, and Tamsyn fell to her knees. Wincing, she looked up when she heard the unearthly screech as another bomber swung low, dropping a second payload.

Just like that, Foxtrot Company was no more. Forty lives, snuffed out in moments. Tamsyn hadn't been a soldier long, but she knew enough to know that no one could have survived that. Half the company had been in looted farm trucks and sedans, but even the armoured vehicles were nothing but melted slag now.

The entire tree line that Griffin had been hiding in was shattered and burning, and there was zero chance she'd survived the attack. Tamsyn prayed that it had been quick and painless but kept her sorrow at bay for now.

Even after being scattered like bowling pins, the undead barely noticed this earth-shattering cacophony, and the charred corpses continued their inexorable advance on Baxter and Eddie, who lay prone near the tangled ruin of the outer fence.

Tamsyn stared at Eddie, numb to her core, willing him to move.

"Get up! Run!" she screamed, finding her feet. Trembling all over, she stumbled across the catwalk and somehow made it down the stairs, the sudden appearance of a helicopter lending speed to her feet. It was sweeping low over the ridge, a searchlight panning the valley floor on the other side. *They're looking for survivors.* A mini-gun spat out death for a few moments, and then the pilot turned the helicopter towards the refinery.

"Don't you dare be dead, Eddie," Tamsyn sobbed. "GET UP!"

She crossed the yard at a sprint, her hands mechanically placing an arrow onto the bowstring, sending it through a zombie skull as if it was an eggshell. Another zombie had hold of Baxter's leg. Weaving through the maddened pack of dead things, Tamsyn stood on its neck, jamming an arrow tip through its eye socket before it could deliver its infectious bite.

"Get up! Get up now!" she shouted, slapping the groggy men until they were up and moving. They'd survived, but the force of the explosion had shaken them around like cloth dolls. The smouldering monsters clutched at them, snagging equipment belts with their blackened fingers, rotted teeth snapping. Sheer terror drove Tamsyn through the gauntlet of decayed flesh, and she barely noticed the unholy stink, slapping away reaching hands and laying about with her hatchet, crying out when one of them had her braid in its dead grip. A moment later, Eddie drove the edge of his shovel through the bridge of its nose, slicing cleanly through its skull.

One of the things tried to wrestle Tamsyn's bow out of her hand, and she buried the little axe in its forehead, so deep that she had to leave it there. Then, the popping of a pistol, as Baxter lay down a panicked screen of lead in every direction.

You forgot your precious Undeath Act pretty quickly, Tamsyn mused. Fighting their way free of the dead refinery staff, Eddie led the way to the fence. The helicopter had spotted them now, and was swinging around, trying to line up its mini-gun.

If they ran, it would drop them long before they reached the tree line. Three more bodies for the worldwide graveyard, just like that.

"This way!" Tamsyn shouted over the racket of the chopper's rotors, and the three of them ran into the tank farm. The gunner only let off a quick burst in their direction, perhaps fearful of striking the fuel tanks. They turned the chattering weapon against the zombies instead, and after a moment the helicopter began its descent. Tamsyn could hear the barked orders of the enemy soldiers and the pop of small arms fire as they finished the undead.

She started throwing levers and opening hatches on the fuel tanks, and the other two followed her lead. Soon a torrent of fuel was pouring down the drains and spillways, and the stink of manmade diesel was thick in the air.

Tamsyn could see shapes flitting through the yard and knew that the American soldiers were surrounding their position, setting up firing lines and waiting for the Texans to make a stupid move. She knew that a small team would be circling the main sheds now, or climbing up to get a good line of fire, the aim to surround them, cut off any retreat.

"Time to nick off, but first let's deny the supply," she said. "Eddie, gimme your matches."

"I don't have any," he said.

"What?"

"You were on at me to quit the smokes, remember?"

Even as Tamsyn was about to have a conniption, she saw the zombie, somehow missed in the Americans' mop-up of the yard. It stood in the shadows of a fuel tank, mummified flesh still smouldering from her failed firebomb, and with a snarl it strode towards them, sloshing into the fuel.

"Run, by the love of god, run!" Tamsyn yelled. Bullets whistled past them as they ran for safety, and then the fuel caught, and everything was noise and an impossible heat. A hot fist slammed her into the ground, sent her tumbling along like a floppy doll, and for a long moment she lay there, too hurt to even move. When she finally drew a breath the air was hot, the acrid smoke setting her to coughing, her ears still ringing.

A pair of hands, and Eddie was drawing her to her feet. When she could stand unaided and had no obvious injuries he was obviously relieved.

"We've gotta go, love," he said. "There's gonna be more of them, we gotta go."

Nodding, Tamsyn knelt down, freeing her bow from underneath a large sheet of stainless steel. Another man-sized shard of metal stood nearby, with one end driven deep into the asphalt. It had landed only a few metres from where she'd fallen, and she shuddered. She'd stumbled over a lip of concrete just before the explosion, a low apron that served as a retaining wall. This was all that had saved her from certain death.

The refinery looked like a war zone now, and barely anything was still standing. Small fires dotted the wreckage, and a secondary explosion made her flinch. The top half of a metal silo had fallen onto the helicopter, which now resembled a squashed bug.

Gunfire. Tamsyn looked up to see Baxter standing over the body of an American soldier, smoking pistol in his hand. The other man had been trapped under a fallen mess of girders and rubble, his gun just out of his reach. Baxter nodded at Tamsyn and limped over to another wounded soldier, delivering the coup de grace with swift efficiency.

"Looks like surrender is off the table," Tamsyn said. "Let's get the hell out of here."

It was almost five hours before Tamsyn let them rest. The three surviving members of Foxtrot Company were beating a hasty retreat cross-country and did not linger on any of the roads they came across.

If bombers and helicopters had found their temporary camp, then the entire American advance was not far behind it. They'd already been stragglers when retreating in a convoy; now they were on foot, and the Yanks were breathing down their necks.

"They got infrared goggles and satellites and god only knows," Eddie puffed, slumped against a fencepost. "It's just a matter of time."

"Shut it," Tamsyn said. "You've watched too many bad movies. They won't find three people in all that."

She indicated the dense pine forest on the other side of the fence. JORDAN LAKE SUMMER CAMP, a sign indicated.

"Well, get a move on," she managed, herself huffing under the weight of extra guns and ammunition, recently prised from the grips of dead soldiers. "Let's not get caught in the open, with all them helicopters and what-have-you."

In moments they had all their gear across the fence and went up and over the wire, rather than marking their passage by cutting through it with pliers.

The moonlight barely penetrated the thick gloom of the forest, and the only sound was the huffing of the other two men, the soft padding of their boots against the carpet of pine needles. Tamsyn had her bow out and ready. She nervously watched the silent ranks of trees and wondered if they were being watched right now.

A slight sound, and Tamsyn gasped, drew back on the string. She nearly launched an arrow at some nervous forest critter, which leapt from shadow to shadow and disappeared in moments.

"Can't believe you just let our supper nick off," Eddie complained. "I'm sure that Buffalo Bill here knows how to cook varmints and roadkill."

A bark of laughter slipped out of Tamsyn's lips, the happy sound carrying throughout the creaking gloom. Biting her lip, she indicated that everyone stop, and for long moments she listened nervously.

"You're both idiots," Baxter whispered, shaking his head. "Follow me, and shut your damn mouths."

He led them to a hiking path, gravel bound with pine logs, and soon they found themselves in a clearing overlooking a large campground. There were a handful of log dormitories, a cluster of picnic tables and an ablutions block.

Time for the three Fs: Forage, Food and Fuel. It was a constant priority for this new army, drummed into them at basic training, and she knew that once any resident zombies were down, they could have anything useful out and stowed in under fifteen minutes.

They'd lost everything at the refinery. Tamsyn thought of their neat stack of packs and gear, blown to bits under that almost-surgical barrage. They'd salvaged some gear from the dead helicopter squad, but there'd been little in the way of water and food. Certainly nothing in the way of blankets or sleeping bags.

Mostly she missed her boots; the sneakers had turned both feet into blisters, and she wasn't game to peel off her socks to inspect the damage.

We need to find some new kit, or we're going to freeze our hungry arses off tonight, she thought. *Which will also be my fault.*

"Watch your zombie numbers in there," Baxter whispered, pointing to the darkened windows, an open door swinging in the breeze. "The law's the law."

"Who's in charge exactly, Private?" Tamsyn said. He met her practiced glare with quiet contempt.

"You're a joke, lady. You shouldn't be in charge of anything. You won't be, once we get back to our line."

"Good. I don't want to do this job anyway."

"Listen here, you useless bitch. You as good as killed Foxtrot Company, lighting fires and blowing shit up. How else do you think the Yanks found us? Don't think I won't be writing you up."

"Baxter, I—"

"You disobeyed Hennesy's orders, and now good people are dead."

Tamsyn's heart fell into her gut. Stunned, she let Baxter push past her. Eddie followed him down to the cabins, delivering a string of northern-tinged threats and retorts to the Texan.

Baxter is right, she thought numbly. *It was all my fault.*

I killed all of those people.

They found one zombie stuck in the ablutions block, the remains of an old man draped all over a toilet, body broken and mangled beyond any mobility or menace. The lock had snapped; the flimsy door had provided no protection when death came for this poor senior, still wearing the tatters of a Hawaiian shirt.

Eddie gave the snarling corpse a swift spade to the face.

"Resurrect that, you daft tosser," he said to Baxter, while scraping the gore from the shovel's edge against the floor tiles.

"There was a person trapped inside that, soldier," Baxter said, loading his pockets with soap and toilet paper. "But that one was a kindness, I'll give you that much."

"This for your kindness," Eddie said, flipping him the bird. "I change into one of those, put a bloody bullet through my head. The end."

"I'll keep it in mind," Baxter said.

Other survivors had picked over the summer camp at some point in the past, but Eddie found a box of canned beans underneath a tangle of mops, and Tamsyn unearthed a handful of practice arrows in an equipment shed. She figured to do something about the blunted tips later, or swap over the heads from her older arrows, scarred and bent from the numerous times she'd wrenched them free from zombie skulls.

Tamsyn had completely lost command of the trio, but a small part of her did not mind Baxter's unofficial coup. *I don't respect myself, either.* Things seemed to have settled into an uneasy democracy for now, but she tried not to think about what awaited her if they managed to escape.

Exhausted from the forced march, they decided to sleep for a few hours and then push on. Shaking the dust out of an abandoned picnic rug, Tamsyn staked out a top bunk for herself, tucking in her makeshift blanket. She protested weakly when Eddie slid in beside her.

"What does it matter now?" he said. "You can fraternise with me all you want. Texas Ranger in the next cabin won't think any less of you."

Tamsyn let out a heavy sigh, sinking back into his embrace. They lay still for a long, beautiful moment, and Tamsyn could almost forget about the world ending, this war, everything horrible she'd seen since the rules of death changed.

Everything came down to just two incredibly smelly people, who were warm and alive, and Eddie soon made her forget everything else.

"We should just run, love," he whispered into her ear later, startling her from a light doze. "We ditch that other dickhead, and we just desert."

"What about Milly?" Tamsyn said frostily. "You just gonna give up on her?"

She tried not to think about the small photo album left in her pack, no doubt burnt to a crisp. Shot after shot of that gummy smile, a mane of golden curls that was growing by the day. She'd been born on the voyage over from England, and with her parents both dead now, Eddie and Tamsyn had adopted the baby girl.

When their draft papers arrived, they made arrangements to keep Milly back in Corpus Christi. There was a nursery and child-carers in the naval base, but Tamsyn thought base-life would be too much confusion for a ten-month-old. Their neighbours the Andertons had agreed to watch her during their deployment. They'd even taken in Scratch, the old moggy from Salt Flat.

The comforts of home, gone forever.

"I know it sucks, Tamsyn, but we're in serious trouble. We are never going to see the kid again. We'll end up court-martialled, in prison or something. Or in front of a firing squad. We need to survive this."

"I'm sick of surviving, Eddie. I want to live. I want a family, not tinned food and jumping at shadows. I don't care if Texas surrenders, if I'm in military prison for five years, or a POW for twice as long. I won't run."

"We should kill him then," Eddie whispered, licking his lips nervously. "Kill Baxter. That way, we get to tell command what happened to Foxtrot Company, not him."

"We're not going to do that," Tamsyn said, after an uncomfortable moment. *Was I seriously considering that?* she wondered. *Have we become this now?*

"Okay then," Eddie agreed, with a note of false calm. "We may only have to scrub dunnies for a week or something. It's not like Baxter's got a great reputation either. So, it's our word against his then."

"Yes," Tamsyn said, her heart racing. Eddie might well be prepared to commit murder to protect her, but in a dark corner of Tamsyn's soul, she was almost eager to see him do it.

It would be a lot easier if something happened to Baxter, she thought, and then she heard three swift taps at the door. They already had their pistols raised and cocked when the Texan slipped through.

"Put those down, it's just me," Baxter said, cradling the looted rifles in his arms. "I'd suggest you get your pants on, lovebirds. We gotta leave."

"Leave?" Tamsyn said, slowly lowering her pistol and easing on the safety. The guns had been pointed at him for a moment longer than necessary, and Baxter frowned.

He knows, Tamsyn thought.

"I can hear a helicopter making passes somewhere nearby," the Texan said, in a low, calm voice, "and there's military vehicles moving on the main road. They'll probably start searching all the campsites and holiday homes round here soon."

"We'll never make it back to our lines," Eddie said, wriggling into his clothes. "They'll be watching all the roads now. We need to find somewhere to hide, wait them out."

"That's not an option, soldier," Baxter said. "They'll have dogs, MPs, spooks with infrared gear, the works. They're looking for deserters and saboteurs."

"Look, mate, I lived through the downfall of bloody England, and I've had every cop and children's service goon after me since I was a lad. No one ever found me when I was laying low."

"Those are special forces, and you've had three months of basic training. They'll find your fart-filled foxhole within five minutes."

"Well, GI Joe, have you got any bright ideas?" Tamsyn said.

"This," Baxter said, putting the armload of rifles onto a nearby bunk. "We jump the first army truck to come sniffing, just inside the entrance to the park, where the trees press in close to the road. We shoot everything we've got, and then we take the truck."

"That's a shite idea," Eddie scoffed.

"We might be all right until we split away from the convoy, but nicking one of their vehicles can only end in tears," Tamsyn said. "Let's try something else."

She led them down through the log cabins, on the path to the lakeside. Jordan Lake stretched out before them, the silvery water of the vast reservoir drinking up the moonlight.

"They'll see us out there, you moron," Baxter said. "God, tonight they'll be able to see us from space."

Ignoring him, Tamsyn made for a nearby equipment shed, raising a rifle butt to snap the lock. Someone had beaten her to it. The place had been picked over, and good. Sporting equipment lay scattered, and anything resembling any of the three Fs had been taken.

"We gonna play lawn darts with the Navy Seals before they haul us off to Gitmo?" Eddie said, kicking over a box of croquet gear in frustration. "God, that bloody chopper is getting closer by the second!"

Just behind a rack of canoes, Tamsyn spotted the little aluminium runabout on a trailer. There was a lick of fuel still left in the tank. Then she found a large box of something else, and a smile slowly spread across her face.

The American helicopter crew spotted the small motorboat almost immediately, and radioed it in to the two squadrons of armoured cavalry sweeping the area. It was running hard, heading north across the middle of Jordan Lake. The rear of the boat had caught fire, and it lit up on the infrared array like a streaking comet.

The chopper shadowed the boat, painting it with a powerful searchlight, and several vehicles were circling the lake, converging on the places where the troubled vessel was most likely to reach land.

That was when the fireworks started. Catherine wheels erupted from the boat, bottle rockets soared in every direction, and geysers of brilliant sparks spooked the chopper pilot, whose hair-trigger instincts had him convinced that they were under attack. The whirlybird swung away in an evasive manoeuvre while the mini-guns shredded the boat until there was nothing left of it.

With all this going on, no one noticed a canoe overloaded with people and old bicycles, headed directly east. Silent paddles drove them across the lake, hugging close to the side of a causeway. Heading for an intercept on the runaway boat, a passing convoy of trucks failed to even notice them.

"I think the fireworks were a bit much," Eddie said later, as the three escapees pedalled their bone-rattler bicycles cross-country. They hadn't seen another vehicle in hours, and it looked like they'd slipped through the tightening cordon for now.

"It was pretty," Tamsyn puffed, taking in the abandoned fields, the silent farmhouses. "Very romantic here, you know. You'd better bring me back to North Carolina someday."

A few lengths behind them, Baxter pedalled like a metronome, looted weapons strapped to every inch of his bike. He made very sure to keep the other two in sight at all times.

He remembered all too well that long moment that Corporal Webb had kept her pistol levelled at him and had read her face like an open book.

"Just you try it," he muttered to himself.

By dawn they'd reached the outskirts of Benson, exhausted and freezing. They'd ridden over thirty miles. Leaving their bicycles in a tangle, they sat on a lookout above the silent town, quickly sharing a cold tin of beans.

"That's highway 40 there, on the other side of the town," Baxter said, pointing to the curlicue of onramps and connecting roads, the black ribbon running through farmland. "From there it's a straight run over to Cherry Point airfield, our regroup point."

"Might be able to spot some stragglers on the road," Tamsyn said woodenly, as Eddie scanned the highway with his spotting scope. Now that they were closer to safety, she could not shake the threat of Baxter from her mind, of what their superiors would do to her. She'd brought the Yanks down on Foxtrot Company.

If we're going to kill Baxter, it has to be right here, right now, she realised.

Aching from head to toe, Tamsyn rested her head against the stone picnic table. In seconds she had slipped into a light doze. The dream came on almost immediately.

As always, she relived the worst day of her life. She was her teenage self, walking the streets of Gravesend with a trashy magazine in her hands.

She'd seen the car slide around the corner countless times, knew every inch of that rusted fender, the way the blue paint bubbled over the wheel arches, even how Simon Dawes was gripping the steering wheel. But she could not look away; the dream never allowed this. The estate wagon took the turn at high speed, and ploughed into the bus shelter, crumpling it like a beer can.

"Mum!" she cried, and was picking through bodies and blood, looking for the broken figure of her mother. Dead at the hands of a drunk driver, some four years before the end of the world. A clean death.

"Tamsyn," she heard someone say, and the tangle of bus shelter and car had been transported to a desolate beach, a winter sea lapping at the carnage. In the logic of the dream the shift made perfect sense. She flinched when a pair of hands fell onto her shoulders and knew without looking who it was.

"Dad," she said, and her father was hugging her. His chest was still a bloody ruin, here at the Isle of Sheppy, the place where he'd met his meaningless death. His eyes were still and dead, the same way they'd been when someone draped a tarp over him.

"They come back," he said, and pointed to the incongruous car wreck. As the salt water touched the first corpse, it rose jerkily, and then all of the crash victims were sloshing forward through the pink froth. Even her mother returned to unlife, thrashing about and snapping her teeth from where she lay, trapped beneath the car.

"There's more to come," and Mal pointed again. Just beyond the wreck, she could see a string of figures, slowly moving along the beach. Undead. Coffin-dodgers, zombies, rank upon rank of the walking corpses. She could recognise her neighbours from Gravesend, broken figures that howled at her with animal fury, shambling towards her. In real life, she'd led an enormous horde to a weak point in their barricade, dooming the town. Tamsyn saw these faces nearly every time she closed her eyes.

"There's more," Mal Webb said, and pointed. A pair of ships had appeared just offshore, an old cargo ship and a superyacht. Tamsyn recognised the *Paraclete* and the *Petty Cash*, their means of escape from England. Struggling through the waves, howling in agony as the salt water licked at their unnatural flesh, all of the people who'd died under her watch came for her.

Then another group of bodies, this one marching in step. The remains of Foxtrot company, charred bodies that were more shadow than shape, slowly blowing apart in the sea breeze.

It's just a dream, Tamsyn told herself. *Wake up.*

"Still more," her dad said, and held her tightly as more of the dead crowded close, brushing at her with their rot-purpled fingers. Old friends, Naomi and Marcus Riley, riddled with bullets. Poor Ali, smiling and chattering wordlessly at her, his slender arms and legs missing big chunks of flesh. Then Clem Murray and Simon Dawes arrived, somewhere between life and death. Re-Humans, the lucky ones who'd been dosed with salt. They put a bow and a single arrow in her hands, one with a big barbed tip.

"He's one man," Mal Webb said, and guided Tamsyn away from the press of the undeath, to a quieter part of the beach. There, standing to attention and looking out to the sea, stood Baxter, every inch of him projecting a calm confidence, even irritating her in this dream.

"There's going to be a lot more," Mal continued, his dead fingers digging hard into her shoulders. He looked as if he wanted to say more, but couldn't frame the words, or something was preventing him from saying something.

Tamsyn tried to break free from his grip. She saw that the hazy strip of sand and water was now filled with thousands of dead people, a clamouring crowd that cried and moaned and pointed to Tamsyn.

There was a dead woman near the front, and she cradled a small figure, a mess of golden curls poking out of a blanket, and Tamsyn thought she was going to be sick when she realised that a dead thing was holding little Milly.

"No, please, let her go," she cried, trying to fight her way forward, praying that the toddler was still alive, wasn't rotting like everyone that pressed around her, wailing and calling out her name.

"He's just one man," Mal pleaded, dragging her towards Baxter, fingers digging, twisting. "They all end up on the beach."

"Dad, no!" Tamsyn cried out, and then she was sitting up groggily on the concrete bench, Eddie shaking her shoulder.

He looked at her sympathetically. Tamsyn knew he'd heard a lot of nightmares coming from her side of the bed, but he never pried. She loved the man dearly, but there were some secrets she would never be able to tell him.

"A jeep, one of ours," he said. "We need to move."

He stood behind her, wrapping her in his arms and giving her a quick squeeze, reassuring Tamsyn more than his clumsy words could ever manage. He handed her the spotting scope.

"Look for a garage, just near that turn-off from the highway. Two of our blokes, having some sort of trouble with their ride."

Tamsyn adjusted the focus until she could clearly see the garage. A jeep was parked in front of the gas pumps, bonnet up and steam everywhere. A Texan soldier was fiddling with the engine, while the other one was using a metal rod to lift the lid of the underground gas tank, siphoning hose uncoiled nearby.

"Damnit. Whole town's come out to welcome them," Tamsyn said. Hundreds of shapes were moving through the streets of Benson, the relentless ant march pattern showing they were anything but alive as the horde converged on the lone garage.

Baxter was already up and sitting on his bicycle at the entrance to the car park, watching them suspiciously. Tamsyn noticed that he'd strapped a pistol to his handlebars, and that his fingers were never far from the hilt.

"After you," he said. "I insist."

Sharing a brief look with Eddie, Tamsyn pushed her bike forward, peddling with her exhausted, shaky legs. Soon the road itself dipped down towards the town, and gravity took over.

"Look out!" Eddie shouted, and a bulk stepped out from a bush and onto the road, reaching for her. Rotten meat wrapped in plaid and reflective orange hunting gear, and a snarling face that was little more than a skull wrapped in cracked leather.

Tamsyn dodged the dead hunter at the last second, but nearly lost control on the down slope, her front wheel shaking with the speed wobbles. The zombie turned and roared defiantly, just before Eddie raced by, knocking it over with a swift kick to the backside.

"That one's for Bambi!" he shouted.

Other figures were stepping out from the woods here and there, the remains of farmers and other hunters. Closer to town, the going got scary. Weaving through the scattered groups of monsters, the bicycling soldiers powered around the edges of the dead town.

"Idiots!" Baxter said when they heard the rapid popping of small-arms fire. The noise drew more of the zombies out onto the streets, and soon the trio were forced to cut through parks and up onto the sidewalks.

Just when Tamsyn was convinced that her muscles would finally freeze up, the garage came into sight. One of the soldiers was holding off perhaps a dozen of the resurrected town-folk, waving his dog-catcher like a man possessed. The other man was holding a carbine, raising the gun in panic, lowering it again, setting off a single shot when a zombie got too close to the jeep for comfort.

"Where in the hell did y'all come from?" the soldier said with disbelief when he noticed the three bicycle-riding Texans. Another zombie reached for him, and he cracked it across the head with his rifle stock.

"We're the cavalry," Tamsyn shouted, popping a wheelie. "Yeehaw."

The man fighting to code had just gone down screaming, dragged underneath a tide of dead hands, slavering red mouths diving down in the press to suckle on the living man's flesh.

"Are they still people, Baxter?" Tamsyn said coldly, snapping off a burst of semi-automatic fire into the knot of writhing bodies. Face set tightly, the Texan joined in, emptying a clip into the feeding frenzy, and then he stood aside, picking off the next wave of death as it walked towards them.

"You, Private, is there anyone else coming?" Tamsyn asked the terrified soldier, jamming a fresh clip into her assault rifle. Baxter was picking off stragglers as they approached the garage, but a mob of dead townsfolk was getting close now, almost two hundred rotters stumbling down the main road from Benson.

"Far as I know, ma'am, we're the last ones," the Texan said, hands shaking as he checked the action on his weapon. "Americans bombed the rest of our squad, everyone else bought it 'cept for me and—and Tod there."

Eddie emerged from the garage shop, his shovel dripping with gore. He had something draped around his neck, and Tamsyn recognised a fan belt.

"Tam, get some water. We need to clean up this mess," Eddie said, dumping a fistful of spanners onto the tarmac around the hood. "Hey mate, see what gas you can tease outta those tanks there. This car is leaving in five minutes, or we don't leave."

Emptying a full clip into the approaching mob, Baxter tossed the empty gun and readied one of the looted weapons, sliding a grenade into the under-barrel launcher. He sent the canister spiralling into that press of grey flesh, and a moment later the explosion came, like God's fat hand slapping at the earth.

A wall of flesh fell, and then slowly rose again.

"It didn't work!" Baxter shouted, firing another grenade. Perhaps a handful of the zombies were too damaged to continue, but the rest came on relentlessly, even with their bodies shredded to pieces and full of metal. The grenade had blown off some limbs, but the dead felt nothing and dragged themselves forward.

Tamsyn found a bucketful of scummy water with a squeegee in it and lugged it to the jeep. She saw that they'd had an accident, a bad one. The bonnet and grille were buckled and wet with a foul slime, a cloud of flies already forming around the site of the impact. It stank like a knackery.

"Oh god, that's disgusting." Tamsyn gagged.

Every inch of the engine bay was slick with gore, and bits of brain and flesh were still baking on the overheated motor. Whatever they'd hit had passed through the radiator fan and been shredded instantly. Everything was coated with a fine layer of jellied death.

"Wash all that shit off now," Eddie shouted from her elbow, and it took the report of another grenade to jar her into action. Fighting back her bile, Tamsyn sluiced the water all over everything, washing bits of bone and chunks of rotten flesh onto the ground below.

"Be careful, don't get it on the distributor cap," Eddie said. "That thing there, with the wires? Don't get it wet."

"We didn't see it," the rattled soldier said to no one in particular. "It stepped out from behind some junked tanker, about a mile back. We just—we pulverised that thing."

"Snap out of it, man, and go get me some bloody fuel!" Eddie shouted. "Well, this is a right mess. Fan belt's snapped, there's a hole in this radiator hose, and I can't even see what's going on with these leads."

"Eddie, we can't drive this," Tamsyn said. "We need another car."

"Do you think any of these other junkers will even turn over now? They've been sat around for years. Trust me, love, it's this jeep or it's nothing."

Cursing, Tamsyn rejoined Baxter, who was leaning across the bonnet of an abandoned SUV, letting off careful bursts of semi-automatic fire. He dropped a zombie almost every time, but it wasn't nearly enough. She lay all of her guns on the bonnet in front of her, passing Baxter a banana clip when his M16 ran dry.

"I'm not that good with guns," Tamsyn admitted. "And I don't have enough arrows to make any difference here."

"So shoot anyway. You can't miss, not from this close."

Tamsyn took up an M4 carbine and tried to hold it steady in the face of that slow, grey advance. She hit collarbones and bone-exposed chests, only getting one clean headshot before emptying the gun. She missed Griffin at that moment most of all – the sniper could have dropped half of that crowd with a peashooter.

"Eddie reckons he can get the jeep going, but I've seen it, it's completely mangled," she said, assembling and stringing her bow. "Baxter, we might not be making it out of here."

"I don't do confessions," Baxter said. Licking his lips, he changed the gun's setting to full automatic, the thunderous chatter of the weapon ending any further attempt at conversation.

Twelve broadhead hunting arrows, she tallied, mentally discounting the other blunted target arrows as little use. Leaving the guns with Baxter, she fell back towards the jeep, sending arrows into undead skulls with complete accuracy.

"C'mon!" she heard Eddie say, and a dropped wrench clattered against the cement. The engine of the Jeep whined briefly but did not turn over.

It seemed ridiculous to Tamsyn that her life was about to end like this. There'd be no more running, the way her body felt after days of physical abuse, days without sleep. She knew she wouldn't even get her bike to move. The zombies were close enough that

Tamsyn could clearly see their hate-filled faces, more than a hundred still up and walking despite everything she and Baxter could throw at them.

Tamsyn thought it might be easier just to lie down and wait for it, to let her aching limbs finally rest, but the thought of being pulled apart by dead hands made her shudder. The weight of the pistol on her hip gained an awful significance. *Nine bullets. Only gonna need four of 'em.*

Feeling an odd sense of composure, she returned to the jeep, to see Eddie madly wrestling with something under the hood. Despite their imminent deaths, the nameless Texan soldier was carefully pouring a bucketful of fuel into the tank.

"Eddie, just leave it," she said, and he looked up from the mangled engine, met her eyes.

"I've got it, love," he told her, but she shook her head.

"I don't want to spend my last moments passing spanners and arguing with you. Come over here, sit down with me," she said calmly. She sat cross-legged on the ground, putting her bow to one side. She reached for the leather snap holding her pistol in its holster.

"Oh no, Tam. No. Get up, love, we're going now."

"I can't run anymore, Eddie. We need to...take care of each other."

Exasperated, Eddie threw up his hands and returned to the jeep. Leaning through the window, he turned a key, and the engine coughed into a rough-sounding life.

"If my old man saw how I'd missed those loose sparkplug leads, he'd have belted me one. I told you, girl, I can fix things. Get up. Get up, we're going!"

Shaking all over, Tamsyn gathered up her things. She slid into the passenger side of the jeep, Eddie already gunning the gas before the doors were even closed. The bonnet was too twisted to close and flapped about like a gore-streaked tongue.

"Wait, what about your friend?" the Texan soldier shouted from the backseat. Baxter was perhaps a handful of steps now from the maddened horde, a barking pistol in either hand.

"He's not my friend," Eddie said, bouncing the vehicle over a stack of brutalised corpses as he made for the highway. Over her shoulder Tamsyn could see Baxter running after them, betrayal and horror written across his face.

"What the hell is going on here?" said the strange soldier in the backseat, staring at them in shock, a nervous sweat beading across his forehead. "They're gonna eat him. You can't leave him! You can't do this!"

What have we become? Tamsyn thought, wrestling with her conscience. *Baxter might put us in prison, but he's still a person. Where does it end? Do we have to kill this poor bloke too?*

This isn't right.

"Stop it," Tamsyn said. "Stop the damn car, Eddie."

"Of course," he said, jumping on the brakes. "I was just having a lend of you folks. You know how much I like to joke."

"Right," Tamsyn said. "There's your punchline in the rear-view mirror, the one who's about to murder us."

The other soldier opened the back door, and Baxter threw himself into the jeep, fury written across his face.

"Have a nice run, mate?" Eddie said. "Did you remember to pick up some ciggies on your way? I'm dying for a puff."

It took Tamsyn, the other soldier, and finally a waved pistol to hold Baxter back. He retreated into a sullen silence, face a thunderhead as the zombies became small specks on the road behind them, and then finally vanished from sight.

They reached the Texan rearguard sometime after lunch. The jeep's wounded engine gave little more than a death rattle by the time they limped past the anti-aircraft guns and mobile SAM batteries. They were jammed into the last troop transport and ferried south at top speed.

A sign indicated that "MCAS Cherry Point" was the next turnoff, but the truck did not slow, weaving through the knots of abandoned cars as it stuck to the main highway south.

"Sir, I thought that was our evac," Tamsyn said to the Staff Sergeant sitting next to her, noting the bloodstained sling holding a shattered arm against his old USMC uniform. "LYNCH" read a name tag above the badly restitched Texan flag.

"Cherry Point's gone," Lynch said. "Our guys got three of their birds, but the place has been bombed to shit. We're regrouping near Wilmington."

Jesus, we've almost lost North Carolina too, Tamsyn thought. Eddie was blissfully snoring away in a corner, but Baxter was still awake, a flicker of hatred flashing across his face when their eyes met.

The stories that man is going to tell about us, she thought, her heart sinking. *Still, at least I'll be able to sleep at night—in prison.*

Slumped uncomfortably on the bench seat, Tamsyn slipped once more into an exhausted doze. The dream came on almost immediately, and she found herself alone in the back of the transport, sitting across from her dead parents.

Her mother was as she'd appeared in the open casket, a miracle of the undertaker's craft. It wasn't her favourite dress, but it had a high enough neck to shield most of the damage from the accident. She made as if to speak to Tamsyn, but stitching still held her mouth closed, and she could only murmur, gesturing wildly as she tried to make herself understood to her living daughter, eyes wide and crazed. Tamsyn's dad held his wife close, patted her arm until her thrashing ceased, and she slumped back into his arms, defeated.

"You couldn't do it," her dad said. Thick clumps of blood and sand were stuck to his damp windbreaker, and something moved within the ruin of his chest—perhaps a lung inflating.

"I'm not a killer, Dad."

"No one sets out to be," he murmured. "Shame. Things won't go easy for you now."

"I don't want easy, Dad. I want what's right."

He nodded, and for a moment they sat in a companionable silence. In the logic of the dream, the rocking of the truck became the constant roll of a boat, and then were walking the silent decks of the *Paraclete*, the cargo boat pushing through a impossible sea of dead flesh, dwarfed by icebergs of frozen blood.

They were alone on the silent deck, and Mal Webb herded his daughter through a corridor lined with blinking lightbulbs, toward the stairs that led to the bridge. She knew, without a doubt, that Baxter was up there, hands clenched around the steering wheel.

"Who's driving the boat, Tam? Who's the captain?"

"I am," she said, and the troop transport went over a heavy bump, stirring her from slumber.

"We're here, kids," Staff Sergeant Lynch said. "Welcome to the new home of Echo Company."

The transport was cutting across a rolling green field, heading to a series of large buildings spread out in the middle of this. The overgrown grass eventually ended in a marsh, and dozens of McMansions could be seen beyond this, blending into a neatly cultivated tree line.

There were neat access roads cutting across the grassy field, but the transport took the most direct path. A stray zombie emerged from a lonely stand of conifers, but the transport steered around it, and the creature wailed at the noise, doggedly trailing the truck.

They landed on a gravel drive, wheels spinning as the driver made for a large sandstone manor. Dozens of army vehicles were parked up against a service door, and a bucket-chain of uniforms was porting in equipment and supplies as quickly as could be managed.

"ST JAMES PLANTATION – COUNTRY CLUB" read a tasteful metal sign.

"You cannot be serious," Tamsyn scoffed. "Are we here to knock in the back nine or something?"

"Negative, Corporal," Lynch said. "This is not a golf course. This is a secure location, with open sightlines in every direction. Not even the Major gets a game in here."

The troop truck rolled to a stop, and somebody popped the back gate. Groaning and stiff from the ride, the soldiers filed out of the bench seats, milling around on the driveway and waiting for orders.

"Listen up, everybody," Lynch boomed in his best parade-ground voice, and the soldiers snapped to attention, falling into line. "We've got five minutes to stow all materiel and vehicles. If the Yanks can see it, they can bomb it. Form a bucket brigade; get every last bullet in through those doors. You two, grab those rakes there, and sweep that gravel. Make those tire marks invisible. I do not want a single stone out of place—am I understood?"

"Yes, Sergeant!" they shouted, and got to work. Pointing Eddie towards the stack of gear, Tamsyn followed the Staff Sergeant, waiting for a chance to speak to him privately. Baxter was already in the human chain, handling guns and cartons with swift efficiency.

Smug bastard. Look at that smirk, Tamsyn thought. *He knows he's got us over a barrel. I'm gonna have to get my side of the story straight, and fast.*

"Why are you not lugging crates, Corporal?" Lynch demanded when he saw her.

"I need to know what's going to happen to my team," she asked. "Our company is toast, and we don't know who to report to now."

"Well, princess, that means you just became my personal property," he said, leaning in close and barking into her face. "Get your arse back into that line and move that shit like it's ticking. Am I understood?"

Jeez, he was much nicer on the truck, she thought, wincing as somebody threw a crate of rations at her.

True to plan, everything was under cover within minutes. Soon after that, the only vehicles visible on the country club grounds were the long-abandoned golf carts. Tamsyn and Eddie were next put to work indoors, where they joined a team swiftly covering every pane of glass with plastic or cardboard.

"Blackout rules," Lynch shouted. "If so much as a hint of light leaks out, you'll all be eating and shitting in the dark, so help me God."

"Where's Baxter?" Eddie whispered, handing Tamsyn another roll of masking tape. "I swear, if that little weasel–"

"Quiet," Tamsyn warned, pasting newspapers over a frosted door panel. Lynch was nearby, taking umbrage with the placement of some blackout sheeting, finally tearing the plastic down with his good arm.

"We should have left Baxter behind," Eddie said when the coast was clear. "I love you, but you're daft. He's singing like a canary now."

"Honestly, two days on your own and it's all Lord of the Flies in your thick head," Tamsyn said. "I can't believe you nearly talked me into–into that."

"We're in a different world now, Tam," Eddie said. "Maybe you're not hard enough yet, but you need to start thinking like me. Survival isn't always nice and neat."

Tamsyn thought of Milly's gummy smile and wondered if they'd allow a toddler into a military prison. By the time they got out, Milly might even be a young woman, might not remember the people who'd spooned muck into her face for a short while.

Maybe it's best if she forgets us, Tamsyn thought, and her heart ached more than the rest of her.

Only the officers were allowed to bed down in the comfort of the members' guest rooms. Rank and file had to make do with camp beds and sleeping bags, and the dining hall was transformed into an impromptu dormitory. Perhaps two hundred men and women playing cards by lantern-light and talking softly if at all.

"There's Baxter," Eddie whispered, nodding in the direction of the first aid station. The Texan was playing poker with a group of MPs and smiled when he noticed the pair watching him.

"Well, he's not stupid," Tamsyn said, yawning. "We'll face the music in the morning, I guess. Promise me one thing."

"What's that?"

"You get to scrub the shittiest toilets."

Staff Sergeant Lynch came for them shortly after reveille, accompanying a Lieutenant with the gold shoulder cord of an aide-de-camp. Tamsyn's stomach fell down somewhere near her new boots, and she stood to attention behind the sack of potatoes she was peeling.

"Fall in, Corporal Webb," Lynch said. "The Major wants to have a word with you. You too, Private."

They left the ground floor of the club, passing a pair of soldiers who guarded the broad curve of the staircase. The guest wing of the manor was opulent, and Tamsyn longed to find the nearest feather bed and throw herself into it. Opened doors revealed officers talking over maps. Runners scurried from door to door with messages.

For a moment Tamsyn considered the absence of MPs–if she was under arrest, they'd be frog-marching her through these halls. But sneaking a quick glance at the grim face of Lynch didn't give her any more confidence. Something had quite recently pissed this man off.

They passed a generator puttering away in the corridor, and Tamsyn noted the fat bundle of power cords running through a new hole in the drywall.

"In here," Lynch said, knocking on the door with his good hand. The door opened, and the Lieutenant shepherded Tamsyn and Eddie inside. He closed the door behind him.

It was an enormous luxury suite, transformed into a command centre. Comms equipment was stacked all over the period furniture, and the other aides were getting into each other's way. Cases lay open on the king-sized bed, and an aide was zipping some spare uniforms into a suit bag.

They just got here, but they're packing everything up, Tamsyn realised, watching as a communications officer was winding up cords, breaking down his equipment for transportation. Aides were stowing computer gear into ruggedized containers, adding these to a growing pile just inside the doorway.

A thickset man in immaculate Air Force blue looked up from a table covered in scattered documents, frowning. His name tag proclaimed him to be MAJOR HOWLETT, just above a thick block of campaign ribbons.

"You're Corporal Webb," he said. Tamsyn stood as still as a rod, praying that she'd get out of this lightly, knowing that she wouldn't.

"I've had a very interesting conversation with one Private Baxter," Howlett said, walking around the table, getting right into her personal space. He began to count off a list on his fingers. "Seems you disobeyed a direct order from your LT. You brought the hammer down on your own people. You threatened your subordinates at gunpoint. You failed to rein in Private Jacobs here while he was bullying Baxter. He was under your watch, Corporal, so you might as well have done it yourself."

The Major leaned against the table, arms crossed.

"Fraternising with your subordinates. Breaching the Undeath Act so many times that you should be locked up forever. Should I go on?"

Tamsyn knew it was a rhetorical question, and kept her mouth shut.

"You're a disgrace to the uniform. God alone knows why Hennesy gave you a field promotion. If I wanted to, I could have you in front of a firing squad for what you did to Foxtrot Company."

As she heard him say the words, Tamsyn thought she was going to wet herself and faint. Her knees felt like they would buckle at any moment.

"So," the Major said, staring her down. "I've spent much of last night and this morning on the phone to Command, figuring out what to do with you and your boyfriend here. I trust you appreciate that I've got much better things to do, given that I'm retreating an entire company?"

"Yes, sir," she said. Eddie was quietly hyperventilating next to her. She could smell his panic. Tamsyn knew from bitter experience that he did not handle authority well, and it was only a matter of time until he did something stupid.

Don't you dare, Eddie, she thought, watching the various aides packing up the suite. All of them wore sidearms.

"Turns out this situation went right up to the top. President Feickert herself was briefed on this, and I've received my orders here," Howlett said, picking up a piece of paper from the desk. Tamsyn wondered if it was an order for their execution, signed by the boss lady herself.

"Seems the Commander in Chief knows you," he said. "Why would Clarice Feickert even remember a scruffy little Brit who likes to make my life hard?"

"I—I did a job for her, sir, back at Corpus Christi," Tamsyn said. *Fetching a truckload of salt that saved her career. A suicide mission that killed two of my mates.*

"It must be nice to have powerful friends," Howlett said, handing her the piece of paper. He'd been gripping it so tightly that the edges were crumpled. "Looks as if you'll live to see sunset. Here are the details of your new assignment."

Tamsyn quickly scanned the document, blinking with disbelief. Howlett watched her with something approaching disgust. He rested his hand on top of his holstered pistol, tapping his fingers against the butt.

...new rank of Captain, effective immediately... officer-in-charge of 6th Requisition Platoon... second-in-command of Echo Company...

Holy shit.

"I am going to dispute this, Webb. I am taking my senior officers and flying to Corpus Christi immediately. When that mad bitch is finally impeached, I will be back, and I will put you in the ground. Now, both of you, get the hell out of my room."

"Sir," Tamsyn said, her throat tight and dry. "I—I didn't ask for this. What am I meant to do?"

"Whatever you want," Howlett growled. "The President just made you my second-in-command, so the moment my ass is up in the air, you're in charge. Lieutenant, show these people outside."

The aide herded them towards the door, and they were efficiently deposited out in the corridor. The door began to close, but Major Howlett reappeared, clearly not done with her.

"One more thing, Captain Webb. I'll be coming back in a day or two to arrest you, so here's your orders: sit tight. Try not to get anyone else killed. That is all."

12

T amsyn watched as the helicopter cleared the treeline. Flying low, it made for the south and Texas, as fast as its pilot could push it.

"If you're lucky, the Yanks will just blow him out of the sky," Eddie said from her elbow. They were in Howlett's room, looking out through the only window not covered in plastic sheeting.

"I'm not lucky," Tamsyn said, fidgeting in her new uniform. Lynch had scrounged a uniform jacket that was almost in her size, and a set of captain's bars from someone too dead to need them.

"He's taken almost everything, ma'am," Staff Sergeant Lynch said, and she found his passive-aggressive obedience a refreshing change from being screamed at. "Most of the comms gear is gone too. There's still a couple of sat phones, radios they were going to junk anyway, nothing that's much use."

"Was that our only helicopter?"

Lynch nodded.

Eddie added a battered laptop with a cracked screen to the meagre pile of electronics on the table in front of her, but it wouldn't even start up. Howlett's people had stripped the room like locusts, and this was all they'd left her with to run Echo Company.

Not that I'll be in charge for long, she mused.

A dozen small problems landed in front of her within the first hour. The cistern water from the indoor toilets was needed for drinking, so latrines had to be dug, out of sight from aerial surveillance.

A group of soldiers had been busted raiding one of the country club's many bars and needed to be given a punishment detail. Tamsyn put them to work on digging the latrines and ordered that the booze be shared amongst the officers.

A patrol had finally caught and brought in the lone zombie, which had once been a groundskeeper. As Company Commander, Tamsyn was provisionally allowed to approve Article 8 kills, but ordered that the infected corpse be given the salt treatment and resurrected into a Re-Human.

"God knows I'm in enough strife when it comes to bloody zombies," she muttered to herself.

"You're just like King Solomon today," Eddie said with a broad smile, appreciating a tumbler full of neat scotch. He wore the gold braid of an aide around one shoulder—she didn't know if she was allowed to hand out new ranks, but Lynch advised that she could appoint anyone as an aide-de-camp, for the short time she was running things.

"It's not the way things are usually done, ma'am," he said, looking at Eddie's bare sleeve with something between disbelief and contempt. "But you're in charge for now. What you say goes."

When she'd finally had enough of the day-to-day running of the base, she ordered everyone out except for Eddie and Lynch. She raised an operator on the sat phone, and after about half an hour of speaking to underlings and political staffers, she finally got President Feickert on the line.

"Tamsyn, this will need to be quick," Feickert said brusquely, her trademark homespun charm completely dispensed with. "I've just come out of a meeting with Command, and they are crucifying me in there. You don't need me to tell you that things aren't going well."

"I'm sorry to bother you, Madam President, but I'm in big trouble," Tamsyn said, and quickly filled her in on the events of that morning, and what Howlett intended to do.

"Well, that explains what that maniac is doing back here, bothering all my people. If he wants to get his bosses to impeach me, well, he can join the damn queue."

Feickert let out a long breath, and Tamsyn could just picture the woman on the other end of the line, pacing around in a cloud of cigarette smoke and perfume. Clarice Feickert was a career politician, immaculately dressed and made-up at all times, the figurehead of a failed rebellion.

"Now listen good, sweetie. I don't trust anyone in a uniform right now, so it was important that I have someone on the ground that I can rely on. Your name came up on that other report, so I pulled some strings."

"About that, Madam President, I–"

"Not important. Do this for me, and we'll call it quits, 'kay?" If they'd been talking face to face, she knew that Feickert would have lightly patted her shoulder, smiling and making her feel like the only person that mattered.

Damn politicians and their fake bullshit. She doesn't even need to be in the room to pull that move off.

"There's been some problems with Echo Company," Feickert said. "I don't have time to go into things, but I've seen some things that Command didn't want me reading. Let's just leave it at that."

Tamsyn realised that someone else was in the room with Feickert, listening in on the conversation.

"6th Requisition Platoon is your baby now, so you look after those folks, you hear me?" Feickert said in a low voice. "I want everyone home in one piece. Everyone."

"I'll do my best," Tamsyn said, mystified. *What is Feickert up to?* "When's the evac?"

"Command have sourced a bunch of small boats. To spread the risk around, keep things safer if the bombers spot you. But the flotilla isn't leaving yet, not till the brass agrees to do the right thing."

"What–what's the hold up?"

"I am the hold-up," Feickert said. "I'm C-in-C, and I'm not letting these bastards leave anyone behind. We cannot let our citizens fall into enemy hands. Tamsyn, I've–I've got to go."

The line went dead.

"Trouble in paradise?" Eddie laughed.

"I don't know what the hell is going on, but I need to see the 6th Requisition Platoon right away. Lynch, where do I find them?"

Lynch checked a clipboard. "Seems the man you are replacing has taken the 6th to the beach for a swim. Yep, says they're swimming."

"Our requisition crew has just–just gone to the beach? We deserve to lose this war," Tamsyn grumbled. "All right, let's go."

Howlett's staff car was still stored in the underground car park, fuelled up and good to go. Lynch stormed around the clubrooms and found Howlett's driver on the winning end of a poker game.

"A stupid man just talked himself out of a cushy job and into digging shitters," Lynch said, tossing the keys to Eddie. "Be an aide and drive."

After their nightmare journey in the tainted jeep, the Lexus rolled along the quiet streets of the country club like a dream, purring through the surrounding resort. Eddie nudged a zombie that got too close, but most of the infected were stuck behind high walls, and no one parked on the streets around here. The roads were clear, and the luxury sedan stayed on the tarmac where it belonged.

They followed the sweep of the main road, and it took them straight to the coast. Tamsyn saw the brilliant sparkle of the water and could have wept for joy. After months of privation and marching, she also found herself wanting to ditch everything to go hang out on the beach.

"Perhaps we'll let the other platoons come down too, on a roster or something," she said. "Could be good for morale, give our people some fresh air."

"If you say so, ma'am," Lynch said.

Eddie took the car to the edge of a boat ramp and killed the engine just short of the sand, next to a pair of Humvees. One of the vehicles was mounted with a large turret, bristling with missile pods and a huge machine gun.

"That Avenger isn't on our materials list," Lynch said, flicking through his clipboard. "Looks like the Major kept that one quiet."

Hundreds of shapes could be seen wading out into the water, and a row of soldiers paced the shore watchfully.

"Something's not right," Eddie said. The soldiers wore the white helmets and armbands of MPs, and some had their guns out. Someone was taking too long to get into the water, and a pair of MPs frog-marched the laggard forward, hurling them into the spray.

"Okay, this shit has to end," Tamsyn said, popping the door. Instantly the sound washed over her, and at first she thought it was gulls.

The people in the water were screaming. Howling as if in absolute agony, the swimmers were in obvious misery. Whenever they tried to come out, the MPs would force them back out into the water.

"Stop it, stop this instant!" Tamsyn said, struggling with an MP who had pinned someone to the sand, and was kicking them hard enough to break ribs. "You let that person go."

The MP turned, the smart retort dying when he saw Tamsyn's rank. The other MPs were gathering to confront the intruder, and Tamsyn felt quite vulnerable until Eddie and Lynch appeared at her side.

"It's not a person, ma'am," the MP said.

She looked down and saw what had actually been knocked into the sand, realised it wasn't a human prisoner. Still weeping and soaking wet, its uniform in tatters, a zombie slowly climbed to its knees.

It looked up at Tamsyn with intelligence and sorrow in its eyes, and she realised she was actually face to face with a Re-Human. A resurrected zombie, dosed with the painful salt treatment, all memory and free will returned to it.

The same went for every single figure in the water. Hundreds of Re-Humans, forced out to swim in the only thing that could cause them pain. Saltwater felt like acid to the undead.

"What in the hell is going on here?" said a lieutenant, puffing across the beach to the gathering of soldiers. "You're letting those rotten motherfuckers climb out of the sea! I—"

Underneath a ridiculous fuzz of moustache, his mouth hung open when he realised who had appeared. He stood to attention. LT RIGBY, his name tag read.

"Ma'am, we've nearly finished giving them their dose. We'll have the 6th out and foraging in approximately ten minutes."

"Their dose?" she said, somewhat horrified.

"We need to give the Re-Humans a daily dose of salt, or the procedure will reverse itself," Rigby said. "We've got a small supply of the stuff, but whenever we're near saltwater we go with the free option."

The Re-Humans were slowly retreating out of the water, and the first ones to emerge were obviously shaken, weakened by the ordeal. They weren't going to be running off anytime soon.

"Damn expensive, running this outfit," Lieutenant Rigby continued. "If it wasn't for how much stuff these dead bastards bring in, I'd keep my salt, let 'em turn wild again."

"And what do these 'dead bastards' bring in?" Tamsyn said, an edge of frost to her voice.

"Everything," Rigby said. "The wild zombies don't even touch them. They can go anywhere, and fetch anything. Wherever there's a heavily overrun location, we send in the 6th, and they come back with toilet rolls, bleach, whatever we need."

"I suppose we should be grateful to them, then."

"Hardly. They're freaks, ma'am. Dead bodies with minds. They should be thankful that we keep them 'alive,' seems fair to me that they earn their keep."

"You know I'm here to replace you, correct?"

"Yes, ma'am," Lieutenant Rigby said. "Can't say as I mind. They're hard to keep in line sometimes, some get all uppity and talk back, you know? Dunno if it was right to bring these things back from the dead."

"Finally, something we can agree on," Tamsyn said. "So take your thugs, and get the hell away from my platoon."

"Ma'am, with all due respect, these things don't have rights," he said, hands raised. "I–I can't just leave you here without any protection. They can still give you the bite, and then you'll be infected."

"Yet none of them have bitten you or your Gestapo here, so what does that tell you? Just fuck off already."

"Well, I sure hope you enjoy playing with your new friends, ma'am," Lieutenant Rigby said, shaking his head as he headed back to the Hummer. "I wouldn't bother remembering their names, if I were you."

She waited until the Lieutenant and his carload of MPs were up the road and out of sight, and led Eddie and Lynch to where the crowd of dead things sat around on the sand, eyes downcast. One or two were still weeping, their companions comforting them.

"Biggest platoon I ever saw," Lynch mused. "There's gotta be almost five hundred of the things. Enough to be their own company."

"What's the difference?" Tamsyn asked.

"If they're a platoon, Major Howlett still gets to be in charge. He's fudged the figures on this little outfit."

The smell was unbelievable. Even though the repeated exposure to salt had cured their skin, the Re-Humans stank like a thousand wet dogs wrapped in garbage.

"Listen up," Tamsyn said, hoping her voice would carry over the pound of surf. "My name is Captain Webb, and I'm in charge of you now."

They watched her carefully, but none of them spoke. Some of the Re-Humans were in pretty bad shape, and Tamsyn wondered if any of the damage had been inflicted under Howlett's watch. From the defeated looks they were giving her, they simply assumed that she was their new gaoler, and that a new regime of cruelty was about to commence.

"No one's going to abuse you anymore," she said. "You follow orders, you'll get your treatments. If you don't want to be treated, you can leave. Right now. I'll let you walk off and you can go wild, if that's what you want."

None of the Re-Humans moved. One the revenants coughed up an entire stomach-load of saltwater, and Tamsyn was pretty sure the horrific sound would keep her awake at nights.

"I'm guessing you've already had folks desert during missions, correct? So, you're all here because you want to be. You get your treatments, and you get to be alive. Kind of."

"If you can call it living," said a familiar voice, a Re-Human that was being supported by another, moving painfully and slowly forward.

"Clem Murray," Tamsyn said with a smile. "Of all the places I expected to see you."

"Young lady, they could not keep me away from the action," the leathery old corpse rasped through a smile. "They hardly needed to round us up at gunpoint, I'd have signed up willingly."

"You're working for me now, Dr. Murray. Come with me, we'll get your things."

"I don't own anything," he said. "I can walk on my own now, Simon, the brine stops hurting when it dries off."

The Re-Human supporting Dr. Murray allowed him to walk unaided, and when Tamsyn saw who it was, her blood ran cold. She saw that figure in her nightmares every night, would forever see the face of the drunk driver who'd killed her mother, back when the world made sense.

It was Simon Dawes, and he stood before her, as dead as a doornail.

"They conscripted all of us, once they realised the wild zombies don't touch the tame ones," Dr. Murray said. He wore a cleanly pressed uniform and sat swirling a glass of brandy in Tamsyn's suite.

"Now this, this I miss most of all," the Re-Human said, sniffing lovingly from the glass. He made no move to drink it but could not keep his eyes from the tannic depths of the liquor.

"We had a great little place going over at Salt Flat, little community of dead-heads that trucked over the salt and kept Feickert's bullshit country going," Dr. Murray continued. "Place is shut down now, when those lying buggers came in and press-ganged us."

Simon Dawes was playing checkers with Eddie on the other end of the map table, the scars of his Glasgow smile even more ghoulish now that undeath had turned his face tight and leathery.

Tamsyn tried to focus on the ramblings of the resurrected veterinarian, but the presence of Dawes set an old anger boiling.

I have tried my best to forgive that man, she thought. *He has redeemed himself and we have made our peace, but I just don't feel it.*

It's not fair. He shouldn't get to keep living, not when Mum and Dad never got that chance.

"So, the Gravesend crew are back together!" Dr. Murray said, raising his glass. "And our young Tam is the head honcho, no less."

"Cheers, you old git!" Eddie laughed. "I'll mix you up some Bovril if you like, probably the only drink that'll give you a kick these days."

"Jesus no," Dr. Murray said, holding his belly and miming the agony the salty drink would have inflicted.

"It's a shame this war went bad," Dawes said, taking two of Eddie's checkers. "I was really hoping to see Washington, DC, or what's left of it."

"We were never going to get there," Tamsyn said bitterly. "I thought you were going to stop taking your dose, Dawes. Wasn't that your plan? Die again, wander off into the sunset?"

"Change of plan," Dawes said quietly. "I guess I kept wanting to know what was going to happen next."

"Here's what happens next," Tamsyn said, sloshing her glass and sending a spray of gin across some paperwork. "Texas loses. We all know it's going to happen. Those of us with pulses, we get put into POW camps. Those of you without pulses," and here she mimed a gun, aimed it at Dawes's' face.

Dawes wisely busied himself with the stack of checkers in front of him, and the bogeyman of her childhood looked nothing more than sad and worn out, a leathery freak with just this crumb of life left to him.

He'd driven the boat that saved their lives, and he'd died for it, died in front of her, but by their own laws the Texans brought him back. Here at the end of things, she found that all of his penance and self-pity just weren't enough.

It never felt like justice, like proper justice. I feel cheated.

The gun on her hip felt heavy and sure, and she found her forgiveness fading one drink at a time. It would be the act of a moment to deliver a second, much more permanent death.

"Folks are saying that the new Yank president is some sort of religious whacko," Eddie said, oblivious to the dangerous look in Tamsyn's eyes. "Thinks it's against God's plan that we keep bringing back the dead."

"It is, and we're all bloody mad. No offence," Tamsyn said as an aside to Dr. Murray, who shrugged. She got to her feet, unsteady for a long moment. "Excuse me gents, I need some air and possibly a painkiller. And then we should drink until they haul us away."

Eddie raised his glass in agreement, and Lynch clinked it solidly. The sour old sergeant had taken a shining to Dr. Murray, and the pair seemed set to chat long into the night.

Tamsyn stepped out into the corridor, immediately stubbing her toe on the generator. Cursing, she hobbled to the stairs, trying to keep moving in a straight line.

Time I fixed a mistake, she thought.

Somehow she got down the grand staircase without breaking her neck and made her way through the indoor camp of the enlisted. She gave droll salutes whenever one was directed at her, which was often.

"I'm looking for Private Baxter," she said, and was directed to a corner that the company's MPs were occupying. A few of them had been present at the beach earlier that day, and she ignored their insolent glares, the angry whispers as she passed through them.

Baxter was lying down with a ration-pack, stretched out on top of his canvas swag. He raised his eyes to the ceiling when he saw who the visitor was.

"Come to gloat, have you?" Baxter said. "Or to hand out some sort of punishment, because you can now?"

"Don't be a dickhead. I came to talk," Tamsyn said.

"Lady, you smell like my granddaddy on Lodge night," Baxter said, waving away at imaginary fumes. "Not surprised. In your shoes, I'd be drinking too."

"Look, cut the crap Baxter. I need your help."

"My help?" he said, amused. "Why would I help you?"

"Because you've got a rod up your arse. Because you do the right thing, even when it's not the easy thing to do. I know you've placed yourself under arrest for breaching the Undeath Act. You're... you're just the sort of nerd I need on staff."

The MPs were mostly ignoring her, but Baxter was close enough to their little camp to be heard. She leaned in close, keeping her voice low.

"Major Howlett is up to something, something bad with the Re-Humans. I don't know who else I can trust here, Baxter."

"What do you want me to do, exactly?" Baxter asked.

"I want you to make me do the right thing," Tamsyn said. "Whatever that is."

Baxter chewed the idea over for a long moment and nodded. Tamsyn gave orders to the MPs, and the man was released into her custody. In a flurry of paperwork, she made all his self-imposed charges vanish, and Private Baxter was a free man.

"Come with me, there's something I want you to see," Tamsyn said, getting more sober by the second. "Time you experienced Texan mercy at its finest."

A pair of medics had the captured zombie strapped to a gurney in the concierge's office. The groundskeeper had been rotting outdoors for almost three years and was little more than a bag of dried skin held together with sinew, the skeleton showing through in a dozen places.

An IV stand stood nearby, a big bag of saline solution slowly pouring into the creature. There was nothing approaching a vein, so the medics had carefully drilled a hole into its skull, running the dose directly into its brain.

One of the medics opened up the valve again, and the zombie began to thrash violently. Tamsyn eyed the leather straps with some concern–the infected dead were unnaturally strong, and this treatment always sent them crazy. The salt brought the undead a pain fiercer than anything felt in life.

"It's almost back, ma'am," one of the medics said. "The third bag of saline usually does the trick."

The groundskeeper's throat-box had been torn out long ago, face and hands chewed down to bone in several places. It could not scream, could do nothing but force out puffs of foul air from its ruined lungs.

Then, it happened. One moment, a monster had been struggling against the pain, snapping its teeth and fighting its bonds, and then the turn happened.

It was both beautiful and terrible to behold, the moment that memory and will returned to the undead. They remembered everything from before, everything they'd done since death, and without fail they would stare up at the lights, confused and scared, the fight gone from them.

"You're in there, aren't you?" Tamsyn said, and the groundskeeper blinked, stared back at her through the blasted grey jelly of its eyes. It was the fifth "birth" she'd attended, and it was always surreal to see that moment, when a veil was lifted in their shattered minds.

"Do you understand now?" she asked Baxter, who nodded, face ashen. Like most Texans, he'd had little to do with the Re-Humans he fought so valiantly for as a concept.

"This procedure is largely responsible for kicking off the entire civil war," Tamsyn said. "We bring 'em back, and the Yanks don't like it. But did anyone think to ask these poor chumps if they want it?"

The new Re-Human looked up at Tamsyn, flinched when it saw the pistol in her hand.

"You're scared and hurt. You remember everything, things you just can't bear. And you'd blow your brains out right now if you could."

Blinking, eyes rimmed with sadness, the Re-Human nodded.

"Goodbye." Tamsyn yanked the saline drip out of its skull, jammed her pistol into the hole and pulled the trigger. A spray of gore spread out across the top of the gurney, and then the Re-Human was just another rotting body.

"We've been at this for hours!" one of the medics protested. "I don't care who you are, I'm filing a complaint with Command."

"Waste your time if you like," Tamsyn said, wiping some muck from the barrel of her gun. "You'll have a copy of my Article 8 paperwork in the morning. Now, clean up this mess."

"Oh, not this prat again," Eddie said on spotting Baxter's aide-de-camp sash. "Did you not forget that he landed us in the shit?"

"Quiet," Tamsyn said. "He's staff now, so pull your head in."

Dawes and Dr. Murray were poring over maps, orders and company inventory, quietly talking together. Without the need for sleep, they'd been at it for hours, and Tamsyn hoped they could untangle the mess that Howlett had deliberately left for her.

If there was something in these records, something that would tell her just what Major Howlett was up to, they needed to find it, and quickly.

Eddie and Tamsyn were hungover to the point of physical pain, and Lynch snored loudly on the nearby sofa. The morning sun was penetrating the gaps around the thick curtain, and Tamsyn blinked wearily, chasing down a handful of painkillers with a warm can of cola.

"Come in," she said to Baxter, who closed the door behind him. He saluted her briskly and stood to attention. Squinting against the throb of her headache, Tamsyn noticed that his shirt and pants were pressed, and he'd attached his new stripes to his sleeve with surgical precision.

Brevet sergeant, a rank probably as temporary as her own, the best she could hand out without applying for outside approval. Eddie wore an identical set of stripes, after Lynch had consulted the General Orders, deciphering the new Republican Rank and Merit Scale. All of the old US forces had been folded into one body in Texas, and the new rules were complicated to the point where no one actually knew them all.

"Cut that shit out," she groaned, pointing to a chair. "It's too early in the morning. Just be normal."

"Yes, ma'am," Baxter said, and sat on the edge of the chair, straight-backed and alert. He could be up and shooting his sidearm in the blink of an eye, and it was all Tamsyn could do to hold her head upright.

"I'm never drinking again," she moaned. "What's going on out there, Baxter?"

"The 6th Requisition Platoon have been resettled into the guest's resort, the next building over. I've handpicked soldiers to guard the Re-Humans, good guys who won't let anyone in, not even the law."

"Good," she said, massaging her temples. "What else you got for me?"

"Some stragglers have just arrived, on foot. It's the Timberwolves, ma'am. 4th Scout Platoon," he explained.

"On foot?" she asked.

"They've been watching the Yankees advance, ma'am, hampering them where possible. Their sarge wants to report in directly to you. It seems pretty urgent."

"Of course. Get that man a drink, hell, get him whatever he wants. There's something I need to do first, but I'll see him straight after."

Tamsyn signalled Eddie to follow her to the dressing room, and she fired up the sat phone, wondering how long it would be before Howlett and his buddies figured out a way of jamming her calls.

"I'm getting nothing out of Command today," she said. "They're up to something, but nobody's telling me squat. If the shit is about to hit the fan, it'll be today."

"Who are you calling then?" Eddie asked.

"Someone I should have spoken to first. I was worried that Command was monitoring our calls, but the truth is that I've been putting it off. I'm–I'm a really shitty parent."

"Milly," Eddie said, sighing. "She's in good hands, love."

"I'm scared, Eddie. What if they've taken her away?"

"There's nothing we can do about it. Let's just find out, okay?"

He took the phone from her shaking hands and raised an operator who connected the call to the somewhat patchy civilian network. When it was ringing, he handed the phone back to her.

"Hello?" came the faint voice on the other end.

"Mrs Anderton! It's Tamsyn! Is Milly there, is she okay?"

"Tamsyn, honey, calm down. She's right here, playing with her blocks. Hey Milly, do you want to say hi to your Mommy?"

The phone made a muffled sound, and she could just make out the sound of a little wet breath, and an excited "ah!"

"Hi Milly!" Tamsyn sniffled, tears streaming down her face. "Hello darling. How are you?"

After a few minutes of a toddler giggling and smearing her handset with slobber, Mrs. Anderton got back onto the line.

"I'm sorry to do this to you, Tam, but I'm going to need to keep the line clear. The Army's on the radio, telling us to make our calls short and free up the exchanges. There's a curfew on as of tonight, no one can go out after dark."

"What–what's going on?"

"A friend of mine who caters over at the Naval Base says the president's being impeached, but it's probably a rumour. There's nothing on the news."

"I haven't heard anything either," Tamsyn said. "I'd better go. You folks keep indoors and keep safe."

"Thanks, Tam. Praying for you, sugar, hope you folks get home soon."

"Me too," Tamsyn said, disconnecting the call.

"That's a coup, that," Eddie said after Tamsyn repeated Mrs. Anderton's words. "Impeachment my arse. The military are taking over."

"If the president has gone down, chances are all of her friends and cronies are getting it in the neck. That's going to include us, unless we can pin something truly vile on Major Howlett."

"That might be easier than you think," said Dawes, standing just inside the doorway. He had the abandoned laptop cradled in his dead hands, the cracked screen glowing fitfully.

"There's all sorts of interesting stuff on this thing."

"I'm guessing they thought this laptop was completely bung, and they didn't have the time to fix it enough to wipe the hard drive," Dawes said. "Took a bit to get the thing going actually, someone trod on the bloody thing with a size ten boot. We jammed a spare battery in there with spit and string, and voila."

The cracked screen of the laptop flickered, even blacked out periodically. It was a pain to use, but it was possible to navigate the file structure. The computer had belonged to one of Howlett's senior officers, part of the crew currently raising hell in Corpus Christi.

"This is your smoking gun," Baxter said. "In some way or another, all of the Re-Humans have been conscripted into forage or repair crews, and Howlett's been quietly transferring all of them into the 6th Requisition Platoon."

"So he's moved all of the Re-Humans here," Lynch said, checking over the company roster. "Five hundred, seventy-three resurrected zombies, from all over the Army. But why's he done that?"

"Because he's been in contact with the enemy, that's why," Dawes said. "They'd deleted these files, and it was hell to get them back, what with this piece of shit blinking and giving me eye-strain. Here, read these." The dead man opened another file folder, his stiff grey fingers fumbling across the keys.

There were a series of transcriptions, ra-tel conversations with the American field commanders, and answers relayed over from their HQ in Hawaii. They were terms of surrender, stating the conditions required for a cessation of hostilities and transfer of power.

"Damnit, Howlett's been talking to Uncle Sam since just after Washington," Tamsyn said, checking the dates. "And he's been moving the Re-Humans around for months before. Looks like the good major was getting together a little insurance policy for himself."

Condition one of surrender was the handover of all Re-Humans for immediate extermination by the Americans. Condition two was the surrender of the remaining field Companies Delta, Echo, and Foxtrot, and the Reserve in Corpus Christi itself.

According to his responses, Howlett haggled for a day or two, trying for wiggle room in the surrender conditions, guarantees for himself and his officers, and leniency for his fellow conspirators in Corpus Christi. He finally agreed to the surrender timetable, one day after Foxtrot was bombed out of existence.

"There was never meant to be an evac," Tamsyn said. "The Yanks know all about this place, and Howlett's got everyone sitting on their hands till Uncle Sam rolls through the gate. The Americans are bringing in two companies of National Guard to Cherry Point, and then they're coming for us."

"Says here that they got Delta Company four days ago. Whole sorry bunch are in a POW camp in Cleveland. Those bastards in Command are selling us up the river!" Lynch growled.

Someone knocked thunderously on the door, and Tamsyn looked up. Everyone that she trusted was in the room with her.

"Oh shit, that sergeant from the Timberwolves has been waiting outside for almost an hour," Baxter said, opening the door. "I forgot about him, with all this..."

"Send him away," Tamsyn said with a frown. "I can hear all his Soldier of Fortune stories later."

"Goddamnit, I will not go away," a man shouted from the door, trying to barge past Baxter. "She's going to want to hear this!"

The sergeant was filthy and had the wired look of someone who'd gone days without sleep. Tamsyn knew the feeling, and grudgingly signalled that Baxter let the man into her suite.

"I'm sorry Sergeant, uh, Willett, but we are neck-deep in the shit," Tamsyn said with a heavy sigh. "I promise I will take your report, but it's just going to have to wait."

"I lost half my squad in Wilmington looking for this goddamn country club, and somewhere between five and ten thousand zombies were hot on our heels," Willett said bluntly. "This place is going to be chewed into matchsticks by lunchtime."

Tamsyn swore, and her command centre erupted into a flurry of planning and packing. The dreaded words *super-pack* were used to motivate the sluggish. Soon the vast swarm could be seen on the horizon, shambling towards the resort.

If anything, Willett had been modest in his estimate.

"We are out of here within the hour," Tamsyn shouted, pacing through the camp beds and yelling up a storm that was almost worthy of Staff Sergeant Lynch. "Anything we don't pack, we don't take. If you're not on the trucks, we won't wait for you. Go!"

Probably a good idea to leave anyways, Tamsyn thought. *I hope those bastard Yanks like the welcoming committee we're leaving them.*

"We'll always attract undead attention, wherever we are," Baxter said. "Five hundred folks gives off a stink that draws those damn things."

Tamsyn borrowed a spotting scope and could see perhaps a hundred infected corpses already crossing the untended fairways. The zombies had formed a super-pack and moved with unerring accuracy and purpose, a slow tide of flesh that threatened to wipe them off the map.

Everyone was set to go, but in the mad panic of packing up all of Echo Company, Tamsyn realised she hadn't actually figured out where to go next. She called her officers in for a quick conference around the front of her Lexus, maps spread out across the hood. Lieutenant Rigby stood behind Eddie, a hint of a smirk underneath his smudge of moustache.

Don't think I won't be waterboarding you the moment we're safe, Tamsyn thought. *You knew about Howlett's plan. What else do you know?*

"We're here," Baxter said, pointing to the map, "and I recommend we hightail it across the channel to Bald Head Island, here."

Tamsyn noted that the area was marked CAPE FEAR, and the island sat at the very tip of the loose delta. She saw the small grid of streets where a village sat, made note of the distance between the island and the mainland.

If they laid low on the island, they might be safe. When it arrived, the American advance would sweep straight past them, right into the welcoming arms of the super-pack.

She shook her head.

"No," Tamsyn said. "It's time we started acting like an army. There's five hundred of us, armed to the teeth, but we're running scared from these arseholes."

She rested her thumb on the map. "We're here, and the super-pack is moving this way. We have to assume that Willett's mob stirred up the whole damn place, and that the entire city's dropping round for lunch."

"We can take Highway 17 west into South Carolina," Lynch offered. "If we can find enough fuel, we'll be back in Texas in a few days."

"No way," Tamsyn said. "Those roads are still clogged to buggery with abandoned cars. We'll be slow and visible, and the Americans could just pick us off from the sky. We need a different plan, one that they're not expecting."

She looked up at the officers, most of whom wore expressions of doubt and barely suppressed panic. If they didn't move immediately, the super-pack would block off the entire headland, and there would be no escape.

"We will circle west, around Wilmington. Back roads, as much as we can. Then we go up north and east till we're here, safe and snug in Croatan National Forest. Hopefully the tree canopy will block any prying eyes from the sky."

She moved her thumb a smudge to the right, until it was resting on a familiar airfield.

"Gentlemen, we're taking back Cherry Point. And then we will head up to Cleveland, and free those sorry Delta bastards. You heard me, they've got our people in the can. And then we will fight on until we're down to our bare bloody knuckles."

Lynch opened his mouth, perhaps to question the plan, but one glare from the hungover and determined Tamsyn was enough to force his disbelieving silence. *There's no time to bloody argue,* Tamsyn thought, *and he knows it.* She scooped up the maps and threw them into the car, indicating that it was time to move out.

There were perhaps thirty vehicles in total, and Tamsyn was forced to jam the Re-Humans back into the darkness of the two semi-trailers originally used to transport them. The Patriot SAM battery led the convoy, sophisticated radar array out and tracking.

Baxter had told her that it was the last version of the Patriot to be made, the PAC-5 system. One vehicle to replace four, with the complex radar and tracking gear built into the launch module itself. It could intercept aircraft and missiles while on the move, the battery could be erected in less than a minute, and it had an astonishing range. At a pinch, they could strike down any aircraft flying over Cherry Point.

They were also down to their last two missiles.

"Wish we had a whole battalion of those," Eddie mused from the driver's seat. "Hold on, love, it's going to be a bumpy ride."

The convoy left the paved roads, cutting across the overgrown golf course. The only access road to the country club was already swallowed up by the advancing swarm, so the line of vehicles bounced across the grounds, pushing through the bush until they found a fire-track. Nature had already half-reclaimed it.

The Patriot snapped through a flimsy iron-wire fence, and consulting her map, Tamsyn figured that they'd come out onto Highway 211. The cracked bitumen snaked westwards, all the way back to Texas, to what passed for home in this dead world.

Tamsyn swore.

Spread across the road and far into the fields on either side, a second super-pack of zombies was lurching eastwards, picking up speed when it heard the engines of the convoy. There were easily five thousand of the undead, kicking up plumes of dust as they stumbled through the rows of dead corn.

"Where in the bright blue fuck did that lot come from?" Eddie said, hands clenching the wheel. Tamsyn madly fumbled for her radio, one eye still on the map.

"Everyone turn right, we've gotta get the hell off the highway. There's an unsealed road just east of here, we follow it north and west. Over."

The convoy fought its way free of the bushland, rejoining the bitumen. The Patriot and both semi-trailers were agonisingly slow to negotiate the turn, and they abandoned one sedan, its axle busted during the rough journey.

"Ma'am, we've got a problem," Baxter piped up on the CB. "Some idiot's broken out of formation, and he's making a run for it. Over."

In her passenger side mirror, Tamsyn could see a Hummer peel away from the convoy, ploughing straight towards the super-pack at top speed. It was their Avenger, and a man was up and mounted in the turret.

"Lynch, who's in the Avenger? Over." Tamsyn asked.

"Lieutenant Rigby, and one of his non-coms," the Staff Sergeant transmitted from his troop-truck. "We should bring that traitor down, ma'am. He's making a run for Texas. Over."

"We're all traitors. Leave him, he's made his choice," Tamsyn replied, putting the CB back into its cradle. Winding down the window, she leaned right out with a spotter's scope, hair flapping around her face as she looked backwards. The curve of the road gave her a clear view of Rigby's freedom run.

The turret operator emptied the missile pack into the horde, the Stinger missiles clearing a path that Rigby followed, bouncing over the smoking craters and scattered monsters. The Avenger struck the undead like a cannonball, scattering bodies in all directions, while the machine gun hammered at the press of undead just beyond the bonnet. The momentum kept them going for almost a hundred metres, and then finally the Avenger was sliding around jerkily, wheels spinning in the grease and guts, until something broke and the vehicle stopped. The modified Hummer was an island of metal, trapped deep within that unnatural sea.

The operator ran the machine gun dry, and it spat lead in every direction. It made next to no difference. A knot of grey arms reached up to caress the vehicle, bashing against the windows, rocking it from side to side. Tamsyn decided she didn't want to see anymore.

13

It was a long drive north, one hundred and forty miles of backtracking along neglected roads. With every mile Tamsyn prayed that the American planes wouldn't spot their winding snake of vehicles, that the Patriot would keep them safe.

We just need a chance, she thought. *That's all.*

Emerging from the ruins of small burghs and abandoned farmsteads, the walking dead were very active, far too active for backwoods North Carolina. Every direction that Tamsyn looked, small groups of zombies were converging on the convoy, as far as the eye could see.

"What gives with the coffin-dodgers?" Eddie said. "They're bloody scaring me, homing in on us like that."

"I'll post double-guards tonight. Hell, I'm cracking open that crate of salt-tipped rounds," Tamsyn said, her throat closing up with panic. *Is this how a super-pack starts?*

Why are all those rotters so interested in us?

Despite the tickle of fear in her gut, Tamsyn found herself nodding off, hands still clutched around the map and radio. In a fuzz of dream, she looked across to see that Eddie was somewhere else, and it was her father behind the wheel, steering them through a nightmare landscape.

Milly was in the backseat, strapped into a baby capsule, a giggling bundle of slobber and thick curls. Her healthy radiant skin contrasted with Mal Webb's dead pallor. Tamsyn found her hands were filthy with grime, coated with something that felt like ash.

Outside, everything burned. Entire forests were blackened and smouldering, and the Lexus fought for purchase on a winding road of cracked bone.

"Last chance, kiddo," her dad said. "Baxter has to go."

"No, Dad, no!" she said, shaken to her core. "We're okay now. He works for me."

"You don't understand," her father said, and made as if to say more. Again, he was struck dumb, and fought to express himself, as if restricted in what he said.

"Don't—Cherry Point—" he managed, and then the dream ended, with Tamsyn sprawled across her car seat and slobbering into Eddie's shoulder.

"Going bloody loopy," she mumbled. "I think I've got post-traumatic stress disorder or something."

"Don't we all, my love," Eddie said, patting her fondly. "We're here."

Tamsyn looked around to see that it was almost dark, and they were passing between enormous pine trees, the trunks wider than her car. The convoy was travelling adjacent to an overgrown ranger's track, making pains to keep every vehicle under cover.

"I hope the Yanks won't see us," Tamsyn said, struggling to find her place on the map. "Okay, I found a site for us. Any closer, they'll be able to smell our pongy socks."

"No, don't do that," Eddie said when Tamsyn reached for the radio. "Lynch says we should be on radio silence from here on in."

Eddie overtook the Patriot, the Lexus's wheels spinning and kicking up a drift of pine needles, and wove through the trees. The Lexus led the rest of the convoy to Tamsyn's chosen campsite.

In minutes the vehicles were huddled under camouflage netting. Clusters of barely visible tents popped up like mushrooms.

"We're gonna have to ditch the semi-trailers," Baxter said. "We don't have enough netting to cover them, and they're probably visible from above."

"What do you suggest?" Tamsyn asked.

"We strip the trucks for anything useful, siphon out most of the fuel, and drive the damn things into the nearest lake. There's three within an hour's walk, deep fishing holes too."

"Done. But let's make sure our smelly friends disembark first."

The rear gates were dropped on the trucks, and almost immediately a concentrated waft of decay swept over that part of the camp. Tamsyn coughed, fought the rebellion in her stomach. During their time in Gravesend, Tamsyn had always carried a bandana to cover her face and a flask of vinegar to ward off the stench of dead things. She still wished the Republican Army would issue these things as standard gear, instead of punishing recruits who took to covering their faces.

"Okay folks, sorry for the cramped ride, but we're here," she said loudly. "There aren't any tents for you, but you're hardly going to catch a cold. Baxter and his men have pegged out an area for you, and we're setting up an aid-station there for your treatment."

"So you're sending us downwind from the fresh folks?" a very grumpy Clem Murray protested. "Sorry that my deodorant doesn't disguise the fact that I'm bloody well dead."

"Oh shit. I didn't know they put you in the truck with the others," Tamsyn apologised. "Didn't you tell them you were on my staff?"

"Buggers thought I was making it up, tossed me and Dawes in anyways," Dr. Murray said. "You know us walking corpses, we all look the same."

"That's enough," Tamsyn said. "Stow the attitude and come with me."

Tamsyn and Dr. Murray walked through the grumbling Re-Humans, looking for Dawes. Despite herself, she felt a shiver, with hundreds of intelligent zombies pressing in on all sides. If they chose to, they could tear her apart in moments, or a dozen foul mouths could pump their disease into her warm flesh...

Just then, the radio on her hip crackled. A strange jittery sound, not the squeal of someone accidentally mashing their transmit key, or the sound of a scrambled signal. Tamsyn realised it was almost like when a working mobile phone was put too close to a speaker.

"You hearing this?" Tamsyn told Dr. Murray, who nodded. She ordered the Re-Humans to halt, and walked through their ranks, sweeping the handset around like a mine-detector.

She finally found the source of the mysterious interference. A fresh-looking Re-Human was causing the radio to go nuts, and when Tamsyn approached the green-tinged leftovers of the young woman, the treated zombie backpedalled, a panicked look on her face. Tamsyn ordered the other Re-Humans to seize her.

"What have you got to say about this?" Tamsyn demanded, holding the radio up to the Re-Human. The jarring stutter of the sound was at its loudest when Tamsyn made a pass over the dead woman's abdomen.

"Please, let me go," the Re-Human begged. The Re-Humans holding her arms pinioned winced, shaking their heads as if in pain. She noticed that the other Re-Humans were retreating to a safe distance.

"What's wrong with you lot?" she demanded of the Re-Humans.

"We've been getting weird headaches near her," Dawes said, appearing at her side. "No one wanted to stand near her in the truck."

"But–but you don't GET headaches," Tamsyn said. "All right, you two, bring her with me. The rest of you, go to your area and await further instructions."

A small field pavilion had been set up for Tamsyn's use, and she took the captive Re-Human here for questioning. Her tags identified her as Nancy Bannon, resurrected four months ago. She looked terrified and wouldn't respond to any of Tamsyn's questions.

"Okay, I've had just about enough of this," Tamsyn said. "Take off your shirt, soldier."

"No, please," Nancy sobbed. "You don't understand."

"That's an order. Oh, sod it. Eddie, Dawes, hold her still."

The Re-Human fought furiously, and even tried to snap at Tamsyn and Eddie with her slime-crusted teeth. They sprayed her into submission with their X-76 water pistols, and Tamsyn ripped the Re-Human's shirt open, popping all the buttons.

There. Underneath the grimy remains of her bra, a large incision began, a jagged cut that went down to just past her navel. Fat steel staples held everything closed, and the smell was horrific.

"You've got five seconds before I riddle you with salt bullets. What the hell did they do to you? Talk."

"I can't," cried Nancy. "They've—they've got my kids. Still alive, back in Corpus Christi. If I talk, they said, they said—"

"Who said?" demanded Tamsyn. "Was this Major Howlett?"

Nancy nodded.

"You forget about Howlett," Tamsyn said. "If you tell me the truth about—this—I'll make sure your kids are safe. I'm friends with President Feickert."

Kneeling down, she leaned in close, got right into Nancy's stink, kept eye contact with the Re-Human. Tamsyn did her best impression of Feickert-in-command, hoping that she looked more trustworthy than hung over and scared.

"Tell me, and I'll make Howlett pay."

Nancy shook, dark, sticky tears leaking out of her dormant tear-ducts. Finally the Re-Human looked up, speaking quietly.

"I was on Howlett's staff, just before the Washington push. I was sent down to the archives, looking for some made up document. I was–grabbed. Some of his aides took me and threw me in a room with one of those things. A wild one," she added.

"His goons let it bite me up good, and then hauled it off in a noose before it could do too much damage. I was strapped to a bed, and I died, and then they pumped me full of salt."

Nancy looked haggard, still wet from the water pistols, slumped on the floor of the pavilion. The pale ruin of her body was still exposed to a tentful of strangers, and Tamsyn realised that a last thread of dignity had just been taken from her.

Tamsyn leaned forward, offering Nancy her hand. She helped the dead woman to her feet, guided her around to her own camp-chair.

"I wish they'd done it while I was dead," Nancy said bitterly. "I was back, back in my head when they brought it in on a trolley. Pulled out all my guts, my insides, and I saw the whole thing. They stuffed me like a goddamn roast turkey."

"What did they put inside you?" Tamsyn said quietly.

"A machine," the Re-Human whispered. "Please, they told me to keep my mouth shut. My kids, my husband– "

"I think we're past that, love," Tamsyn said. "Baxter, bring me some pliers, hell, bring a whole tool-box. Nancy, if you want me to help your family, I'm going to need you to cooperate."

With pliers and adjustable spanners, Eddie and Baxter pulled out the metal staples. Pulling on a pair of latex gloves, Tamsyn gently folded back the flaps of Nancy's severed abdomen, carefully peeling back the dead flesh. The Re-Human pleaded with Tamsyn the whole time, intently watching the operation on her dead flesh. Tamsyn found the whole process unnerving.

There, strapped to her ribs and spine with wire, a fat metal cylinder lay, completely featureless. UR-14 PROTOTYPE, a nameplate proclaimed.

"Is that a bomb?" Eddie stammered. "We gotta get out of here!"

"Don't be so bloody daft," Tamsyn said, snipping away at the supporting wires with her pliers. "Why would Howlett go to all this trouble? He's already got bombs."

"I hope you're right," Eddie said.

They kept Nancy in custody, but Tamsyn didn't think she'd get much more info from the brutalised dead woman. Her service records showed she was amongst the last shipment of Re-Humans to the 6th, and there the paper trail ended.

The device itself was isolated on the very edge of the camp, guarded by five slightly nervous looking soldiers.

"Dawes, do something useful. Get onto the laptop and look for anything on this UR-14," she said, an uncontrollable wave of loathing rising up when he looked at her with his sad smile. "I can't handle that stupid, broken screen."

Night had long fallen, but there wasn't a fire in sight. In Tamsyn's absence Lynch had organised the double guard around the camp, and even sent out a recon patrol towards Cherry Point, less than five miles to the east. The Timberwolves had already returned, and as Tamsyn peeled off her latex gloves, she took Sergeant Willett's report.

"They've got crews repairing the damage from the US bombing run," the scout said, flicking through the images on a digi-cam set to night-vision. "Looks like they're securing the base for long-term use. One company of infantry has landed and is based in this dormitory here."

"Fuel tanks are largely untouched, our boys didn't get a chance to blow them when we got the hell out of Dodge. The Yanks have cleared away most of the destroyed hangars, and it looks like most of their birds are out in the open."

"How many?" Tamsyn asked, flicking through the images. The airbase was positively enormous, more of a small town than a runway with sheds.

"One company regular infantry, and at least six platoons' worth of special forces. There's almost a full squadron of birds, transport planes, various bombers, Raptors, whatever those losers in Hawaii could put in the air. There's also two Longbird Apache gun-ships, and the ground crew needed to keep all that scary shit up in the sky."

"How many?" Tamsyn asked again, feeling a muscle work in her jaw. Now that they were here, her bold plan seemed ridiculous, doomed to failure.

"Perhaps two thousand," Willett said, looking thoughtful as he considered the number. "And forget the direct approach. My boys nearly got tagged by an IR array. Infrared. The whole perimeter is painted."

"Leave this with me," Tamsyn ordered, taking the camera. "That's some good work, Sergeant, go get yourself and your men something to eat."

Leaning against her camouflaged car, Tamsyn tucked into the mush of an MRE ration pack, looking up and spotting the occasional star peeking through the roof of the forest. She wanted to cry, wanted someone else to take over all of her responsibilities.

"I just want to go home," she whispered to herself, before realising that she didn't really have a home, not anywhere.

"The smart money's on surrendering, ma'am," Baxter said, interrupting her maudlin train of thought as he walked over from her tent, that ever-present suggestion of a swagger. "You know, we're only five miles from warm prison beds, hot showers, better food."

"Don't kid yourself. They're eating the same shit we are," Tamsyn said, offering her ration pack to Baxter. He took the spoon and fell in with gusto.

"Tell me something, Baxter. Why on earth are you working for me? I seem to drag us from one clusterfuck to the next."

"Do you really want to know?" Baxter said through a mouthful of mush. She nodded.

"My family's always been Army, four generations now. We've got a five-star general, two Congressional Medals of Honor, and our family barbeques are like a Purple Heart reunion."

He paused, lost in thought. The ration pack was forgotten in his hands.

"My granddaddy was a hero back in 'Nam, and my Pa went to West Point. This is all I was ever going to be, ma'am. But let's just say that 'Don't Ask, Don't Tell' hasn't been kind to my career."

"Oh," Tamsyn said.

"This new Army, no difference. You're the first person who ever gave me a chance," Baxter continued. "We might be dead this time tomorrow, but at least I'll die with stripes on my sleeve."

"Let's hope you get to keep them," she said. She fished the camera out of her pocket, showed Baxter the photos. "It's hopeless, isn't it?"

"Well, it's not going to be easy," Baxter said. "Don't give up, ma'am. We can really do some damage here."

"How do you figure? We're outnumbered 4-1, and they've got some serious hardware over there."

"No. Think 2-1, ma'am."

Baxter flicked over to the shot of the airbase perimeter, long grass peppered by regularly spaced infra-red arrays.

"To you or me, that'll bring the whole joint out and gunning. But to Dawes and all his stinky buddies? That's officially the world's shittiest fence. It won't even pick them up."

The penny dropped. The undead were as cold as the grave, as would be the resurrected Re-Humans. Completely invisible to IR, they'd be able to walk right up to the front door, undetected.

The notion of these monsters used as shock troopers sent a chill down Tamsyn's spine. *This changes everything*, she realised. *If we give them guns, we've just made ourselves obsolete.*

"Don't doubt that there isn't some sort of motion sensor closer to the wire, something to bring a patrol should a stray zombie wander in. But our lot don't need to get that close."

Baxter pointed to the dormitories, the ones Willett reckoned on being home to an entire company of infantry, and more Special Forces than Tamsyn felt comfortable thinking about.

"You get one big group here, armed with assault rifles and M203 launchers. They keep low and raise hell. It'll take headshots to drop our undead friends, so they can do a lot of damage there. Shame we lost the Avenger, would have been handy there too."

He flicked to another photo.

"The rest of the Re-Humans hit the squadron parked on the tarmac. Give 'em all the heavy machine guns, our undead are strong enough to lift them and fire. That will get Uncle Sam's attention pretty fast and keep our first group effective."

Tamsyn boggled at the plan. She'd had five hundred super soldiers at her disposal all along. They wouldn't feel pain, could take dozens of bullets without missing a beat, and wouldn't tire under heavy loads.

"Hopefully it will stop those fly-boys from scrambling too. It would be nice to capture some birds, but if this second group takes them out of commission, that's just as good. If they manage all of that, then they can secure the fuel. That leaves the rest of us, the folks with pulses."

He pointed out a shot of the command compound, with the gun-birds nearby, equipped and ready to go.

"While they're busy dealing with armed zombies, every living member of Echo Company takes on this command post, with everything we have. We absolutely have to drop those choppers early on in the piece, or they'll chew us to bits. Hopefully the Patriot can do something about that."

Baxter looked at Tamsyn expectantly, and she blinked, dazed at the audacity of his plan.

"Okay," she said numbly. "We'll do it. Tomorrow night."

Eddie shook her awake sometime close to dawn. Grumbling, she tried to burrow back under her covers, but he stripped her cot and left her shivering in her underclothes.

"Get up, ya skinny witch," he scoffed. "Our Dawes has found something on the computer. It's about that gizmo."

"That wasn't necessary," she mumbled, wriggling into her crumpled uniform. "I'm your boss, you know."

She found Dawes sitting near the generator, a dangerous looking wire running directly into the laptop. Lynch and Baxter leaned around the Re-Human's shoulders, their tired faces reflected in that flickering glow.

"What did you find?" she asked.

"Nancy's little surprise came courtesy of Undead Research. You'll know these folks as the ones who've figured out the salt treatments."

"And the salt bullets, salt water as a weapon, etc., etc.," Tamsyn said. "So, nice blokes all round."

"Look, Tam, I'll cut to the chase," Dawes said, rubbing at the cracked bridge of his nose. An old habit, and now he'd almost worn through to the cartilage beneath. "You'll need to act quickly with this thing. The UR-14 is making the super-packs and bringing them to us."

"What?"

"This brief here says the canister emits a microwave in a certain frequency. It's like a dinner bell for any wild undead within 15 miles. Just gives my lot a slight headache, has done ever since Howlett flicked the remote switch yesterday."

"He wants Echo company destroyed?"

"Scorched earth policy, I guess," Baxter said. "I know he wants to take you down, ma'am, and there's a few folks here that know too much about the Re-Humans. Tidying up loose ends before the Yanks can ask too many questions?"

"And when Uncle Sam follows the plan, rolls in to the country club to take prisoners–presto, everyone's already been eaten. Sad, but not surprising. What a clever son-of-a-bitch." Tamsyn leaned over Dawes to take control of the computer, scrolling through the technical specs of the device.

"It can be activated remotely, most likely via satellite," Lynch said. "Which also tells us that Major Howlett knows where we are right now. We dump this thing in the same lake as the trucks, and we take off in a random direction within the hour. We're all in terrible danger."

"Oh, no no no," Tamsyn said absently, reading quickly. "This is actually a good thing. Howlett thinks the canister is still strapped to Nancy's insides, and that she is right near Cherry Point. If it looks like we've already been taken prisoner, he's not going to switch off the signal. He'd want the super-packs to do their worst."

A satisfied smile crept across Tamsyn's tired face.

They had the base commander down and zip-tied, a stocky bald colonel still in his pyjamas. Sporadic gunfire could still be heard outside. Waggling a pistol in his face, Tamsyn demanded that the furious Colonel Turley get onto the P.A. system and order all his personnel into an unconditional surrender to the Republican Army of Texas.

She felt elated; ten feet tall; a bulletproof Boudicca. Tamsyn had lost only 23 of her living soldiers, and 57 of the resurrected dead had gone on to their final peace.

Baxter's plan had worked almost perfectly. It didn't hurt that a Re-Human volunteer had launched the assault by pushing the UR-14 into Cherry Point on a hand-truck, closely followed by two thousand swarming zombies.

In the face of this terror, the armed assault from the flanks had come as a complete surprise, and the Yanks were caught with their pants down. The UR-14 was now speeding away on a captured jeep, and the device would be destroyed 100 miles west of here. Slowly but surely, the bullet-ravaged super-pack followed the signal away from the captured airfield.

"You'll hang for this, lady," Turley croaked, tied to a chair in his old office. "Our people won't stand for it. You've armed those damn monsters, and there's no stepping back from that abyss."

"Shush. Some of my best friends are dead," Tamsyn said. "Now tell me again, where is Delta Company being held?"

Turley spat on the open map, and Tamsyn slammed her pistol against the desk, making the man flinch.

"You're being very stupid, Colonel. Take him away, I'm sick of his stupid face." A pair of MPs hauled the American commander away, and Tamsyn rubbed at her temples.

They'd been in charge of Cherry Point Airfield for less than two hours, and already her problems were mounting. They'd captured almost 1500 American personnel, and they needed to be processed and secured. Those killed in the assault needed to be identified and readied for burial.

One of the Harriers had escaped the barrage before bombing the Patriot out of existence, roaring into the dawn sky on a due west bearing. Hawaii would soon know about this.

"We need to get this place ready," Tamsyn told Baxter. "The Yanks won't dare bomb the base, but they'll be coming."

"What's going in your report to Corpus Christi?" the Texan asked, a flicker of worry dancing across his smooth-shaven face.

"I'll tell them the truth," she said. "We've all disobeyed our orders and broken the Undeath Act big-time, but to hell with those idiots. We've crossed the Rubicon now."

"Yep. No going back from this," Baxter said softly, busying himself with something else when Eddie walked into the room.

Looking out the window, Tamsyn saw a small group of Re-Humans patrolling the tarmac, cradling heavy machine guns as if they were toys. Her skin crawled. After what they'd seen them do, no one was game to ask the undead soldiers to give up their guns.

Once the airfield was completely secured, Tamsyn called in a meeting of her chief officers, convened in a captured strategy room that was complete with charts and routes to the country club, as well as pins marking the planned advance southwards to Texas.

We've turned the tide, Tamsyn thought. *Time to make this victory stick.*

They considered a variety of strategies. Lynch proposed they hold the base and arrange a prisoner swap, Delta Company for the captured Americans, but Eddie disagreed.

"No deals. Those tossers won't talk, anyway. Not after what we did with the Re-Humans. We've hit 'em hard, so let's keep hitting 'em. I say we blow Cherry Point sky-high and go spring out our lads in Cleveland."

Fingers steepled, Tamsyn gave serious thought to the plan. They'd just captured some serious hardware, the latest weapons platforms, and more aircraft than they could fly. With Delta and Echo companies, as well as a shock force of Re-Humans, they could retake all of the ground Texas had lost.

"What about the prisoners?" Baxter asked. "We'll need a lot of personnel to move them and guarding them on the road's going to be a bitch. We'll need to keep a small force here."

"They're eating all the food, probably trying to escape. Prisoners are a liability," Eddie said, drawing his finger across his throat. To Tamsyn's dismay, no one actually disagreed.

"Turn them," Dr. Murray said, wincing as he chewed on his daily salt ration. "Send our boys into the pens to give the Yankee prisoners a little nibble, and offer them salt or death. They'll have no choice but to fight for you."

"No!" Tamsyn cried. "Absolutely not. No more Re-Humans."

"After all we've done for you?" Dr. Murray said with a wry grin. "Thought we dead codgers were useful now?"

Annoyed, Tamsyn dismissed the meeting. *As usual, I'll just have to half-arse my way through to a decision. I keep making the mistake of thinking this job is a democracy.*

It's my call now.

Between one of the captured techs and her own specialists, they had managed to get the comms centre working again, re-scrambled to Texan codes. Ordering everyone out, Tamsyn girded herself. She raised an operator, placing a call with Republican Command.

She demanded to speak to the head of Command, and briefly explained the situation. Expecting to speak to a mid-level functionary, she was surprised to find General Bachman himself on the phone.

"Captain Webb, have you lost your goddamn mind?" Bachman yelled. "I'm sending Major Howlett up on the next available chopper. You are to place yourself under arrest and await his arrival."

"Sir, Howlett is a traitor, and I've got proof," Tamsyn said, her throat dry. "He's been talking to the Americans, going behind the President's back. He's sold three companies up the river, and all the Re-Humans too."

"Listen carefully," Bachman said. "Howlett works for me. We've cleaned house, and now that Feickert is being impeached her illegal war ends. We were meant to sign the surrender documents today, but there you are, disobeying your orders, poking around where you shouldn't."

The world seemed to fall out from underneath her.

"No. Hell no," Tamsyn said. "I've had it with you and your pack of liars. Here's what's going to happen."

She took a deep breath and thought of Caesar at the Rubicon. *No going back.*

"I'm going to do your job, you fat slug. I'm going up to Cleveland, and I'm rescuing the men that you betrayed. Then, we are going to win this war. I'll swim to Hawaii with water-wings if I have to."

"You and your rogue company are finished," General Bachman growled furiously into the phone. "I'll see all you Feickert sympathisers in front of a firing squad. Shit, I'll pull the trigger myself."

Tamsyn punched the console in front of her, fighting off the panic attack, blinking away her tears. *It can't end this way. Not after everything.*

"We've got better hardware than you, and enough planes to bomb you back into the Stone Age. Do you think the Reserve can hold off two pissed off companies and hundreds of Re-Humans with guns? Think about that."

"You stupid girl," Bachman said. "You don't know what you're doing. We've already lost the war, but the moment you put a gun into a dead man's hand, you landed all of us in the shit. You're a disgrace."

"Sir?" Tamsyn said. "Fuck you, sir. I'll be seeing you in Corpus Christi, real soon."

She disconnected the call and vomited all over the floor.

"We're on our own," Tamsyn told the packed briefing room, fists clenched tightly around the lectern. "Command has arrested our lawful president and is about to surrender to Uncle Sam. I will not accept this surrender, and neither should you."

The officers and non-coms of Echo Company were up in their chairs, shouting and shaking their fists. Lynch whistled through his teeth, and the noise eventually died down as they waited to hear the rest.

"We are the Army. We're the ones who've bled for our nation, sacrificed our own lives for a just cause. The way I see it, those weak bastards have lost the right to call the shots."

Wolf-whistles, and soldiers stood in the chairs, cheering. The new Re-Humans officers probably cheered the loudest, wearing their new stripes with pride.

"We are taking back Cleveland, and freeing our soldiers, good people that the generals have given up on. We will push those Yankee pricks right off the map. And then, then we are going back home, and I will put those treacherous bastards into a deep black hole."

The whole place went batshit crazy, and Tamsyn grinned at the applause. She was so caught up in the moment that she didn't see the worried look on Baxter's face, or the way Lynch narrowed his eyes as he watched the armed zombies.

She whisked her staff into the planning room. Now that she had the grunts on her side, she needed to act quickly. For all intents and purposes, this was going to be the new Command in exile.

"Listen. Major Howlett is coming up on a chopper, and he means to arrest us. This man has betrayed our republic. I want that helicopter to be a burning wreck."

"Too much, ma'am, too much," Baxter said. "Those other folks onboard with Howlett are just following orders. We can arrest the major, and then we get to keep the chopper too."

The others agreed, and swallowing, Tamsyn nodded.

Wow, give me one military victory and I go all Genghis Khan. I need to settle down a bit.

"So the Yanks will be coming here for their men, that's a given," she continued. "We leave a token force here, but we're going to have to play hardball with the American prisoners. Get used to thinking of them as hostages.

"While these folks play Mexican stand-offs, we haul ass north. We tear apart Cleveland and bust out Delta Company. We arm our men, secure the city, and come back here to mop up."

A runner came for Tamsyn. There was an urgent call for her in the CENCOM. It could only be bad news, and the operators figured it best that she hear it first. Tamsyn left her underlings to figure out all the details of the Cleveland manoeuvre, and crossed the tarmac to the radio room, nervously watching the sky for helicopters.

She ordered the radio operators out of the room, and making sure the door was closed, she picked up the headset and mike. She connected the call.

"Captain Webb here," she transmitted.

"Captain Webb, this is Major Havelock, officer in charge, Reserve Company," a man said, the patchy signal making his words difficult to hear.

"Major," she said.

"As the senior surviving member of Command, I've assumed control of the Republican Army," Havelock said. "I order you to release your prisoners and surrender yourself and your forces to the American officer in charge. Immediately."

"Now, you listen here," Tamsyn said. "I've told that idiot Bachman, and now I'm telling you. We're going back for our men, and then we're coming down to arrest the whole damn lot of you."

"Captain Webb, please listen. It's—it's done, we're finished. Corpus Christi is gone."

14

Tamsyn stared numbly up at the ceiling, barely noticing as Eddie leaned over her, asking her questions, finally wrapping her in his jacket.

She could still hear Havelock's words. His description of the atrocity had been clinical, almost deadpan.

A long-range bomber reached Corpus Christi about an hour ago, the American President authorising two tactical nukes. A last-straw reprisal following Texas arming its Re-Humans. One bomb wiped the Naval Base off the map, the other shattered the makeshift Texan capitol and the surrounding neighbourhood to its foundations. The explosion had happened at roughly the same moment that Clarice Feickert took the stand to defend herself.

The blast dropped several of the city barricades and blocked off part of the saltwater moat. The permanent horde camped on Corpus Christi's doorstep flooded into the smoke-filled streets. The Americans had destroyed the military and government targets, and the zombie horde had killed everyone else. Havelock estimated the horde at tens of thousands of zombies.

Worried about reprisals from the Americans, and fearing their own rebel companies, Command had sent Reserve Company out yesterday on "naval manoeuvres." From the water, the Texans watched their city burn, helpless, knowing that to go in was to kill themselves.

It made the fall of Gravesend sound almost trivial.

"I killed her, Eddie," Tamsyn said, almost catatonic. "I killed Milly, and Mrs. Anderton, and those kids in the school down the street, and everyone at the farmer's market. They're all dead."

She heard Eddie talk to someone on the radio, and then he was cradling her in his arms, carrying her towards the door.

"We've gotta run, love," he said. "I'm taking you out of here, and those other two dead sods can come too, if they've got any sense."

To avoid suspicion, Eddie put Tamsyn back on her feet, made sure that she could walk. She felt the grip of his hand on her elbow as he guided her back into the command centre, turning into the wardroom he'd claimed for himself. He sat her on a cot and frantically began to pack a kit bag. Blinking dully, she noted him throwing in guns, ammunition, and tins of food.

"My bow," she heard herself say.

"It's still in the Lexus," Eddie said. "Quick, love, we gotta go. The news is bound to get out."

Walking briskly across the compound, Eddie led Tamsyn to the motorpool. All the captured vehicles had been lined up here, and a pair of engineers were nearby, inspecting one of the new weapons platforms.

"Where are you going?" someone said, and Tamsyn noted that Baxter was leaning against the driver's door of her staff car.

"We're leaving, is what's going on. Get out of the bloody way."

"We heard what happened," Baxter said, a distant look on his face. "The Americans are on the radio right now, demanding that you surrender. I call that one hell of a time to drop your bundle, ma'am."

"Baxter, please," Tamsyn managed. "Just let us go."

"I can't do that," Baxter said, drawing his sidearm. "Captain Webb, I'm placing you under arrest."

"The hell you are," Eddie said, eyeing off the pistol held dead level with Tamsyn's heart.

"Ma'am, when you gave me this job, you asked me to make you do the right thing," Baxter said, holding his ground. "No matter how hard it was."

"Don't do this," Tamsyn begged.

"Baxter, what the hell are you doing?" Lynch shouted, the staff sergeant huffing over from the command building. Baxter turned his attention from Tamsyn for that one moment, long enough for Eddie to whip out his own sidearm. He emptied half the clip into the Texan.

Face white, his eyes fixed upon some impossible distance, Baxter let off one shot, discharging the gun somewhere near his feet. Slumped against the Lexus, Baxter twitched, sitting in a pool of his life as it leaked out of him.

"Eddie, no!" Tamsyn cried. Fighting her way free of his arms, she rushed over to the fallen soldier, who stared up and through her, just the same way her father had.

"You damn fool," Lynch shouted, fumbling out his sidearm with his off-hand. Crouching behind a captured jeep, the staff sergeant let off potshots in their direction. Eddie was down on one knee, returning fire, but Lynch was too far away for Eddie to hit with the pistol.

"Tamsyn, help me out," Eddie grunted, scrabbling backwards, opening the back door of the Lexus for cover. "Get your bow! Don't just stand there."

Silence. Lynch was probably moving through the vehicles, hoping for a better shot, or he was going for help. Tamsyn remembered the engineers working nearby and wondered who else was close enough to stop their escape.

She passed her hands over Baxter's eyes and laid him down on his side, leaving a bloody smear running down the side of the car.

For some reason she placed him in the recovery position. *Too late for that.*

"Get in the car," she said. "We're leaving, before anyone else gets hurt."

"Righto, then," Eddie said, and cursed as a bullet smashed out the window, inches from his face. He dove through the window, *Dukes of Hazzard* style. Tamsyn gripped the door handle, wincing as a bullet hole appeared, inches from her hand. She opened the door and crawled across to the driver's seat.

Lynch had circled around them, and the motorpool engineers were with him, advancing from car to car, darting forward when their companions were firing at the Lexus.

Thankfully Lynch and his press-ganged attackers only had their service sidearms to hand. With assault rifles, Tamsyn knew they would already be dead.

"Get us going!" Eddie said, lying across the backseat and reaching up to fire out blindly through the shattered window. "Move this thing, love, before they hit the petrol tank or something."

"Where are the keys?" Tamsyn said, frantically searching through the glove box, behind the sun visor.

"They're still in my pocket," Eddie said, rooting around in his pants, throwing the keys at her. They hit her in the face before landing somewhere on the floor. Tamsyn couldn't see where they'd gone and felt around under the seat.

Gripping the chunk of keys, Tamsyn looked up to see that the three men were advancing on the car in a loose line, pistols held level. Panicked, she froze, and held her hands up, defeated.

This is it, she thought, a moment before the men disintegrated in front of her, chunks of meat flying in all directions. Lynch got off one shot before he too was chewed apart by mini-gun fire.

Emerging from behind a troop-truck, a dozen Re-Humans stood in front of the Lexus, armed with the big guns. Tamsyn felt almost sick and hoped that it would be over quick.

They've finally risen up, she thought. *These are the most dangerous creatures on earth, and we've backed them into a corner.*

She saw that Dr. Murray and Simon Dawes were with the decaying cadre. She rolled down the driver's side window, shaking as she beckoned them over. She prayed that they were all still on the same side.

"All right then, Tam," Dr. Murray said.

"All right then," she replied, relieved.

"Good thing for you that Dawes here spotted all this from the traffic control tower," Dr. Murray said. "He was up there watching for your helicopter, saw the whole thing."

"Thanks," she said, looking dubiously at Dawes, who was nervously checking the action on his heavy gun.

"We heard what happened in Texas," Dr. Murray said. "Figure it's every dead man for himself now. Our lot are seizing what they can and shooting anyone who tries to stop us. We don't have any friends now."

"You've still got me," Tamsyn said. "Come with us. You and—and Dawes."

"What about our mates?" Dr. Murray said, waving his hands around. All about, dozens of resurrected soldiers were climbing into the vehicles, and someone started firing a turret gun into the command compound.

"Looks like they're doing fine," Eddie said from the backseat. "We going or what?"

"Going where?" Dr. Murray said with a chuckle, but he and Dawes got into the battered Lexus just the same. Tamsyn put her foot to the floor and found herself driving through a furious firefight. The Re-Humans were doing their best to seize the base from the living.

I don't blame them, Tamsyn thought, her heart pounding. She kept low in her seat, hoping the car body would stop any stray bullets. *We deserve it.*

They could still see the airfield when the first of the American bombers soared overhead, and then another, and soon the planes were too many to count. The last four people to escape from England heard the explosions, and soon the horizon was a wall of fire and smoke. Hundreds of parachutes could be seen against this hellish backdrop, drifting slowly groundward.

Tamsyn kept driving.

The car ran out of fuel somewhere west of Atlanta. Ignored by the dwindling population of local zombies, Dawes and Dr. Murray poked through the nondescript suburb, looking for supplies, and came back with the barest lick of fuel, siphoned from a lawnmower. It would give them another ten miles at best.

"I know of at least one Company came through here on the trip to Washington," Dawes said, poking his almost mummified head into the window. "Stripped this place to the bone."

Tamsyn ignored him, picking at a loose part of the steering wheel, worrying at the vinyl with her nails. The Re-Human shrugged and helped Dr. Murray load the other supplies into the trunk.

Eddie sat next to her, torso wrapped in bandages. In the firefight, Lynch put a bullet straight through one of Eddie's love handles, and during their escape Dr. Murray put his half-forgotten veterinarian skills to use.

"We need to talk, love," Eddie said. "You've said hardly a word about where we're going, what we're going to do."

"We're going home," Tamsyn said firmly.

"Tam, there's no home," Eddie said, exasperated. "Far as I'm concerned, we should be as far away from Texas as possible."

"I need to see it. I need to see what I did," Tamsyn said. Her jaw hurt from grinding her teeth, and her muscles ached from countless hours in the wheel. She wouldn't sleep and refused to let anyone else drive.

"Milly's dead, my love," Eddie said gently. "And it's sad, but that's just how it is. There's nothing we can do for her now."

"I don't even have any photos of her," Tamsyn said, and then the dam burst. She hugged the steering wheel, great heaving sobs tearing through her, and she wailed.

"Why am I still alive? Why?" she screamed, pounding at the dashboard, shaking the wheel till it seemed it would snap off in her hands, tears and snot running down her filthy face. Finally, she slumped forward, the whole mess running into her lap. She continued to weep softly.

Eddie held her close, sniffling himself. Dawes and Dr. Murray kept a respectful distance until some minutes later, when Tamsyn straightened up, wiped her face, and turned the key.

The bullet-riddled car coughed into a final silence on a lonely road, and Tamsyn sat behind the wheel for a long moment, staring straight ahead at the cracked asphalt.

"Okay love, well, we gotta start walking," Eddie said, popping open the passenger door. "C'mon then. A walk always cheers me up."

Every muscle aching, Tamsyn climbed out of the Lexus. She did not even bother to close the door behind her. The Re-Humans had found a wheelbarrow at the last stop, and it sat beside the abandoned car, piled high with supplies. Tinned food, flour, water, and as many saltshakers as they could find.

"We've had a talk, Tam," Eddie said. "Us three, about what we need to do now. We've come up with a plan."

"You have, have you?" Tamsyn said absently, hands clenching and unclenching. She turned from her consideration of the road ahead and stared woodenly at the trio.

"Look here, young lady, you stopped being in charge of us the moment we nicked off," Dr. Murray said. "We're all deserters, so don't think you can tell us what to do now."

"Wouldn't dream of it," she said snippily.

"There was a plan. The Re-Humans came up with it, should we all need to go AWOL," Dawes offered. "We thought of heading south, put millions of zombies between us and pursuit. Mexico maybe, somewhere the Americans wouldn't want to follow."

"Suits me," Tamsyn said. "Drop me off at Corpus Christi on your way through."

"Don't be facetious," Dr. Murray said. "We've had to come up with a different plan. Mexico wouldn't be safe for you living folks."

"The Bahamas," Eddie said. "You saw it on the way through, there's a bucketload of little islands down there. Clear all the zombies from one rock, and we can live safe and sound on an island paradise for the rest of our days."

"Come on. You know how I feel about going all *Blue Lagoon*?" Tamsyn scoffed. "What if we have a baby, Eddie? What if I have problems? Who's going to look after it if we get sick?"

"We won't be on our own. Not for long," Eddie said.

"Once you kids are settled in, Dawes and I will start making trips to Cuba," Dr. Murray said. "Making some neighbours for you. We reckon the Americans won't even realise that a nation of Re-Humans is existing quietly, right on their doorstep."

"Communist zombies. Oh goody."

They walked south, following the quiet back roads that threaded from town to dead town. The first leg of their journey meant long days on foot towards Jacksonville. This endless trudge was sometimes interrupted by the occasional knot of zombies. Going by the number of empty houses and farms, almost all of the zombies around here had formed a swarm, heading for parts unknown.

Tamsyn found it eerie, walking through this almost empty world. She took to sleeping with her bow, convinced that a super-pack to end all super-packs lay just ahead. She could just picture it, a million or more of the dead, a walking city that would catch their scent and dog them relentlessly, dragging them down when they could walk no more.

Every night brought her the nightmares. Bad ones, dreams of fiery apocalypse, crowds of accusing faces, pointing, calling out her name. She would wake lathered with sweat, Eddie snoring away, the two dead men staring at her from across their campfire.

I'm cursed, she began to say to herself. *Everything I touch goes bad. People die when I'm around.*

Maybe the world would be better if I wasn't in it.

As they slowly made their way across the state, the two Re-Humans became churlish, snapping at each other over the slightest offence. Dr. Murray's stores of dry wit had run out days ago, and Dawes's usual martyr act became something darker. Every movement had an edge of violence to it, a jittery energy that he could barely contain.

The two humans became very nervous.

As they passed by a tree on the roadside, a pack of birds took flight. Quicker than thought a spooked Dawes had his mini-gun up and tracking, shredding the tree with a quick burst of lead. When Tamsyn protested the waste of ammo he hurled the enormous gun to the ground, stalking off the road and into the bush.

"Leave it," Tamsyn told Eddie, and followed Dawes. Following the Re-Human down a hillside, she found him sitting by a trickling stream, trailing one purpled hand in the water.

"I can't feel this," Dawes said, not looking up. "I mean, I know it's water, and I can scoop it up and even drink it, but it's not wet to me, it's not even cold. It doesn't feel like anything."

Tamsyn sat on the bank next to Dawes. The damp clay stuck to her pants, and her arms rose in goosebumps. Down here, out of the autumn sunlight, Florida was actually cold.

"What's going on with you, Dawes?" Tamsyn finally asked.

"Running out of salt," he said. "Me and the old bugger, we've been on half rations for days, and today we halved that. It's driving me bloody loopy."

Tamsyn looked into his dead fish-eyes and saw that the spark of intelligence was dimming, that Dawes was starting to get the vacant look of the wild undead. The Re-Human procedure was starting to reverse itself.

"If you can hold on four, maybe five more days, we'll be at the coast," Tamsyn said. "I know it hurts more, but you could swim into the sea, get your dose that way."

"No," Dawes whispered. "I can't do this anymore."

Tamsyn nodded and touched his shoulder. She left him there, slouched by the creek, a twin trail of dark tears sliding down the ruin of his face.

I cried a river because of what you did, she thought, a flash of hatred filling her.

"Well?" Eddie asked as Tamsyn emerged from the bushes. She plucked her bow and arrows from the wheelbarrow and hunted around for a length of rope. Dislodging a box of bandages, she saw the tiny plastic bag of salt at the bottom, the precious crystals held in with a rubber band.

There were perhaps two teaspoons worth of salt left.

"Dawes is staying here," Tamsyn said, and Dr. Murray nodded mournfully. *A noble sacrifice.* Eddie checked the action on his pistol and made as if to follow.

"I'll be okay. He wants to turn, go wild again. I'll sit with him until it happens." She held up the coil of rope. "I'll tie him up a bit, but eventually he'll get loose, do whatever the wild ones do."

"It's what he wants, Eddie Jacobs," Dr. Murray warned. "Let this happen, lad."

Tamsyn returned to the stream, holding the loop of rope down by her side. Dawes saw this and smiled, his scars pulling the tight leather into a horrible grimace.

"Smart girl," he said. "Over here, this looks like a nice spot."

He found a thick tree at the bank of the stream, a silver birch with thick roots running down into the water. Sitting against the trunk, he let her run the rope around him, tying a loose knot over his belly.

"This won't hold long," he said.

"You'll break out of that eventually, after you turn," Tamsyn said. "That's your chosen penance, right? For all the bad shit you did, to my mum, to those other people you killed?"

Dawes nodded. "Thank you, Tamsyn."

"It's going to happen soon," Tamsyn said, looking into his eyes. The speck of life, of will and reason, was slowly fading. "You'll get to make good on what you've done."

They sat there for what seemed like hours. The sun crossed the sky, the barest lick of its light touching Tamsyn in the cool glade.

"I have always hated you, Simon Dawes," Tamsyn said, breaking the companionable silence. "I thought I had a good reason, but it turns out that I'm a much bigger monster than you."

"How do you mean?" mumbled Dawes, his speech already slurring. His head was slumped forward, and a faint tremor was causing his feet and hands to shake slightly.

"You were driving drunk and ran a car into a bus shelter. I have killed an entire city of people, everyone on that boat trip, my comrades, everyone who served under me. I killed my step-daughter."

"That's not your fault," Dawes began.

"It was," she snapped. "Corpus Christi was wiped off the map because of me. So was Gravesend. I led the horde to a weak point in the barricades. God, I killed my best friend. You're the only person I've ever told that to."

He said nothing, but watched cautiously as she rolled back her sleeve, waved his arm in front of her face.

"I want you to bite me, Dawes. Give me the infection, and I'll turn with you. We can roam the world together, a pair of monsters."

He shook his head, turned away when Tamsyn tried to pry open his mouth. She slapped him hard, then again when the first had no result.

"Can't feel it," he said woodenly, smiling loosely. "Carn –feel nuffin."

The smile slowly fell from his face, and for a moment he was perfectly still. Then Tamsyn saw the shift, watched as the eyes fixed on her, predatory, hungry. The shell that had been Simon Dawes snarled at her, reached for her with grasping fingers, pulled against the flimsy knot-work that would give in seconds.

Still wallowing in her own internal darkness, Tamsyn wanted to lunge forward, jam her fingers into that snapping mouth, but she couldn't do it. She wanted life more. Wanted revenge most of all.

Tamsyn fitted an arrow to her bowstring and calmly drew the fletching to her cheek. One moment a monster roared defiance at her, the next a sad dead man was pinned to a tree, an arrow squarely resting between his eyes.

Tamsyn left Dawes next to the bubbling stream and went to rejoin the others. She felt cleansed, felt that justice had finally been delivered. After years of sorrow, she'd never intended to grant the last request of Simon Dawes.

Rejoining the other two, Tamsyn quietly slid her bow and quiver into the wheelbarrow. Neither of them asked her what had happened down in that quiet glade. For the first time in months, Tamsyn slept deeply and did not dream.

Miami proved tricky. A super-pack roamed through the beach-side city, finally moving on to devastate other parts of post-apocalyptic Florida. From a high-rise, they observed zombies of the dormant variety abandoning their old routines, drawn away by their rabid brethren.

Tamsyn wondered if Texan research had caused this, if the boffins had found a way to empty the cities of zombies, with a view to reoccupation.

Not that it matters now, she thought. *Uncle Sam gets to enjoy the results.*

"It's like the Beatles are in town or something," Eddie said, flicking his cigarette butt over the side of the building, down onto the horde passing below.

"Thought you'd shaken that filthy habit, young Jacobs," Dr. Murray said. "What does your lady have to say about that?"

"I figure he's earned the right to enjoy a puff," Tamsyn said, soaking up some rays on a deckchair. "I'm not his keeper."

They crossed the abandoned city before dusk, Tamsyn zipping around joyfully on a pair of rollerblades. They swapped the wheel-barrow for a shopping cart and looted the largely untouched shops with vigour.

"Listen to that racket," Eddie said, wincing as the metal cart crashed and clattered along the sidewalk. "We're daft for walking around with this thing."

"No matter," Dr. Murray said, lobbing a brick through another plate glass window. "We're the only ones here."

They took a leisurely stroll towards the nearest marina, meaning to supply their chosen boat until it rode low in the water. Remembering the disastrous voyage over from England, no one was keen to go without anything this time around.

"I'll be in this pharmacy," Tamsyn said, waving off Eddie when he made to follow. "Girlie things."

Clattering through the broken glass on her blades, Tamsyn quietly pocketed a pregnancy test, carrying out two boxes of pads and roughly a lifetime's supply of paracetamol.

You might be a dad, Tamsyn thought, wondering how she'd break the news to her man-child of a boyfriend. He was just wandering out of a jewellery store, a sheepish grin plastered across his face. When he saw her, his hand dived into his pocket, but not so quick that she couldn't spot the ring. It was a huge stone that, in the old world, would have been far beyond the salary of a normal mortal.

"What are you up to, Edward Jacobs?" she said, rolling alongside him. Her grin matched his.

"Nothing, ya snoopy cow," he laughed. "Go and do something useful. Lift me some grog or something."

"Kids, you need to get a wriggle on," Dr. Murray said, pointing back the way they'd come. The broad city street was filling fast with coffin-dodgers, the very edges of the super-pack. The wave of decaying bodies slowly bore down on them, pushing them towards the beach and freedom. Whooping, they pushed the trolley towards the boats, holding onto the sides and riding it down the hill.

Tamsyn laughed until the tears came. She'd never felt more alive.

PART 4:
BETTER RED THAN UNDEAD

15

When the world ended, Tamsyn's new house had still been on the market. The flags and dusty sandwich boards invited her in for an open inspection, almost four years since the zombie pandemic put an end to real estate.

Eddie found the house keys in the pool. The estate agent was long gone, most likely dead now, but she'd left the mini-mansion neatly locked up. Brochures and floorplans were neatly laid out on the kitchen counter, the glossy paper coated with dust. The asking price was five million dollars.

"We'll take it," Eddie said. He made a point of yanking out the "FOR SALE" sign, throwing it over the neighbour's high fence. They took care to wrap a fat chain around the wrought iron gates, on the off chance that a dead millionaire might come knocking.

Sunset Keys was as quiet as the grave. Isolated and safe, but the rich islanders had still managed to destroy themselves. Before Tamsyn and Eddie found the empty mansion, each house on the luxury island told the same story. Wars between neighbours, bare larders, evidence of suicide parties and empty boat slips.

Apart from a handful of zombies, the whole island was empty. No one would bother them here.

Tamsyn loved every inch of the new house. She loved the cinema room, the big airy bedrooms, and the ocean views from the balcony. Most of all, she adored the pool. When her ankles felt like fiery hinges and her back seized up, she could sink into the water. Here, she could escape the cruelty of gravity for a while, and hold the sticky Florida summer at bay.

The little person in her tummy kicked, and Tamsyn smiled.

"Oy! That's all meant for garden water," Eddie yelled at her, a shovel across his shoulder. "Stop floating about and do something useful, ya daft cow!"

She poked her tongue out at him and swam a gentle lap. She figured she was about six months pregnant now, give or take a week or two. Wouldn't pay to overdo things.

While Eddie drank beer and worked on the garden, Tamsyn spent most of her time in a happy hormonal daze, painting or reading. When they got the generator going in the evenings, she main-lined the house's extensive DVD collection.

She slept through most afternoons now, the hot Florida sun too much for her to handle. Windows open, she rolled about on the bed, trying to find comfort in a world where she had the belly of a whale, where every internal organ was now a percussion instrument.

The air was thick with heat. As she dozed off, the dream came almost immediately, a recurring nightmare her mind forced her to sit through from start to finish.

The whole town was lined up on the pier at Gravesend. Her neighbours were calm-eyed and living, though in her last memory of the place, the pier was awash with blood and rot, people screaming as they plunged into the freezing Thames, dying of the shivers or just drowning.

Ali, grinning and waving. Will Dwyer and his family, smiling and safe. Naomi and Monica, reunited and blissfully in love. Eddie's dad was there, fishing next to her own father. Poor old

Mal Webb, shot dead on a beach, but here he looked off into the distance, lips curled slightly as if smiling at some secret joke.

"You killed us," her father said.

Nearby, her mother shared a sandwich with Gravesend's famous statue of Pocahontas. The bronze woman picked at the food with otherworldly grace. Two big boats coasted by in unison, a cargo ship and a luxury yacht. The *Paraclete* and the *Petty Cash*, and in this dream their decks were lined with smiling faces.

In reality they'd almost starved, stuck out in the ocean on the dead cargo ship. They'd lost over half their number boarding the drifting superyacht, a desperate gamble in wild seas.

"You killed us," these people said, and they were right. The voyage to America was her risky plan, her failure. Their blood was still on her hands.

The Gundersons. Little Millie. Marcus Riley and Simon Dawes. She walked on those doomed decks and begged for forgiveness, but they all turned away, shrugged off her hands.

Simon Dawes she could happily kill again. That one was a fair call. He'd killed her mother, after all. He waved at her, and she mimed a pistol at his face, *bang.*

The far side of the Thames became the other side of the Atlantic Ocean, and then she was walking through Corpus Christi, Texas. She knew the place was a ruin now, nuked out of existence, but here she saw the Navy base, the neat streets. Waiting for the ships were an army of murdered ghosts, here pink-skinned and happy.

Clarice Feickert, President of the Texan Republic. She'd started a civil war on behalf of the Re-Humans, fed them the salt they needed to remember life. Kept the mindful dead locked up in ghettos.

"You killed us," Feickert said around a cigarette, all makeup and shoulder pads and bluster. Dead, a radioactive smear, and of course this was her fault too.

Next to her, the soldiers Tamsyn had served with, dead to the last. Colonel Dekker, the enormous Marine who sold them out for a truckload of salt. Her buddies from Foxtrot Company, boozing and playing cards. Staff Sergeant Lynch, scowling into his clipboard, counting inventory even in this fantasy.

Finally, Private Baxter, blunt do-gooder, a paladin in an age where noble deeds got you killed. Here, he wore the medals he'd never earnt in life, bore a general's star.

"You killed us," he said, and he was right.

"I didn't mean to," she protested.

They closed in, smiles fading and flesh rotting. All that was left to the world were zombies with familiar faces, reaching for her, biting at her arms and legs, demanding justice, demanding that she listen.

"You're still alive," they all said, and she tried to convince them that no, she was already dead, always had been.

"Tam! Come down here!"

Eddie?

"Tam, we got a coffin-dodger!"

Eddie's excited cries brought her completely out of the nightmare, crying and heart pounding. She muzzily noted how her rich cotton sheets were soaked with sweat. Her breathing slowed. There was a worrying twinge from her womb, the sense that something was squeezing her insides in a vice.

Throat dry and heart racing, Tamsyn touched her belly gently. She was rewarded with the kick, the motion of the baby rolling over within her. Breathing a shaky sigh of relief, Tamsyn wiped her eyes, tried to put the moment behind her.

"If something goes wrong, we're on our own, little one," she whispered to the life inside her. "No National Health here."

Frowning and holding the small of her back, Tamsyn waddled out of the house. The front lawn was completely dug out now, converted into a vegetable garden. Filthy from turning the beds, Eddie stood by the front gates, leaning on his shovel and pointing.

"You wouldn't read about it, love. We missed one!"

There were no cars on the island, and the streets were empty but for the occasional abandoned golf cart. Taking the shortest possible path to their house, a dead man walked, clothing worn to rags. The balmy summers had baked its flesh to leather, and the zombie looked like a skeleton draped in beef jerky. A mummy, unwrapped and set to walking.

Clutching at the air with fleshless hands, the creature moaned, a low cry of hunger, frustration. As it gripped the bars of the gate and shook them, Eddie smashed the dead man's fingers with his shovel. He laughed at the snapping teeth and reached for the chain.

"I'll sort this chap out," Eddie began, and flinched as something blurred past his cheek. An arrow punched into the dead man's forehead, and with a final sigh the zombie sank to the ground, unnatural life passing from it.

Tamsyn stood on the front steps, lowered her bow. Even as Eddie goggled at her, white-faced and mouth working, she gave a shrug.

"Gotta keep my eye in, love," she said, placing the bow next to the small arsenal of guns on the porch. "Relax! I could still shoot an apple off your head, and you know it."

"You're a bloody maniac," he gasped. "Don't fire an arrow anywhere near me. I bloody mean it. Shit."

Eddie dragged the body across the street. Tamsyn lugged out a canister of fuel, ignoring his objections that she was pregnant and shouldn't lift anything. They sipped warm soft drinks back at the house, leaning on the balcony as they watched the corpse burn.

"He must have been in a cellar or something. Banging around in the dark, and then he found a way out." Eddie ran a hand over his head, leaving dirt smears mixed with sweat. She'd finally convinced him to grow his hair out, but it was still stubble for the most part.

"No way," Tamsyn countered. "He had a nice tan. Mark my words, our dead friend has been enjoying a tropical apocalypse since day one. I say he was stuck in a backyard, or on a roof."

"Well, only he knew," Eddie said. "Shame. All this posh shite, and he had no one to share it with."

Tamsyn leant against her man, smiling and happy, nightmare already forgotten. For about the tenth time that day, she admired her engagement ring. Back in Miami, she'd caught Eddie looting it from a jewellery store. The stone was so big, she thought she could cut her way through plate glass.

Definitely some benefits to the world ending, she decided.

"Stop looking at your ring," Eddie scoffed. "You'll wear it out."

"Shoosh. Let me have my moment," Tamsyn said, and Eddie smiled. They kissed then, and there was nothing to the world but two kids from Gravesend, with the squirm of a baby between them.

Tamsyn spent the afternoon up on the observation deck, watching Key West through a telescope. Less than a mile away, the island chain swarmed with undead. Thousands of walking dead filled the streets, milling about aimlessly.

She watched the horde with morbid fascination, and a faint tickle of excitement. She knew that if she or Eddie were to set foot on that shore, they'd be torn apart in seconds. The place was completely overrun by zombies, most of them too stupid to follow the highway back through the Keys and onto the mainland. The island chain seemed to work like a flypot; drawing in dead things, but not letting them go.

Then, a movement near the marina. Something pushing through the crowd of rotten flesh. It was Dr. Murray, wheeling a sack truck piled high with forage.

"Hope you got me some chocolate," Tamsyn muttered, watching as her friend climbed back onto the boat. Once the goods were loaded onto the runabout, he used a gaff pole to push away the curious zombies, lifting the gangplank before any of the corpses could turn stowaway.

The pack of undead only seemed to notice him in a puzzled, distant kind of way. He smelt the same, looked the same. But it was in his eyes, in the way he moved. A memory of life, wrapped in dead meat.

Not quite a zombie, not quite alive. Dr. Murray was a Re-Human, his mind brought back from undeath with a painful salt treatment. The closest thing to a cure that anyone had found.

He ran the boat gently across the mile of muggy ocean, and even from here Tamsyn could see how low it rode in the water. He'd filled it almost to the gunwales, and as the runabout got closer she could make out big canisters of drinking water, sacks of flour. Boxes, neatly stacked and held down with cargo webbing.

"Ah, c'mon," Tamsyn moaned. "I'm pregnant here. Not really interested in baked beans and powdered milk."

She tracked the boat past the first row of houses, and through gaps in the palm trees she saw him circumnavigate the island. A pair of small docks faced Key West, old berths for the water taxi and the ferry from the mainland. But they were too close to the island chain. It wouldn't do for someone to spot their boats in the moorings, wonder who was living on the island.

Especially the Americans. It was only a matter of time till they came sniffing.

"Eddie, he's back," she called down to the garden. Waddling down the staircase and out through the front doors, Tamsyn fetched a floppy hat, wheeling the spare sack-truck towards the front gate. Shaking his head, Eddie took it from her.

"Are you bloody daft? You're knocked up. I said no lifting."

"I'm pregnant, not disabled," Tamsyn said.

Eddie put a pistol into the waistband of his shorts, and Tamsyn picked up her bow, gently strapping the quiver onto her hip. The belt was snug around her big belly, and she had to let it out another notch, shifting it lower.

Unlocking the gate, they stepped out onto the street. A handful of flies were still buzzing over the charred corpse, and Tamsyn fought the rebellion in her stomach. A whole island to choose from, and her lazy fiancé left the body straight across the street.

Eddie and Tamsyn took the main throughfare, passing through the opulent weekenders and guest cottages. Though the gardens were overgrown now, the effect remained. Luxurious real estate, far beyond the reach of most mortals.

Crossing the communal tennis courts, they made it to the north shore of the island, skirting the resort. Tamsyn watched every broken window carefully. She sat an arrow on the string, ready to pull and release.

For all their care when clearing the island, they'd missed one. Where one dead thing lurked in the shadows, there could be a dozen more, watching her hungrily...

It would only take one bite to turn her into a monster, to corrupt the life growing inside her. Tamsyn shivered, almost willing a coffin-dodger to show itself.

"Cor, look at all that stuff," Eddie said as they reached the shore. Dr. Murray already had the runabout moored at the resort's private dock and was stacking the supplies onto the pier.

"Load it straight onto the cruiser," Dr. Murray said. "Enough here to make another run."

Tamsyn felt sad at the thought. Nice as it was, this island was only a temporary home for them. The Republic of Texas was in ashes, and she was a war criminal. The plan was for Dr. Murray to poke through the shops and the homes in the infested Keys, foraging everything that wasn't nailed down.

Then, get the hell out of town before Uncle Sam got here.

Home was actually going to be Fort Jefferson. It was a ruin on the Dry Tortugas, an island cluster one hundred miles to the west. It was isolated, completely safe, and absolutely boring. Once Dr. Murray scrounged up enough supplies to last them five years, they were leaving Sunset Keys forever.

Five more years. The time they reckoned it would take the wild undead to rot down to bone, to slip into a final death. Till then, she would wait them out behind stone walls, raise her child in ignorance of these monsters.

The Re-Human worked like a metronome, heaving heavy crates over the side. When he effortlessly threw a five-gallon water bottle directly into Eddie's chest, his supernatural strength was most evident.

"Sorry, lad," Dr. Murray said, as Eddie picked himself up from the pier, winded. "Keep forgetting that you folks with pulses are a bit soft."

"Sod off," Eddie managed, fighting to get his breath back. "You stinky bastard."

Clem Murray was the only other survivor of Gravesend, though *survive* wasn't the most accurate word. The old drunk was as dead as a door-post. What flesh remained to him was taut and leathery, tanned from sunlight and frequent dosings of salt-water.

Even as the Re-Human teased Eddie, Tamsyn saw the weary cast to his eyes, the way his shoulders slumped. She thought of the painful treatment that kept him going, the only thing Dr. Murray could feel now. Not for the first time, she wondered if it would be kinder to put a bullet through his head.

"Now, as for you, lass," the Re-Human said sternly, crooking a skeletal finger to beckon her closer. "I fetched some essential supplies for those in the family way."

"Clem, if this is another bottle of folate or bloody fish oil, I'm going to scream. Seriously."

Reaching into the boat, the Re-Human held up a box, still stamped with import and quarantine stickers. Somewhere, Dr. Murray had found a cache of honest-to-God English chocolate, unopened and preserved in all its tooth-rotting glory.

"Yanks don't know how to make a good chocolate," the Re-Human mumbled. Dr. Murray feigned protest as the pregnant girl clambered into the boat, squeezing him tightly and squealing with delight. Right there and then she tore open the box, stuffing her mouth full of chocolate sweetness.

"Mad as a meat-axe, your missus," Dr. Murray said to Eddie. "You'd think she'd never seen a Mars Bar before."

Laughing through a mouthful of sweet goo, Tamsyn tossed a chocolate bar up to Eddie. Before the world ended, this was the simplest of pleasures, a luxury she'd almost forgotten. Survival did not always mean living.

Even as she and her fiancé devoured the sweets, Tamsyn noticed the way that the Re-Human looked on, almost wistful. The dead man occupied himself with tying down the runabout, fixing a tarp to keep out the monsoonal rains.

"Don't you worry none, Tam," he said, waving away her concern with a mummified hand. "I found a jar of Bovril and that's good enough for me."

"You're gonna try and drink that salty muck?" Eddie said.

"I'd rather hit the Glenfiddich, but we make do," the Re-Human said curtly. Arms loaded high with heavy boxes, the Re-Human shuffled onwards, heedless of the weight or the strain on his muscles.

Re-Humans aren't actually strong, Tamsyn realised, shamefully tucking the chocolate bar into her pocket. *They just don't know when they're damaging themselves.*

She saw the need for haste; a fat cloud was bearing down on the island, and in minutes the boxes would be soaked through. Tamsyn helped to ferry the lighter crates onto the cabin cruiser, stowing down the supplies for the voyage west.

The boat used to be known as the *Christmas Bonus*, but Tamsyn rechristened it *Pocahontas,* using a stencil to apply the new name. It was an old weekender with flaking paint, liberated from a marina near Miami. Between Eddie and Dr. Murray, the motor was in as stable a condition as these amateur mechanics could make it.

After three years rotting in dock, the engines in the newer boats wouldn't even turn over. It was the *Pocahontas* or nothing.

The fuel tanks were big enough to take the cruiser to Fort Jefferson and back. The boat had a small kitchen and a toilet, as well as a deep-freeze for storing fish. Last of all, the *Pocahontas* had a sleeping berth and a TV complete with DVD player.

Tamsyn hated Fort Jefferson, but she never minded the boat ride. Everything else made her nauseous, but thankfully sea travel no longer bothered her—a weird but welcome side-effect of being knocked up. Once the boxes were stowed she got out the makings for a cup of tea, and put her feet up. This time around, she planned to watch the first two Godfather movies, and as much of the Gilmore Girls as she could get away with.

"Not today," Dr. Murray grumbled. "We're not sailing through that squall."

"You let me sit down before telling me that?" Tamsyn said, struggling to rise. Grudgingly, she accepted Eddie's hand, and waddled away from the boat.

The trio were only ten steps away from the pier when the storm hit, soaking every stitch within seconds. The others ran for shelter, but Tamsyn could only hobble and curse, miserable as the baby kicked her again.

"You hurry up and fix me a golf cart, Eddie Jacobs!" she shouted. "This is bullshit!"

Eddie put on the power that night, the summer storm muting the generator as it clattered away underneath the veranda. Dinner was the pair of whiting that Eddie hooked that morning, accompanied by canned vegetables and powdered sauce. For their dessert, Dr. Murray produced a tinned pudding with a flourish.

"Cheers to the international import store. Here's hoping Clem remembers the address!" Eddie toasted. He was drinking scotch and poured a tumbler for Dr. Murray too. The Re-Human never drank the stuff, but every now and then he held the glass to his nose, took a deep and loving sniff.

Tamsyn noticed that as Eddie drank, Dr. Murray's hands shook. He still suffered from a life-long addiction to the grog, denied now by the cruelty of his bizarre new existence. His was the body of a zombie, rejecting anything but salt and human flesh.

Eddie cleared away the dishes, and Dr. Murray brought out some cards, dealing for whist. Tonight was Eddie's turn to pick the music, and he cranked up Oasis, singing along with more enthusiasm than skill. The hidden speakers in each room did their best to fight off the storm's fury.

"God, you're such a chav," Tamsyn complained. "Turn it down a bit."

"What, the neighbours gonna complain? I hope they do," Eddie scoffed. Dr. Murray tried to teach them other games that he knew, and they settled down for several rounds of gin rummy. Eddie changed the Oasis for some Arctic Monkeys, and Tamsyn dropped her cards with a laugh.

"That's it. Unless there's a sudden injection of culture, I'm going to bed."

"Before you do, let's try the Bovril out," Dr. Murray said seriously. "See if it works."

Worried, Tamsyn stayed.

Boiling up a kettle on the gas ring, Eddie drunkenly fumbled the black extract into a mug, stirring vigorously. He planted the mug in front of the Re-Human, sloshing the contents onto the expensive walnut tabletop.

"C'mon, down the hatch old son," Eddie crowed. Dr. Murray wrapped his hands around the mug, the grey slug of his tongue emerging to lick cracked lips.

"I don't know if I should," he said.

"You don't have to do this," Tamsyn said.

Dr. Murray peered into the curling steam, working up the courage. All of a sudden he snatched up the mug and poured the contents straight down his throat, heedless of the scalding liquid.

"Yeah!" Eddie shouted. "I knew you could do it!"

Dr. Murray's cloudy eyes watered with pain as the salty drink burnt his insides. Salt was the only thing he could feel now, a daily torture that kept his monstrous nature at bay.

The Re-Human smiled, and then a moment later he gagged. A black geyser erupted from his mouth to splash across the table, his body heaving as it rejected the broth.

Tamsyn pushed away from the table but was too late. Even as she ran for the toilet, her dinner sprayed through her fingers. Eddie stood in the middle of the carnage, laughing and air-guitaring to a blistering guitar solo. Furious with him, Tamsyn turned off the stereo and sat next to Dr. Murray. The Re-Human sat covered in filth, quietly weeping.

"I'm sorry, Clem," Tamsyn said, wiping her mouth. She sat next to the Re-Human, rested her hand on his shoulders. Apart from the smell of sick, the dead man was tanned and salted to the point where his skin was now pliant leather. At a time in her life where even food smells set her off, the dead body of Dr. Murray smelt like varnished wood, or a closet full of old clothes and blankets.

Tamsyn secretly found Dr. Murray's smell to be quite comforting. She used a napkin to wipe his face clean, sponging off the vomit, soaking up his dark, sticky tears. He'd been kind to her father in Gravesend, back when both the men had been alive. It was time for her to repay the favour.

"I couldn't even taste it," Dr. Murray sobbed. "I can't taste anything."

The morning was clear and brilliant, and when the sunlight touched Eddie's face he groaned like he was a zombie himself. With a vicious satisfaction, Tamsyn whipped the curtain all the way across, bathing the room in pure light.

"Stop that," Eddie moaned. "You horrid woman, make it dark again."

"You know, Eddie, I feel fine. Perhaps it's because I didn't drink a bottle of scotch all on my own."

"You're just jealous," he said, face muffled by the pillow. Relenting a little, Tamsyn pulled the curtain across, and she sat at the foot of the bed. Composing her thoughts, she wondered how best to berate her fiancé for his meat-head behaviour.

Besides, poor Clem doesn't need to be reminded that he can't drink now.

"You won't be behaving like this when our baby comes along," she began, only to be rewarded with a snore.

The palm trees along the street dropped several fronds during the night, one of which lay across the charred zombie. Their house was sturdy, and not even the tiles had moved under the onslaught.

Tamsyn caught up with Dr. Murray as the Re-Human shuffled towards the beach. She didn't fit into her bathers anymore, and ventured out in an oversize t-shirt and some old shorts with a sagging elastic band. Even decked out with a sunhat and flip-flops, Tamsyn carried her bow, one arrow nocked on the string.

"Leave me alone," the Re-Human grumbled.

"It's a free country. I'm going for a swim too," Tamsyn said.

"I do this on my own," he continued, but the protest trailed off when he realised Tamsyn meant to follow. He huffed across the island in silence, boots scuffing up leaves and sand.

They reached the beach, a magnificent crescent of white sand. Apart from a handful of mildewed deck chairs, they had the whole place to themselves. Laying out a towel, Tamsyn carefully put her bow and arrow on this, keeping the mechanisms free of sand. Opening a tube of sunscreen, she caked it onto her eternally pale skin.

"Want some?" she said without thinking, offering the sunscreen to Dr. Murray. Even as she stammered out an apology, he waved it aside, fumbling out of his clothes with stiff fingers.

"Might as well rub varnish into this," he grumbled. He stood before the rolling surf, naked and miserable. He'd been an old man when he died, a drunkard with his ribs hanging out and perhaps a few years left before the booze did him in altogether.

Now, immortality.

He was luckier than many of the Re-Humans she'd seen, poor individuals found with missing limbs, flesh gone to rot, guts bloated or hanging out in foul ropes. No, Dr. Murray was lucky to die in Texan captivity, and when he rose as a man-eating freak, he received the salt treatment almost immediately. He was perfectly preserved.

Clem Murray always hid his fatal injury behind long sleeves, but when he took his daily dip the zombie's bite was revealed. It wasn't much of an injury, just a semi-circle of grey marks, the indents barely visible in his dark hide.

"Rude to stare," Dr. Murray said.

"Would it make you more comfortable if I took my clothes off?" Tamsyn said, and made to lift off her tent of a shirt. She'd always been self-conscious around boys, but he just felt–safe. Not a threat. Not even a man now.

"Don't be ridiculous," the Re-Human snorted. "I had a grand-daughter about your age. I'm too old and too bloody dead to perve on some knocked up kid."

"Your loss," Tamsyn said with a grin, and slid into the water. It was still early, and the water was chilly enough to make her gasp. The baby kicked in protest, a steady flutter that pleased her on some primal level.

She sank into the foam, freezing by inches until she had the depth to swim. Apart from the grisly creature hovering at the water's edge, the beach was a perfect scene, a postcard picture. Palm trees, and mansions, and standing amongst it all, a crime against nature.

Dr. Murray paced around on the shore, working up courage. Finally, he stomped into the water, determined to meet his elemental enemy. The moment his foot touched the foam left behind by the last wave, he gasped, began to limp.

Then another wave pushed against his lower legs, and the gasp became a low keening, a cry that the Re-Human tried to hold inside. As he pushed forward, the water rose up his thighs, and then the cry became a scream.

Tamsyn thought she'd offer him moral support by being here, but now she understood. Salt brought a level of pain that unmanned him. This was an intensely private moment, and she was treating it like a day at Brighton.

Howling in agony, Dr. Murray sluiced the seawater against his limbs, and then Tamsyn was amazed to see him dunk his entire head under the water. He stayed down there for over a minute, with only the occasional bubble floating to the surface. A thread of panic wormed its way through her chest, and every instinct screamed at her to get over there, pull him out of the water.

"It's not like he has to breathe, my little pumpkin," she told the baby.

Sure enough, Dr. Murray jerked out of the water almost two minutes later, still screaming and vomiting the gutful of water he'd swallowed. Tamsyn knew enough that the seawater burnt like acid to the undead. The Texan army had force-bathed its Re-Human regiment, torturing the dead every day, but they all went willingly.

They needed the salt. Only a few days without it, and the Re-Humans reverted back to mindless zombies, slavering for human flesh. It was the nearest thing to life, and many of the Re-Humans embraced the pain, made their own mysticism out of the experience. There'd even been a new religion in the ghetto before President Feickert was forced to shut it down.

When Tamsyn considered the sheer willpower it took for Dr. Murray to stay submerged, to let the magic mineral soak into his lifeless flesh, it staggered her.

Shaking, body wracked by sobs, the Re-Human made for the shore. Tamsyn followed, ashamed that she'd gate-crashed Dr. Murray's daily ritual. He stood in the sun, arms outstretched, and turned to let the sun slowly dry his damp flesh.

"Don't," he warned as she approached him with a towel. "That just rubs the salt in. Hurts like buggery."

When the beads of water dried and ran from his taut carcass, Dr. Murray brushed the last crusts of sand from his skin, wincing a little. Then he accepted the towel, wiping off left-over salt with quick, economical movements. His dose received, Dr. Murray laid the towel out on the sand, rested next to the girl. Tamsyn settled down with the hat over her face, wriggling her toes in the sand.

"Thank you," he said. "It's embarrassing, but I'm glad you came."

"Don't be ashamed," she said, patting him on the arm. "Not like you can help it. I couldn't put myself through that, not all the time like you do."

They sat in a companionable silence for many long minutes. As the sun slowly turned the beach into an oven, Tamsyn relaxed, soaking up the warmth. Her baby fluttered again, turning somersaults in her stomach.

"I lost a finger today," Dr. Murray said calmly. Tamsyn sat bolt upright, staring. He had his hand held out flat, and the middle finger dangled, attached only by a strip of sinew. After a moment of consideration, he tore it loose, cast it out into the sea.

"What did you do that for? We might have been able to put it back on!"

"Pah! It's not a tooth, girl."

Still shocked, Tamsyn looked at the gap in his hand, the way the Re-Human calmly surveyed the damage. He gave his body a quick inspection and found a toe in a similar condition. This he managed to skip across the water, the squishy digit bouncing twice and then sinking.

Tamsyn noticed that two other toes were already missing. His foot resembled a bruised fruit now, and despite everything that salt could do, decay was finally claiming Clem Murray's body.

"Saw it happen to some of the others," Dr. Murray said quietly, almost calmly. "Ones who came to the Re-Human program with more miles on the zombie clock, more damage to their bodies. Happened for them much faster. Thought I might avoid it, but I was wrong."

"What happened? What are you saying, Clem?" Tamsyn asked.

"The salt can't hold it off forever," Dr. Murray said. "You start dropping bits like a leper, and then you're naught but a snapping skull attached to a torso. Worst of all, you're still stuck in here." The Re-Human tapped a bony finger against his temple.

"We're not really immortal. It's just a cheap trick, Tam. We get a few more years, perhaps a decade or two if we eke out the treatment."

Tamsyn was stunned at the revelation. She'd observed the way the salt was curing his flesh; she thought he'd been going very well, better than ever. He'd been charging into the overrun towns with gusto, hauling out more supplies than she or Eddie could even hope to carry. Almost every day Dr. Murray was out on the forage, working like a man obsessed while she and Eddie soaked up the rays and played house.

Then, it all made sense.

"You're going to kill yourself," Tamsyn said. "Once you're sure that we've got enough food and we'll be all right, that's when you'll do it."

"It's not like that," Dr. Murray began, but couldn't find the words or perhaps the spirit to argue. Tamsyn was on her feet now, kicking sand and shouting.

"Were you going to leave a note?" she shouted. "Or just a body?"

"It's my time, lass," Dr. Murray said, standing up to face her fury. "You don't need me anymore. You've got your Eddie, he's a good lad."

"No! I want you around! I want you to meet my baby, and be an uncle, and grumble about everything, and just *be there*! I need you, Clem," she said, the final words falling out as sobs. She hit him, fists bouncing against the knotty wood of his chest, and then he had her wrapped up in his cold embrace, where she cried.

"I'm not your dad, Tam," Dr. Murray said gently. "He's gone, love, and I need to go too."

She cried, unable to say anything else. Apart from Eddie, Dr. Murray was the only reminder of home. Everyone else from Gravesend was gone now. They'd followed her here, and now they were all dead.

A low sound grew, barely audible above the waves and her own sobs. A plane, droning over the Keys. They pulled apart, staring up at the aircraft as it hung in the air like a fat dragonfly. A bomber, painted with the USAF logo. A machine from a forgotten world, dipping lower and lower.

"Americans," Dr. Murray said. "We've got to go, Tam."

She stared at the plane, horrified. It made a pass over the old Naval airbase, just north of Key West. She saw the doors open, watched as a cluster of bombs fell from the plane's belly.

The other island erupted in fire. Even on Sunset Keys, the thunder of the detonations was clear, a sound Tamsyn remembered all too well from the war. They were less than five miles from the airbase.

More aircraft, half a dozen at least. B-52s and stealth bombers, even jet fighters armed with missiles. This motley squadron made pass after pass, bombing the airbase with precision.

"They'll be clearing the airfield of dead folk," Dr. Murray said, dragging her across the sand. "Making a beachhead for themselves. Hurry up, girl!"

Then helicopters, fat dragonflies bobbing in the humid air, and the distant chatter of mini-guns. Wiping away the tears, Tamsyn stared in shock, just able to make out the rappel lines, the dots of soldiers as they fell to the tainted earth.

"Quickly, we have to leave," Dr. Murray urged.

Tamsyn could only look on in horror as a huge ship rounded the tip of Key West. Water cannons pounded the coastline and the docks, the high-pressure saltwater as good a weapon as any gun. Hundreds of zombies fell before the spray, washed away like leaves from a driveway.

The warship flew the United States flag, high and proud. The *USS Chimaera*. Finally, they'd found her, and now they were going to slap her in chains.

"Move!" Dr. Murray insisted. "Do you want them to spot you larking about on the beach?"

"No," she began, and then a fierce pain gripped her womb, clenching like a fist. She sank to her knees with a gasp, terror gripping her by the throat. It was far too early for a contraction, almost three months until her due date.

"It hurts," she cried. Tamsyn saw a thin trickle of blood running down her thighs, and she whimpered.

"We need to get you to a doctor, Tam," Eddie said. His face was pale, and he cradled her in his strong arms, carrying her to the *Pocahontas*.

"No," she said. "We're not going to the Americans. We've got to leave, Eddie."

"They've got medics! They can help you!" he pleaded. "I can't lose you Tam, I won't."

"They'll shoot Clem and put us up before a military tribunal," she said. "War crimes, desertion, all of it. Eddie, if you signal that ship, we all die."

"What about our baby?" Eddie asked. His usual bluster was replaced with worry. If the world hadn't ended, she had no doubt he'd be speeding them through traffic now, in a stolen car if he had to. He'd threaten the doctors at the emergency department, bullying and shouting until she got the care she needed.

There weren't any hospitals now. If they ran, her baby's life rested on the skill of a resurrected vet, with scavenged medical supplies.

"It doesn't hurt as much," she said, trying to convince herself as much as Eddie. "I felt another kick a minute ago, a little one. It might be okay, love."

It was tempting to send off a flare, to wait for the troops to arrive. Every motherly instinct screamed for her to go to the Americans, cap in hand. But they'd found a supply drop in Miami last month, with food parcels and news meant for survivors. Her face was on a wanted poster, along with a hefty reward.

The Americans had nothing but frontier justice waiting for her, baby or not.

Dr. Murray came down from the resort's clock tower with a telescope in hand, making for the pier at a limping jog. Tamsyn absently wondered if the Re-Human had damaged something lately, perhaps a tendon. There was only so much punishment his dead body could take.

"Yanks are all over the Keys," he said. "Aircraft carriers, patrol boats, even a destroyer. I saw them blow up the bridge to the mainland, and there's more planes landing at the old Navy base. Looks like we got new neighbours."

"So much for hiding in plain sight," Eddie said. "Let's get the fuck out of here."

With a last lingering look at Sunset Keys, Tamsyn sighed. Eddie lifted her across the gangplank, and carefully carried her into the belly of the *Pocahontas.*

"We're on the blind side of the island, away from the aircraft carriers and all that," Dr. Murray said. "Damn unlucky if a plane spots us once we get going. They've got a few million zombies to keep them busy."

The boat engine coughed and turned over. Eddie quickly untied the cruiser, shaking his head as more bombs fell.

"Uncle Sam is going to pop us like a floating turd," Eddie grumbled. "I swear, we're idiots."

Dr. Murray said nothing, carefully easing the throttle to full. They pulled away from the island, the prow pointed due west. An eight-hour boat ride, and they'd be safely behind the walls of Fort Jefferson.

It looked like the next five years involved playing house in a crumbling ruin, a home birth that would hopefully go to plan, veggie gardens and fishing. And at some stage, Dr. Murray would quietly check out of this life.

Caught in these thoughts, another cramp tore through Tamsyn, more painful than the first one on the beach. It left her doubled-up and gasping, and Eddie rushed to her side. Tears leaked from his piggy eyes as he gripped her hand.

"Eddie, I need a doctor," Tamsyn whispered. "Something's wrong."

"Clem, turn the boat around," Eddie shouted. "Tam's in trouble."

"No," she shouted. "No Americans."

Once more, the pain passed, and she was able to uncurl herself. The baby kicked again, a faint flutter that didn't resemble its usual acrobatics. Despite Eddie's protests, Tamsyn levered herself out of bed, headed for the bridge.

"Where's your navigation charts?" she demanded. Dr. Murray pointed a wrinkled finger at the centre console, and Tamsyn fetched out a fistful of maps. Smoothing them out on the dashboard, she found the tip of the Florida Keys, and drew an invisible line south-west.

"We go here," she said, wincing as another small twinge passed through her womb. "Take us to Cuba."

"What? You want cigars or something?" Eddie said from her elbow. "You're bloody mad, love."

"Cuba has more doctors than anywhere in Latin America."

"And do you know what? They're all bloody dead!" Eddie said. "So are we if we land in some tinpot country. It's just not safe."

"Eddie dear, I love you but you're not too bright. How much salt have we got, Clem?"

"Enough to keep me going awhile," the Re-Human said. "Bit extra in case the boat conks out."

"That's settled then. We go here, to Havana. If Michael Moore was right, there's a clinic on every corner. We find some dead chap in a white coat, pump him full of salt, and bingo!"

"No more Re-Humans," Dr. Murray said. "I thought that's what we agreed, after–after Dawes died."

After I put an arrow through his rotten brain, Tamsyn thought.

"I need a doctor, Clem," she said. "No offence, but I'm not exactly dropping a litter of kittens here."

"Fine," the dead man said, swinging the wheel left. The boat slid around in the surf. The compass in the dash twitched and rolled, finally pointing south-west.

Tamsyn went into the little bathroom, checking for blood. There was nothing new, but she wondered if the damage was already done. Perhaps she was miscarrying right now. She waited a long and nervous minute, praying for movement, for anything. Finally the baby twitched, nudging at her almost half-heartedly.

"Hang in there, baby," she whispered. "We'll get help."

Blinking at the wind and the spray, Tamsyn walked out onto the deck. She pointed the binoculars back at the Keys, noted with some alarm that a cordon of small boats was already surrounding Key West. Even now, a solitary patrol boat slowly drew up to Sunset Keys, spotters scanning the mansions for signs of life.

They'd missed discovery by a matter of minutes.

"Helicopter," Eddie said at her side, and Tamsyn twitched the binoculars skyward, catching the chattering machine as it cleared the resort. For a long moment she held her breath, watching as the machine hovered over the island, expelling soldiers down rappel lines. The pilot only needed to turn slightly, and for someone to see their little boat speeding across the waves...

Cargo dropped, the helicopter returned to Key West, flying low across the humid stretch of water. Tamsyn watched the Keys until they were a smudge of land on the horizon. The explosions had stopped, and she could just make out a pair of water-bombers, dropping plumes of salt water onto the land.

"Good time to move," Eddie observed. "Whole neighbourhood's gone to shit."

Once the Keys vanished from sight, Dr. Murray eased back on the throttle. They hadn't run the cruiser that hard since fixing it, and now there was a nasty rattle in the engine. Worried as she was about the baby, Tamsyn remembered the motors dying on the *Paraclete*.

"Don't worry, love," Eddie said with false cheer. "Sometimes it takes ages for a baby to come, right? Better a boat than some dingy waiting room."

In her mind, she already knew what needed to be done. Dr. Murray would need to walk into a city, searching out a walking corpse that was hopefully a doctor. Then, he'd need to restrain the undead, and somehow bring them back to the boat.

Next, they would have to pump a saline mixture into its brain, and over a period of several hours keep the salt at the exact level needed to start the Re-Human process.

If they got it wrong, they'd fry the zombie's brain, and would have to start from scratch with a fresh recruit. If it all worked, a rotten pair of hands would help bring her new baby into the world.

Or the new Re-Human would emerge, crazed and screaming. Four years of undeath, and they'd remember every moment with complete clarity.

What's the correct mixture of salt and water? Tamsyn tried to think of the proportion, and with some panic she realised that she didn't know. She'd overseen the reanimation process once when she served as a Captain, but the boffins at Undead Research kept that information close to their chests. And she'd been drunk.

They eventually figured it out. So can we.

She put on a Seinfeld DVD and tried not to think about the ticking time bomb in her uterus. Eddie held her close, and the canned laughter of the old world washed over them.

Four hours later, they spotted Cuba's coastline. Palm trees fringed perfect beaches, and further inland, a bizarre geology of square hills thrust up from the rainforest.

Tamsyn thrilled at the sight of the verdant mesa, but a faint throb from her stomach reminded her of what needed doing. Biting down on the bubble of sudden fear, she swept her binoculars across a small coastal village. The place was run-down, shabby looking.

Unsure if the settlement had fallen into disrepair since the pandemic, or had been derelict to begin with, Tamsyn looked closely. She tried to spy something that might have been a medical clinic, or perhaps a hospital.

"What's Spanish for hospital?" she asked, trying to spot a sign. There was something that looked like a town hall, and a neat church. Everything else was a shack, or a farmhouse, or both.

Already, the rainforest was reclaiming everything. Another ten years, and there'd be little evidence that people had even been here.

"Blowed if I know any Spanish," Dr. Murray said. "My brother went to Majorca once. Furthest I ever got was Blackpool."

"Here's the locals," Eddie said excitedly, looking through a riflescope. Thousands of undead were emerging from the rainforest, a slow migration that passed through the overgrown plantations.

Most of their clothing had rotted away since the outbreak, and there was little left to say what each person had been when alive. If there'd been a doctor for the district, he'd dressed plainly, or wasn't here.

"This is a waste of time," Dr. Murray said. "When I did my country rounds as a vet, I didn't dress any differently from anyone else. Your chances of finding a doctor in that? Hopeless."

Referring to the map, they tried to guess where they were in relation to Havana. With her limited navigation skills, Tamsyn guessed that they'd landed slightly east of Havana.

"It might get hairy, but we try the city," she said. "Much less chance we'll nab a farmer by accident."

The *Pocahontas* limped along the coastline, the motor definitely misfiring now. If Dawes or Riley were still with them, she knew they'd have the engines stripped and reassembled within the hour. Eddie's idea of maintenance involved him lifting the cover and belting a rattling engine part with a hammer.

"That'll do it," he said with false bonhomie, coughing when blue smoke leaked out of the engine port. Dr. Murray wound the throttle back even further, until they were barely crawling along.

"Never had this old thing above half-throttle," Dr. Murray shouted back at them. "We've gone and bloody wrecked it, we have."

The farms and villages gave way to suburbia, grimy buildings packed in close. The narrow streets were still strung with abandoned washing, bleached rags now. And everywhere were undead Cubans, filling the streets and wandering in eternal confusion.

As they rounded a final headland, Havana proper appeared. The skyline was a bizarre mixture of old and new. Dirty skyscrapers and tenement housing thrust up from a landscape of churches and historic buildings. Everywhere were huge banners depicting Castro and Che Guevara, draped from crumbling buildings, plastered across billboards. Dour looking signs in Spanish, revolutionary slogans in place of advertising.

Havana was a battlefield. Everywhere, the burnt-out wreckage of vintage cars and trucks, barricades and razor wire blocking off the broad avenues. There were more broken windows than whole, and in places the buildings had been bombed to rubble or razed to the ground. The damage seemed almost random, like a tornado had licked through the hot streets, dropping buildings at whim.

There were burnt out tanks, military trucks rammed into store-fronts, even an upside-down jeep. In the parks, most of the trees had been cut down, dragged off for fuel.

A war then, but the only winners were the zombies, wandering aimlessly through the ruins. A handful of walking corpses stood on the mangled wreckage of a fighter jet, their dead eyes following the passage of their noisy boat. Tamsyn's heart fell. She'd secretly been hoping for evidence of survivors, but Cuba was a graveyard.

Just like everywhere else.

Slipping past an ancient seawall, Dr. Murray guided the *Pocahontas* into the port. They passed beneath an old fortress, a relic set deep in the clifftop. Tamsyn thought she saw a flicker of movement on the battlements, but a moment later it was gone. She wrote it off as just another zombie, perhaps still stuck in the tourist attraction it died in.

We could clear that out later, hide in it, she thought, watching for more movement. *Sea access, thick walls, access to supplies.*

Control of the harbour.

Echoing across the still water, the rattle of the boat-motor resounded from the harbour walls. Tamsyn watched nervously as hundreds of zombies were drawn by the noise, lining the far side of the inlet and staring at them hungrily.

The inlet let them into a vast natural harbour, with piers and docks in all directions. The port was littered with wrecks, freighters and pleasure craft, even a cruise liner. Dr. Murray had to weave the *Pocahontas* through the debris, even as they cast about for a suitable place to land.

"Look at that," Eddie said, pointing to the side of the half-sunk liner. Charred craters above the waterline showed where the ship had come under heavy fire, explosions buckling the thick hull. Similar damage could be seen on the other big ships. All of the sunken vessels bore the Cuban flag.

Like everywhere else in the world, once the dead rose and attacked the living, people took to the sea in a panic. Here, someone had sunk these ships before they could even clear the harbour.

"I'm beginning to think we should have gone over to the Americans," Dr. Murray said. The southern side of the port fed an industrial area and seemed less populated with undead. Even as he steered them towards a pier, there was a noise behind them, a faint whine that they could soon hear over the laboured struggles of their own motor.

Tamsyn saw a motor launch speeding out of the inlet, full of armed men. They were riding the boat hard, and the pilot weaved them through the wreckage expertly, homing in towards the *Pocahontas*.

"There's survivors here," she began, just as one of the men fired a warning shot at them. Another hollered into a megaphone, Spanish words that needed no translation. *Stop where you are. We're gonna take all your stuff, and then we might just kill you anyway.*

Tamsyn cursed her stupidity. She wasn't the only one to think that the sea fort was a good place to live. And it was a time-honoured tradition, held by bandits all over this savage new world. Wait for the victim to pass, cut them off from escape, and then move in at your leisure to take whatever you wanted.

"Don't stop," she shouted to Dr. Murray. "Drive this thing into the dock if you have to, but we have to run."

"Tam, listen. These people might be able to take you to a doctor," Eddie said.

"Maybe they'll just put a bullet in my head and save themselves the trouble," Tamsyn snapped. She quickly strapped on her quiver, wincing as another cramp shot through her belly. A pistol went into her shoulder holster, and lastly she buckled a combat knife around her leg.

Eyes wide, Eddie quickly kitted up. He jammed guns and ammo into a satchel and made sure to pack all of their salt.

Now that their warning shot had been ignored, their pursuers opened fire in earnest. Their boat was bobbing in the wake of the *Pocahontas*, and the first fusillade of automatic gunfire went wide. Three rounds cracked into the stern of the cabin cruiser, like a demented woodpecker trying to latch on. Thick blue smoke poured out of the engine bay now, and the motor was misfiring badly.

With a grimace, Eddie picked up an assault rifle, emptied half a clip towards the boat behind them. Their driver veered to the right, putting a sunken freighter between them. In moments, their attackers would swing around the wreck, strafing them along the starboard side.

"Hang on, kids," Dr. Murray said, guiding them towards a smaller pier at full speed. "This might hurt."

At that moment, barely thirty yards from the pier, the engine on the *Pocahontas* coughed once, and then it was silent. Cursing, Dr. Murray thumbed the ignition switch, and was rewarded with nothing more than a sullen chug.

"Damnit!" the Re-Human shouted, abandoning the controls to snatch up a gun. Tamsyn watched hopelessly as the *Pocahontas* coasted forward on the last of its momentum. The jetty got closer and closer, each yard a slow eternity.

Eddie threw a loop of rope towards a docking post, missed. Quickly bringing in the line, he tried again, but the pier was still too far.

"You call that a throw?" Dr. Murray snarled, snatching the rope from Eddie. Wincing as the salty hemp bit into his dead flesh, the Re-Human hefted the thick line with no effort, looping it over a piling.

The three of them frantically drew the line in, hauling the ship alongside the pier. Even as the bandits' boat rounded the freighter, they had the *Pocahontas* alongside the jetty. Eddie wrestled with the gangplank, even as bullets whistled around them.

They ran for cover along a jetty littered with crates and dead forklifts. Tamsyn tripped over a coil of rope, and she struck the pier hard, skinning her knee. With her womb still twinging painfully, she crawled across the cracked pier, bullets cracking into the boxes all around her.

Before the world ended, Tamsyn would never have believed anyone would shoot a gun at her. There was a time when she'd have been terrified. In the old soft world, she'd have submitted to these people, given them whatever they wanted.

Now she was a combat veteran and had a baby and fiancé to protect. Her army training kicked in instantly, and all panic was replaced with a cool readiness, the determination to make these bastards pay. She signalled to Eddie and Dr. Murray, ordering them to spread out and keep low. *Minimise the risk to your personnel, maximise the damage to the enemy,* her old instructors said.

Even though it had been months since she'd worn a captain's bars, the other two obeyed her, darting across the dock and scrabbling for new cover. Old habits died hard.

The boat came past the pier in a broad sweep, guns chattering. The hail of lead pattered against the wharf equipment and the crates, indiscriminate fire that didn't even come close to hitting them.

Tamsyn had been shot at by the best and knew that these gunmen were far from professional soldiers. Most of them wore olive-coloured fatigues, but they were fairly young, gaunt with hunger. Green soldiers then, most likely conscripts.

She felt almost insulted.

As the boat passed them, Tamsyn signalled to Eddie. Nodding, he rested his rifle on the back of a forklift, drew a careful bead. He gave three tight bursts on semi-auto, and two men fell, another wounded. The boat wobbled in the chaos, and Eddie sank back into cover before the survivors could return fire on his new position.

As they concentrated their gunfire on where Eddie had been, Tamsyn sent one arrow winging across the narrow gap of water. It sank deep into a man's throat. He flopped about in the rear of the boat, screaming as his comrades tried to yank the arrow loose.

She heard the whine of another engine in the distance. Two more boats coasted through the inlet. One was another motorboat full of shooters, a mop-up crew. The second was a big patrol boat, with a deck mounted mini-gun. It cut its engines and set to blocking the inlet. There'd be no escape by water, not even if they could get the *Pocahontas* started.

If they got out of this mess, there was nothing for them but Havana. They were trapped here.

Motor whining, the nearest boat made a tight turn. The excited gunmen were still shooting at the pier, even though it was now out of range. Tamsyn quickly shouted out her new plan, insisted when Dr. Murray objected.

The second boat was bearing down on them, and within a minute or two they would be outgunned. It was now or never.

"You've already got a death wish, Clem, so just bloody do it!" she shouted. Nervously, the Re-Human stood, blinking as the first bullets winged past him. When a lucky shot punched into his gut, Dr. Murray touched the entry hole, staring as the boat bore down on the pier.

"Move, soldier!" Tamsyn shouted. The command stirred Dr. Murray out of his daze. The Re-Human lumbered towards the main wharf, making a rude gesture at the attackers and shooting token rounds in their direction.

As Tamsyn suspected, the soldiers ignored her and Eddie, every single one of them going for the easy target. Dr. Murray took three more bullets to the chest before they realised what he was.

"En el cerebro!" she heard one of them scream to his comrades, the man tapping himself in the temple. *Head shot!* Even as the gunmen understood that a zombie was somehow shooting at them, Eddie was in his new position, flush with the edge of the pier itself. When the boat passed beneath him, he leant out, firing on the bandits at almost point-blank range. He emptied a full clip and turned the boat into a bloody knackery.

He's perfectly fine with this, Tamsyn thought, watching as her fiancé calmly murdered a boatful of men. *Eddie Jacobs was made for this awful new world.*

The boat's driver was slumped against the wheel, his lifeblood flooding the deck. The motorboat crashed into the stern of the *Pocahontas,* and as the motor continued pushing the boat forward, the broken hulls ground together with a squeal.

Two of the attackers survived Eddie's onslaught, fuzz-stubbled teenagers with coffee-coloured skin and wide eyes. Wounded and shaking, they raised their hands in surrender. Tamsyn lifted her bow, drew the barb-tipped arrow back to her cheek.

"Do it!" Eddie shouted at her. "It's them or us."

"No," she said, lowering her bow. "They're just kids."

Pushing her aside, Eddie hauled out his pistol, stitching the frightened boy soldiers full of bullets. When one of the lads let out an awful gurgling scream, Eddie eased him over with a headshot.

"Let's go," Eddie said, shepherding her along the pier with a hand on her elbow. She shrugged her way loose from his grip and slapped him across the face.

"You just killed those boys, Eddie! They surrendered, and you shot them anyway. What the hell?"

"They'd have done for us the moment we looked away," Eddie said bluntly. "Love, in this world…you need to be more ruthless. If you can't do the nasty stuff, I have to step up."

The second crew were almost halfway across the harbour now. They had to move. Eddie touched Tamsyn's belly gently and smiled. She turned away from the bloody boat, fought down her fury. Eddie was just protecting his family, the only way he knew how.

She knew he was right and wondered how long until she became as brutal as him. What kind of cold-blooded killer would they raise together? Could they give their baby any kind of childhood, or just memories of violence and hunger?

Eddie hustled her towards the main wharf, calmly reloading the assault rifle with a fresh banana clip. A quick walk was the best she could manage, and even this rolling motion put a lot of pressure on her tender uterus. Tamsyn thought she needed to pee, felt like she was going to be sick.

She could see Dr. Murray on the waterfront now, executing the handful of curious zombies drawn by the shooting. The undead let him walk right up to them, and he calmly fired one mercy round into each skull, dropping them like the horses he'd once put down for a living.

"Clem understands. We've gotta survive, Tam," Eddie said. "That's the only rule now."

16

The second boatload of men did not leave the docks. Tamsyn watched through binoculars as olive-uniformed men poked through the *Pocahontas*, looting it of everything they'd been forced to leave behind. She scowled as the bandits stacked their supplies on the dock, overjoyed at the surprise bonanza.

No one would be hunting them. The robbers had what they'd come for, and they seemed happy to trade their dead men for almost a tonne of food.

"We should have sunk the damn boat," Eddie grunted. "Look at those smug bastards."

Tamsyn and the others were on top of what looked to be wheat silos, following a high catwalk. A sensible precaution, but the warehouse district was safe enough. They'd only dropped a handful of undead, quiet kills from Tamsyn's bow that did not attract any attention. Silent was best.

There seemed to be two types of zombie, the static kind that stuck to familiar surroundings, and those that formed into large hordes, mindless nomads scouring all life from the earth. Havana seemed firmly stuck in the first category, the resident corpses unwilling to stir far from home and hearth.

Good. Better that than a super-pack, she thought.

Apart from the resurrected bodies of functionaries and dockhands, the whole area was deserted. Not so the nearby city. Tamsyn swept the binoculars across a million dead faces, despairing at the number of health clinics she could see. They might as well have been on the moon.

"I'll have to go in alone," Dr. Murray said. "Too dangerous for you two."

Even as he said this, Tamsyn saw how much the prospect scared the old Re-Human. The chances of him stumbling across a doctor were next to nil, and dragging a bound zombie through a million of his friends would be less than fun.

They wouldn't hurt him, but getting through that press would be hard going, let alone with a struggling monster in tow. It wouldn't be a pleasant task.

Dr. Murray could pass for a zombie at first glance, but what if there were any more of those soldiers? A smart zombie would attract bullets at the very least, but Tamsyn thought it more likely that those warlords would try and capture him. Take poor Clem apart in their big fortress, cut him open to see what makes him tick.

She'd made plenty of half-arsed plans in the past, but this was the dumbest one yet. Even as she cursed her own impulsive nature, she felt another twinge through her belly. Whatever was going to happen, she didn't have long. She needed medical help, and fast.

Eddie was several silos over now, pacing the catwalks and scanning the city through his riflescope. Whistling between his teeth, he waved them over. The metal grating swayed beneath her and Dr. Murray, and she noted with worry just how rusted through the grating was. It had been unsafe decades before the apocalypse.

"Forget the city," Eddie said. "Check this out. Just left of that little castle there, off the main road."

He was pointing to an area south of the city proper, where the high buildings petered off and became an inner suburb. Tamsyn quickly found the ruin with her binoculars, panned slightly left. A wide road led past what looked like a baseball stadium, the grass dead now. Opposite this, set back from the road and surrounded by large grounds, an enormous building in stone.

The signs were too far away to read, but she could make out a red cross, and a beat-up white van with bubble lights on top, with all the doors left open. An ambulance!

"Not as many coffin-dodgers neither," Eddie said. "Probably only fifty on the whole street, couple on the grounds. We go in like the clappers, all of us. We'll find a doctor in no time."

"Still too dangerous," Dr. Murray said. "Besides, young Tam is hardly able to run around."

"Don't worry, I've figured that one out too."

Perhaps ten minutes later Tamsyn was bouncing around in a Soviet-era wheelbarrow, wincing at every small bump. In place of a pneumatic tyre, they'd used a wheel of cast iron. It made an absolute racket. Eddie propelled the contraption along at a slow trot, which was about as fast as Dr. Murray could move now.

"Be ready, love," Eddie said. "Kinda got my hands full."

She held both their pistols, one in each hand. The wheelbarrow rattled across the pitted asphalt, and dozens of zombies were drawn by the sound. Apart from these unnatural monsters, it was easy going out here. In England, the main roads were choked with abandoned cars, but apart from one wrecked bus, this "Calzada Del Cerro" was clear.

"It's just like rugby, pet," Eddie puffed, weaving them through the forest of reaching arms. Mouldy claws snatched for his flesh, and the locals looked like dead heroin addicts, eyes wide and hateful, broken teeth snapping.

Four years in the Caribbean hadn't been kind to these bodies. They were little more than mummies now, bones held together with skin and sinew. Rudimentary muscles drove them on, and even though their bodies were slowly failing, they seemed as hungry for human flesh as they ever had.

"I feel like meals on wheels," Tamsyn began, and broke off as another cramp gripped her. She cried out, and before she knew it she'd dropped one of the guns over the side of the wheelbarrow. Cursing, Eddie steered them wide of a gathering corpse-knot, and the gun was lost.

"Don't worry, I've got it," Dr. Murray said dourly, ignored by the zombies as he pressed through their ranks. He jogged back to the wheelbarrow, pressing the heavy steel into Tamsyn's hand. His limp was much more pronounced now, and through the haze of pain she absently noted how even his good leg seemed stiff.

Dead tendons can't take it.

"Sorry," she gasped. "I'm sorry, Clem."

It took almost an hour for them to reach the hospital. By this stage a rotten crowd was following them along the main road, only a short distance behind them. Dr. Murray struggled to move faster, his dead limbs disobeying him with every step.

"Go on without me," he told Eddie. "I've gone and bloody blown something in my legs. I'll catch up."

"Rubbish," Eddie said. "We're still faster than this lot."

"Eddie, please," Tamsyn said. "He'll be okay."

"If it all goes wrong, we'll meet you on the hospital roof, yeah?" Eddie said. Dr. Murray nodded, and Eddie picked up the speed. Tamsyn bounced around in the wheelbarrow, and as Eddie weaved around a trio of dead Cubans, she looked back.

Dr. Murray gave her a cheerful wave, even as the ravenous horde parted around him, swallowed him up. The undead didn't even notice him.

Bouncing down the main access road to the hospital, they finally encountered a logjam of traffic. Old cars from the fifties, complete with zany tail fins. Military vehicles, even a handful of ambulances, looted and now open to the elements. Eddie swore when a zombie fell out of a truck, and he nearly dropped the wheelbarrow. Startled, Tamsyn emptied half a pistol clip towards the dead soldier before she made a headshot.

Eddie steered Tamsyn across the grounds, the broad lawn now patchy and given over to weeds. Three zombies came for them, none of them dressed like doctors. Pausing to take a breath, Eddie took one of the pistols and cleared a way to the front door. He struggled to manoeuvre the wheelbarrow over the earth, and by the time they reached the front doors he was panting like a racehorse.

"HOSPITAL SALVADOR ALLENDE," the first sign declared. "EMERGENCIA" read another, with a red cross and an arrow pointing to the far end of the log-jammed road.

"Not that way," Tamsyn said, climbing out of the wheelbarrow. "They'd have taken the first victims there. Coffin-dodgers from floor to ceiling."

The front doors were chained from the inside, and through the plate glass Tamsyn saw a rough barricade, furniture stacked up high. Official notices were plastered on the glass, and Tamsyn didn't have to read the language to know that people were being warned away, that this hospital was no longer safe.

Bow at the ready, Tamsyn circled the building. The spasms were less intense now, but every now and then she had to squat, shaking as a wave of pain washed through her. Eddie hovered nearby, helpless and bewildered.

"Keep looking," she gasped. "A quiet wing, cancer ward or something. A dead doctor might still be lurking around."

He helped her to rise, and they looked for a quiet way in. The windows were wire-grilled, and secure. Eddie found a small service door, complete with an upturned bucket for smokers to sit on. Locked.

They'd left a solid jimmy-bar on the *Pocahontas*, and Eddie had nothing to force the door. Even as he kicked it in frustration, Tamsyn saw a figure crossing from the next courtyard, drifting towards them on shattered legs. The zombie moaned woefully, dragging something in its wake.

"Wait, Tam, it's wearing a coat," Eddie said. "Could be a doctor or a nurse."

Tamsyn saw that it was dragging a mop and let her arrow fly. The arrow struck the dead orderly just above the temple. The zombie fell to the ground, fluttering and finally still.

"This way," she said. "Our friend here obviously ducked out for a cigar or something."

Several wings jutted out from the main hospital building, and retracing the zombie's footsteps brought them to an open door. A storeroom, the lino floor now littered with dirt and leaves.

Treading carefully, Eddie stepped over the debris. At some stage in the past, the shelves had been stripped of supplies, and only empty boxes remained. Cracking open the inner door, he carefully leaned out into the hallway. Giving a sign that all was clear, Eddie led Tamsyn into the hospital.

She remembered the public hospitals in England and thought they'd been grim and depressing. Compared to the dinge she saw here, these places now seemed a beacon of Hippocratic efficiency. In Salvador Allende, it seemed the décor wasn't even an after-thought. Cracked and peeling paint, stained cement floors, and the only decorations were grim signs, perhaps warning people to wash their hands, or to be good Communists.

Occasionally, they came across a lone chair for visitors, scuffed and broken. Passing an empty nurse's station, Tamsyn wondered at the lack of people, how this half of the hospital wasn't teeming with monsters.

She had her answer when they found the first ward. At least forty beds lined the long room, all the curtains swept back. The windows were closed, and the stink was unbelievable.

Every bed held a corpse. Each pillow was crusted with a brown rose of old blood, and the patients stared into eternity through a bullet-shaped third eye.

As Tamsyn walked forward, she kicked a brass shell with her feet. It danced musically across the cement floor, and that's when she noticed that all of the bodies had silver hair. A ward full of old people, executed in their beds.

"They must have turned," Eddie said, pulling Tamsyn outside. He closed the door, but the stink still came through.

"Nope," she said, fighting back the urge to vomit. "None of them were tied down. When things went wrong, when there was no evacuation coming, they—they triaged the oldies." Here she mimed a gun to Eddie's forehead.

"Mercy killing," Eddie said. "Makes sense."

More of the same, the further they got into the hospital. Rooms full of the "triaged," spared the horrors raging through the emergency wing. Once they found a body in a robe, slumped in the corridor; a patient who'd wandered out of bed, shot against the wall like a political dissident.

When they reached a children's ward, Tamsyn didn't even want to open the door. Search as they might, all the staff had fled in the wake of this massacre. There were no dead nurses or doctors here, no one left behind to watch over these murdered charges.

"We're gonna have to try the emergency ward, love," Eddie said. "Might get a bit hairy in there, but we'll manage. Maybe Clem can help us, when he catches up."

"Let's use this to flag him in," Tamsyn said as she grabbed a clean sheet from an orderly cart. "It's a big roof."

They made for the northern end of the wing, hoping to spot Dr. Murray on the road. They were barely twenty feet from a door marked "SALIDA" when they heard a banging sound from the outside.

"Damn coffin-dodgers! They sniffed us out." Eddie lifted the assault rifle from his shoulder, checked the clip with a worried frown. Tamsyn wondered how many bullets he had left.

The door banged again, and whatever lay on the other side was serious about busting it open. Tamsyn fumbled an arrow onto her bow, breathing away the panic, praying that the cramps wouldn't foul her aim. They were backing down the corridor now, making for the storeroom, when the door gave with a squeal of wood. It swung open to reveal a figure wreathed in sunlight.

A man, crowbar in hand. He was clean-shaven, and wore a neat checkered shirt tucked into tan pants. She guessed him to be in his early twenties. When he saw them, he gawped in shock, as surprised as they were. He had a rifle slung over one shoulder but made no move for it.

"Eddie, don't," Tamsyn warned. Eddie already had the gun level with the stranger's heart, so she pushed the assault rifle aside, held it there.

"Could be that same mob from the harbour," Eddie growled, snatching the gun out of her grip. She stood in his way, giving him the I'm-in-charge-here look that ended most arguments. Eddie backed down, lowering his gun with a sullen grunt.

The man raised a hand in a cautious greeting, and called out a rapid greeting in Spanish, an enquiry that she couldn't even get the gist of. Unnotching her arrow, Tamsyn waved back.

"No Spanish. English."

"Inglés," the man repeated doubtfully, and ducked back outside. Two other figures returned inside with him, similarly dressed. They peered down the corridor with similar looks of surprise.

"Hello," one of them called out in halting English. "We come for supplies only. Please, don't shoot."

"It's okay," Tamsyn shouted. "We won't shoot you."

"Speak for yourself," Eddie mumbled, before Tamsyn dug her elbow into his ribs. Holding his big gun low but ready, Eddie walked up to the man, eyeballed him good.

"You're not a Party man," the neatly dressed looter said calmly. "*Comunista?*"

"No, we're not communists," Tamsyn said. "Boat, from America. We were attacked in the harbour."

"*Comunista,*" the man said with a nod. "You should not have come here. Especially you, señorita. Not safe for you."

The third man brought out a sack-truck. Ignoring them now, the young men went about stripping the hospital of any remaining supplies. Sheets, towels, even boxes of soap.

"I don't believe this," Eddie said, scoffing as the looters stepped around him to make a neat pile of goods by the door. "They could at least offer me a smoke or something."

"Please, I need help," Tamsyn said, waddling along and trying to keep up with the English speaker. "Just stop, okay. I need to talk to you."

"We don't have long," the Cuban said. "Many walkers, coming up the road now. *Avispas Negras,* they watch these places too."

"Who?"

"The Black Wasps. Very bad people."

When the man made to pick up a box of disinfectant, Tamsyn clutched his arm. He politely peeled away her fingers, moved around her with eyes downcast.

"Look. I need help. I'm having trouble with my baby. Blood, cramping. I came to Cuba looking for a doctor, and I'm going to get one."

The looters held a rapid conversation in Spanish and appeared to be in disagreement. The man with the crowbar seemed to win the argument, and the English speaker addressed her with a resigned smile.

"You'd better come with us then. Quickly, we don't have time to wait."

"You have a doctor?" Eddie blurted.

"Señor, we are all doctors," the young man said.

The men had an electric golf cart parked in the courtyard outside. They loaded the looted supplies with efficiency, strapping down boxes over every square inch of their silent transport.

"A seat for the lady," the man said. "You will have to hold on, señor."

"We've got a friend," Tamsyn said. "He was right behind us. We have to wait for him."

"If he is not out the front, we go. Black Wasps like to wait near the hospitals."

It was a tight squeeze in the golf cart. Tamsyn was packed in between two of the men, and the English speaker held onto one of the roof poles. Warily slinging his gun over one shoulder, Eddie gripped the opposite pole, planting his boots on the running board.

The driver cursed as the overloaded cart struggled across the hospital grounds. Occasionally the English-speaking doctor alighted from the cart to ease the weight, jogging alongside. Reluctantly, Eddie copied him, huffing across the overgrown lawn.

Passing around the furthest corner of the hospital, the road came into view. The doctors swore, and the man to Tamsyn's left readied his rifle. The swarm of zombies had caught up to them, in the hundreds now.

There, in the forefront, lumbering along and trying to outpace the other undead, Dr. Murray slowly broke away from the pack.

"You have to stop! That's our friend," Tamsyn shouted, but the driver ignored her. The golf cart made a bumpy progress through the ruin of a flower bed and dropped down from the kerb with a metallic crunch. The cart gave a worrisome whine, but everything still seemed to be working. Jogging alongside the cart, the English speaker gave an instruction to the driver, who slowed down and stopped.

"Your friend is dead," he told Tamsyn, looking at Dr. Murray through his riflescope. "I'm sorry for your loss, but he's not a person anymore."

"Stop, he's different from the others!" Tamsyn shouted, struggling to rise from the seat. A cramp stole through her then, and all she could do was shout at the doctor, cursing as her legs disobeyed her.

Even as Eddie stalked towards the Cuban doctor, the man fired. What was intended to be a mercy kill went down and left, just below Dr. Murray's collarbone.

It all happened at once. Eddie knocked down the doctor with the butt of his rifle. Shouting, Dr. Murray fired back, a wild shot that pierced the golfcart's canopy. And a bright flash appeared from a distant roof on the opposite side of the street.

A man in camouflage gear, complete with a green hood, had just taken their photo. Another figure could be seen up there, moving through the chimney pots and TV antennae. He held a huge sniper rifle, one she recognised from her training as a Soviet-built Dragunov.

Neither of these observers even attempted to hide.

"Munéca! He is Munéca!" the winded doctor cried, scrabbling away from Eddie with his hands and feet. The other doctors were yelling, pointing towards the roof.

"Black Wasps," the doctor said. "We've got to go."

"Not," Tamsyn said through gritted teeth, "without my friend."

She hip-and-shouldered the driver out of the way, pushing him right out of the cart. Even as the other doctor protested, Tamsyn grabbed the wheel, put her foot flat to the floor. With wheels squealing, she drove the golf cart in a wide circle, aiming towards the zombie-pack. It was top-heavy with supplies, and at one point threatened to tip over.

Cutting between the zombie pack and Dr. Murray, Tamsyn slowed down long enough for Dr. Murray to grab onto the poles and hang on. The Cuban stared at him with horror, flinched when the Re-Human grinned.

"Bad manners to shoot at the tourists," Dr. Murray said, and then the man wailed in fear. Tamsyn felt a warm flood on the bench seat as the man released his bladder. He tensed, ready to jump out of the golf cart. She lashed out with her hand, snagging the man by the collar.

"He's my friend. Mi Amigo. Sit down."

"Nice wheels, lass," Dr. Murray said.

She spun the golf cart around, driving back to Eddie as fast as the cart could move. The doctors and Eddie were in a firefight with the men on the rooftop, trying to pin the soldiers down. From the roofs came the crack of a rifle, and the original driver fell to the ground, wailing and clutching at his bloody leg.

"Smart," Dr. Murray said. "He could have gone for the kill, but he's wounding those chaps. Trying to slow everyone down."

Tamsyn pulled up alongside them, rolling slowly. Even as the men piled on, she fumbled with the straps holding on the supplies. Despite the doctor's protests, she pushed everything over, and the looted goods fell in the golf-cart's wake.

"You can have band-aids and die, or go without and live," she said, taking the golf cart off-road. They bounced around in the flowerbeds, bullets singing around them. Once they reached the tree line at the edge of the hospital, the gunfire stopped. She guided the cart behind a row of shrubs, always keeping cover between them and the other side of the street.

"You, give me some directions," she said to the man next to her, and froze. He lolled in the seat, blood gushing out of his ravaged throat. With a final rattling gasp, he bled out. A perfect kill, barely two feet to her left.

Then she realised the gunmen on the roof had been toying with her. They could have wiped them all out at any moment. Which left only one alternative: they'd been instructed to follow the foreign visitors and capture them if possible.

The doctors were nothing but target practice. She'd seen the easy posture of the men on the roof, recognised the arrogance and contempt writ large in every gesture. They had to be Special Forces, and didn't even regard these looters as a threat.

Keeping to every scrap of cover, they finally reached the far side of the hospital grounds, and she spent some minutes weaving through side streets, backtracking and watching for pursuit. She came to something that looked like a university or a high school, courtyards and long buildings laid out in a grid. Pulling up in the shade of a stairwell, she promptly vomited over the side.

"I'm sorry," she said, wiping her mouth. "Your friend, we need to leave him here."

The English speaker nodded, tears running down his swarthy face. Tamsyn still had the sheet they'd intended as a signal cloth, and they laid the dead man out on the ground, wrapping him in a makeshift shroud. There was no time to bury him, and they didn't even have a shovel.

"It was a good death," she said. "A clean death. Do you understand?"

"Death is death," the doctor said numbly.

They made their introductions then, over a round of potent cigarettes that made Tamsyn's nose sting. Waving away the smoke, she sat at a distance and glared at Eddie, who was throat deep in nicotine heaven. The English-speaker was Hector, and his friend with the wounded leg was Rodolfo. They'd recovered from their fear of Dr. Murray, who was now something of a curiosity for them.

Dead man talks and shoots, Tamsyn thought. *So why aren't they asking ten thousand questions?* The Re-Human kept his own counsel, probably wondering the same thing.

I don't like the way they're looking at him.

"We were medical students during the pandemic," Hector said. "ELAM. Uh, Latin American School of Medicine."

"What happened after?" Tamsyn asked. "Where did you go?"

"We are still there," Hector said. "We graduated too."

Grinding out his cigarette, the Cuban pulled a grimy map out of his pocket. It showed Havana, and several locations were penciled across the streetscape. Forage sites, places overrun and marked with a X, other notations in tiny handwriting. He pointed west of the city, to a small peninsula bordered by a river.

"When the dead come, our director blocked off the south-western approach. Last year we divert the river, so now this," and here he ran a fingernail along the watercourse, "is a salt moat."

"Hang on a minute," Eddie said. "Why isn't your hospital like that place? Each one I've seen lately looks like a zombie disco."

"It's a training hospital," Hector said. "Limited patients. The director sent half of the teaching doctors to help at the main hospitals, and then locked ELAM down."

"Smart man," Tamsyn said.

"Señora," Hector corrected with a smile. "Maria Ramirez."

Rodolfo was in a lot of pain from his wound, but all Hector could give him were codeine tablets, redressing the wound with strips torn from the dead man's sheet.

"We need to go," he said, binding Rodolfo's leg in a tourniquet. "The wound is worse than I thought. How are your cramps, Tamsyn? Time them please."

It took them almost two hours to skirt zombie-ravaged Havana, doubling back through ruined streets, passing around large concentrations of the undead. Hector drove them into a safe house in an outer suburb, a sprawling old manor built in the pre-Revolution days.

Under the porch were half a dozen golf carts, ready to be hooked up to a generator. Hector left the cart, did not connect it to the jerry-rigged recharge system.

"No time. The next guy will have to do it," he said. They piled into a monster of a Chevrolet, complete with bench seats and sweeping fins.

"We take golf carts into the city from here. This is too noisy," he said, and the car's engine roared into life. Eddie was in ecstasy, poking at the controls and fiddling with the radio until Hector slapped his hands away. Tamsyn sat with her bow between her knees, wincing as another pain jagged at her belly.

Please be okay, she thought. *Please baby, please just kick for me.*

This time, there was no kick. A lone tear fell down her cheek, and she let it fall. Eddie noticed and gripped her hand tightly.

"We must be careful now," Hector said. "If the Black Wasps find this place, they will wait here for our next supply run."

"Who were those soldiers?" Tamsyn asked, trying to keep from dwelling on the baby. She had to focus on the now, on the immediate threat. The moment she dropped her guard, she would cry hysterically.

"Black Wasps, they are the worst of the *Comunista*," Hector said. "Special Forces. The rest, office boys, lower Party officials. Conscripts. Not much of the Army left. The Black Wasps, they run everything now."

"So the men in charge shot your friend," Dr. Murray said. "If they run everything, why don't they run you?"

"Those *hijos de puta*, we do not answer to them now," Hector said forcefully. "We are independent. The *Comunista*, they have failed the people."

"Please, god, not another bleeding civil war," Eddie said, miming a prayer to the heavens. "We've had enough of that malarkey."

"What does he mean?" Hector asked.

"America is fighting itself," Tamsyn explained. "Was. We lost. And now we're here."

"Ah," he said, and noticed her wincing as the pain rose. "Are you timing those?"

Hector took them on a thunderous tour of post-zombie Havana, following a twisting route with familiarity. Tamsyn could see blockages and trouble-spots on some of the side streets, and it seemed that these doctors had mapped out all heavy populations of static undead.

Occasionally, a lone zombie would appear on the road, snarling with arms outstretched as the solid automobile bore down on it. Instead of avoiding it and climbing the footpath, Hector would put his foot down and twitch the steering wheel so he hit the body dead centre.

Rotten mincemeat, every time. The Chevy did not even miss a beat. Tamsyn wondered how many tonnes of steel this was, thundering along an empty road. She'd never have driven this way in a modern car; hit a body the wrong way, and the front was just as likely to crumple as anything else.

"They don't build 'em like they used to!" Eddie crowed. "If my dad were here to see this, he wouldn't bloody believe it! A proper Yank tank!"

"Damnit," Tamsyn sobbed. "It really hurts. Eddie, please just shut up about the car."

Rodolfo moaned weakly from the backseat. Hector looked in the mirror, arching an eyebrow. He pushed the fat gas pedal almost to the floor, and the big car leapt forward, knocking bins over as it drifted around a tight corner.

"You. Loosen the tourniquet for ten seconds," he told Dr. Murray. "Keep your hands away from his wound."

"I'm dead, not rotten," Dr. Murray snarled. "These hands prepared plenty of meals for those two, and I never made them sick."

The Re-Human fiddled with Rodolfo's bandages, let the blood briefly flow back into his leg. The man screamed at the sudden pressure, and when Dr. Murray cinched the knot tight, he turned white and fainted.

"Try to keep him awake," Hector snapped.

"All right, keep your knickers on," Dr. Murray grumbled. He hauled the unconscious man up, slapped his face gently. The man stirred, momentarily startled when he saw his undead neighbour had him by the shirt-front.

The two doctors gabbled at each other in Spanish, Rodolfo eventually fighting his way out of Dr. Murray's grip. He slid across the bench seat, putting as much blood-soaked leather between them as he could.

"How far?" Tamsyn cried. "Please hurry."

"Are you timing the cramps? Are you, señor?"

"Um, she gets them every ten or fifteen minutes," Eddie said, referring to his looted Rolex. "Is that bad?"

"Listen to me," Hector said, looking briefly to Tamsyn as he negotiated a turn. "The bleeding, we will investigate. But this cramp that you have is called the Braxton Hicks."

"Rubbish!" Tamsyn shouted. "This hurts like buggery! I think I'd know if it was a false contraction!"

"Have you had a baby before?"

"No," she admitted.

"You can still talk. When you have a contraction, you will not be talking."

"You're — you're just a jumped-up med student!" Tamsyn grunted, wincing as her uterus clenched. "I've got a serious problem here."

"Listen to me," Hector said, voice raised, all patience gone. "My cousin was just killed. My best friend back there, he is bleeding to death. You, you will be okay."

Hector swung the Chevy out of a side street and onto a main road, wheels squealing. It was a straight run of potholed asphalt, completely empty of traffic. The vintage auto danced across the blacktop like a chrome stallion.

He drove through an outer suburb, recent housing that looked austere and flimsy. It soon gave way to an industrial zone, with a skyline of still cranes and rusting warehouses. They passed within metres of a large undead swarm, a few hundred nomads spilling out of a sand quarry. As the Chevy roared past, the crowd turned as one, stumbling towards the blacktop.

"Oh no," Hector moaned, one eye to the rear-view mirror. Tamsyn turned around to see what the problem was and swore. Rumbling out of a side-street came an enormous tank, the gun turret swinging to face them.

Most of the roving horde was on the road now. Heads turned at the thunder of the tank's engine, their blasted eyes drawn towards the booming rattle of steel treads on asphalt. The juggernaut did not deviate and cut a rotten swathe right through the zombies. Skulls and bloated bodies popped like grapes, and dozens of the undead were ground into the tarmac, twitching like squashed bugs.

Face white, Hector put his foot to the floor. The Chevrolet responded with a confident roar, chewing through fuel as the panicked doctor put distance between them and the rolling Soviet-era hulk. Tamsyn watched in horror as the turret rotated, raised slightly.

A crack of thunder, and the gun barrel spewed smoke and fire in their direction. Hector twitched the wheel, weaving and swearing in Spanish. Just behind them, the road erupted in a geyser of asphalt and stone. Too close.

"Jesus!" Eddie shouted. "This mob don't fuck around, do they?"

"I missed the turn-off," Hector said, fumbling with the map. "We'll need to take the highway now."

A second shell sent a plume of dirt flying to their left as a crater appeared in the road verge. The third shot landed so close that the force sent the car skidding sideways for a moment, even as stones and shrapnel rained around them.

"Tam," Eddie cried, gripping her upper arm tightly. For a moment the hard man of bluster and bravo was gone, and clutching wordlessly at her was a frightened boy.

Then the tank stopped in the middle of the road, barrel still tracking them. From what Tamsyn had seen of armoured combat during the war, this gunner had their number. They were sighted in, and still well within range.

The rolling killer squatted over that last intersection like a dog at bay, and then she knew.

"They want us alive. They're herding us," Tamsyn said. The industrial belt gave way to the first of the farms and plantations, and they'd officially left Havana behind them.

Hector swore and jammed on the brakes. The big car shuddered to a halt.

Waiting for them at a crossroads was a roadblock, complete with rolls of razor wire and sandbags. Two army vehicles waited; an APC that was as old as Clem, and an off-road vehicle with a machine gun mounted on the back. Half a dozen soldiers pointed a mixture of guns in their direction. Tamsyn noted that all were dressed in the same olive fatigues as the men who'd attacked them in the harbour.

A Black Wasp barked at them through a megaphone, his camouflage hood making him look like a pilot *sans* helmet. The conscripts looked nervous, and Tamsyn wondered if the man with the machine gun might accidentally fire at them. Her father had died that way, and it seemed a fitting end for her.

Another alternative came to mind. Tamsyn had a horrifying vision of a jail cell, of Eddie beaten, the pair of them shot dead in some rude corner. Poor Clem, dissected and broken, watching these people as they carved secrets out of his immortal flesh.

"They won't take us," Eddie promised, resting a hand on his gun. She nodded, and a tear fell onto the gentle roll of her belly. There was no room in this world for her little family, nothing but death and misery at every turn.

Time to kiss a pistol.

Then, underneath her despair, a cold fury rose. It pushed aside all thoughts of a romantic suicide. This was a stupid place to die. She would not die, would not surrender to these maniacs.

After all she'd been through, after everyone who'd died in her place, she was finally down to Eddie's level. It was all about survival now, her and her child.

"Drive," she told Hector, the iron of command in her voice. "Drive at them, man!"

"Oh, Maria will never forgive me for this," Hector whispered, and jammed the Chevy into first gear. He punched the gas and drove the big car straight for the barricade. Tamsyn saw the soldiers back away from the sandbags, and a stray rifle-shot winged in their direction. The machine-gunner tracked their movement, watching the Black Wasp commander and waiting for the order.

At the last minute, Tamsyn leaned into Hector, turning the steering wheel hard right. The tires squealed, but the heavy auto kept level, where a lighter car might have flipped. Crying out, Hector pushed her away from the wheel, fought to correct their steering as the Chevy left the road and ploughed through a wire fence.

"This is the director's car," Hector said, flinching as the Chevy bounced across the corner of a sugar field, destroying several fence posts and snapping the cane. Then they were through the overgrown plantation and back onto the road, side-mirrors dangling.

They roared around the roadblock, and the soldiers looked at them in a mixture of confusion, perhaps admiration. Eddie flipped them the bird.

A mess of wire and wood dangled from the front grille of the Chevy, the barbed wire scratching into the immaculate paintwork. A woody spear of sugar cane protruded from the radiator, and steam began to curl up from under the hood.

By some minor miracle, the tires were intact, and they hadn't snapped an axle. Even mortally wounded, the antique Chevrolet rolled on.

Behind them, the vehicles backed out of the impromptu roadblock, turning around to give chase. Soldiers piled into them, and the man who'd fired at them was beaten by the Black Wasp. She'd called their bluff and won. What was left of the Cuban government definitely wanted them alive.

The crumbling road parted what had been farmland. Before them was the ocean, shining white as the Caribbean sun sank towards the horizon. Hugging the coast was a thick ribbon of road, well-maintained and at least four lanes wide.

The APC and the off-roader were closing in now, but the machine-gunner did not fire, even though he could riddle the car with bullets. The army vehicles swung out wide, slowly gaining as the Chevy fought against its mortal injuries. Tamsyn could see that they would swing out to either side, blow the tires, somehow force them off the road.

They reached the main highway in one piece. The engine clattered in protest, and Hector took the turn tightly, cursing as the machine-gunner fired a brief burst at them. The rear window shattered, covering Rodolfo and Dr. Murray in glass shards.

Leaning out of the window, Eddie fired his assault rifle at their pursuers. The big gun bucked wildly, and all of the bullets went wide. Still, the off-roader's driver was green, and panicked under fire. The vehicle weaved erratically and eventually left the road altogether, ploughing into a stand of shrubs. Eddie pumped his fist in victory, whooped.

Resting his rifle on the parcel shelf, Dr. Murray drew a bead on the APC, and the Re-Human looked grimly at the forbidding metal plate, the view ports. Tamsyn saw as he took the only shot he could; a fluke that wounded the man in the APC's gun-turret, drove him back into the vehicle's innards.

The armoured vehicle rolled forward, nudged the back of the Chevy. Fiddling with the choke and downshifting, Hector gave the dying car another ounce of power, prayed as the steam began to pour out from under the hood.

"We're almost there," Hector called out. Through the veil of steam, Tamsyn could just make out the wide sweep of a river, and beyond that, an enormous facility. She recognised the peninsula from Hector's map, saw a compound of long buildings connected with neat streets, surrounded by spacious grounds.

A huge wall cut the school away from the mainland, a mess of cinder blocks shored up with car bodies. It reminded her a little of Gravesend's fortifications, a jerry-rigged barrier to Keep the Bad Things Out.

The highway curved around, and Tamsyn's heart sank as she saw the smouldering remains of a bridge, cement and steel cracked and buckled. A ruined tank sent flames and diesel smoke into the sky, and dead soldiers lay on both sides of the river. Same uniforms, different sides.

On this battlefield, a few dozen undead walked, moaning hungrily in the direction of the citadel. The besieged doctors made no attempt to clear them, and they shuffled with impunity.

"What the hell do I do now?" Hector said, looking with disbelief at the bridge. He rolled to a slow stop, thumping the steering wheel in frustration. "I can't get across that."

They were trapped on the same side of the river as the APC. The armoured car rolled up slowly, stopping a short distance away. Soldiers hustled out of the rear hatch, advancing slowly on the Chevy with guns ready.

The Black Wasp climbed up into the machine gun nest and smiled. It was one of the nastiest things Tamsyn had ever seen.

"I thought doctors were meant to be smart," Tamsyn said, and pointed to the river. "Drive."

Putting the Chevy into gear, Hector punched the gas, the engine whining in protest. The big car lurched and shuddered, and thick fingers of steam poured out from under the hood. They couldn't see a damn thing now, but Tamsyn felt the car bounce around, felt the rough terrain as Hector took them off-road.

Then, the mad rush down to the river, the back-jarring collision as the car burst through the reeds and struck the water. The over-cooked motor hissed and finally died, and the Chevy was as dead as the rest of the world.

In the next few moments, they were out of the car, a mad scrabble as the soldiers came running. Tamsyn struggled through the shallows, trying to hold her bow overhead. Eddie dragged her forward, heedless of wetting his guns, and Dr. Murray staggered forward, screaming in agony. Tamsyn dimly noted an obstruction upstream, realised that this was the part of the river they'd turned into a salt moat.

Rodolfo was shouting from inside the car, and the context was all too clear. *Leave me, go on!* Hector followed them into the water, sorrow written across his face. A gunshot rang out from the car, and then another.

The wounded doctor shot the first of the conscript soldiers to descend the riverbank and sent the rest scattering, diving for cover. Even as Tamsyn and the others pushed out into the depths of the river, Rodolfo held these unwilling soldiers at bay with nothing but an old rifle.

Then a return volley, the sound of bullets striking metal. A low cry from the car, and then silence.

"Quickly, Tam," Eddie cried, helping her across the slimy shallows on the far side. Several times she slipped, fought to regain her balance on the rocks. "Drop the stupid bow." But she wouldn't.

Dr. Murray's head creased the surface, and he resumed his air-raid wailing, sobbing as the salt continued to wrack him. He'd walked across the bottom of the river, emerging like a creature from a B-grade horror movie. Water poured out of his rifle barrel, and he threw the useless gun to one side.

A rumble from the opposite bank. Even as they climbed away from the water, the APC stood on the other side, machine gun tracking them. Tamsyn saw how exposed they were, and squeezed her eyes shut, waiting for the bullets to stitch across her body.

What she thought was her final moment passed in an infinity of silence. She opened her eyes to see the Black Wasp jumping down from the turret. The APC lurched into reverse gear, swiftly making for the highway. Moments later, the opposite riverbank exploded into a fury of earth and fire, as shell after shell rained around the escaping enemy. When the smoke cleared, the broken bodies of the conscripts could be seen on the bank.

"We've got big guns too," Hector said, panting. "Come."

Next came a flurry of armed men and women, and rapid conversations in Spanish that she couldn't follow. Tamsyn put herself in front of Dr. Murray, terrified that one of Hector's friends would misunderstand and kill the Re-Human out of hand.

An officer interrogated the Re-Human in Spanish, pistol out and held low. Dr. Murray responded with a choice set of swear words, and the man nodded, as if the old grump had just passed an important test.

Stripped of weapons, they were let through the gates and searched again. Tamsyn saw uniformed soldiers patrolling the piece-meal walls, their numbers bolstered by civilians. Artillery pieces faced the river and the ocean, and a handful of military vehicles sat fuelled and ready.

A huge tank waited just inside the gate, the crew lounging around on the treads and playing cards.

Dusk fell as Hector gave his report, and Tamsyn heard a hidden bank of generators kick into life. Floodlights painted the court-yards and long buildings, and in some of the buildings the interior lights came on.

On the walls, the guards swept spotlights across the approach to the school, occasionally hurling something onto the ground below. Round, wobbling grenades, with a chicken crest of fingers. Latex gloves, pressed into service as water balloons. From the inhuman howls that washed over the wall, Tamsyn guessed these were filled with salt water.

Most worrying to Tamsyn was the fact they were being ignored. The trio huddled together in the courtyard, half-blinded by the bright lights. A pair of men had been assigned to watch them, but they conversed quietly in their own language, smoking cigarettes and not responding to any of Tamsyn's questions.

"I think I get it," Eddie said quietly. "These arseholes have seen Re-Humans before. Why else have they just let a zombie into the henhouse?"

"Shut the hell up," Dr. Murray said tensely. "Those two might know English."

There was nothing to do but play gin rummy down in the dirt, the Re-Human fumbling out each card with shaking hands. Being a vague curiosity to these people was worse than the hysterical reaction they'd all been expecting, and Dr. Murray knew it too.

He'd just become a commodity to these people, which meant of course that they were now locked into this conflict. Whatever future the school held for him, it wasn't doing yardwork.

The next Tamsyn saw of Hector was when he arrived with a nurse and a wheelchair. He'd talked his superiors into providing her with immediate care. She was off to the obstetrics wing.

"I'm coming too," Eddie insisted, but Tamsyn shook her head, even as she sank into the wheelchair with a grunt.

"I'm sorry love, but I need you to stay here," she said. "Do not take your eyes off Clem, not even for one second."

Eddie nodded, confliction washing across his punch-sculpted face. Tamsyn found the situation vaguely ridiculous and tried not to laugh. After everything that had happened to them both, Gravesend's most promising thug was just another petrified dad-to-be.

"You'll see our baby soon enough, I promise you. We're safe now."

She squeezed his hand, and then the nurse rolled her across the courtyard and into the dark maw of a building. Hector jogged ahead, wrestling open a pair of doors and flicking on the lights.

"We have to ration out our resources," he explained. As they travelled through the halls, he constantly switched off the lights behind them. She was the only patient, moving through the silent ward in a bubble of light.

"Last year we had five babies, all at once," Hector said. "Now, none for six months."

The place was musty, and the noise of their movement boomed around the empty hallways. It was in stark contrast with every hospital Tamsyn had ever seen. Here, the doctors vastly outnumbered the patients, and there was no queue, no waiting room full of ferals and drug addicts.

She saw shadowy rooms lined with small desks, and the sudden appearance of an instructional skeleton in a doorway caused her to cry out, to reach for her absent bow. It was a school, she had to remind herself. They swept past a handful of classrooms with spartan furnishings. From what light spilled in through the doors, Tamsyn saw that the instructors taught medicine with chalkboards and out-of-date equipment.

"In here," Hector said, shepherding her into a small examination room. There was a single gurney and a handful of medical machines nearby. At a guess, Tamsyn wouldn't have put anything in that room under thirty years old.

"Are you–" Tamsyn began nervously. Hector was a doctor, but they'd shared the bond of battle, the intimacy of death. His cousin and best friend were dead because of her. The thought of him poking around her private parts made her feel uncomfortable. A little worried at the thought of being invaded by a man who must hate her now.

"No. The obstetrician is coming. A lady."

"Thank you, Hector," she said. "I mean it."

He hovered at the doorway, as if he needed to say something else, some meaningless homily to paper over the day's events. But he was rescued by the presence of a new face, a woman who walked the hallways with an electric torch. As the lady bustled in with a broad smile, Hector quietly slipped away.

"You are Tasmeen?" she said with a pleasant lilt. The obstetrician was a woman in the full glow of Latino life and could have been anywhere between thirty and fifty years old.

"Tamsyn," she corrected, and the woman nodded, smiling broadly at her mistake. Between her and the nurse, they activated the equipment, wheeled over a machine that turned out to be an antique ultrasound.

"I am Dr. Valdéz, but you can call me Flora," she said. "You, you are my first patient in a long time."

With the nurse's help, Tamsyn got out of the chair and changed into the hated cotton gown. Flora parted the gown, squirted a foul-smelling gel out of a small bottle and all over Tamsyn's belly.

"Sorry, it is cold," she said. When the ultrasound finally hummed into life, the obstetrician waved the wand all around her bulging belly, smiling and cooing.

"See there?" she said, pointing to the screen. "Your baby is okay."

Tamsyn saw the green figure moving around on the clunky monitor and broke down, tears of joy rolling down her face. She wished she'd brought Eddie in, wished she could share the vision of this little face, the chubby little hands that moved around, confused and grasping at nothing.

"Do you want to know?" Flora said with a sly smile, and Tamsyn nodded. She pointed to the relevant part, and both she and the nurse burst into raucous laughter and cooing.

"I knew it," Tamsyn said with a smile. It seemed that boy children in Cuba were a very good thing.

"Hector says you had a bleed this morning. I am guessing about a tablespoon full?"

"Yes," Tamsyn whispered, terror climbing up her throat. She wasn't out of the woods yet.

"The placenta looks okay." After a brief minute of indignity, Flora declared Tamsyn's cervix to be in good shape.

"A marginal bleed," the obstetrician said. "You will be fine. And those cramps, they are definitely Braxton Hicks. There is nothing wrong with this baby or you."

Relief flooded through her. She'd brought her friends through fire and peril, terrified that she was miscarrying, but now, everything was okay.

Those men in the harbour, Hector's friends, the soldiers. People are dead now because you panicked, she thought suddenly. The realisation dulled her moment of joy, but neither the doctor nor the nurse noticed her smile fade.

"So, you will stay here until the baby comes?" Flora said hopefully.

"We — we hope to leave," Tamsyn said. "If we stay for three months, we'll definitely wear out our welcome."

"Three months? Your maths is wrong, Tasmeen."

Flora wielded the ultrasound wand once more and showed Tamsyn the hidden life in her womb. She pointed out some measurements and other signs that her practiced eye had picked up.

"You are over eight months pregnant," Flora said. "Any day now, that gorgeous boy of yours will arrive."

A nurse wheeled her through the grounds, handling the old wheelchair like a pro. The school was a confusing mass of buildings that made no sense in the darkness, and Tamsyn was sure that the nurse steered these dark pathways by memory alone.

The other woman spoke no English, and so they traversed the fortified compound in silence. The faint strains of music and laughter reached them. Those on point sweated and strained their eyes into the night, but the off-duty base life seemed much more relaxed.

A dark night, with the moon a thin pinpoint behind clouds. Tamsyn sweated profusely, and her exposed skin stuck against the vinyl seat. Summer in Cuba was brutal, even after the sun fell.

They were headed for the one building where every window blazed with light. A low-roofed administrative compound, complete with dingy staff-room and a cubical farm.

"Director," was all the woman could say, and she left Tamsyn at the doorstep with an apologetic shrug. Woman and wheelchair disappeared into the night.

Tamsyn was spotted by a young man with an armful of files, and politely shepherded into the heart of the office. She took in the bizarre mixture of high-ranking military officers and academics, buzzing around the cubicles and talking on top of and around each other. From what she could glean, the medical studies were continuing. On one wall, what looked to be a lesson plan, slightly adjacent from a pinboard festooned with maps and troop movements.

"Oy! We're in here, love," she heard Eddie say, and she saw him standing in the doorway of an office. Behind him, Dr. Murray sat in a chair, arguing quietly with someone on the other end of a desk.

No guards.

"All right then?" he asked, and a relieved smile spread from her face to his. *It's all okay.* She melted into his arms, but Eddie pulled away after a moment.

"You'd best come in here," he said, *sotto voce.* "Clem's in strife."

Tamsyn entered the office of Director Maria Ramirez, her name and title etched onto the glass of the door in no-nonsense block lettering. Ramirez was a wiry old woman who'd entered this broken new world at the end of a career. Her head was crowned by a thatch of grey hair, pulled back taut and pinned in place.

The woman in charge was as far from Clarice Feickert as it was possible to get. Ramirez was the very picture of austerity. She wore a plain blouse underneath a battered old doctor's coat, and no jewellery or make-up. Apart from a framed degree on the wall, there was nothing in this office approaching a decoration, not even a single photograph.

Dr. Murray sat on a chair before the battered desk, arms crossed and face drawn into a scowl. He nodded once when he saw Tamsyn and pushed the other chair towards her with his foot.

"So," Ramirez said in perfect English. "Finally, I get to meet the girl who wrecked my car."

"I am sorry," Tamsyn said. "We had no choice."

"Hector was most concerned that you be examined immediately. Are you okay?"

Tamsyn nodded.

"I'm very glad," Ramirez said, pinning Tamsyn rigid with her flinty eyes. "I would hate to think that two of my doctors died for nothing."

Tamsyn bowed her head, shame flushing her face. In a world where dead people tried to eat you, she'd panicked at the sight of a little blood. With a cooler head, they would already be in Fort Jefferson, safe and hidden.

"Don't you worry none, Tam," Dr. Murray growled. "This rotten cow has worked out a blood price, no fear of that."

"Control yourself, Dr. Murray," Ramirez said. "You are my guests, but this is a communist enclave. Everyone who lives here must contribute."

"You say guests, I hear prisoners," Eddie shouted. "Tam's all right now, so we're going. Tell your goons to open the gate!"

"We both know that isn't going to happen, Mr. Jacobs," Ramirez said, looking meaningfully at Dr. Murray. The Re-Human slouched in his chair, dried ligaments creaking. In the harsh fluorescent light, most of his fingers had that worrisome bruised hue, black threads running up the back of his hands. His leathery hide was beaded with condensation, and the whole office stank like wet dog.

"Wait, wait. You're communists? I thought you were the rebels," Tamsyn said, confused and tired. "Aren't the communists the ones who tried to kill us?"

"We are all revolutionaries," Ramirez said, with the air of someone tired of explaining things. "Those others, little more than bandits in uniforms now, scrabbling for food and bullets. The Party has lost its way."

The sombre decor made sense now. Director Ramirez was old school Communist, through and through. This mob hadn't broken away from Communism; they were trying to enforce it, preserve it behind a thick wall.

Outside, the barbarians roamed, and the dead looked on while humanity destroyed itself. The players were different, the reasons too, but some things were universal. If Gravesend was anything to go by, they had to get out of here, and fast.

"We had a man in Texas," Ramirez said. "Intelligence agent. Brought back footage of the ghettoes, of dead people with minds and voices. Your colleagues, Dr. Murray, penned up like criminals."

The Re-Human said nothing.

"The outbreak swept through Cuba, east to west, but we survived here. More than that, we never forgot our mission. Heal the sick. Resist imperialism. Teach our people to do what is right."

"Really? Do you think keeping us prisoner is right?" Tamsyn said, and the others voiced their approval. "We're leaving."

Ramirez leaned forward, sweeping her iron gaze across the sullen trio. She was only a tiny woman, but even Eddie bit his tongue. With practice borne from years of facing down unruly students, she silenced them without a word.

"Imagine my thoughts when I discovered that a rogue nation was keeping slaves, right on our doorstep," Ramirez continued, as if Tamsyn had never spoken. "Hoarding the cure. Repressing the workers, even after the world ended."

"Spare me that pinko gob-shite," Dr. Murray groaned.

"Look at yourself," Ramirez said. "You are the ultimate communist. You consume no resources, save for salt. You can produce labour tirelessly and will live for as long as your body can hold out."

Dr. Murray snorted, held up his decaying hands.

"In almost every way, you are superior to a mortal human being. Dr. Murray, the wilful undead are the next wave of the communist revolution."

"You want all the dead folks to be like me?" Dr. Murray said incredulously. "Plant your fields, milk your bleeding cows? Why would any of us do that, if we didn't have guns to our heads?"

"You misunderstand. The rehabilitation of the infected is paramount, above all else," Director Ramirez said. "Everybody has looked at the apocalypse as if it's a disaster. I say it's an opportunity. You, Dr. Murray, are an opportunity."

She fished out a file from a desk drawer, splayed it out onto the desk. Tamsyn saw page after page of tabled figures, but the report was in Spanish and meaningless to her. Ramirez unclipped a sheaf of photos and laid them out like a tarot.

Undead, strapped to gurneys and straining to bite the nearby medics. IV bags, pumping salt into dead flesh.

"We went through thousands of patients, trying to copy what the Texans had done. It's not as simple as inserting salt into an infected corpse. The amount must be exact for the treatment to stick, and the saline ratio changes at least twice during the course."

Tamsyn felt foolish; the idea she could sail over here and resurrect a dead doctor seemed ludicrous now. If hundreds of Cuban doctors couldn't replicate the cure, why did she think she and two friends could?

More photos. Shot after shot of still corpses, overdosed on saline, brains burnt out. Enormous pits full of burning bodies, bulldozers pushing them in like smouldering logs.

"We only got it right once."

She pulled out one final photo, and Tamsyn gasped. She recognised Raul Castro, here grey-faced and obviously dead. An obvious propaganda shot, the deceased President of Cuba was seated with other officials, looking at the camera with intensity. A big chunk of flesh was missing from the side of his throat.

"One of the generals put a bullet through Castro's head the next day. The Black Wasps killed our researchers, destroyed the lab under Havana. The Party did not want an immortal corpse as president."

With a polite knock on the doorjamb, an officer entered the room, apologising quietly. Ramirez looked over the document he handed her, signed off on it and handed it back. The high-ranking soldier was festooned with junk medals, but he seemed almost scared of Ramirez, relieved when he left the office.

"Three Army divisions realised the importance of our research and came over to us. War ever since."

She shuffled the photos back into the file, locked it in her desk drawer. The de facto leader of Cuba walked around her desk. Kneeling in front of Dr. Murray, she clasped his dead hands.

"We will not ask you to be anyone's slave," she said. "But we need your secrets, the ones locked inside your body."

"All I've got is slow rot, lady," Dr. Murray said. "I wouldn't wish this on anyone."

"Imagine a world where the last generation of humanity makes things right," she said quietly, fervently. "All of the pollution, cleaned up. Forests replanted, roads and cities torn up, given back to nature. The last of the war-mongers and tyrants, starved out of their bolt-holes and made to pay for their crimes."

"You're going to give the virus to everyone, aren't you?" Tamsyn said quietly. "Me, my baby, everyone who made it through this mess."

"We're not monsters, Miss Webb. If you refuse the Re-Human treatment, you'll be allowed to live out your life on a reserve. Sterilized, of course. It has to be this way. All human life must end."

Tamsyn was too shocked to even speak.

"When we have the process perfected, all who volunteer can become like your friend here," Ramirez said. "No one will want for anything, none will be favoured. Communism, perfectly realised."

17

"C lem, we have to get out of here," Tamsyn whispered. "These people are freaks."

Dr. Murray sat on a gurney, letting the nurses withdraw syringes full of viscous goop from his veins. It was all off to the new lab, where the surviving researchers waited to analyse every ounce of fluid.

What had once been the Oncology School was now Dr. Murray's home. He had furniture, books, even a record player. What comforts remained in the school were placed at the Re-Human's disposal, and he wanted for nothing.

Tamsyn was furious with him. When she asked Ramirez what the cancer patients were meant to do now, she discovered that almost a dozen terminal cases were waiting for this salt-cure.

The first of Ramirez's undead force, simply grateful to survive.

A doctor walked around Dr. Murray with a power-drill, running the fine-tipped drill into strategic locations. He ran the drill straight into Dr. Murray's heart and put the drill bit straight into a sample bag. The next sample came from Dr. Murray's left thighbone, and the Re-Human looked almost bored as the drill whined, worming into his marrow.

"It's for the best, lass," Dr. Murray said. "Besides, a deal's a deal."

When the doctor finished his extractions, he handed the drill to a nurse, and summoned another helper with the sharp click of his fingers. A nervous young woman stood as close to Dr. Murray as she dared, presenting a tray full of fat syringes. They looked big enough to dose a horse, each of them filled with a clear liquid.

"You changed your tune quick smart," Tamsyn accused. "I hope your fingers fall off, you arsehole."

Frowning, the doctor summoned a pair of orderlies, who politely herded Tamsyn out into the corridor. As the doors swung shut, she saw the doctor slowly slide the syringe into Dr. Murray's index finger.

Embalming fluid. Ramirez reckoned on saving Dr. Murray's rotting parts. With regular dosage and some excision of tainted flesh, she predicted his Re-Human body could last anywhere between another fifty to two hundred years.

The school's chief prosthetist had already planned the fitting of false limbs to Dr. Murray when his own began to fail. Given the proper attention and maintenance, Ramirez gave the next wave of deliberately infected Re-Humans a conservative "life span" of somewhere between two and five hundred years.

More than enough time to clean house, to put the world to rights. Sombre attendants, cold hands that would one day put the last of the humans into the ground.

Fuming, Tamsyn waddled out of Oncology, the morning sun almost blinding her as she threw open the outer doors. Another summer day in Cuba, and Tamsyn felt like someone was beating her about the head and shoulders with a hot wet towel.

She walked the grounds, willing the baby to arrive. The Braxton Hicks contractions were still happening, but less and less now. Tamsyn wanted the big pain, wanted to know that her baby was on his way. The moment she was stitched up and her baby was fit for travel, she and Eddie were busting out of this place.

As for Dr. Murray, he could stay here and literally rot.

Tamsyn kept to the shade whenever she could and watched five swarthy boys running around shirtless, an impromptu soccer match that wound through the trees and even onto a staircase. Outside of the main cafeteria, a soldier played a bolero on a guitar, accompanied by a teenager with a powerful voice, who beat out a rhythm on a packing crate. The song was toe-tapping and incredibly sad, all at once.

Tamsyn wondered which of these people had chosen to die.

Ramirez assured them that over three-quarters of the school would be taking the treatment. One injection to bring undeath, then the salt treatment to bring the living mind back, to lock it in an eternal body. Only one hundred of Ramirez's people were refusing the treatment, and it disturbed Tamsyn to realize that the bubbly Dr. Flora would soon be sterilising these people.

"I won't let her touch us," she swore to the life inside her.

One of the medical classes was being held outside, underneath the shade of an enormous tree. When Tamsyn realised that Hector was running the class, she changed direction, but he spotted her, waved. Hector ended the lesson and followed her, easily catching up to her pregnant gait.

"Tamsyn, wait," Hector said. She wouldn't look at him and kept her face forward as she stomped away. She'd as good as killed his cousin and his best friend, but the clean-cut young doctor seemed glad to see her.

Tamsyn didn't want to make friends. Friends got killed. This way was just easier.

"There's something really wrong with you people," Tamsyn finally said. "Are you going to take the treatment?"

Hector nodded.

"Well, you're an idiot."

"We can do the best good this way," Hector said. "Overthrow the last of the tyrants, heal the earth."

"You are going to die," Tamsyn said, stopping short and prodding him in the chest. "You won't be able to feel, to love, to even taste anything. It's just you and your dead mates at the end, shuffling around on your immortal coil. *Comprende*?"

"Tamsyn, it's okay," he said with a gentle smile. "When we don't have to worry about survival, we can focus our energy on more important things."

"There is literally no point to life as a Re-Human," Tamsyn said. "Clem showed us that. I've seen those poor buggers go mad inside of a year, but here you are wanting to sign up."

"Come on, I want to show you something."

She gave up, didn't have the energy to deflect the cheerful young man. Hector led Tamsyn through the school until the buildings gave way to a baseball field overlooking the sea. The entire field had been ploughed up, even the diamond itself. Vast rows of vegetables grew under the hot sun, and Tamsyn saw several figures pottering around, dragging sprinkler hoses and tending to the garden beds. She saw a pair of big water tanks at the end of a service road, designed to keep the sports grounds green.

The school had grown a market garden here to commercial scale, and Tamsyn guessed there was enough food for everyone. Surplus, if three-quarters of these people suddenly died.

"We do things differently in Cuba," Hector said. "If something doesn't work, or if we don't have the parts, we work around it."

There was an old bench-seat nearby, from when this field hosted friendly games of baseball. Her back twinging, Tamsyn made a beeline for this seat, easing down with a sigh of pleasure.

"When we couldn't copy the Texans, we—we tried other ways," Hector said, sitting next to her. "It didn't work how we hoped, but we still learnt much."

One of the gardeners came close, dragging a hose to a nearby cluster of water fittings and pipes. Tamsyn saw that it was a woman, emaciated and filthy. Completely dead.

Her eyes were vacant, and she regarded the young people on the bench-seat with the dull stare of the mindless undead. This was not a Re-Human. Tamsyn realised the dead woman wore latex gloves, and a wire muzzle strapped to her jaw.

Gasping, she made to rise, to put as much distance between her and the zombie as possible. Hector put a hand on her shoulder, pressed down gently.

"You are safe," he said. "Watch."

The zombie knelt by the water fittings, slowly connecting the hose. She dropped the hose several times and then pondered the fittings for a long moment. With a low grunt, the zombie remembered what to do, and screwed the connection together.

The dead woman turned on the tap, and the sprinkler began to work. Regarding the flow with quiet satisfaction, the zombie rose, wandered away to collect a rake.

"What the hell was that?" Tamsyn breathed.

"A failed treatment," Hector said. "We combined the saline treatment with a measure of embalming fluid. It works, but only to a point."

A man with a broad-brimmed cowboy hat could be seen striding through the zombie workers, directing them about their tasks. One of the undead seemed to baulk, shaking its head and almost mulish in this refusal. The living man pulled out a cattle prod. Even as the corpse mewled in confusion, he touched the prod to its throat, filled it full of volts.

It twitched on the spot, moaning pitifully. Tamsyn watched, fascinated and revolted as the dead nerves conducted electricity. It seemed effective in a way, a punishment that the zombie could feel, but less cruel than a spray of salt water.

The overseer did not seem to enjoy the torture, and only shocked the creature for a second or two. He pointed again, as if encouraging a toddler to follow instruction.

Still shuddering, the corpse accepted the shovel, trudged off as ordered. It looked back at the overseer once, almost sullen, but when the man raised the cattle-prod the zombie quickly bent to its work.

"Zombie slaves," Tamsyn said.

"We call them *muñecas*. It means dolls," Hector explained. "Their minds are gone now, and they cannot be brought back. If they were alive, we would say that the formaldehyde has pickled their brains. Made them into idiots."

"Are you still making these...things?"

"No. The Party, they wanted to make soldiers of the *muñecas*, send them in boats to America. Ramirez said no."

They watched as the undead went about harvesting the food, working slowly but steadily. This strange new breed of undead seemed able to follow simple instructions, and they even appeared to enjoy each other's company when their work brought them close.

"They do not hunger for human flesh," he said with a shrug. "The *muñecas* do as they are told, and most of them seem happy enough. Better than a bullet, *si*?"

"Why do you show me this?" Tamsyn asked.

"You say that we are mad for wanting to become Re-Human. Proof, then, that things can always be worse."

At first it looked like Tamsyn and Eddie would be slated into a student dormitory, but a cramped bedsit was found for them. As "special guests," the young Brits were surrounded by the rooms of billeted officers and senior lecturers.

Ramirez was keeping them right under her thumb.

The teachers all had houses once, off-grounds. Now, there was nothing for them but the school, and folks too slow to claim a bunk were dossing down in class-rooms, cafeterias, and gyms.

On the way in she'd seen old wards divided into rooms, tarpaulin curtains strung up and doing little to filter the coughing and chatter of one's neighbours.

In London, this bedsit would be a slum rental filled from floor to ceiling by expat Australians. In post-apocalyptic Cuba, it was an absolute luxury. Part of Dr. Murray's deal with the devil, along with a private medical team for Tamsyn.

"You better appreciate this, kid," Tamsyn told the baby, frowning as the naked lightbulb flickered again. She put down the Spanish textbook and rubbed at her sore eyes. She found the lessons frustrating, and the language wasn't coming to her easily.

Eddie returned shortly after dark, tired and scowling. He was required to contribute labour to the commune, and quickly volunteered to join the guards. If they were going to break out of this compound, they needed to get access to guns.

"Did you get one?" she asked quietly.

"I did nothing but throw water balloons at coffin-dodgers. All day. They don't trust me with a gun yet."

Sleep was hard-won; the ancient pedestal fan did little to move the sticky air, and when the power failed altogether the room became unbearable. She sweated and fumed, and poked Eddie in the ribs when his snoring reached buzz-saw levels.

Eventually she slipped into a restless slumber. The dream came almost immediately. She sat on a park bench in Gravesend, looking up at the statue of Pocahontas. Her hands rested on a flat belly, yet to know stretch marks or the impatient thumping of a foetus. Tamsyn turned to see her father sitting beside her.

Mal Webb. His chest was still shattered and bloody, hair damp and clogged with beach-grit. He looked at her mournfully, shaking his head slowly. He took her hands and laced his cold fingers through hers, and she felt the seawater and grit on her skin.

"The Jacobs boy," he said. "You have to leave him."

"Dad," she sniffled. "Eddie's different now. I love him."

Her father opened his mouth to say more, but something caught in his throat, words that perhaps he wasn't allowed to say. For a long moment he struggled to frame his intent, and he clutched her hand tighter, grey lips moving silently.

"You have to leave him," he managed.

"I won't. We're having a baby."

"Send him away, Tam. Please."

Mal Webb released her hand and stood. He walked to the statue, rested his weight against the stone plinth. Behind the bronze Pocahontas, something unseen lurked, a menacing force that waited to snatch her father. In the logic of this dream, she knew that he'd broken some sort of rule. A punishment was coming for him, and her too if she could not wake up.

"The dolls," he said with a tremor. Fingers of shadow crept out from behind the statue, swallowing Mal whole, reaching for her. She woke with a start. Tamsyn sat bolt upright in her bed, heart pounding, face slick with tears.

Writing off the nightmare as another episode from her damaged psyche, she shuffled off to her appointment with Dr. Flora. Much to Tamsyn's surprise, the obstetrician recommended that she be given back her bow and arrows.

"Gentle exercise can be good," she said, scrawling out a note. "Only a little bit, and some walking, okay?"

The woman smiled, but Tamsyn saw a fanaticism in the depths of her eyes, the soul of a surgeon committed to ending humanity. Dr. Flora was no friend to her.

The quartermaster had no English, and handed over her gear with a bored expression, unconcerned at giving a bow to a heavily pregnant woman. Nearly every soldier walked the grounds armed to the teeth, while the archery kit looked more like camping equipment than a true weapon.

"Shows what you lot know," she muttered. Looking for a safe place to practice, Tamsyn walked out on the bluff, next to the old baseball field.

She spent a long moment watching the waves roll in, and the ribbon of beach looked inviting, a postcard picture complete with a stand of palm-trees. The scene was made disturbing by the inclusion of the undead gardeners, who might well have continued their toil throughout the night.

The soldiers had the tank parked by the beach today, a man in the turret scanning the sea with his binoculars. Two artillery pieces waited nearby, already aimed at Havana. Tamsyn shook her head as the illusion fell away. No peace here. None anywhere.

When the overseer saw her watching, he walked over. The man was an enormous brute with a greasy cowboy hat and a thick grizzle of beard that almost reached his navel. He had the ripe smell of someone not acquainted with bathing and seemed to wear generations of dirt quite cheerfully. The cattle prod swung from his belt. It could probably drop a buffalo on half-charge.

The zombie-herder seemed almost simple, a bumpkin, but there was something approaching a deep cunning in his eyes. Was that a flicker of recognition? The overseer looked at her with some amusement, asked her a question in Spanish.

"No Español," Tamsyn said. "Inglés."

The man nodded. When he saw her bow and arrow, he pointed to a nearby stack of pea-straw bales, mimed the shooting of a bow. She nodded, and he helped set up a target for her. Fetching a can of spray paint from a nearby shed, he painted a bull's-eye ring onto the straw bales.

"*Flecha, flecha!*" he cried out with delight, and Tamsyn emptied her quiver into the bale. He whistled appreciatively at her accuracy and took away one of the bales. Tamsyn laughed and stepped back another ten paces.

Her arrows flew. Even as she eased into the peaceful commune of draw and release, Tamsyn saw the *muñecas* out of the corner of her eye. Two of them had ceased work, watched her archery until the big overseer waved his cattle-prod meaningfully.

The overseer seemed to enjoy the company of a pretty young girl, even if she was heavily pregnant. He fetched a half-melted chocolate bar out of his overalls and offered it to her.

"Gracias," Tamsyn said, wolfing it down. He smiled and nodded, patting his own belly enthusiastically. "Yes, I've got a baby. Uh, bebé."

He tried to ask her something else, but the language barrier proved frustrating. He shrugged and made to return to his work.

"Tamsyn," she said suddenly, pointing to herself. "Me llamas Tamsyn."

"Jorge," he said with a broad smile. "Jorge Delgado."

Despite herself, Tamsyn had made a friend. The next day, she came back to the field and found a trio of targets already waiting for her. Jorge sauntered over with a broad grin and even enlisted a spare *muñeca* to retrieve her arrows.

Tamsyn spent almost every day out on the bluff. Jorge traded words with her, and soon enough they could hold a halting conversation. Tamsyn brought some of her daily rations, and Jorge traded chocolate and fresh fruit for her unwanted cigarettes. Even Eddie came out for cigarettes once or twice, on the rare times he was relieved from duty.

"Your amigos?" she asked Jorge, pointing to the obedient zombies.

"Dogs," he said, fumbling for an unfamiliar word. "Uh, my pets."

It made sense. He wasn't unkind to his charges, simply firm. Much like anyone working with beasts of burden, he set boundaries and enforced these. Tamsyn remembered the Re-Human ghettoes, the brutalities inflicted by the Texans, and decided that Jorge was okay.

He showed her the *muñecas'* favourite game, and Jorge and Tamsyn took it in turns to drag a bent coat-hanger through a grimy bucket. He'd laced the water with detergent and blew through the metal loop, launching soapy bubbles into the air. The undead went crazy, snatching at the iridescent globes, gasping with delight as they popped.

Tamsyn laughed till she snorted, and going by the squirm in her gut, it felt like the baby was laughing too.

Sharing a lunch of flatbread and beans, Jorge asked haltingly after Tamsyn's friends, and seemed quite interested in Dr. Murray. Given his close work with the *muñecas*, this made some sense. Tamsyn told Jorge what she could about the salt treatments, of the hardships Dr. Murray had faced. She absently related how the Re-Humans had even fought in the war, a detail he took in attentively.

When her cramps played up, she spent a sweat-soaked day in bed, yelling at Dr. Flora and convinced that labour had arrived. It was almost two days until she next ventured out to the garden, but Jorge was nowhere to be seen.

He'd been the school's groundskeeper before the outbreak and still kept to a little shack just past the clay basketball courts. These had been repurposed into a piggery. The sows and their litters were clamouring at the gate, excited when they saw her approach.

It was almost noon, but Jorge hadn't fed them yet.

Worried, she walked around Jorge's shack, trying to peer in through the grimy windows. The *muñecas* were still in their flimsy pen beneath the veranda, pushing at the chicken wire and moaning woefully.

"Hola?" Tamsyn called out. She knocked on the door, but there was no answer. Fearing the worst, she turned the handle, stepped inside.

She'd only been as far as Jorge's front door once. The big man liked his privacy, which Tamsyn definitely understood. But he could be stuck in there, sick or even worse. From what she'd gleaned of his arrangement with Ramirez, no one cared what he did out here, so long as he kept the food coming in.

Few had time for old Jorge Delgado, and no one visited.

Throwing back the curtains, Tamsyn looked at the interior of the shanty. Jorge lived in here like a bachelor, the counter lined with empty tins and tools. Dirty clothes littered the floor, and his simple bed resembled a rat's nest.

The smell inside made Tamsyn's stomach turn over. Everything was sour and unwashed. A pot on the simple cooktop smelled of rotting cabbage, and he'd probably never attended to the pile of dishes in the sink.

"Jorge?" She checked the tiny bathroom. Nothing. He wasn't here. Tamsyn had an eye for detail and noted that his boots weren't there, and neither was his favourite hat. The ancient strata of mess was covered by a more recent layer; junk that had been kicked around, drawers torn open and partly emptied.

Papers scattered across the table and even the floor, as if he was looking for something in particular.

He'd packed a bag, left in a hurry. Something spooked Jorge Delgado, and she'd bet he wasn't even near the school now. Over the walls and far away, or more likely on a boat, sometime during the night.

The soldiers patrolling the perimeter were new arrivals to the Latin American School of Medicine, but the old groundskeeper would know every inch of this place. If anyone could sneak out, he could.

Poking through a mess of newspapers and old records, she found what Jorge missed. A notebook, bound in string and bulging with extra pieces of paper. Fishing a craft-knife out of a glass jar, Tamsyn sliced open the bindings, opened the book.

Notes in Spanish, a surprisingly neat hand that filled every inch of every page. Tamsyn could hardly make out any of it and felt slightly guilty for invading Jorge's private diary. Perhaps this would give a clue to his whereabouts. Maybe she could find where he'd gone and help him.

Then she found the documents. Pages from a report, meaning-less numbers. Letters, signed off by Director Ramirez, and what looked to be the minutes for some sort of meeting.

Jorge had been building a dossier on something, quietly lifting files while people thought he was changing lightbulbs and fixing windows.

As Tamsyn frowned over the book and tried to decipher it with her beginner's Spanish, something fell out of the back. It was a photo, a crisp printout on good paper. Tamsyn turned it over idly, and then an icy hand gripped her chest.

It was a picture of the *Petty Cash*, cruising into the harbour at Havana. She saw herself on the rear deck, staring up at the castle walls. The photo captured her likeness perfectly.

Jorge Delgado was a Party spy.

"What did you tell him?" Ramirez shouted. Her office was filled out to the doorway with officers and faculty heads, leaning over Tamsyn and yelling heatedly at each other.

Jorge's notebook lay gutted on the desk, pages unstitched and neatly arranged for investigation. The groundskeeper had stolen dozens of confidential reports, taping relevant sections into the notebook itself. Research notes for the Re-Human project, notes on the abandoned *muñeca* formula, inventory and troop dispositions for the school forces.

The file clerks were constantly at the door, yelling out new discoveries. Jorge had been nicking records for months. Tamsyn fought the panic, tried to rise. She needed to get out of this craziness, to find Eddie. An officer pushed her back into the seat, yelled at her until spittle flecked her face.

"Enough," Ramirez yelled, slamming the tabletop with her wrinkled old fist. "Give the poor girl some air. All of you, get out."

Tamsyn smiled weakly as the heads of the school filed out of the room. Maria glared at her, and Tamsyn swallowed nervously, looked down at her big belly.

"If you weren't in the family way, for what you told that man, I—I would have you shot," she said. Tamsyn felt a cold knot in her stomach.

Several of the stolen reports were unaccounted for. The thefts pointed towards a second and maybe a third notebook, more recent information that Jorge had taken with him.

"A fishing boat was stolen from the old boathouse," Ramirez said. "Your good friend Jorge is on his way to Havana right now, and he will give the Party our research."

"You should be thanking me!" Tamsyn said. "I uncovered a bloody spy."

"Listen, you stupid girl," Ramirez said. "You told him everything. Re-Humans used as soldiers, salt dosage, everything the Black Wasps need to know."

"We could barely talk to each other," Tamsyn protested. "He probably didn't understand half of what I was saying."

"Jorge Delgado speaks perfect English," Ramirez said. "He was pensioned out to the school after being injured in combat. He commanded a tank squadron once."

"Oh." Blood ran to Tamsyn's cheeks. Jorge had played her like a master puppeteer. No doubt the latest notebook contained all the detail of their conversation, the strengths and weakness of Re-Humans, her own recollections of the time she'd armed the undead and used them to seize an enemy base.

At the time, it had felt good to chat to someone who just listened, who offered little but smiles and chocolate. Now she wanted to be sick.

"I was a little suspicious when Jorge wanted the *muñecas*," Ramirez said. "But they did good work on the garden. We were so busy trying to solve the salt issue, we let a spy learn how to train zombie slaves."

The older woman sighed, deflated. Her anger at Tamsyn seemed to dissipate, and she realised it for what it was. A Latino temper, brought to the boil and aimed at the nearest outsider.

"We should have shot those poor wretches." Ramirez produced a bottle of rum from the innards of her desk, made to offer it to Tamsyn but thought better of it.

"They will come now," the director said, taking a belt straight from the bottle. "They have our troop numbers, and they know the salt-cure is in our grasp. The Party will throw everything at us."

"Maybe it's best if they do win," Tamsyn said, hands clutched protectively over her belly. "They can stop you from ending the human race."

"You are young, Tamsyn, and I do not expect you to understand." Ramirez took another slug. "I have seen many things in my life. Batista's thugs, the Revolution, the Americans and the Russians, all chewing on Cuba like dogs."

Ramirez leaned forward, caught Tamsyn's sullen glare.

"Do you know what I learnt, during my long life? The men with the guns, they never change. Flags, creeds, countries, all mean nothing. It all comes back to this."

She slapped a revolver onto the desk, and the barrel seemed to regard Tamsyn with a deadly eye.

"Killing. My tribe can beat up your tribe. The walking dead have brought us back to the oldest way. The rule of might."

Frowning a little, Ramirez put the pistol away. She handled it awkwardly, proof that she rarely held one. Tamsyn wondered if she could overpower the woman, take the gun from her. Bargain her way out of the school.

But then what?

"We have the chance to reinvent history, to break this cycle of violence," Ramirez continued. "The Party, the Black Wasps, they are nothing but barbarians, banging on the gate. They want the *muñeca* formula, and they will make the zombies into a slave army, big enough to conquer the world."

"They're no worse than you lot," Tamsyn grumbled.

"We are humanity's saviours," Ramirez said. "One day, it will all make sense to you. When you have your baby, and he is weaned, I want you to reconsider the treatment."

"Absolutely not."

"You could do a lot of good. Why live for mere decades in a camp when you can exist for hundreds of years? You can fix the world, stamp out the Alexanders and the Caesars. I see that fire in your eyes, your drive! You want to make things better. Here is your chance."

"You are gonna have to put me in chains," Tamsyn said, struggling out of the chair. "I mean to live. That's all that counts for a damn now."

Night found Tamsyn wide awake in her bed, wide-eyed and worried. Eddie crept in at the end of his shift, exhausted and filthy. Wash-water had just gone down to half rations, and everyone stank.

He wriggled into their bed, nuzzled against the curve of her back. By long habit his calloused hands found her baby bump, and the three of them lay in close contact, a family unit.

Tamsyn let the bubble of headquarters noise wash over her, paid no more mind to the squeak of shoes that passed their room.

Messengers came and went throughout the night, rapping on doors and stirring the commanders from their sleep.

The school was on high alert. Once she heard the distant crack of a rifle, but no sound followed other than the pounding of her heart.

"I still couldn't get a gun," Eddie said, when it was clear that both of them were far from sleep. "Bloody water balloons, fetching ammo and shit. I feel useless."

Rumours were flying around on the walls, each worse than the last. Some were translated for Eddie's benefit. The Party were coming. They were already here. The gardener was a spy. The Castro brothers were back from the dead, and the entire school had been found guilty of counter-revolution.

Thrown as he was by most of the rapid chatter in Spanish, Eddie knew the moods of soldiers as good as anyone else. The general vibe was this: *shit about to meet fan.*

"We need guns before we can bust out," Eddie said. "Or we'll get chewed up in seconds."

"Let's run anyway," Tamsyn said. "We take Clem if we can, but tomorrow, we run."

"They're going to evacuate," Dr. Murray said quietly. Tamsyn moved closer, watched the nurses as they rushed the latest round of samples out for analysis. The Re-Human looked like Swiss cheese now, torso riddled with holes.

"An island, south of Cuba. *Isla De La Juventud.* They're gonna ditch the soldiers, everyone but the research team and the director's mates. They're close to cracking the treatment, lass, and it looks like they're cutting their losses."

There were no doctors in sight. Tamsyn saw the panicked look in the nurses' faces, the discreet way that they were packing up their equipment.

Then she and Dr. Murray were alone, with only the clatter of the nurses' sneakers in the hallway. Not a minder in sight.

"I've asked that you and Eddie be allowed to come too," the old Re-Human said. "That hard-nosed bitch in charge, she'll only take you on one condition. Tam, once the baby comes, you and Eddie need to take the treatment."

"No way in hell," Tamsyn said. "Clem, we're gonna bust you out of here."

Then the first contraction gripped her, a terrible squeezing that made her scream. She slid out of the chair, skinning her knees on the painted cement floor. The pain was like nothing she'd ever experienced, and the wild flexing of her uterus made her old gunshot wound seem like a bee-sting.

"Nurses! Help!" Dr. Murray called. She looked up to see him unclipping the IV drip, climbing out of the tangle of tubes and equipment. There was a hand-buzzer nearby, and he drove his grey finger into it repeatedly.

The distant sound of a bell. Tamsyn felt dampness, but not blood. Her water had broken. She heard the sound of running feet from the corridor, but she couldn't tell if they were coming or going. She reached up for Clem with shaking hands, and then the second contraction hit her. Was it two minutes apart?

"Hang on, Tam," Clem said, and Tamsyn gripped his cold hands as hard as she could. He cradled her on the floor, and she sobbed as the pain shot through her body.

"Nurse!" Clem roared. A third contraction gripped her, and that's when Tamsyn heard the stutter of gunfire, the distant *crump!* of a shell landing. Random hands appeared through the pain, lifting her into a gurney.

"They're attacking the school," she gasped, and someone told her to hush. She looked up to see Dr. Flora fussing over her, attended by a sole nurse whose eyes kept creeping towards the door.

Time lost all meaning. There was nothing to Tamsyn's universe but agony, punctuated by explosions and the rattling of windows. Twice the power failed, and dimly she noted how Dr. Murray lit a bunch of candles, lining the shelves and windowsills.

It was dark now. She'd been in this room for hours, straining and swearing, calling for Eddie until her voice got hoarse. He was on the walls, Dr. Flora said, and his commander would not release him.

Then the lights came back on. Dr. Flora dragged over the ultrasound machine, cursed as it whined into life. The lights dimmed once, but the power held out as she ran a quick scan.

"Your baby is in breach," the Cuban doctor said, flustered and beginning to panic. "We will need to cut him out."

Caesarean. Tamsyn's heart sank. There was no time for this. It would take weeks for her to recover. Eddie would have to find her a wheelchair, somehow get them out of here before the Party overran the school.

She felt useless, scared.

Another explosion, and the power died out altogether. More shells, so close now that they painted the walls in a lightning flicker.

"They're at the wall," she said weakly, even as Dr. Flora applied a local anaesthetic to her. After the pain of her futile labour, the needle felt like nothing.

"Hold on love," Dr. Murray said, gripping her sweaty hands tightly. Dimly she noted the tearing sensation as the obstetrician carved her open, felt something pull as she drew the baby out.

Then a little shape was on her chest, bloody and bawling. The room shook as a shell landed in the courtyard outside. Glass broke, equipment fell, and Tamsyn's son howled his sorrow at this horrible world.

She looked down at him and sobbed with relief. His face was scrunched up and slimy, and he was perfect. With toes and fingers where they belonged, her son wailed loud enough to eclipse the battle outside.

The nurse approached with a pair of scissors, and Tam slapped her hands away. She had horrid visions of a forced sterilisation, Ramirez's policy for the last generation of humans. The woman looked at her with confusion.

"Don't touch my baby," she shouted. "You leave him alone. If you hurt him, I'll kill you."

"It's just for the umbilical cord, Tasmeen," Dr. Flora said. "Don't fuss now, we have to stitch you up. Quickly."

The nurse cut her baby's cord, even as Dr. Flora attacked her with needle and thread. Tamsyn only looked down once at what the Doctor was doing, and the sight of her open belly almost made her faint.

"He's a beaut," Dr. Murray cooed, waggling his grey fingers at her boy. "A real little bruiser. Your Eddie will be right proud of him."

Dr. Flora tied off the final stitch, and between the three of them they got Tamsyn from the gurney to a clunky old wheelchair. They left the room as it was, bloody bed and all. A mad race down the darkened corridors, the explosions urging them faster. Tamsyn clutched at her newborn, the baby howling and just as confused as she was.

Dr. Murray booted the final doors open, and then they were out in the chaos. A nearby building was in flames, and the stutter of gunfire was too close for comfort. The shooting was inside the school, and Tamsyn dimly noted a tangle of masonry where the outer wall had been.

Eddie had been at that wall. He didn't even have a gun.

"Quickly," Dr. Flora gasped, and led them deeper into the school, away from the fighting. Ahead of them two doctors ran, white coats flapping. They yelled back in Spanish, beckoning them on with urgency.

Tamsyn was so numb with fear and exhaustion that it took her a second to realise what she was looking at. The outer doors to an old gymnasium lay open, and people were madly clearing tarpaulins from a hidden vehicle, hauling it outside with ropes.

A plane. It was an old biplane with an enclosed cabin, and she saw someone turning the big propeller, checking it for obstructions.

"You lot are pulling my leg," Dr. Murray said, dragging one leg and struggling to keep up. "That thing must be as old as Stalin."

"Antonov AN-2, most reliable plane in the world," Director Ramirez said from behind them. "If we get past their guns, we will escape. Somebody, help this girl. Vamanos!"

Two men carried her up the steps and into the dusty interior of the plane. She counted twelve seats, and perhaps twenty people milling around outside. It was going to be a tight squeeze.

"Eddie!" she shouted, scanning the faces. "Where's Eddie?"

No one answered her. Doctors squeezed into the seats, some hauling medical bags or personal belongings. Even as the baby continued its air-raid screech, she fumbled with the window.

In places they were two to a seat. The plane wouldn't get off the ground. She needed fresh air. She needed her son's father.

"Eddie!" she sobbed. "We can't leave without Eddie."

Through the press of passengers, she could see Dr. Murray up the front, arguing with Ramirez and Hector. Ramirez hauled out her pistol, and with a glum look on his face the Re-Human settled into his seat.

Hector settled into the pilot's chair, reaching up for switches, tapping at uncooperative gauges. He shook his head. Then the director hauled the door shut, and Tamsyn screamed.

"You horrid bitch, you're gonna leave them!" she shouted, and then the engine coughed into life. She felt the hum of the motor through the simple bench seat, and oddly enough this seemed to calm her baby.

He suckled at her arm, and she realised that she needed to feed her baby now. Tears streaming down her face, she opened her gown and planted him against her breast, heedless of the people around her. The baby latched on with no issue, drained milk from her like there was no tomorrow.

Propeller whining and gaining speed, the plane bounced across the school grounds. Tamsyn saw the buildings flash past, some burning and broken from stray shells. Hector opened the throttle right up, and the old plane narrowly cleared Jorge's vegetable garden.

Then they were up and over the sea, climbing higher and higher. Through the window, Tamsyn saw a flotilla of boats pulled up on the beach. Party soldiers were moving around the burning wreckage of a tank, and several of them opened fire on the plane.

Hector jinked the biplane from left to right, dumping several of the passengers into the aisle. Tamsyn held onto her baby and prayed, wincing as a stream of lead pattered against the hull.

When they reached a safe altitude, Hector turned the plane around, flew over what was left of the school. Tamsyn saw enemy tanks bouncing over the rubble, and foot troops marching over the fallen wall.

A small group of school soldiers stood in the courtyard, arms raised. The enemy made a stack of captured rifles, and apart from sporadic gunfire, the battle was over. Tamsyn pressed her nose against the glass, hoping against hope to recognise her fiancé from this height.

They're taking prisoners. He might be okay.

I'll come back for you, my love. I promise.

There was one final explosion, a spectacular eruption that reduced the administration building to matchsticks. Ramirez led a ragged cheer, and Tamsyn knew enough Spanish now to divine the bitter cries of her passengers. *Deny the supply, burn all the notes. Give those bastards nothing.*

Dr. Flora appeared, forcing her way through the other passengers. She examined Tamsyn's stitches and took some time now to check over the baby.

"He is beautiful," she said. "Healthy and strong. What are you going to call him?"

"Malcolm," Tamsyn whispered, thinking of her father. The burning school vanished into the darkness. "His name is Malcolm."

Tamsyn worked the rocking chair like a grim-faced metronome, soothing the baby on her breast. The wood creaked and squeaked, and young Malcolm drank deeply.

Tired to the bone, she stared across the porch and through the overgrown rose garden, eyes unfocussed and numb to what lay beyond. Five enormous turrets dominated the plain, an old prison called the Presidio Modelo. She'd been inside once and vowed never to return.

Ramirez had finally gleaned the salt-cure from Dr. Murray's flesh. Her horrid project went on inside that dreadful place, and the survivors from the school worked around the clock.

The full scope of this undertaking was staggering. Crumbling structures were repaired. Museum wings were repurposed into living quarters. Dug into the magnificent bay, a new evaporation pan lay just one mile from the prison, and a misfiring truck made the trip daily, dumping tonnes of salt in the courtyard.

Each of the turrets held one thousand cells, facing inwards to a single guard-tower. For the first time since the 1960s, the historic jail was at maximum capacity. When the wind blew this way, she could hear the screams, like a chorus of tortured gulls.

Malcolm grizzled a little, and Tamsyn jiggled him on her shoulder until he burped. Another row of shambling bodies walked out of the nearest turret, ant figures led by someone in a white-coat.

Recruitment was going well.

Even in autumn, the heat was oppressive, but the shade under the porch gave some relief. Near as she could tell, this had been an officer's cottage, back when the jail housed dissidents and counter-revolutionaries. The garden was half dead and running wild, but she supposed it was first planted by that officer's wife, to block out the view, to bring cheer to this dour place.

Sliding Malcolm into his crib, Tamsyn slumped back into the rocker. Motherhood was brutal, and she'd had so little sleep just lately that she felt like a zombie herself. The motion of the chair lulled her into a doze, and soon she dreamt.

She still sat in the chair, but the tiny cottage and its garden were full of her dead friends. Ali and the others from Gravesend, everyone who'd died on the crossing from England, soldiers she'd served with.

Naomi and her mother clucked over the baby, and Baxter threw her a wry salute. All were hale and healthy, and cups of tea were in evidence. Then through the press of remembered faces came her father, and Mal Webb loomed before her, worried and frowning.

He was the only one of the visitors who actually looked dead. His grey lips were sewn together, ugly black threads that prevented him from speaking. He paced around on the porch, gesturing at Tamsyn, pointing north, back to the Cuban mainland. He gave up and sank to the boards, prying at the stitches on his mouth and weeping.

"Your dad's in disgrace," Simon Dawes said, appearing at Tamsyn's elbow. He wore the cheap suit she'd seen him in at his sentencing, years before a cellmate carved his face into a Glasgow grin. Before she'd forced this man into captaining a ship, into undeath, into that quiet glade where she put an arrow deep into his brain.

Poor, mealy-mouthed, washed-up Dawes. Killer of mothers, martyr and sorrowful pain in the arse. Even knowing it was a dream didn't lessen her hatred of this man.

"Don't," she warned. "You don't get to talk to me."

Dawes shrugged. He accepted a cup of tea from Clarice Feickert. The chatty Texan was working the room, smiling and doing her best to make a lie of the tactical nuke that ended her life.

"I'm losing my bloody mind," Tamsyn said.

"Seems there's a lesson to this party," Dawes offered, sipping daintily. "Not sure what your old man wanted to say, but I bet it's got something to do with vengeance."

"Very funny. Fuck off."

"How about you tell that to him?" he said, nodding towards the garden gate.

Standing there, framed by dead roses, Eddie lurked at the edges of the gathering. He looked at her, licked his lips. Tried to step forward.

"You can't rescue Eddie," Dawes said. "Run, girl. Grab that kid of yours and run like fuck."

Then Tamsyn woke up and saw grey hands reaching for her baby. She was on her feet in a heartbeat, a fat revolver clenched in her shaking grip. Hector stammered, stepped back from the crib with hands raised.

"I'm sorry Tamsyn. I thought you were sleeping," he said. "Just came to check on you and Malcolm."

"We're fine," Tamsyn said through clenched teeth. She held the gun level with his temple, fought to control her anger. Hector's beautiful coffee-coloured skin was a yellow-gray, his soulful eyes now like those of a hooked fish. Blasted and empty.

They'd all gone and done it. Dr. Flora, Ramirez, all of the people who'd caught the plane. They'd taken it in turns to die and to return, and now these resurrected doctors worked around the clock to end humanity.

As far as she knew, she and Malcolm were the only living people on this entire island.

"Tamsyn?" Hector said, and she apologised, lowered the gun. Ramirez's old revolver, given to her on the strength of Dr. Murray's lie. He assured the Cubans that Tamsyn would take the Re-Human treatment too, once Malcolm was weaned from her milk. It was the only reason a seat was saved for her on the plane.

Just go along with it, Tam, he'd whispered in her ear. *Better red than undead.*

"We're almost ready," the doctor said with a grin. "Three thousand Re-Humans now, and more each day. We find walking dead in the towns and farms, tourists from the resorts. The director thinks we can raise fifty thousand Re-Humans, right here!"

"Forget numbers, you need to source more guns if you want to take Cuba back." Tamsyn said. "You've gotta stop thinking like doctors."

"Che Guevara was a doctor," Hector said solemnly.

Dr. Murray came over to play cards that night. He was a hero to Ramirez's extinction movement, and they gave him the finest quarters, anything he wanted. But when he wanted to be left alone, absent himself from the planning and speech-giving, he paid a visit to the only people onsite with pulses.

"He's a bonnie lad," he said, smiling over the crib. Malcolm cooed up at the dead man, not at all horrified by the taut leather of Dr. Murray's face. Tamsyn doubted her kid even knew what a living man looked like.

"Your dad would have been proud, Tam," Dr. Murray said. "His namesake and all."

Tamsyn smiled sadly, dealt out the cards. They played by candlelight for long hours, comfortable with the long silences.

Pausing their game to change a horrific nappy, Tamsyn saw Dr. Murray wince over his daily salt drink.

"What actually changed your mind?" she asked. "I thought you'd had enough of this life. Why'd you give these sods the cure?"

"I met someone, back at the school," he admitted. "Flora and I, we—"

"You and Dr. Flora?" Tamsyn snorted with laughter. "How does that even work?"

"I'm dead, not blind," Dr. Murray said. "She's got a nice smile. You get my age, that counts for a lot."

Smiling, Tamsyn opened her mouth to rib the old man, when a rifle shot sounded through the open window. The warning klaxon by the main gate sounded briefly and was just as soon silenced. Two more whipcracks, and the distant stutter of a semi-automatic.

Cards fell to the table, dropped from senseless fingers. Dead eyes met living. Tamsyn knew that the Black Wasps were here, and that they were already inside the complex. Quick, professional insertion, no fuss. Neutralise the guards, mop up any resistance.

"How the hell—"

"Jorge," Tamsyn said. "He knew about this place all along. Shit!"

She was already up and moving, tossing the baby gear into a kit bag. By the time she strapped on her bow and arrow and tucked Malcolm into his sling, she felt like a pack mule.

Over the whole mess, she strapped the gun-belt. She couldn't shoot worth a damn, but the weight was reassuring. Dr. Murray fussed around in the kitchen, absently grabbing supplies for the living, much as he'd always done.

"So we're giving up on Eddie," he mumbled, and Tamsyn paused, one foot through the door. She turned and pointed a finger at the old Re-Human, tempering her rage only when she realised Malcolm was finally asleep.

"No," she whispered. "No. I'm going to capture one of those scarily competent soldiers and beat the location of the prisoners out of him. That's the plan, that's—that's all of the plan."

"Sounds good," Dr. Murray said nervously. He fetched a crowbar from the garden, gave it an experimental swing. Chances were he could kill a whole squad of living men with it before they got lucky with a head-shot.

Slipping away from the cottage, Tamsyn and Dr. Murray headed towards the sporadic gunfire. Some of the outer buildings were on fire, and groups of Re-Humans stood nervously with rifles, watching for the Black Wasps even as they ran circles around them.

She saw Dr. Flora on the steps of the governor's manse, struggling to free a jammed bullet from her rifle. A sniper pinned her neatly with a bullet to the head, and she fell, life-delivering hands flopping uselessly.

Dr. Murray moaned, held a hand against his mouth. Tamsyn saw the black trail of sticky tears.

Ramirez tried to rally her new recruits. They fought like the press-ganged farmers and tourists that they were and died again. The enemy had already won, and they knew it. The rest of it was just special forces being arseholes, having their own deadly brand of fun.

The soldiers knocked Ramirez to the ground, hog-tying her and breaking her legs in several places. They did nothing to help her. Her revolution was at an end, and the Party would end her twisted scheme with brutality and style.

Tamsyn's plan suddenly seemed wise. Those bastards wouldn't expect anyone to come hunting them, let alone a girl and a mouldy old man. Most of her fear went away, replaced with the thrill of the chase.

It was an overcast night, and visibility was next to nil. There were snipers by the front gate, picking off stragglers. No doubt fireteams were beginning to sweep through the jail, clearing each building. If she was in command, she'd have a hammer force, a crack squad held in reserve. To drop the boot on any resistance if things got ugly.

And somewhere, a command post. Whoever was in charge would want to keep an eye on things, make sure the job was done properly. The chief of this raid would be up high, in one of the guard towers perhaps. That's who she needed to grab. Now *that* they would not be expecting.

Building to building, moving in the opposite direction to the fireteams. The best Tamsyn could manage was a low jog, and the scar of her incision gave a low throb. She ignored it, pressed on through the darkness. After having the baby, she'd lost a lot of her fitness.

A grenade, followed by curses. These did nothing to the undead, and she heard the triumphant cries of the Re-Humans as they flushed out a Party shooter.

The Black Wasps responded with heavy machine gun fire, and the knot of resistance disintegrated into a spray of flesh and bone. Tamsyn saw the broken remains of a dead man, little more than a spine with a skull and still cursing.

Lit by smouldering wreckage, a soldier appeared, driving his boot through the Re-Human's skull. She was close enough to recognise the empty shell of Hector, his face now a broken agony. Tensing up, Tamsyn made to move in, but Dr. Murray held her arm, hauled her back.

Such a nice boy, barely a man. Always helping others. Tamsyn fought to get out of Dr. Murray's grip, wanted to wing an arrow towards his killer.

A moment later, four more soldiers followed the boot-stomper, creeping towards the next building like a pack of camouflaged cats.

"Flora's gone too," Dr. Murray whispered. "You don't see me acting stupid."

The good news was that Tamsyn's half-remembered tactics got them through the cordon. The fireteams had missed them. She stole forward, sticking to "cleared" buildings, angling towards the entrance and hopefully the command post.

She walked around a corner, only to hear the scratch and hiss of a road flare. The light revealed the bottleneck of barracks buildings around them, with nowhere to hide. In the sudden light a dozen dead things appeared, less than ten feet away and watching her warily. *Muñecas*, dressed in olive-green fatigues, armed with hatchets and clubs.

She saw other flares go up, casting light across the battlefield. This was the hammer group she'd been expecting. A final crushing blow, the shock force intended to mop up the last of the doctors' resistance.

Squads of zombie infantry, spread across the grounds. There'd be no escaping this slow advance, and dimly she found herself approving of the tactic.

Complete victory, and a chance to show off a new military toy. This was special forces, to the letter.

They'd been spotted, and there was little point trying to hide now. Tamsyn backed away, looking for escape, somewhere out of the snipers' line of fire. There was nothing. Malcolm squirmed in his sling, and Tamsyn felt the urge to murder, to strike down anyone who came near her baby.

She nocked an arrow, held her old bow ready. Beside her, Dr. Murray raised his crowbar in disbelief, perhaps wondering if it even made a difference now.

The brain-blasted zombies paused, unsure of what to do next. Tamsyn saw a spark of electricity, the flash of a cattle prod being applied. The zombies moaned, shuffled forward with weapons raised.

Behind the undead ranks, a familiar figure, driving them onwards with shouts and jolly encouragement. It was Jorge Delgado, the olive-green uniform fighting to contain his bulk. Flare in one hand, cattle prod in the other, he looked at the pair with genuine shock. Then, the same broad smile she'd seen at the school, the spy posing as a kindly idiot.

Gritting her teeth, Tamsyn drew back on the compound bow. Pulleys turned and drew the string to maximum tension, ready to launch an arrow through skull and brain. Terrified, Jorge dropped the flare, scrambled for the pistol on his belt. Before the gun could clear leather, the big man fell with an arrow protruding from his eye.

The *muñecas* stepped closer, still following Jorge's last command. Tamsyn and Dr. Murray retreated, but the way back was blocked by a trio of men in green hoods, who looked at them and laughed. Black Wasps, guns at the ready. The nearest man indicated with his rifle that they head back, face the advancing undead. It was clear that they intended to watch her die, see the walking corpses tear apart her baby son.

From what she knew of Spanish, she heard the men placing bets between themselves. How long will the *norteamericano* last? Will the dead man kill his own kind?

Malcolm stirred and ended his nap with an impressive wail. She fought down the hysterical bubble in her gut, the urge to cry at the futility of her maternal protection. It all came back to one arrow, followed by another. Zombies fell, and in some numb part of her mind, Tamsyn wondered how many of the living dead she had dispatched. Once, she had known that number.

Draw, and release, and when she next reached for an arrow, Eddie stepped forward. He was pale in the flare-light, his eyes dead jelly. A ragged sliver of flesh was missing from his neck, and nothing but a mournful groan came from his mouth.

Somehow, Jorge laid his hands on the *muñeca* formula, and someone in the Party decided to turn her wonderful fiancé into an unnatural killer, into one of their dolls.

The hands that once caressed her body held a claw hammer, and as he got closer to her, he raised it. Tamsyn felt hypnotised, unable to move in the face of that cold stare. She dropped her bow, and the bubble of hysteria climbed out of her throat. Tamsyn screamed his name with their son clutched to her chest, begging for Eddie to please, please stop.

Dr. Murray stepped into his path, crowbar raised. Eddie barrelled through him without pause, shattering bones and sending the pry-bar flying. He stepped over the Re-Human's broken body and raised the gore-streaked hammer over Tamsyn's head. There was no emotion to this murder, nothing in front of her but a robot with a tool.

Malcolm screamed, and it stirred Tamsyn into motion. She drew the revolver, stepping back from the flurry of hammer blows. Clutching the sling tight to muffle the sound, she sent two rounds into Eddie's chest before she corrected her aim, putting a bullet through his forehead.

With a final sigh, Eddie crumpled to the ground, and then he was still. She regarded the pistol in her hand, the slave zombies that were mere feet away. Dr. Murray, finally broken beyond repair.

The soldiers, cheering her on.

Her baby, scared of the thunder of guns. God only knew what she'd just done to his hearing.

She could not reach her bow and gave it up with a twinge of regret. The last gift from her father, lost now, but this paled in the face of what she'd just done. *Eddie.* She spent one bullet on the nearest zombie, and helped Dr. Murray to rise, dragged him away from the dead advance.

"Stay behind me," Dr. Murray wheezed. There were great holes torn from his lungs with the claw hammer, and he needed to lean on Tamsyn, like a dry bundle of sticks with no weight to it. One arm hung uselessly down his side, and Eddie had pounded half of his face into a sagging mess.

He turned from the *muñecas* and took one step towards the soldiers. The Black Wasps mocked him, set to catcalls and creative insults. Dr. Murray was barely quicker than Jorge's doll-zombies, and as he shuffled towards the men, the threat must have seemed comical.

Tamsyn kept behind Dr. Murray, and fumbled open the revolver, pulling out the spent rounds. She plucked extra bullets from the bandolier, dropping two of them. Malcolm cried, her breasts ached, and somewhere behind her, the love of her life lay dead by her hand.

Eventually she had the chambers full, and clicked the barrel shut. Dr. Murray was perhaps ten steps from the soldiers, and now they raised their guns, held them casually in his direction.

"Hedor!" one of them cried out, waving his nose. *Stink.*

Dr. Murray stepped closer, took a bullet to the guts. One more step, and a trick shot separated the useless arm from his body. They knew they could finish him with a head shot, and Tamsyn realised these men were like sadistic boys, taunting a wounded animal with sticks and stones.

They would break Dr. Murray and leave him for the hatchets of the *muñecas*. God only knew what horrible things they would do to her then. Soothing her boy as best she could, Tamsyn hid the gun in the baby's sling, wincing as the cold steel pressed against his little tummy.

She stepped away from Dr. Murray, hands held up and empty. A woman with a baby, obviously disarmed. The soldiers paid her no attention.

"Shoot!" Dr. Murray screamed, and brandished his crowbar at the soldier. "I'm not even a man!"

Laughing, the men took him apart. They shot away his legs, knocked his only weapon away, and took to him with boots and rifle-butts, even as he snapped at their toes and cursed them.

He's sacrificing himself for you, Tam. Make it count.

Tamsyn used the time to open her shirt and put Malcolm against her breast. He latched on, screams replaced with content suckling. She pressed her baby close, covered his tiny ear with her hand.

The soldiers ignored her, and she crept around their carnage, watched them reduce her old friend to paste. One of them looked up stupidly at the sight of her bare breasts, and he was the first to die, Ramirez's revolver out and barking until it was empty. Finally, all of the men were still.

The leaderless *muñecas* were still advancing. Tamsyn took one step towards the outer fence and realised that someone was calling her name.

She looked down and saw that Dr. Murray was still alive, even though the soldiers had staved in his face. He looked up at her through his one remaining eye, and his lips trembled. There was nothing left to the man but a broken skull in a stack of dead meat, yet still, an unholy life lingered in him.

"Tam," the misshapen mouth managed, a quaver. Most of the sound was lost in the punctured lungs, his trachea squashed almost flat.

"I'm sorry, Clem," Tamsyn said, foraging through the dead soldiers with shaking hands. She plucked out a Russian sidearm, fumbled for the safety. The *muñecas* were close enough to smell, and a second group came at a swift walk, drawn by the gunfire.

"Go," the broken Re-Human said, the effort at speaking visible. "Live."

"I love you," she said, and pressed the muzzle of the gun against his temple. One sharp clap, and the unnatural second life of Clem Murray came to an end.

She made to prise an assault rifle from stiff fingers but gave it up as excess weight, left that place with monsters snapping at her heels. Manoeuvring through the buildings by instinct, she felt a tickle in between her shoulder blades, expected the slam of a sniper's bullet at any second.

Given that she'd just dispatched the two people dearest to her, the universe finally gave her a break. The baby suckled in silence, and she reached the chain link fence, stumbling across a Black Wasp insertion point by dumb luck. The mesh was neatly severed, rolled back to admit Party soldiers.

Young Malcolm continued to drain her of milk, eyes closed peacefully, oblivious to the fact that the bottom was falling out of her world. Her heart was nothing now but a cold stone. If it wasn't for the baby at her breast, Tamsyn would have put a bullet through her brain, there and then.

Tamsyn barely remembered that nightmare journey across the Isla De La Juventud. Behind her, a patter of small-arms fire erupted from the old jail. Rhythmic volleys rolled across the plains, the kind that spoke of firing squads, the neat despatch of a captured foe. She couldn't mourn the foiling of Ramirez's mad scheme, but the echo of the executions made her skin crawl.

Back to business as usual in Cuba, she thought.

Her blind escape became an exhausted shuffle, and she walked throughout the night. It felt like every last teardrop had been wrung from her. She passed through plantations and winding jungle paths, pausing only to hide from the occasional wild zombie. Tamsyn fell into a place beyond thought, numb to the slow breaking of her heart. Instinct drove her forward, and she felt in tune with her surroundings, as much an animal as the creeping things she heard in the undergrowth.

Scaled things watched her in the balmy darkness, but she passed by, unmolested, barely noticing as other small creatures were eaten in the night. The swaying of the travel sling lulled Malcolm into a peaceful rest. She watched him with a broody eye, and a small part of her envied the baby for his innocence and rest.

It rained for about an hour, and then the moon pushed aside the clouds. The landscape was silver now, and clean. When her feet brought her out of the wilderness and into the outskirts of a resort, she noted the cluster of buildings as if through someone else's eyes. She passed through hostels and beach huts smashed by an old hurricane, the caretakers too dead to put things to rights.

All that remained of the dock were the splintered uprights. Charter boats with staved in hulls lay scattered across the sands. The hurricane had driven one big fishing vessel several meters inland, burying the prow in the ruins of a hotel.

She saw the dinghy through reptile eyes, the aluminium hull snug against a sand dune. It would float, had to float. Tamsyn placed Malcolm in the boat, and he looked up at her like Moses in the basket, blinking and confused. Even as she struggled to free the boat from the sand, she heard them coming. A handful of undead, climbing over bricks and beams, arms outstretched as if in welcome.

She drew out the dead soldier's pistol, hands shaking as adrenaline wracked her tired muscles. She had the presence of mind to step away from the boat, but Malcolm screamed at the loud crack of gunfire.

Dead things staggered into her wild volley, heedless of Tamsyn's loose grouping. Only one fell to a head wound, and then the clip was empty. Dimly she mourned the loss of her bow, even as she drew out Ramirez's revolver. Three of the rotters left now, close enough to breath their foul stink at her, and she emptied the revolver into their faces, shaking off their dead hands.

The hammer fell on a spent shell. *Shit, no time to reload!* She snatched up a chunk of cement, and drove the jagged stone against their rotten heads, grunting as she broke their skulls into paste.

A sound. Tamsyn turned to see that one coffin-dodger remained, wily enough to creep around her and make for the boat. Leathery claws reached out for the squealing bundle, and Malcolm howled fearfully.

Tamsyn flew across the sand, shouting and wild-eyed. She brought the paper-thin monster down with a wild tackle, pinning the sticky torso to the grit with her knees. Even as the zombie snapped at her, she brought the stone down, over and over.

Long after it stopped wriggling, Tamsyn continued to hammer at its face with the masonry, shaking with sobs. Heedless of the gore on her arms, she snatched at her baby, checking him all over to make sure he was safe.

She scanned the buildings, worried that more zombies would come. Tamsyn didn't know if she had the energy to fight anymore, and her stomach hurt. With the last of her strength she hauled the dinghy across the sands, looking fretfully at her little man.

He'd already settled after his zombie scare, looked up at her peacefully. Three months old, and already a veteran. Tamsyn checked the fuel tank and scavenged through the abandoned jet skis to return with a half-full jerry can.

They needed to go a long way.

If it had been an onboard motor, she might not have got it going. The squat box on the tiller was no more complex than a lawnmower, and likely to still work after all these years unfired.

She was at the limits of her physical strength, almost delirious. Eddie seemed to be in her ears, telling her to check the sparkplug, to clean some of that bleeding sand out of the workings, to stop pissing around and give it a good old belting with the butt of her gun.

Even as she did these things, she turned to retort, closing her mouth when she realised she was talking to a ghost. Her fiancé was cold and still, miles behind her. It sank in then; she was utterly alone, and responsible for another life. She needed sleep, a good cry, a hot bath. Someone to take little Malcolm off her hands. What she had was a leaky old boat, a hungry baby, and almost a dozen zombies coming through the ruins.

"No, no you don't," she gasped, hauling frantically on the motor's pull start. Even as the undead made for the waterline, the motor roared into smoky life.

She swung the tiller, the boat bouncing across the gentle swell. Clutching the baby against her skin, Tamsyn looked around in the rotting fish nets and junk, hoping to find a map. Nothing.

Charting by instinct, Tamsyn steered away from Cuba, pointed the boat away from America and everything that had ever hurt her. Vaguely she thought of her geography, and despite all common sense she twitched the tiller southwest.

"Let's try Mexico or Venezuela," she told the baby, who blinked at the sea-spray. "We can see zombies in sombreros. Maybe your Mummy might find a stash of tequila."

The little boat ran throughout the night, and once or twice Tamsyn slipped towards sleep. Each time she woke with a start, desperately clutching to Malcolm, terrified that he might fall out of the speeding boat. The motor was warm beneath her hand, and when it began to cough and splutter, she tipped the last of her fuel into the tank.

They had no food, no water. One revolver with maybe four bullets. Tamsyn peered into the night winds with fading spirits, wondering how far she'd get before the fuel ran out.

She spotted an oar in all the junk and laughed until she wheezed with laughter. The image of her paddling for hundreds of miles? Ridiculous.

Shortly before dawn, the little motor ran rough, began to misfire. The sun rose on an empty ocean in all directions, and Tamsyn felt the first tickle of panic rise in her chest. She should have reached Mexico by now. They should have been safe.

Malcolm began to cry.

Sometime before lunch, she'd pitched the revolver into the ocean. It was too tempting. She raised up a little tarpaulin shelter to keep off the sun, tried her hand at fishing with the mouldy old nets.

Her breasts were sore, and every bit of her felt drained. If she didn't get water and food soon, she wouldn't be able to feed her child. While the baby slept on a bed of ropes, she paddled the boat onwards, trying to navigate with the sun. A tangle of net trailed behind the little runabout, which she brought it in from time to time. She didn't even know what she'd do with a fish if she caught one.

Delirious, lips cracked, Tamsyn spent her hours fussing over the baby, making sure he was under shade and fed. She slipped in and out of dream and spent hours arguing with ghosts. Eddie scoffed, told her she'd taken a wrong turn. Baxter and Dr. Murray told her to try and turn back, to find a quiet corner of Cuba if she could.

"You'll be half dead, love, but you'll make it," Eddie said, red third eye leaking fluid across his grey face. She couldn't look at him, couldn't face what she'd done.

Her dad simply sat in the stern, mouth filled with stitches, cold hands caressing his sleeping grandson. He stared forward, like a drug-sniffing dog with a clue, and he pointed to the blue horizon. He nodded at her, as if to say "job well done."

She woke, almost dropping the oar. A shape in all that wet flatness, hard to see against the sunlit water. A shape with something rising above it. A lighthouse, maybe a turret.

Gritting her teeth and staring into the glare, Tamsyn paddled. She ached to the bone, and her arms felt like fulcrums flexing in some distant galaxy. Malcolm cooed softly, eyes fixed on the rippling tarpaulin above him.

A grey bulk, cutting through the swell. A big warship, with a scrap of red and blue flying above it. Tamsyn wheezed with laughter, even as she stood up and waved the oar, praying that they would spot her.

"After all that, the Americans found me," Tamsyn told her child. It no longer mattered. She would hand over her Malcolm to the first person with an honest face and go to the firing squad willingly. She'd saved her son.

The boat veered from its course, came towards her like a grey iceberg. Tamsyn settled into the seat, coaxed out some more milk for baby Malcolm. As salvation bore down on them, she took in his little wrinkled face, drank in every detail of her precious son. She was determined to leave this broken world with one good memory, one moment of peace.

Here was life in her arms, so precious and fragile. Even as her executioners came for her, she felt radiant, more alive than ever. Everything led to this moment, to the survival of her son against all odds.

Even as she resigned herself to a trial and death, Tamsyn looked up from her boy, regarded the approaching ship. It was close enough now that she could see figures on the upper deck, the launch being winched down to water-level. But when she looked at the flag, she was honestly stunned.

This warship, neat as a pin, was flying the Union Jack. Painted across the bow was the name *HMS KENT*, and several of Her Majesty's sailors were waving to her. Speeding out to meet her, a launch full of her own countrymen, armed but relaxed.

Even as she thrilled at the sight, the smile faded from her face. The last Tamsyn had seen of England was a mouldering graveyard, from tip to tip. Apart from the prisons on the Isle of Sheppy, there was no government anywhere.

All of the survivors had been left to fend for themselves.

The Marines pulled alongside, eyeing her cautiously. She croakingly identified herself as a British citizen and allowed them to search her and Malcolm for bites. When they were declared uninfected, the boats were tied together, and she was lifted onto the launch.

"It's your lucky day, miss," their officer said. "Didn't expect to find anything on patrol, let alone one of our people in a leaky old punt."

"I was trying to get to Mexico," she rasped, guzzling from a flask of drinking water and getting it all over herself.

"You got lost. Nothing for one hundred miles in any direction. One more hour, and we were going back to base."

She'd lost her passport years ago, but it seemed her accent was enough. With nothing but the clothes on her back and a baby in her arms, Tamsyn found a warm welcome onboard. Everyone on the *HMS Kent* seemed clean and well-fed, and she was pressed with questions by many of the curious sailors. Where had she been? How did she get so far in such a little boat?

Begging exhaustion, Tamsyn politely declined all conversation. Her escorts cleared a way through the well-wishers and the curious, taking her to see the lieutenant commander.

The first thing Tamsyn noticed about the crew were their relaxed attitudes, fresh faces that didn't have a thousand-yard stare. If the crew of the *HMS Kent* had seen any zombies, she was sure it had been from a safe distance.

When she remembered what it felt like to starve, to hide from unspeakable monsters, a coal of fury grew in her gut. Grateful as she was for her rescue, Tamsyn found herself hating these people, simply for having missed the whole show.

The master of the HMS *Kent* briefly met with her. Even through her exhaustion, she drew on her experience as an officer, relating her story in a concise but complete manner. When the lieutenant commander noticed how tired she was, he ordered she be given quarters and allowed to rest.

After her mad flight from Cuba, the regulation bunk felt like heaven. No sooner had her head hit the pillow but she was out, waking only when Malcolm squalled for a feed. She spent the whole day in a muzzy doze, gratefully accepting a hot lunch from the cooks.

An ensign came to fetch her much later, and she noticed the sun was well across the sky. She'd slept almost all day. She was brought to the officer's mess, where the lieutenant commander invited her to an early supper at the captain's table.

"I've made my report to Command," he said, spearing a finely sliced veal steak with his fork. "We'll be home in an hour, and a lot of people want to talk to you. You'll be able to fill us in on the new neighbours, for starters."

"Home?" she said, poking at her meal. The meat looked fresh, not canned. Five years ago, veal was just another item on the shelf at Tescos, but seeing it here in the post-apocalypse? Ludicrous.

"Well, not *home* home. Royal Navy's based at the Cayman Islands now. Probably the only place in the world missed by those unholy monsters."

"Lucky folks," Tamsyn said, her contempt giving way to hunger. She wolfed the meal down without regard to etiquette, and when Malcolm fussed she fed him at the table.

"You might want to watch your manners on land," the lieutenant commander said stiffly. "His Royal Highness might not want to see your tits during the briefing."

"Royal Highness?" she said.

"We've still got a royal in charge, Miss Webb," he said. "Far as I'm concerned, it's business as usual."

As the sun crept towards the sea, Tamsyn saw Grand Cayman. The island was attended by a cordon of grey shapes, big ships of every description. She spotted an aircraft carrier, several frigates and destroyers, even a submarine.

There were at least twenty big ships here, all flying the Union Jack. The *HMS Kent* eased into the port at George Town, the crew working with efficiency and familiarity.

On the docks, she saw a fish market, and small children ran around at play, dodging their parents' calls for dinner as long as possible. Cars drove about on the island, and the first streetlights were flickering on. Apart from the extreme Naval presence, the Cayman Islands were the picture of normality.

They were met at the docks by a high-ranking officer with a driver, adjutant, and more junk medals on his chest than she'd ever seen. Tamsyn blinked as she was introduced to Admiral Sir Charles McKenzie, First Sea Lord, Chief of Naval Staff and head of the Royal Navy.

"Tamsyn Webb," she mumbled, juggling Malcolm in her arms. "I was a captain once."

Bidding her farewells to the master of *HMS Kent*, Tamsyn was driven into the George Town Naval Base. It was a modest compound, originally intended for a token presence. Quarters were found for her, and a set of clean clothes were brought.

"You have one hour," the admiral told her. "Privy Council is already in session, and your presence is requested. I'd suggest you bathe before meeting his Royal Highness."

"Aye aye, Captain Dickhead," she muttered, throwing a salute to the closed door. A warm bath had already been drawn, and Tamsyn made sure to bathe Malcolm before herself. The outfit seemed to be an old dress uniform for a woman sailor, removed of all insignia. Skirt, blouse, stockings, and sensible shoes, just a little bit too loose. With a sigh, she examined herself before the mirror.

"You'd better not chuck up on me," she told Malcolm, and then the knock came. She braced herself to meet the de facto government of the United Kingdom, sitting *in absentia*. Not to mention a prince.

"Oh no you bloody don't," she said, waving away the ensign who made to take Malcolm from her arms. "I'm not letting him out of my sight. Mitts off."

The next few minutes were a whirl. Once more a jeep ride with the admiral, this time through the streets of George Town. Neat streets were faced with palm trees, and every third building seemed to be a bank. Passing through the government district, the jeep pulled up at the front of the Government Administration Building.

"I'll not pluck the child from your arms, Miss Webb, but do try to keep it quiet," the admiral said. They swept through the modern office block, passing through a phalanx of security until they were at a thick set of double-doors, guarded by Royal Marines.

They were admitted at once, and Tamsyn felt nervous. It was ridiculous how many heads of state she'd met, considering she'd only just turned nineteen, but it never got easier. The room contained a fancy conference table, ringed by men in suits and military uniforms.

The Privy Council of the United Kingdom. Tamsyn's heart skipped a beat. At the head of the table, hair beginning to thin, Prince Harry sat behind a sheaf of paper, glancing up at her briefly.

His Royal Highness. The only royal left, and England's future king was a playboy helicopter pilot. *Great.*

Her rescue from the ocean was a minor item on the agenda, but of state importance was the information she held. She remembered some of these faces from the newspapers and television, folks from the House of Commons, even a few from the House of Lords. The old prime minister was there, and even the opposition leader.

She was grilled at length about the situation in America, the zombie research, the outcome of the failed civil war. Tamsyn described the Cuban threat, and for many minutes the Council debated the best course of action to take. While a few pushed for military intervention, the consensus slowly swung to *hold back, observe the situation.*

"That's it!" Tamsyn shouted, pushing back her chair. "Just sit on your bloody hands, then. You lot are fucking useless."

"Mind your tongue," the admiral thundered. "This is the Privy Council, not some mothers' group. Show some respect."

"Respect? There are people in England right now who are starving, when zombies aren't killing them. Where is the government? Larking about in the Caribbean. You should all be ashamed," she said, pointing to the members of the Council.

"Everybody out," Harry said, quiet and firm. The councillors looked at the prince, only leaving when he repeated the order. Soon it was only Tamsyn and Harry, who indicated that he sit next to her.

"I'm—I'm sorry, Your Highness," she managed. "They just made me angry. An army of zombie slaves on your doorstep, and they want to just ignore it?"

"Tell me more about what you saw," Harry said. "Not like an army report. Just talk to me."

And so they talked for a long while, Tamsyn and the future king of England. They compared stories, of lost loves and friends. When baby Malcolm cried out in hunger, she fed him without apology, comfortable in this man's presence. He listened to the story of Gravesend without interruption. After a long moment, he apologised deeply for leaving his subjects to fend for themselves.

"I've spent too long listening to these frightened old men," the prince said, burping Malcolm. "We will make this good. I promise you."

The next time that the Privy Council met, Tamsyn was back in attendance, but this time she took a seat next to Prince Harry. He'd offered her military, she'd accepted advisor. "Specialist Consultant to His Royal Highness" was her official title, which sure beat anything else she'd ever done.

She talked to the Council about Cuba's zombie slaves, of an America grown cold and feudal. She spoke about going home and putting England to rights. Of being an example, in a world that needed one.

"It's not enough to survive this," Tamsyn said firmly, staring down men twice her age. "Animals survive. People live."

THE END.

Tamsyn will return in
The Tamsyn Webb Chronicles #2
Go to Hell

Read on for an excerpt
from the sequel...

Who here has killed someone?"

Tamsyn was dressed in a black vest and cargo pants, hair pulled back into a severe ponytail. Dozens of soldiers and sailors stood before her, at ease, and she recognised the quiet contempt. She was the civilian "expert" brought in to tell the military how to do their job.

Another lifetime ago, she'd worn a uniform too. She'd killed her share of people, too, far too many to bear thinking about. Tamsyn Webb was not quite twenty-one years old, and she carried her past like a sack full of rocks.

"I asked a question. Who here has ended the life of a human being by force?"

Half a dozen people raised their hands. She pointed to the nearest, a commando twice her size. He was a tough looking customer, face marked by a jagged scar. The man was all muscles and when he looked at her, his lip curled up slightly.

"You. Tell me who you killed, and why."

"I shot five Taliban when they hit our convoy near Logar. A roadside bomb took out our vehicle, killed the driver. I was the only one able to return fire."

"How did you kill them?" Tamsyn said, and she got right into his personal space.

"Machine gun mounted up top. Sent twenty of those bastards running for their lives. Five confirmed kills."

"Machine gun. Hmm," Tamsyn said, not breaking eye contact.

"So, Mr. Afghanistan, have you killed any zombies?"

"No," the man said, the sneer visibly falling from his face. Tamsyn stepped back, looking over the group.

"Anyone? Anyone here kill a zombie? No?"

She let the group chew on that for a moment, and then continued.

"You are the luckiest bastards on the face of the planet," she said. "Out there? It all went to hell. 99% of the human race, wiped out. Not just killed either. Attacked by people who were dead. Corpses, moving and trying to eat you alive. It is bloody scary."

She saw it then, washing across their faces. Survivor guilt, writ large. These leftovers of the Royal Navy had seen out the entire outbreak at the Cayman Islands, turning boats away at gunpoint. Three years in hiding, never once in danger.

"You haven't seen them. You're all soft. If a zombie came at you, all your training, your tough guy bullshit? It's all useless. You will panic, and you will die."

She gestured behind her at the training ground. The Royal Cayman Police Force had a paramilitary arm, and they'd set up a mock urban assault course for the British military, the type where people could kick in doors and rescue hostages.

"I have fought a lot of zombies. So, I'm here to give you my expertise in surviving an attack. I want you six to come forward, the ones who put their hands up earlier. Everyone, muffs on please, this is a live fire exercise."

The marines and commandos stood at the spray painted line, readying their assault rifles. In the distance was a bullet-pocked shopfront, glassless windows facing the group.

"You know how this goes. Kill the bad guys, spare the living hostages. Okay Paul, hit the switch please."

Cardboard targets started to appear in the doorways and windows, rapidly appearing and disappearing. The six shooters peppered the targets with ease, shooting cartoon zombies that lurched out, hands stretched into claws, mouths open. Expert shots, tight groupings on the head like they'd been told, and they spared the token "survivor" who leapt out.

Tamsyn waited until the all clear, and then gave a slow, sarcastic clap.

"Yep, you nailed 'em. All right killers, we're going onto the next part of the course. This one is where you meatheads get to boot the doors in, and clear a building like you're playing Call of Duty. Except I'm going to raise the difficulty level."

She handed out a bunch of random pistols, in various states of disrepair. The veteran she'd mocked before checked the clip, eyebrows raised when he noticed it was half-empty.

"Leave the big guns here. Out there in the real world, you dropped them days ago. You're hungry and scared, and you're down to a handful of bullets, your combat knives, and then your bare hands. Now, imagine that you have a horde of walking corpses closing in on you. I'm talking tens of thousands, maybe a hundred thousand zombies, and they've cut you off. The only way you are going to live is if you get through this building."

Tamsyn gave a signal to the control tower, and a recording started playing through the loudspeakers. A low moaning, rising from thousands of rotten throats, cribbed from every horror movie Tamsyn could get her hands on. It started off low, but grew in volume until Tamsyn had to shout to be heard. All the swagger from her volunteers was gone now, and they stood with their pistols in hand, trying not to look rattled.

"All you have to do is get through that building in one piece," she said. "In fact, don't even bother engaging with the targets. Go!"

They set off at a slow advance, approaching the assault course by rote. Tamsyn started screaming at them through a megaphone.

"You don't have time for this fancy bullshit! Ten thousand zombies are right behind you! Enter the building now!"

The first Marine kicked in the front door, and they poured in, yelling as they cleared the first room, and then they started crying out, all discipline gone. Tamsyn heard a pistol shot, and then someone screaming. In no time flat the group had broken through the back door, and one Marine fell to his knees, retching onto the ground. The big veteran from Afghanistan came storming over to Tamsyn, red with fury.

"Goddamn sicko," he screamed into her face. "I should kill you."

"You need to wake up, mate," she said, perfectly calm. "What's in there is your world now. If you can't deal with that, then yes, you are going to die."

Something in her eyes broke through the man's anger, and he backed away, shaking his head.

It had taken a little doing, but Tamsyn had gotten approval from the island's coroner to exhume several fresh corpses from the town cemetery. The bodies were strapped into remote-control dollies. The moment anyone entered that part of the course, actual dead meat came at them, stinking and awful. Death, up close and personal.

"Next six volunteers, you are up," she shouted, tipping out a big bag of pistols. "No one goes home till you all go through that door."

Over the loudspeakers, the undead horde cried out for living flesh, and the men and women in uniform turned pale.

A bus came for the Marines, who slunk up the steps, robbed of all bravado. Tamsyn watched them leave the training compound, giving them a cheery wave that nobody returned.

"What are we going to do with the bodies, miss?" the sergeant she only knew as Paul asked. He looked at her as if she was unhinged, and Tamsyn supposed that on some level she actually was.

"Leave them hooked up to the dollies. I'm training another group on Wednesday, and I want those corpses to really stink."

"There is something wrong with you, lady," the policeman grumbled, hitching up his belt. He whistled through his teeth, and a trio of constables set to fixing the course. They swept up the bullet casings, handkerchiefs over their faces to ward off the stink.

"Hey, don't blame me for making it realistic," Tamsyn said. She fetched her bicycle from where it leaned on the fence, and she rode away from the training grounds, ringing the little bell.

Tamsyn Webb was important these days. She was on the Privy Council, a special advisor to no less than Prince Harry himself. Even though fuel supplies were getting low on Grand Cayman, she still rated a vehicle with a driver, which she almost never used. She simply preferred to cycle home, alone with her thoughts, soaking up the endless sunshine.

Times were tough in the post-zombie Cayman Islands. Fuel rationing meant that few drove, and on an island that used to import almost everything, most things were now in short supply. As she rode through George Town, she passed dozens of empty banks, now just a reminder that the Caymans were a tax haven in the old world.

Turning onto her street, Tamsyn rode into her front yard, dumping the bicycle on the front lawn. It was a modest home, but it suited her needs, and there was enough laughter inside to forgive the peeling paint. She threw open the front door, her face splitting into an instant smile.

The excited cries, the patter of tiny feet slapping against the tiles, and then Tamsyn caught a flying toddler, who was all giggles and smiles.

"Malcolm, you little scallywag," she laughed, and tickled her son mercilessly. They lay in the hallway, laughing themselves stupid. They were still that way when Olivena found them. The heavyset Jamaican woman wore rubber gloves and looked exhausted.

"Your little angel has been drawing on the walls again," she scolded. "I have to scrub every wall in this house. If he were my child, I would use the wooden spoon. So naughty!"

Tamsyn tried to keep a straight face. Olivena made out that she was strict, but she had a soft spot where Malcolm was concerned. Tamsyn's son was running rings around his nanny, and Olivena secretly loved it.

"I'm very sorry, Olivena. I'll try to keep the markers locked in a drawer." The nanny grizzled in response, her complaints following her up the hallway and to the kitchen. Tamsyn and Malcolm broke into laughter again.

They made peace over tea, enjoying fish stew. Olivena had a good hand with the spice, and Malcolm rarely refused anything that she put in front of him. Malcolm sat in his high chair, face and bib covered with food, babbling about his favourite toys.

Tamsyn smiled sadly. Her little man was growing by the day, and some days she could see her father in his profile. Malcolm Webb, the boy's namesake, who died trying to get her to safety. Then she saw Eddie Jacobs in his face, the way little Malcolm was quick to smile and laugh, and she felt a dark bubble rise up from her chest.

Eddie. God, how she missed that man. He'd been a meathead from the start, but he'd been *her* meathead. They'd finally found love, he'd given her Malcolm, and now he was gone. Just like everyone else in her life, their lives ending in her wake. It was like she'd sucked up their opportunities, all of their remaining days like some sort of vampire, continuing on when everyone else simply stopped...

Malcolm flicked a spoonful of food at her forehead, and she snapped out of her melancholy. Olivena clambered out of her chair, grumbling and already reaching for a dishcloth, but Tamsyn saw the suggestion of a smile in the corners of her mouth.

"Good shot, mate," she whispered to Malcolm.

—◖●◗—

A storm hit Grand Cayman that night, rolling in from the west. Once Malcolm settled down in his cot, Tamsyn sat on her porch to watch it. Drink in hand, she marvelled at the storm's power, the driving wind and rain. The lightning show was spectacular, and it suited her somber mood.

The power flickered, and then it finally cut out around 9 pm. Navy engineers had hooked up the nuclear reactors from two of the Vanguard-class subs to the George Town power grid, but it was patchwork at best. Tamsyn happily sat there in the dark, drinking rum and watching nature scour at the world.

She drank most of the bottle and sang pop songs to herself, crying drunkenly when she realised that all of these people were now dead. After her service in the Texan Republican Army, Tamsyn could sleep almost anywhere, and she fell asleep on the porch decking, the warm rain tickling at her toes.

The nightmare came almost instantly. In the dream she opened her eyes, and her house was surrounded by the dead. Not the slavering corpses tearing up the world; these were *her* dead, and they were packed up against the edge of the porch, staring at her. Their faces were pale and bruised, eyes sunken, beady, drinking her in as they crowded around her. They stretched across her front yard, and down the road, as far as she could see.

She could not move in this dream, and it was like their attention had her pinned to the wall. Tamsyn was a butterfly flush with life, and it frustrated these dead, a parade of familiar faces who'd made a special trip just to see her.

Tamsyn recognised many from Gravesend, everyone she'd doomed. It was her fault the zombies got through the town barricade. Her one stupid mistake had killed hundreds, had led to the massacre on the docks. She saw Ali, her best friend from school, and he stared at her, nothing human left in his eyes. She'd left him behind. Watched him die.

"You're not safe," he said.

Others pressed forward. She saw people who'd died on that awful voyage from England to Texas. Ones who'd died in the war, others who died in nuclear bombing of Corpus Christi. Again, her fault. She saw Baxter, poor doomed Baxter, and her loyal soldier shook his head, not unkindly.

"You're not safe," and he tried to say more, but his mouth worked uselessly, and he gave up with a shrug. Naomi and old Clem Murray tried then, and pleaded with her earnestly, assuring Tamsyn that she was not safe.

Then her father stepped forward, and Tamsyn cried out. His lips were still stitched up with black thread, the same as she'd last dreamt of him, and he held little Milly in his arms, her foster daughter who'd died in a mushroom cloud. Her little face took Tamsyn in, and she mouthed the words "not safe."

"I bloody get it, okay!" Tamsyn cried out. "What am I meant to do?"

The ghosts parted then, and Tamsyn's heart skipped. Eddie stepped onto the porch, wincing as if the effort cost him dearly. He was arm in arm with her mother, who looked angry.

"Tam, you gotta go love," he said. "Please. It's the boy."

Behind the crowd there was a soft glow, like a sun rising, but the light was all wrong, unnatural. The storm began to fail, and Tamsyn's personal crowd of ghosts fell aside, wailing, unable to look upon the approaching light.

"Go!" her mother screamed, and then Tamsyn woke up with a start. She was still sitting on her porch, but it was dawn, the storm long since passed. Heart still racing, she climbed to her feet, back and legs aching from the awkward way she'd slept.

Always with the dreams. She'd had vivid nightmares for years now, even before the zombies came, but they were getting worse.

Sometimes a good drink kept them at bay, but this was happening almost every night. Too often she woke screaming, setting off the neighbourhood dogs, and little Malcolm would join in from his cot, confused and crying. Olivena would hustle in, warm milk already in hand, soothing them both back to sleep with old Jamaican lullabies.

If she had too many bad nights in a row, Tamsyn drank on the porch, or hid in the toolshed while she worked through a bottle. Olivena did not approve of Tamsyn self-medicating and kept trying to drag her to her church, to meet a selection of her friends' sons. Tamsyn could think of nothing she wanted less. Her heart still ached for Eddie, and she turned away anyone who looked like a gentleman caller.

If it wasn't for her work and for her son, Tamsyn had the feeling that she just might fall off the face of the earth.

"I've gotta get my shit together," she muttered, stretching her back. Then she saw the jeep turning into her driveway and swore. The driver was a young ensign in Navy whites, which only ever meant one thing. She threw open the front door and ran into her kitchen in a panic.

"Olivena. Olivena! Where did you put my skirt?"

Olivena was sitting next to Malcolm's high chair, spooning goop into his face. The boy squealed with delight when he saw her, and the sight made her feel like the worst mother on the face of the earth. Too drunk to get up and feed her own son...

"I ironed your skirt this morning. It is hanging up behind your bedroom door," Olivena said pointedly. Tamsyn hit the bathroom at a run, splashing water on her face and attacking her boozy mouth with a toothbrush. She scrubbed at her armpits with a wet cloth, wishing she had time to wake up under the shower.

"Privy Council isn't meant to be till tomorrow," she mumbled. In under two minutes she had her hair up in a bun and wriggled into the smart skirt and blouse that Olivena had picked out for her.

Jamming her toes into her flats, she whirled through the house like a dervish, snatching up papers and folders.

"I'll be home later," she shouted, planting a big kiss on Malcolm's face, and even giving one to Olivena for good measure. The Jamaican pushed her away, waving at her face.

"You smell like rum. Drink this," the portly woman said, pushing her own coffee into Tamsyn's hands. Smiling gratefully, she drank it as fast as she could.

Opening the door, Tamsyn held herself high, trying not to look like the wretched drunk who'd run inside bare minutes ago. The ensign looked at her with barely veiled amusement as he opened the passenger door for her.

He drove her through George Town, the town streets empty except for some children on bicycles and palm branches knocked down in the storm. Tamsyn tried to go over her papers for the day, fighting off the urge to vomit whenever the ensign took a corner.

"Big day today," he began, and Tamsyn held up her hand.

"Look, mate, I know you're being polite. I'm trying really hard not to throw up right now. Please, can we just have a quiet ride today?"

"Yes, ma'am," the random ensign said with a frown. She wasn't winning many friends in the armed forces. With a sigh, she returned to her items for the Privy Council.

Resources, dwindling. Almost no diesel left on the island. Bankers and hedge fund managers were being pressed into farm work, with work crews clearing away the rainforests and jungle for more farmland. A report on her own efforts at training the Royal Navy in zombie combat, and another raft of motions and reasons why the government-in-exile were too scared to leave the Cayman Islands.

All she wanted to do was take this fragment of civilisation and go home. Tamsyn remembered the horrors of Gravesend, the knowledge that no one was left to help, to reclaim the island from the zombie hordes. All along, the leftover government had been here, hiding with the coconuts and all the world's money.

She gripped her files and papers, anger bubbling in her gut. She had no doubt that today's meeting would be just as pointless as the last one. When the jeep pulled up outside of the Government Administration Building, her hangover was replaced by the will to fight, to knock some heads together.

The driver opened the door, and Tamsyn bustled out, gritting her teeth when the ensign didn't salute her. Her whole existence on the Privy Council was due to Prince Harry's goodwill, and even the rank and file of the Navy knew it. Part of her relished the battles over the Council table, the way the pompous old shits resisted any of her ideas.

One of the few things that keeps me going, she thought. She worked her way into the building, past the complicated ballet of assistants with more paper, guards on every door, and then finally into the Council chamber itself, various talking heads and military brass now finding their seats.

Sliding into her own chair, Tamsyn looked to Prince Harry, her one champion. She stopped cold. Sat to his right were a trio of strangers, men in uniforms she'd hoped to never see again.

Americans. One was a five-star general, the other an admiral with acres of fruit salad and medals hanging from his chest. The third was a man in suit and tie, and Tamsyn recognised him from the TV, back in the old world when her dad forced her to watch the news before her homework.

President Wycliffe. He'd spent the last few years hiding out on Hawaii with the remainders of the US government. When a zombie ripped out President Palin's throat, he got the top job.

The man looked too perfect. He had a strong jaw, and when he spoke his teeth were white and straight, a clashing wall built just for photographs. Wycliffe kept his hair neatly combed over a precise part, with just a touch of white at the temples. Tamsyn had heard stories of the man's religious convictions, and when the Texans brought life back to the zombies, he'd come for them with guns blazing.

Only Jesus was meant to come back, right? she thought, worrying at her nails.

"We'll be blunt, your Highness," Wycliffe said. "We need your boats, and we need your men."

Tamsyn saw Prince Harry share a look with Terry Fallot, his prime minister, who gave a slight shake of his head. The other members of the Privy Council looked guarded, almost terrified. As always, the governor of the Caymans sat self-importantly in his chair, but today even he had the rare sense to keep his mouth shut.

Secret Service agents hovered around the edges of the meeting room, watching everybody. Tamsyn sat very still and hoped that nobody noticed her. That none of these Americans realised who she was.

"We are getting slaughtered over there," Wycliffe said. "Damn zombies are clumping together, hordes that are millions strong. We've got the Cubans nipping at us wherever we try to set up shop, it's—it's a damn mess."

"President, we lost our country too," Prince Harry said. "We'd like nothing more than to go home, but it's just not safe yet."

"We are allies!" Wycliffe suddenly shouted, banging on the table with the flats of his hands. "Are you just going to sit on this island while we all die?"

"We have to look at the safety of our personnel, the protection of our remaining assets," the prime minister began, but Wycliffe waved off the excuses.

"I've heard enough of this. You're a bunch of damn cowards." He stood, even as the general lay an impressive sheaf of papers on the table. An agreement, complete with empty signature page.

"We'll give you one week to come to your senses. If you will not participate in our joint survival, I will dissolve all alliances between our countries."

Prince Harry stood, followed a heartbeat later by the rest of the table. He shook the President's hand, face a thundercloud. Tamsyn knew how much it galled him to wait on this island, to let the undead stink up England while he sat here in safety. Tamsyn guessed that he alone wanted to help the Americans, and badly.

The Americans started to leave the Privy Council chamber when the five-star general stopped in front of Tamsyn, recognition washing across his face.

"You're Tamsyn Webb," he said, and drew his sidearm. The room erupted into pandemonium. Secret Service agents leapt into action, guns already drawn, and the British Marines posted by the door responded in kind, rifles up and tracking. Everybody was shouting, and Tamsyn was frozen, staring into the black mouth of the pistol pointed at her chest.

"Captain Webb," the general shouted, "For your war crimes, I am placing you under arrest."

THE ADVENTURE CONTINUES IN "THE TAMSYN WEBB CHRONICLES #2 - GO TO HELL".

— ABOUT THE AUTHOR —

Jason Fischer is a writer who lives near Adelaide, South Australia. He has won the Colin Thiele Literature Scholarship, an Aurealis Award and the Writers of the Future Contest. In Jason's jack-of-all-trades writing career he has worked on comics, apps, television, short stories, novellas and novels. Jason also facilitates writing workshops, is an enthusiastic mentor, and loves anything to do with the written or spoken word.

Jason is also the founder and CEO of Spectrum Writing, a service that teaches professional writing skills to people on the Autism Spectrum.

He plays a LOT of Dungeons and Dragons, has a passion for godawful puns, and is known to sing karaoke until the small hours.

— ACKNOWLEDGEMENTS —

Many thanks go to the original patron of the Aussie zombie, Baden Kirgan, who took an active role in bringing this story back to life, first as a magazine serial, and then in book form. Black House Comics may be gone, but never forgotten.

More thanks go to Jason Franks, whose many insights saved this book since it first lurched into life, and more so when it rose from the dead as an Argonautica Press title—a true zombie book!

Next, a gush of appreciation goes to Jeremy, Alana, and everyone else at Outland Entertainment for taking on the Tamsyn Webb series, bringing it to a new audience. You guys rock!

Thanks to Jason Paulos, Demi Thorpe, and now Ann Marie Cochran, designers of the cover art and posters for various editions of this book over the years. You've all given life to my favourite heroine, and I thank you.

Finally, thanks to all the fans of the original print-runs of *Gravesend* and then *Quiver*—there are (finally) sequels on the way, and I hope they were worth the wait!

As always, my love to Kate, Logan, and now to Lottie.